SILVER BIRCH, BLOOD MOON

Other Fairy Tale Anthologies Edited By
Ellen Datlow and Terri Windling

BLACK SWAN, WHITE RAVEN
RUBY SLIPPERS, GOLDEN TEARS
BLACK THORN, WHITE ROSE
SNOW WHITE, BLOOD RED

SILVER BIRCH, BLOOD MOON

EDITED BY
ELLEN DATLOW &
TERRI WINDLING

AVON BOOKS ◆ NEW YORK

AVON BOOKS, INC.
1350 Avenue of the Americas
New York, New York 10019

Copyright © 1999 by Ellen Datlow and Terri Windling
Cover illustration by Tom Canty
Published by arrangement with the editors
ISBN: 0-380-78622-2
www.avonbooks.com

Library of Congress Cataloging in Publication Data:

Silver birch, blood moon / edited by Ellen Datlow and Terri Windling.
    p.   cm.
  Contains 21 stories by different authors.
  1. Fantasy fiction, American. 2. Fantasy fiction, English.
3. Fairy tales—Adaptations. I. Datlow, Ellen. II. Windling, Terri.
PS648.F3S58   1999   98-54639
813'.0876608—dc21   CIP

First Avon Books Trade Paperback Printing: March 1999

AVON TRADEMARK REG. U.S. PAT. OFF. AND IN OTHER COUNTRIES, MARCA REGISTRADA, HECHO EN U.S.A.

Printed in the U.S.A.

OPM   10 9 8 7 6 5 4 3 2 1

For the Rasmussen sisters: Pat, Cindy, Sally and Sue, with love.

—TERRI WINDLING

For my aunt, Helen Schwarz, who introduced me to magical things with annual excursions to *The Nutcracker*.

And for my editor and friend, Jennifer Brehl.

—ELLEN DATLOW

Contents

CONTENTS

Contents

INTRODUCTION

TERRI WINDLING AND ELLEN DATLOW

Silver Birch, Blood Moon is a collection of adult fairy tales: traditional stories spun, woven and stitched into enchanting new shapes by twenty-one contemporary writers. You'll find "Beauty and the Beast," "The Frog Prince," "Hansel and Gretel," and other such classic fairy tales within these pages—but here, Beauty lives on a sugar plantation, the Frog Prince lounges in an English garden, and Gretel moves between foster homes; here, there is no guarantee of a happy ending or of a timely rescue; here, appearances can deceive and transformations are not forever.

There are two common misconceptions modern readers often have about fairy tales: first, that they are stories about fairies, which is not necessarily the case. Although some fairy tales actually do contain such enchanting otherworldly creatures, many of these tales do not; rather, they are tales about mortal men and women in a world invested with magic. (The misnomer comes from the

French *conte de fées*, a name given to a literary style popular at the court of Louis XIV.) A more appropriate term for these stories might be "wonder tales" or "magical tales"—or "fantasy," as we call an entire genre of fiction today. Fairy tales from all around the world share common imagery, plots and themes, generally concerning the nature of illusion and the process of transformation, recounting dark journeys and perilous quests which mirror (as the great mythologist Joseph Campbell has reminded us) the journey each of us embarks upon from birth to death. Like poetry, fairy tales speak to us in a richly symbolic language, distilling the essence of the human experience into words of deceptive simplicity. The imagery found in fairy tales is rooted in the ancient oral folk tradition, giving these stories a mythic power and resonance few art forms can match.

The second common misconception is that fairy tales are—and always have been—stories meant for children. Not only was this not the case prior to our own century, but the whole notion of childhood as a time of simple innocence, separate from our adult lives, is a relatively recent development in human history. In ages past, magical tales from the oral folk tradition were told to audiences of all ages—while literary fairy tales (like the original "Beauty and the Beast" by Marie-Jeanne L'Héritier de Villandon, or the early, sexually explicit version of "Sleeping Beauty" by Giovanni Straparola) were written for audiences of aristocratic, educated adults. Advances in printing technology resulted in a publishing boom in the nineteenth century—a time when the idea of childhood became romanticized by the English upper classes (in stark contrast to the lives actually lived by all but a small number of privileged children). It was during this time that Victorian publishers created the separate field of children's literature. Magical tales drawn from folklore, and from literary publications of centuries past, were adapted by these publishers in editions aimed at a young audience. True to the values of the day, such adaptations were duly stripped of the moral complexity, sensuality or downright bawdiness characteristic of older fairy tales.

It is unfortunate that these Victorian children's stories are the fairy tales most of us know today—or versions even further watered down in Little Golden Book editions and Walt Disney cartoons. Today, many readers don't know that the tales have ever been otherwise. They think that Cinderella has always sat meekly in the cinders, awaiting a rich prince; that the story of the Little Mermaid has always had a happy, romantic ending; that Snow White's murderous rival has always been a wicked step-parent; or that Sleeping Beauty has always been awakened by a chaste, respectful kiss. Uncovering the older versions of these tales, we find ourselves in darker territory: the Italian "Cat Cinderella" coldly plots her stepmother's death, while Sleeping Beauty is raped and impregnated during her enchanted sleep; in Germany, Snow White's own mother orders her heart cut out and cooked for dinner; in Denmark, the Little Mermaid dies when her fickle prince grows tired of her love; in Africa, the Armless Maiden loses her limbs resisting her brother's sexual advances; in South America, Beauty is enraged when her Beast transforms into a simpering prince. The older tales were unflinching in their portrayal of frank sexuality, brutal violence and complex family dynamics; they were often morally ambiguous, and relished bloody retribution to a degree that is disturbing to our modern sensibilities. These were tales addressing adult concerns, or the concerns of children far from innocence—tales rooted in real life, not the soil of Nevernever Land. It has been a great loss to our mythic, cultural and literary heritage that we've allowed such tales, passed on for centuries, to be turned into sweet, simplistic pap.

The good news is that in recent years creative artists in many different fields (writers, painters, dancers, dramatists) have been turning back to fairy-tale themes, reaching past Victorian stories to older, darker, more powerful variants. Contemporary artists like painter Paula Rego, sculptor Wendy Froud, feminist poet Olga Broumas, harpist/composer Loreena McKennitt, mask-maker/dramatist Julie Taymor, filmmaker Neil Jordan, and a host of others are using fairy-tale symbols to create art both fresh and timeless, speaking of modern life in language as old as storytelling itself. At the same time, folklore scholars are making the older tales available once again in works such as Angela Carter's *Old Wives Fairy Tale Books*, Italo Calvino's *Italian Folktales*, Jack Zipe's *Spells and Enchantments* and Marina Warner's *Wonder Tales*.

In the past, many accomplished writers drew inspiration from fairy-tale imagery to create classic works of adult prose and poetry: Shakespeare, Spenser, Blake, Keats, Goethe and the German Romantics, Yeats and the Irish Renaissance writers, to name but a few. Today, this literary tradition continues in the work of Margaret Atwood *(The Robber Bride)*, A.S. Byatt *(Possession)*, Sara Maitland *(Angel Maker)*, Marina Warner *(Indigo)*, Robert Coover *(Briar Rose)*, Salman Rushdie *(Haroun and the Sea of Stories)*, Susanna Moore *(Sleeping Beauty)*, Berlie Doherty *(The Vinegar Jar)*, and other writers whose books can be found on the "mainstream" shelves. Fairy-tale symbolism pervades the work of modern poets like Anne Sexton *(Transformations)*, Olga Broumas *(Beginning With O)*, Sandra Gilbert *(Blood Pressure)*, Gwen Strauss *(Trail of Stones)*, Lisel Mueller *(Waving from the Shore)* and Randall Jarrell *(The Complete Poems)*. In particular, the fantasy genre has provided a home for many fine writers creating contemporary literature with mythic or folkloric motifs, such as Patricia A. McKillip *(Winter Rose)*, Tanith Lee *(Red as Blood)*, John Crowley *(Little, Big)*, Jonathan Carroll *(Sleeping in Flame)*, Robin McKinley *(Deerskin)*, Jane Yolen *(Briar Rose)*, Delia Sherman *(The Porcelain Dove)*, Ellen Kushner *(Thomas the Rhymer)*, and Sheri S. Tepper *(Beauty)*. Writers in all three fields owe a great debt to England's Angela Carter, whose sensual, darkly magical tales (collected in *The Bloody Chamber* and, posthumously, in *Burning Your Boats)* have profoundly influenced many of us working with fairy-tale themes today.

It should be noted that it is probably no accident that the majority of contemporary writers listed above are women. Previous volumes in this anthology series have been variously praised and castigated for the number of women writers whose work we've published in their pages, and for the distinctly feminist subtext to be found in many of their tales. Although it has never been our intent to focus these volumes *exclusively* on women's stories, the fact that so many women writers are drawn to fairy-tale material is also part of a long and honorable historic tradition: folk tales and magical tales (like other largely anonymous arts) have long been associated with women. As Alison Lurie has pointed out (in her essay "Once Upon a Time"): "Throughout Europe (except in Ireland), the storytellers from whom the Grimm Brothers and their followers collected their material were most often women; in some areas they were all women. For hundreds of years, while written literature was almost exclusively the province of men, these tales were being invented and passed on orally by women." For centuries, fairy tales have been the voice of disenfranchised populations: not only women, but also the old, the poor, and social outcasts (such as the Gypsies—famed throughout the world for their wealth of magical tales). Fairy tales speak covertly, symbolically, about the hard realities of life; and these symbols are proving as potent to artists today as in centuries past.

Poet Gwen Strauss described the appeal of ancient tales to modern writers in the foreword to her collection *Trail of Stones.* "Whether it is a princess calling down a well, a witch seeking out her reflection, children following a trail into the woods, falling asleep or into blindness, a common thread . . . is that each of these characters is compelled to turn inward. Though each confronts different issues—fear of love, shame, grief, jealousy, loneliness, joy—they have in common a time of solitude. They are enclosed within a private crisis. They have entered a dark wood where they must either face themselves, or refuse to, but they are given a choice to change. The momentum of self-revelation leads them toward metamorphosis, like a trail of stones leading them into the dark forest."

In the stories that follow, you'll read of magic, illusion,

crisis, peril and transformation. You'll find many trails into the wood—and even a few back out again.

Enjoy.

—Terri Windling
Tucson and Devon

—Ellen Datlow
New York City

Kiss Kiss

TANITH LEE

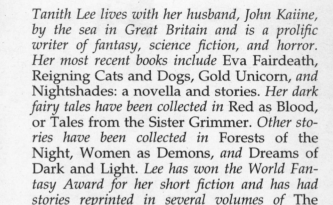

*Tanith Lee lives with her husband, John Kaiine,
by the sea in Great Britain and is a prolific
writer of fantasy, science fiction, and horror.
Her most recent books include* Eva Fairdeath,
Reigning Cats and Dogs, Gold Unicorn, *and*
Nightshades: a novella and stories. *Her dark
fairy tales have been collected in* Red as Blood,
or Tales from the Sister Grimmer. *Other stories have been collected in* Forests of the
Night, Women as Demons, *and* Dreams of
Dark and Light. *Lee has won the World Fantasy Award for her short fiction and has had
stories reprinted in several volumes of* The
Year's Best Fantasy and Horror.*

*Lee, along with the late Angela Carter, has
been one of the major purveyors of adult fairy
tales during the past decade. Her fiction is lush
and dark. Her story "Kiss Kiss" is the first of
three variations on "The Frog Prince." In it,
Lee gracefully examines the social and political
realities of a young woman who would be the
envy of most of her contemporaries.*

Kiss Kiss

You see, I was only eleven when it began. I'm twenty-three years of age now. Just over twice that lifetime. But did I know more when I was younger? Was I more wise then than now?

The estate was small, and although my father was a prince, we were by no means rich. That is, we had fires in winter, and furs heaped on the beds. There was plenty of game in the forests for my father and his fifteen men to hunt and bring home as dinner. We had wine and beer. And in the spring the blossom was beautiful. And all summer there was the wheat, and afterward the fruit from the orchards. But I had holes in all but my best dress, as my mother did. One day, I would have to have something fine, because I would need to be married. I didn't question this, the only use I was, being a girl: the princess. Sixteen was the normal age. My mother said I was pretty, and would do. It was all right. And on my eleventh birthday, my father gave me an incredible present. Since we didn't have so very much, seeing it, I knew, despite appearances, he must think I had a proper value. My mother gasped. I stood speechless. I really didn't need him to say, "It's gold. Gold over bronze. Be careful with it."

I said nothing. My mother said, "But, dearest—"

He cut her short, as usual. "It can be part of her dowry. They're popular in the city. They're lucky, apparently. You may," he said, "throw it up and catch it. Don't roll it along. It would get scratched."

"Thank you, Papa."

I held the golden ball in utter awe. It was very heavy. It was, I think, for strong young lordlings to throw about. My slender wrists ached from its weight.

But I took it out through the neglected garden, and walked with it down the overgrown paths, to the lake among the pine trees where, in the worst winters, the wolves came, blue as smoke, and howled.

I've heard it said that sometimes when a man stands near the brink of a cliff, he may think, What if I step over? Just such an awful thought came to me as I stood by the lake, which was muddy and rushy in the summer evening. Suppose I let go the golden ball, and let it roll, scratching itself, over into the deeper water?

No sooner had I thought it than a bird screeched in the trees of the forest on the lake's far side. And I started, and the ball dropped from my tired hands.

It rolled, flush, through the grass, in through the reeds with their dry, brown-purple flowers. I ran after it all the way, calling to it, stupidly crying, "No, no—"

And then it slid over the water's edge, straight in and down. Under the surface I saw it glimmer for one whole second, like a drowned sun. And then I saw it no more.

What could I do? I didn't do anything. I stood staring after the lucky golden ball, lost in the brown mirror of water, sobbing.

My father hadn't ever beaten me, at least not with his hands. He had a hard tongue. I dreaded what he would say. I dreaded what I'd done. To be such a fool.

Gnats whined in the air. One stung me, and I scratched my neck, still crying. The scratching made a noise in my ear that suddenly said, "Little girl, little princess, why are you weeping?"

I stopped in amazement. Had I imagined it? The voice came again. "Can I help you, little princess?"

No one was there. Only the gnats furled over the dry flowers. At the edge of the water, in the shallows, something was stirring.

The sun was among the pines now, flashing. It caught the edges of the ripples in brassy rings. And two round eyes.

"Have you lost something precious?"

What was it? A frog . . . no, it was too big. The round eyes, colored like the duller flashes of the sun.

"Yes—I've lost—my golden ball."

"I saw it go down. I know where it is."

I thought, blankly, I've gone mad. It's the fright. Like the girl last year when the wild horse ran through the wedding party. She went mad. She was locked away. They'll lock me away.

I turned, to rush off up the sloping ground, toward my father's disheveled towers.

The voice called again. "Here I am. Look. You'll see, I'm well able to go after your precious ball."

Then I stopped and I did look. And it came out of the water part of the way, and I saw it.

I gave a squeal.

It said, "Don't be afraid. I'm gentle."

It *was* like a frog. A sort of little, almost-man thing that was a frog. Scaled, a pale yet dark green, with round, brownish glowing frog's eyes. It had webbed forefeet that might be hands. It held them up. They had no claws. And in its open mouth seemed nothing but a long dark tongue.

I was terrified. It was a sprite, a lake-spirit, the sort the old women put out cakes for in the village, to stop their mischief.

It said, plaintively, "Don't you want your golden ball, then?"

My first adult decision, perhaps, was between these

two evils. My angry father, and the uncanny creature from the lake.

"I want the ball."

"If I fetch it," said the frog-demon, "I must have a favor in return."

"What do you want?"

"To be yours."

It was so unequivocal—and yet, as I found out soon enough, so subtle. "Mine? How?"

"To belong to you, princess."

Was it pride or avarice, a desire for some power in my powerless existence? To have a spirit as my slave. No. I think I only knew I had to get back the ball. And because it hadn't said to me, I must have your virtue, or, I must have your firstborn child, as in the stories they do, I was just relieved to say, "All right. You can be mine. Please fetch it for me!"

After it had gone down, with one treacly little *plop*, I stood there thinking I'd been dreaming. I even started to search about for the golden ball, in case that too was a dream, a bad one.

The sun went into the blacker, lower third of the forest, and the sky above grew coppery. Crickets started across the fields. An owl called early for the shadows.

Then the water parted again, and up came the necessary golden ball, real and actual and there. It was clasped by two scaly frog hands.

I went gingerly down and took the ball, snatched it. I held it to my breast with all my fingers.

Then the frog-thing's face broke the water. Even then, I could see how sad its face was, the way certain animal faces are. Its eyes might have been made of tawny tears.

"Remember your promise."

"Yes."

As I hurried back toward the pile of the house, I heard it coming, hopping, after me. Not looking, I said, *"Go away!"*

"If I belong to you," it said, "I must be with you. Every minute. Day and night."

Then I saw, the way the maiden does, always too late
in the tale, what she has agreed to.

"You can't! You *can't!*"

"You promised me."

I started to pray then to God, in whom I believed, but
from whom I expected nothing, ever. He'd never answered any of my youthful prayers. And didn't do so
now.

But the frog-thing came to me, quite near. It stood as
high as my knee. It had frog legs, huge webbed feet, without claws. Sunset gleamed on its scales. In its scratch of
a voice it said, "I won't speak to them. I won't tell them
you lost the ball. I can do things they'll like. Find things.
It will be all right."

But I ran away. Of course. Of course, it ran after.

In the garden, by the broken statue of a god, an old
god even more deaf than God, I had to stop for breath.
The golden ball had weighed me down. I hated it. I hated
it worse than the frog-demon. In that moment I knew,
too, how much I hated my father.

The frog had reached me without trouble. It hopped
high, right up on the stone god's arm. And out of its
mouth it pulled a most beautiful flower. Perhaps it had
brought it from the lake. Creamy pink, with a faint perfume, thinner and more fresh than a rose.

The demon leaned, and before I could flinch away, it
had put the flower in my hair.

I thought, out of my new hatred for my father, Anyway, he'll kill this thing as soon as he sees it.

I tossed my head, and the flower filled the air with
scent. I hated everyone by now, and all things. Let them
all kill each other.

"Come on, then," I said, and went toward the house,
and the frog-thing hopped along at my side.

They called it Froggy. That was their way. They used to
throw it scraps from the table. It wouldn't ever touch
meat. It had a little fish, and it liked green things and
fruit, but I don't know how it ate, for it seemed to have
no teeth. And this I never learned.

In the beginning, they were more circumspect with
it—after, that is, the first outburst.

When I came into the hall, the women were at the
hearth, and the boy was turning the smaller spit for the
dead hares my father had taken in the forest. The house
had a kitchen, but it was used only when there were
guests. Half the time the bread was baked there too.

The owl-shadows were gathering, red from the fire,
and one of the men was lighting the candles. In all this
flicker of red and dark, no one saw the frog for some
while.

I went up to my mother, who was wearing her better
hall-dress that had only one darn in it. She took hold of
me at once, and called her maid to comb my hair.

It was the maid who saw the frog first. She screamed
out loud and pulled out a clump of my hair.

"Uh—mistress—ah! What is it?"

I was too ashamed to speak. My mother naturally
didn't know. She peered at the thing.

It stood there patiently, looking up at her with its sad
face. It had vowed not to speak to anyone but me.

The maid was crossing herself, spitting at the corner
to avoid bad luck.

At the fire, they had turned and were gawping. And
just then my father stormed in with his men and three of
the hunting dogs, stinking of blood and unwashed mascu-
linity. One of the dogs, the biggest, saw the frog at once.
He came leaping for it, straight across the hall. As this
happened, the frog gave a jump. It was up a tree of lit
candles, wrapped there around one of the iron spikes, and
the wax splashed its scales, but it didn't make a sound.

The dog growled and drooled, pressed against the
candle-tree, its eyes red, its hair on end.

My father strode over at once.

He said to me, as I might have known he would,
"Where's your golden ball, girl?"

"Here, Father."

He looked at that. Then up the candle-tree. My father frowned.

"By Christ," said my father.

Although I hated him, hate can't always drive out fear, as love can't. In terror I blurted, "It came out of the lake. It followed me home. I couldn't stop it. It wants to be with me."

My mother put her hand over her mouth, a gesture she often resorts to, as if she knows she might as well not cry out or talk, since no one will bother.

My father said, "I've heard of them. Water demons. Why did it come out? What were you doing?" He glared at me. This must be my fault. And it was.

"Nothing, Papa."

He folded his arms, and glowered at the frog. The frog eased itself a little on the stand. Leaning over from the waist, it bowed, like a courtly gentleman, to my father. Who gave a bark of laughter. Turning, he kicked the dog away. "It's lucky. They bring good luck. We must be careful of it."

He ordered them to carve some of the half-raw hare, and offered it to the frog, which wouldn't have it. Then one of the women crept up with a cup of milk. The frog took this in a webbed paw, and had a few sips. Despite its frog mouth, it didn't slurp.

Once they had driven the dogs off, the men stood about laughing and cursing, and the frog jumped onto the table. It got up on its hands and ran about, and the men laughed more, and even the women slunk close to see. When it reached the unlit candles at the table's center, it blew on them. They flowered into pale yellow flame.

This drew applause. They said to each other, See, it's *good* magic. It's funny. And when it scuttled over to me and jumped out and caught my girdle, hanging on there at my waist so I shrank and almost shrieked, they cheered. I was favored. They'd heard of such things. It would be a *good* year, now.

It was. It was a good year. The harvest was wonderful, and some gambling my father did brought in a few golden coins. Also, the frog found a ruby ring that had been lost—or hidden—by an ancestor in the house. All this was excellent. And they said, when they saw me com-

ing, the demon at my side, "Here's the princess, with
her frog."

But that was after. It took them a little while to be
so at home with it. And that first night, after my father
encouraged me to feed it from my plate, let it share my
cup of watered wine, when it started to follow me up the
stone stair, where the torches smuttily burned, he stood
up. "Put it outside your door," he said. "We don't know
it's clean in its habits." This from one who had, more than
once, thrown up from drink in my mother's bed. Who
defecated in a pot, who occasionally pissed against indoor
walls. The servant women being expected to see to it all.

When we reached my room, I tried to shut the frog-
demon outside in the passage. But it slipped past.

"I must be with you," it said, the first time it had
spoken since we came in. "Day and night. Every minute."

"Why?" I wailed.

"Because I must."

"Horrible slimy thing!"

I tried to kick it aside. Did I say I was a nice girl? I
hadn't learnt at all to be nice, and was almost as careless
and cruel to servants and animals as the rest of them.

But it eluded my foot, which anyway was only in a
threadbare shoe, not booted like the feet of the dog-
kicking men.

It wasn't slimy. I'd felt it. It was dry and smooth, its
scales like thin plates of polished dull metal. When it
sprang lightly on my bed, I took off my useless shoe and
flung it. But the frog-demon caught my shoe, and put it
on its head like a hat.

At that, finally, I too laughed.

I didn't want it on my pillow. But onto my pillow it
came. Its breath was cool and smelled of green leaves. In
the dark, its eyes were two small lamps.

It sang to me. A sort of story. At last I lay and listened.
The story was the accustomed kind my nurse had told
me, but I was not yet too old for it. A maiden rescued
from her brutal father by a handsome prince. Even then,
even liking the tale, I didn't believe such men existed. I
knew already what men were, and, without understand-

ing, what they did to women, having seen it here and there, my father's men and the kitchen girls. It had looked and sounded violent, and both of them, each time, seemed to be in pain, scratching and shaking each other in distress.

Even so. No one had sat with me and told me a story, not for years.

In the night, I woke once, and it was curled up against my head. It smelled so green, so clean. I touched its cool back with my finger. It was mine, after all. Now I too owned something. And it would talk only to me.

Already when I look back, my childhood seems far away, my girlhood even farther. Old women speak of themselves in youth as if of other women. Am I so old, then?

During the time they all came quite round to it, and called it Froggy, and the Princess's Frog, I must have been growing up with wild rapidity, the way the young do, every day a little more.

While it performed tricks for them, found for them things that had been lost, seemed to improve the hunting, the harvests and the luck, I became, bit by bit, a woman. You see, I don't remember so much of it, because so much was always the same. It's all, in memory, one long day, one long night. The incidents are jumbled together like old clothes in a chest.

I recollect my bleeding starting, and the fuss, and how I hated it—I do so still, but the alternative state of pregnancy appeals less. I recall the bear in the forest that winter who mauled one of the men, and he died. I remember the priest coming on holy days and blessing us, and that he too liked to touch the buttocks of the maids, and once those of the kitchen boy, who later ran away.

The priest looked askance at Froggy. He asked was it some deformed thing from a traveling freak show, and my father prudently said he had bought it for me, since it was clever and made me laugh. Also, he said, it was fiercer than the dogs and would protect me. That was a lie, too. The frog was only gentle. Although, in the end, the dogs respected it and gave up trying to catch it. The

biggest dog would let Froggy ride him, and all the while
Froggy would murmur in the dog's ear. This was after
the big dog was bitten by a snake in the forest, and ran
home yelping, with terror in his eyes, knowing he would
die of snakebite, or the men would cut his throat.

But Froggy, when the dog fell down exhausted, scuttled over and latched its wide mouth on the bite. Froggy
sucked out the poison, and dribbled it on the floor with
the blood. Everyone stood back in astonishment, one of
the men muttering, stupidly, that if the dog died it would
be Froggy's fault. But the dog recovered, and never forgot.

The women took to tempting Froggy to lick cuts on
their hands to make them better. Froggy never refused.
They said it was because they rubbed on honey first. They
called this a "frog's kiss."

It never spoke to anyone but me.

And I remember one afternoon, when I had the familiar black pain of menstruation in my belly, I was lying in
the spring grass, and Froggy was sitting quietly on my
stomach, where the pain was, kneading me gently, until
I was soothed and the pain died. The sun was in the
orchard trees, which were just then losing their blossom,
and all this yellow-white-green shone behind my frog, all
puffed with light. The frog sang or chanted. Some old tale
again. What was it? A knight who rescued a maiden. I
saw for the first time how beautiful it was, this creature.
Its amber eyes like jewels, the smooth pear shape of its
body like burnished, carven, pale, dark jade. The paws
that were webbed hands and feet, and had no claws. The
sculpted mouth, with its rim of paler green, toothless and
fragrant. The healing tongue.

I smiled at the frog, not from amusement, but from
love. I loved it. It was my friend.

After this, I seemed to learn things. The meanings of
birdsong. The ways of animals, and of weather. I was
more gentle too. Who had I learned that from but Froggy?
There was no one else.

My mother pulled me to her about this time. She was,
despite the luck, still unchilded, and my always-
displeased father had slapped her. There was a bruise

under her eye where one of his rings had cut her skin. She seemed proud of the bruise, often touching at it in the hall, as if to show off that her husband still paid her attentions.

"Look at you, such a big girl. You must have more binding for your bosoms. And you mustn't run about so much." Sometimes I would receive these lessons; no one else took any notice of her. Finally neither did I. But now she added, playfully tweaking my ear, "You must have earrings. He'll want to find you a husband soon. He's mentioned it. A man with land and soldiers. You're a pretty girl, if only you'd leave off these sluttish ways. Do you ever comb your hair? I'll send you the girl to brush it every night with rose oil."

I thought of my father, planning to marry me to some large, uncouth and appalling landowner, someone like himself. From my thirteenth birthday until now, I'd tried never to think about it. But I was fifteen. The awful appointment approached.

I ran off as soon as I could, the frog bouncing after me like a jade ball—the golden one had long ago been put into a coffer.

In fact, I don't remember I ever spoke of my troubles to Froggy. He was always there. Every minute. Night and day. He knew. And when my stomach hurt he kneaded it, or when I woke crying from a nightmare he comforted me, or made me laugh. I'll say He, now. I might as well.

I sat on the old stone horse statue at the foot of the garden, which now I was tall and agile enough to climb, and Froggy sat in my lap, plaiting for me, web-fingered, a crown of red daisies. Butterflies danced, and the willows by the lake looked very bright. Later there would be a summer storm.

Froggy told me a story. It was new. A prince was cast into a dungeon. His lady came to find him and rescued him by putting magic on the bars.

At first I didn't know why the story was so strange.

Then I said, "But it's the man who rescues the maiden. She's weak and helpless. She can't do anything. He's strong and clever. It has to be him."

"Oh, no," said Froggy. "Not always. A man may be made weak, and overthrown. And do you think men are so clever, then?"

I shook my head. I gabbled, in sudden horror and fear, "I'll have to marry one of them. He'll take me away." And then I said, "He may be unkind to you as well."

"But I shan't be with you," said Froggy softly. "If you marry this man."

Astounded, I stared. He raised his wonderful topaz-amber eyes. "Not be with me—but you're always there."

"Then, it would be impossible. He'd kill me, you see. Or I'd die."

I put my arms round Froggy and held him. He never struggled, as an animal, a puppy or a cat, would do. I laid my cheek against the crown of his head, the scales of smoky jade. "You're my only friend. Don't leave me."

"It must be. If you marry the man your father finds for you."

My tears would have streamed over him. But I said, at last, "It won't happen. I'll stay here. I won't be married. Ever."

I might as well have said, Night won't fall, or, The sun won't rise tomorrow. Before I first bled and ran about screaming, thinking I was dying—no one had bothered to prepare me; it was Froggy who calmed me instead—before I bled, I'd never have thought such a filthy thing were possible. And with marriage, the threat had always been there, as long as I could recall.

My husband-to-be visited us just before Christmas that winter.

He was like the bear they said had killed my father's man, and clad in a black bearskin cloak with clasps of gold. He had a gold stud in his ear too. His boots were leather, his shirt embroidered. His men were well turned out and well armed. He stank of everything. I can't begin to itemize his smells. He was about forty, and I nearly sixteen.

I, contrarily, had been bathed in the porcelain chair-bath, and my hair had been washed and brushed with rose oil. I had on my best, newest dress, without darns, and earrings of gray-white pearl, and a ring of gold.

When he saw me, he struck a pose, my intended husband; he bowed and fawned, as if I were some great lord, or a bishop, or a king. Everyone laughed heartily, and he straightened up, all good nature.

"You see, I like her. I'll take her." Then he kissed me. He had shaved, but already his skin was rough and he scraped my mouth. But that would be nothing.

The dinner was lavish. My frog did wonderful tricks, lighting the candles, cutting a fruit with a tap of his hand, finding things people had hidden and juggling the bones of some poor little birds we had eaten.

In the end, we were able to go, the women and Froggy, to leave the men to get spectacularly drunk. My mother took me to her bower, the shabby room that led from the bedchamber. She sat me by the fire to pat my flushed face and feed me sugared walnuts.

"What a good girl. He liked you so. Oh, it will be a lovely wedding. The church all hung with flowers. The day after your birthday. And you must have three new gowns, your father says. He's a generous man. And your husband will shower you with things in your first months. He's rich. Be careful to please him and you may even see yourself in silk!"

"How do I please him?" I asked, sullen with terror.

"It's simple, child. Never, ever say no. God said women must be obedient. Do whatever your lord wants. And—well, I'll speak of that later, your wedding night. But you must always pretend that you like what he does. Recollect always, he's your superior. You owe everything to him."

I couldn't say that he made me sick, that I wished to throw up from his kiss. I knew about sex, although she had tried to hide it from me, as she had successfully hidden menstruation. The thought of that struggling and grappling and the obvious pain, with *him*, repelled me so greatly I couldn't even think about it.

I said, "I see, Mama." And at my feet, the frog ate a

little sugar, staring into the fire that made his eyes look, also, green.

When she sent me to bed—I must be at my best to see the monstrous husband off tomorrow; in fact, she knew my delighted, drunken father would want intercourse with her tonight—I ran, Froggy in my arms, and shouted at the woman with the rose oil to go away.

Then, rocking Froggy, I wept, until needles seemed to be drawn through my eyes.

My own fire was out by then. It was growing stealthily and awesomely cold. I said, "Let's go into the forest. The wolves may kill us or we'll freeze. Let's do it. Anything. Anything instead of *him*."

There was a long silence. I heard the stars crackling like icy knives in the black sky. Then the frog spoke back to me.

"There's another way."

"No. No other way. Nothing."

"Yes. Do you remember the maiden who was rescued?"

"Oh, that story—"

"Do you remember the prince that the maiden saved with her love?"

"Shush," I said. I would say today, But this is true life. This is real, and inescapable. Here, there are no miracles or magic. Then I said, "Don't talk about those silly things. They can't help me."

"Yes. I'll tell you how."

I held him in my arms and he spoke and I listened. His voice—the very voice he used to charm the dog, to charm *them*—scratchy and little, mesmerizing in the silence.

"A spell can be broken so simply, princess. Do you love me by now?"

"*Yes.*"

"Then all you need do is kiss me. On my frog's mouth. Is that unthinkable?"

"I had to kiss *him*."

"I'm not like that."

I looked down at him, my slumbrous, umbrous jewel.

His holy frog face. My friend. "I'd have done it—I just thought you might not like me to—"

"*I?*" He couldn't smile. His eyes smiled, half closing, like a cat's. "Do it now," he said.

I never in my life did anything more easily. I lifted him up and kissed him. His mouth was like a summer leaf, cool, a little moist, smelling of fresh salad, and with a crumb of sugar from the walnuts—*sweet*.

When I opened my eyes it was because my hands and my arms were empty.

"Who are you?" I said. I was so afraid, I was numb.

He said, "My God, it hurt so much. Worse than before. Oh, God."

He leaned on my wooden chair, and then dropped into it. His shining golden hair fell long over his pale face. I had never seen a man who was so beautiful. He wasn't like a man. An angel, perhaps. I heard him breathing. Presently, in his musical voice, he said to me, "Little princess, my enemies worked against me. They changed me to the form—of what you saw. But your loving kiss—has brought me back. Now I'm yours forever, and you're mine."

His eyes, as he looked at me, were not amber or green. They were very dark, the color of night, just as his hair was the color of day. His garments too. Fur, gold, steel, gems.

What did I feel? I was excited. I tingled all over. The fairy story had come true.

I didn't need to hear the sound of hoofs below, galloping, bells ringing from the village, to know his men were coming, all glorious as he was, washed, perfumed and brave, armed to the teeth. Spell broken, he could drive the unwanted husband away. And my father—he would never cease to be grateful to me for the alliance I had brought him instead, this other husband, a prince who had been a frog.

And yet, I went back to him slowly. He was now far larger than I. My head, when he stood up, reached just below his shoulder. The enormous rings on his fingers were icy. He had a smell like fire, not water. But it was very cold.

My arms were empty, but he took me into his instead. What was wrong? What did I miss?

Oh, I missed my friend.

There was never such a wedding. They still talk about it, seven years after. Of course, I left my father's house. A bride does. She belongs to her husband. But he owns a princedom. My father cried large tears of greed as he bade me farewell.

There's everything here. A bed all my own, with a canopy shaped like a firmament and stitched with diamond stars, a different bath for every day of the week— marble, rose quartz, cinnabar and so on. There are foods, and drinks, I'd never heard of. He has a menagerie, with lions. His people, now he has come back, worship him like a god.

It was almost a year before he began to eat meat again. This was advised to make him strong, and it worked, because soon after I conceived a child and it was a son. I've given him three sons now, and my body has changed shape a little. This happens. A woman's lot. Sex remains a mystery to me. But yes, it does hurt.

In our third year together, he struck me for the first time. It was over some small quarrel—I'd forgotten my mother's rule of obedience. I mean, God's rule. My husband was gracious afterward, said he was sorry and sent me a rose made of rubies, just the color my blood had been from the broken tooth.

Despite the baths, he's just a little understandably lax that way. He smells of health and meat and wine, sweat, lust, sometimes of other women. From politeness, he says, he shuns me during menstruation. He never sings to me, or tells me stories, being very busy. He kicks the dogs.

I don't know why he changed so much, changed spiritual shape as pregnancy and birth physically have altered me. Was he always this way when human? Yes, naturally. A fine, noble, virile man. A prince. He doesn't juggle,

never lights candles himself. Evidently, he's mislaid all
the magic.

Every night when I'm alone, as increasingly now,
thank God, I am, in my heavenly bed, I say a prayer for
the one I had. He taught me so much. He was my friend,
my frog. He never left me. I loved him. Not like a baby
or a pet, not like a man. A unique and crystal love, all
shattered now in pieces. I didn't know what was happening, and he must have suffered, being that other one. And
so we wasted it, that perfect time. Now it's forbidden to
all of us to speak of it, the period of his life when he was
enchanted. When he was a frog.

Nevertheless, I dream of it still. Sometimes. All that
we did when I was slender, young and free, and how I
loved him so. And how I lost him forever to that hateful
betrayal of a kiss.

Carabosse

DELIA SHERMAN

Delia Sherman is the author of the novels Through a Brazen Mirror *and* The Porcelain Dove. *She has published short fiction and poetry in various anthologies, most recently a collaboration with Ellen Kushner for* Bending the Landscape *and an erotic fantasy story for* Sirens. *She is consulting editor for Tor Books and co-editor (with Ellen Kushner and Donald G. Keller) of the anthology* Horns of Elfland.

According to Sherman, bad fairies may create problems, but they often offer the young princes and princesses they curse the opportunity to become more than they would have otherwise been. In her opinion, they do everybody a favor by stirring things up a bit, and should be given some credit—and some sympathy—for their subversive roles.

Carabosse

There were twelve fairies at the feast. Never
Thirteen. The day the queen gave birth, the king
Sent out twelve messengers on horses,
One to each of us, begging us
To bless her, name her, crown her with our favor.
So we came.

There was a banquet—well, there'd have to be,
With jeweled plates and cups, the usual fee
For fairy-godmothering. My sisters returned
The usual gifts: Beauty. Wit. A lovely voice.
Goodness (of course). Good taste (that was Martha,
Wincing at the jeweled cups, the queen's gown).
Grace. Patience. An ear for music. Dexterity
(To help her learn Princessly skills, as sewing,
Dancing, playing the lute). Amiability.
Intelligence.

I had meant to give her a long life.
I raised my wand and caught her eyes. They were
Gray and awake. Her cheeks were flushed with pink,
Her hair transparent down. She batted at
My wand and laughed. The court transfixed me
With expectant eyes—the king and queen,
My sisters, ladies, nobles, serving men,
Waiting for my gift. I considered
Her life, her marriage to a prince raised
Blind to the world behind the jeweled cups,
And said, "Sweet child, I give your life to you
To lead as you will, to go or stay, to use
My sisters' gifts, or let them be. Rule
In your own right, consortless and free.
If you choose."

The king raged; the queen wept; my sisters
Stood aghast. Not marry? The kiss of death,
A harsher curse than marriage to a frog,
Or kissing a hedgehog, or serving a witch, or even
Herding geese, since all these led to mating.
As a good fairy, I did what I could; I gave her
A hundred years' sleep, a hedge of briars, a spell
That would sort her suitors, test them for grace,
For patience, for wit and intelligence and good taste,
For amiability and a lovely voice.
A man who would be her mate,
Not her master.

The Price

PATRICIA BRIGGS

Patricia Briggs was born in Montana, and has lived in the Northwest most of her life. Her first novel, Masques, *was published in 1993 and she has since published a second,* Steal the Dragon. *She lives in Benton City, Washington, with her husband, three children, a bird, two cats, and a horse.*

Briggs grew up with fairy tales—her mother was a children's librarian—so when she decided to try her hand at reworking one, she initially looked at some of her favorites and discovered, to her dismay, that while she could expand on them, she really didn't want to change them. Instead she chose one of her least favorite tales. In its original version, "Rumpelstiltskin" has what Briggs considers a number of preposterous circumstances (what was a miller doing talking to a king anyway?), a doubtful cast of villains and heroes, not to mention several offensive themes that our society still perpetuates. She decided the tale was ripe for a rewrite. "The Price" is the result.

The Price

Molly couldn't recall just when the first time she'd seen him had been. Never before this summer certainly.

She did know that it wasn't until the fourth market of the season that she'd begun to watch for him. It was then the market steadied to a trickling flow of people rather than the flood that came initially. Sitting at her booth, she had time to observe things that on busier days escaped her notice.

He would wait until she was occupied with a customer before coming to her small booth and touching the weaving on the tables. If she stopped to talk to him, he turned away and melted into the crowd as if he were uninterested.

Her first thought was that he was a thief, but nothing was ever missing. The next explanation that occurred to her was that he was too abashed by her looks to approach. She knew that many men, even ones she'd known in childhood, were intimidated by her looks.

Being beautiful was better than being ugly, she supposed, but it caused quite as many problems as it solved. For instance, it cost her several weeks before the idea that he might be worried that she would find *him* frightening crossed her mind.

It wasn't that he was ugly, but he didn't look like anyone she'd ever seen either. Small and slight—he moved oddly, as if his joints didn't work quite the way hers did. He reminded her of the stories about the fauns with human torsos on goat's feet that ran through the hills. She'd even stolen a quick glance at his feet once, when he thought she was haggling with a customer—but his soft leather boots flexed just as hers did.

If she'd been certain that he was frightened of her, she would have let him choose his own time to approach her. But she had watched him closely last market day, and he didn't seem the sort to be easily intimidated. So she brought her small loom with her, the one she used for linen napkins, though usually she preferred to work with wool since wool caught her dyes better. The loom made her appear to be busy when there were no customers about—and so she hoped to lure him to the booth.

He wandered over casually, and she pretended not to notice him. She waited to speak until he became engrossed in a particularly bright orange-patterned blanket before she spoke.

"It's my own dye," she said without looking up. "There's a plant in the swamp that a marsher collects for me each spring. I've never seen a color that can match it—rumpelstiltskin, they call it."

He laughed, before he caught himself; it sounded rusty and surprised, as if he didn't do it often. She wasn't certain what the joke was, but she liked the sound of his laughter, so she smiled into her weaving.

"I know it," he said finally, when she thought that he'd decided to leave. "A wretched-looking plant to be responsible for such beauty."

She looked at him then, seeing his face clearly for the first time. His features were normal enough, though his nose was a bit long for the almost delicate mouth and

eyes. His skin was mottled and roughened, as though
someone had carved him from old oak and forgotten to
sand the wood smooth. The effect was odd and unsettling.

He stood still under her regard, waiting for her judgment. She smiled, turning her attention back to her weaving. "Beauty is as beauty does, sir. A blanket will keep
you warm whether it is orange or dust-colored."

"But you made it beautiful."

She nodded. "That I did, for I must sell it, and most
people look for pretty things. My face calls more people
to my booth than might otherwise come here, and I am
glad of it. But the blanket I sleep with is plain brown,
because I find that it suits me so. Your face, sir, would
not cause me to cross the street to look at you, but the
way you touch my weavings led me to tease you into this
conversation."

He laughed again. "Plain-spoken miss, eh?"

She nodded, then inquired mildly, "You are a weaver
as well, sir?"

"And you are a witch?" His voice imitated hers.

It was her turn to laugh as she showed him the cal-
luses on her fingers. "Your hands have the same marks
as mine."

He looked at her hands, then at his own. "Yes," he
said. "I am a weaver."

They talked for some time, until he relaxed with her.
He knew far more than she about weaving in general, but
he knew hardly anything about dyeing. When she asked
him about it, he shrugged and said that his teacher hadn't
used many colors. Then he made some excuse and left.

She wondered what it was that had bothered him so
as she packed the merchandise that hadn't sold in the
back of the pony cart with the tables she used to display
her goods.

"Patches," she said to the patient little pony as he
started back to the mill, "he never even told me his
name."

On the next market day, a week later, she brought some
of her dyes with her in a basket, making certain that she

included some of the orange he had admired so much. She left it out in the open, and it wasn't long before he approached.

She kept her gaze turned to the loom on her lap as she spoke. "I brought some dyes for you to try. If you like any of them, I'll tell you how to make them."

"A gift?" he said. He knelt in front of the little basket and touched a covered pot gently. "Thank you."

There was something in his voice that caused her to look at his face. When she saw his expression, she turned her attention back to her weaving so that he would not know she had been watching him: there were some things not meant for public viewing. When she looked up again, he was gone.

She didn't see him at all the next time she set up her booth, but when she started to place her weavings in the back of the cart, there was already something in it. She pushed her things aside and unfolded the piece he'd left for her.

Her fingers told her it was wool, but her eyes would have called it linen, for the yarn was so finely spun. The pattern was done in natural colors of wool, ivory, white, and rich brown. It was obviously meant for a tablecloth, but it was finer than any she'd ever seen. Her breath caught in her chest at the skill necessary to weave such a cloth.

Slowly she refolded it and nestled it among her own things. Stepping to the seat, she sent Patches toward home; her fingers could still feel the wool.

The cloth was worth a small fortune, more than her weavings would bring her in a year—obviously a courting gift. To accept such a thing from a stranger was unthinkable . . . but he didn't seem like a stranger.

She thought about his odd appearance, but could find no revulsion in her heart—perhaps only someone who was very ugly or very beautiful could understand how little beauty mattered. The man who had created the table cover had beauty in his soul. She thought of the clever fingers caressing her weaving when he thought she wasn't looking, of the man who had been so afraid to frighten

her, of the man who had bared his ugliness so that she
would not be deceived into thinking he was something
other than what he was. She thought of the man who
gave her a courting gift and the gift of time to go with it.
Molly smiled.

The path she took approached the old mill from behind, where the pony's field was. With an ease that was
half skill and half habit for both of them, Molly backed
the pony until the cart was sheltered by an overhang. She
unharnessed him and turned him loose to graze in his
paddock. She covered the wagon with a canvas that fastened down tightly enough to protect her goods from rain
or mice until the next market day. She left his gift there
until she knew what to do about it—but she was still
smiling as she walked through the narrow way between
the mill and the cottage where she lived with her father.

The millpond's rushing water was so loud that she
had no warning of the crowd that was assembled in front
of the mill. Half a dozen young nobles gathered laughing
and joking with each other while her father stood still
among them with an expression on his face she hadn't
seen since the day her mother died.

Fear knotted her stomach, and she took a step back,
intending to go for help. Two things brought her to an
abrupt stop. The first was that she finally recognized the
colors that one of the young men was wearing—royal purple. There was no help to be had against the king. The
second was that one of the young men had seen her and
was even now tugging on the king's shirt.

She'd never seen him herself, though he had a hunting
cottage nearby, for he seldom bothered to approach the
village, generally bringing his own amusements with him.
She'd heard that he was beautiful, and he was. His clothing showed both the cost of his tailor and the obsession
with hunting that kept him fit. His hair was the shade of
deepest honey and his eyes were limpid pools of chocolate. Despite the warm color, his eyes were the coldest
that she had ever seen.

"Ah," he announced. "Here she is, the fair damsel for
whom we have waited. But she starts like a frightened

doe. I weary of speech. Kemlin, I pray you, remind us of why we are here."

Molly saw the boy for the first time. A page, she thought, though she really knew nothing of court rankings. He looked frightened, but he spoke clearly enough.

"Sire, you asked me to wander about the town and tell you something amusing. So I walked the streets from cockcrow to sunset and returned to your lodge."

"And what did you report?" asked the king.

"I saw a spotted dog run off with a chicken from—"

The king held up a hand, smiling sweetly. "About the miller's daughter, I pray you."

The rebuke was mild enough, but the boy flinched.

"I am sorry, sire. I came upon three men eating bread near the fountain at the center of town. Each apparently had a daughter who was passing fair. Each father tried to outdo the other as he spoke of his daughter, until at last the miller—"

"How did you know it was the miller?" The king's voice was soft, but the titters of the other aristocrats told her that he was baiting the poor boy.

"I knew him because you sent me to the mill last week to find some fresh flour to powder my hair with, sire."

"Ah, yes. Continue."

"The miller, sire, stood and said that not only was his daughter the most beautiful woman in the kingdom, but that she was such a weaver as might spin flax into silk, wool into silver fit to bedeck a queen's neck—nay, she might even spin straw into gold if she so chose."

Molly couldn't help glancing at her father, who stood so silently in the courtyard. His gaze when it met hers was full of sorrow. She smiled at him, a small smile, just to tell him that she knew it was not his fault that the bored nobles had decided to prey on something other than deer.

"After you told me your story this morning, what was it I said?" asked the king in a faintly puzzling tone, as if he couldn't quite recall.

"Sire, you said that if the paragon of maidenly virtues existed so fair, and so skilled: that she must be your bride." The boy looked at her now, with a wealth of guilt in his eyes.

Poor baited lamb, she thought, so tormented himself, but still able to feel compassion for another victim.

When the laughter died down, the king turned to her. "Fair maiden, I see that the first claim was not exaggerated. You have hair the color of mink and eyes like the sky." He paused, but she did not respond, so he continued. "Therefore, you and your father will come to my lodge as my guests. Tonight, after we dine, you will be shown a room full of flax that you may spin into fine silk thread. If you do not . . . what was it I said, Kemlin?"

Molly knew, and she was certain the boy did, too, that the king remembered perfectly well what it was he had said.

"Sire," said the page reluctantly, "you said that if she did not, you would have the mill torn to the ground, her father's tongue put out for lying, and the girl herself beheaded in the town square."

The king smiled, revealing a pair of dimples. "Yes. I remember now. You will come with us now."

Though the king offered her a seat pillion behind one of his nobles, Molly asked to walk with her father. The king seemed ill-inclined to press the matter, so she clasped her father's hand in hers and he returned her grasp until her hand hurt—though nothing of his torment showed on his face.

The king's hunting cottage was a castle in its own right, filled with assorted young men and women. Molly and her father sat together at the dining table, two ducks in a room of swans. Swans are vicious animals for all their beauty.

After the meal, she was taken to a room as big as her father's cottage filled waist-high with flax, with a small spinning wheel in the corner. She was given a small, closed lantern to light the chamber. She nodded goodbye to her father and waited until the door shut before she allowed her shoulders to droop.

The flax was high quality, and there was more of it than she would ever be able to afford if she saved for the rest of her life. But it was flax, and no matter how good the yarn she spun, it would make fine linen cloth, but not silk. Even if fine linen thread would have been acceptable, she would never be able to spin so much in a single night.

Despair clogged her throat and misted her eyes and she kicked a pile of flax and watched it drift to the top of another pile. Wiping her arm across her eyes, she waded through flax to the spinning wheel and sat down to spin. Hours passed, and weariness slowed her quick fingers.

"Miss?"

She cried out in surprise.

The man from the marketplace shrank back as if to fade to wherever it was he'd come from.

"No," she said quickly, reaching out to him. She didn't know how he could have entered this room, but it was good to see a friendly face. "Please don't go, I was only startled. How did you get in here?"

"I heard . . ." he said hesitantly, watching her as if he expected her to scream again, "that you were here and why. It sounded as if you might need help."

She laughed; it sounded forlorn, so she stopped.

Shaking her head, she said, "There is only one wheel here—and even if you can spin faster than I, you cannot spin flax into silk."

"You might be surprised," he said, pulling back his hood, revealing funny tufts of red hair. "Let me tell you a story. Once upon a time there was a boy, not a bad boy, but not particularly good either. In a mountain near his village were caves that all of the village children had been warned against, but, as he wasn't as smart as he thought himself, the boy decided to go exploring in the caves. He got lost, of course, and spent a long time wandering through the caves until his candle burned to nothing. He tried to continue and fell down a hole, breaking any number of bones."

Molly thought about the odd way that he moved and winced in sympathy. "How did you survive?"

"Ah," he said, "that is the crux of this story. I was saved by a dwarf, an outcast from his own people, who was very lonely indeed to want the company of a human.

He used magic to save me, to let me walk and speak normally and to repair my addled wits. He taught me how to weave, an odd talent for a dwarf, I know, but he was quite good at it. I stayed with him until he died, several years ago—of old age, I should add, in case you suspect me of any foul deeds."

She hadn't, but it was nice to know.

He was quiet for a moment; then he said, "He taught me magic as well. If you like, I can spin your flax into silk, but magic always has a price. The price for my life was to live it as you see, something not quite human, but clearly nothing else."

"What would be the price of spinning all of this to silk?"

"Something you value," he replied.

She bowed her head in thought and removed a copper ring from her finger. "This belonged to a young man I loved, who loved me in return. He was called to fight in the king's army. Last year his brother brought back his body. Will this do?"

"Ah, miss," said the strange little man, a wealth of sorrow in his tone. "It will do very well—but I'm not certain I'm doing you any favors by my magic."

"Well," she said with a smile, though it wobbled a bit, "I would rather lose the ring than see my father lose his living and his tongue; and dead, I would value the ring not at all."

The man nodded and rolled the ring between his hands, spat on it once and muttered to himself. He opened his hands and the ring was gone.

Without speaking another word, he gestured for her to give up her place at the spinning wheel and set to work. His fingers flew far more swiftly than hers, and she wasn't able to see exactly when the flax turned to silk. She watched for a long while, but finally she slept, her head pillowed upon a pile of silken thread. She didn't feel the gentle touch of his clever hands against her cheek, nor did she hear him leave.

She awoke to the sound of a key turning in the lock.

She looked swiftly to the spinning wheel, but there was no one there.

The king was the first to enter the room. He had been laughing, but as he stepped through the door and saw the silk, his face went blank with astonishment.

Molly came to her feet and curtsied. "Sire."

"It seems," said the king slowly, "that your father was not overly hasty in his words—I will leave him his mill. Tonight we shall see if he keeps his tongue. Come, you will break your fast with my court."

Breakfast was not as bad as dinner had been, maybe because Molly was so tired she was able to ignore everything but her plate and her father, who was once more seated beside her. They didn't speak, though he held her hand tightly, under the table where no one would see.

That night the king took her to the same room, but this time it was filled waist-deep with fine-combed wool.

"Tomorrow," the king said, "if you have not spun this wool into silver, your father shall have his tongue removed."

Molly raised her chin, fatigue banishing her normal caution. "I will have your word before the court that if the wool is spun to silver tomorrow morning, you will leave my father alone from that moment forward."

The king's eyebrows rose at her speech. "Of course, my dear. You have my word."

"And I will witness to it," said a woman's voice.

"Mother!" said the king, astonished.

Molly looked at the woman who had approached. She didn't look old enough to have sired the king; only the slightest touch of gray sparkled in her golden hair. Her hand rested gently on the shoulder of the young page Molly recognized from the day before.

The queen smiled at her son, though her eyes were shrewd. "Sir Thomas sent a message to me, telling me what you were up to. When I heard there was a child here who was credited with such marvels, I had to come and see. Kemlin tells me that she has already spun flax into silk."

"Why did Sir Thomas go whining to you?" asked the king in a dangerously soft voice.

The queen shook her head. "My dear, it's harvest time and you have the mill closed down because of some fantastic story you heard; of course he was upset. He had no way of knowing that the girl would be able to accomplish such a feat—she has no reputation for magic."

"I see," said the king in a voice that boded ill for Sir Thomas.

"Sir Thomas," said the queen in a soft voice, "is a particular friend of mine. I would be very displeased if anything were to happen to him." She smiled. "Now, shall we let this child get to work?"

Molly stepped into the room with her lantern and waited until the door had shut behind her before taking the narrow path cleared through the wool to the spinning wheel in the far corner of the room. The wool that she walked past was of far higher quality than she'd ever worked, as if someone had combed through all the fleeces in the land and chosen the very best. She thought it would be far more beautiful spun and woven into cloth than it would be changed to cold silver.

She wondered if he would come back tonight, and if he did, whether he would be able to help her. She didn't know anything about magic, but she thought there would be a significant difference between changing flax into silk and changing wool into silver: wool and silver are not very much alike.

"Miss," he said from the other side of the spinning wheel, though he hadn't been there just a moment ago.

This time she didn't jump or start at all, but smiled. "Good evening to you, sir. I'm very glad to see you, though I could wish it were under different circumstances."

He nodded, glancing around the room. "It seems a shame to waste this; he could have chosen lesser wool."

"Shall we leave it, then?" she said softly. "I would like to see how you are able to spin it into fine yarn for weaving."

He looked at her, light blue eyes dimmed by the shadows in the room. "You will die if it is not spun to silver."

"And my father will lose his tongue." She took off her necklace. It was a cheap thing, made of beads and copper wire.

"Here," she said. "This was given to my grandmother by a traveling wiseman upon her marriage. Mother told me that it held a simple charm, just the blessing of the old man who made it, but she wore it from her marriage to her death even as her mother had."

He took it from her, weighing it in his hand. "It has magic still. Some from the maker, but more from the warmth of the women who have worn it—this will do nicely."

He cupped the necklace in his hands and blew on it gently. Then he touched his lips to his hands, whispering words she couldn't quite make out, though they sounded soft and sweet. When he opened his hands the necklace was gone. Without a word, he sat on the stool and began to spin.

She watched for a while as silver chain grew on his spindle; then she lay down in the soft wool to sleep. When she awoke he was gone and there was not a wisp of un-woven wool in the room. Instead silver chain, as finely wrought as Ian Silvermaker had ever worked, sat in a pile that was taller than she was.

She realized that her head was resting on something soft and lifted it hurriedly, expecting a find a mound of wool. Instead she found his cloak. Even as she caressed it with her fingers it faded until it was no more.

"I know," she said to the empty room. "He must not know you've been here."

When the king entered the room there was expectation on his face. Molly watched as the courtiers filed in to finger the silver, and looked up to meet the queen's specu-lative eyes.

That morning, at Her Majesty's request, Molly ate be-side the queen.

The older woman fingered the soft, woven brown-and-cream wool of her shawl and said, "I know a man who might be able to spin wool to silver."

Molly looked at the shawl and knew who had woven it. She'd seen such weaving only once before. She nodded her head. "I know a man who might weave wool into a shawl that fine."

"It was a gift from my son."

Neither smiled, but they understood each other well. The queen would not tell her son who was responsible for the magical transformations, but her first duty was to her son.

Molly's father was sent home without his daughter. He kissed her forehead before he left, and she held that kiss in her heart.

That night she was led to a different room, twice as large as the previous one. Inside was enough straw to bed down a sizable dairy herd every day for a year.

"If you can spin this into gold by morning," said the king with as much passion as she'd ever heard him speak, "I will marry you before nightfall. If you do not, you will die; this I swear on my father's bones."

She nodded at him and stepped into the room, pulling the door shut behind her. As she heard the key turn in the lock, the little weaver emerged from one of the stacks, dusting off his shoulders.

"How do you know the queen?" she asked.

He smiled. "She knew my master; he did a little magic for her and some weaving as well. Since his death she's commissioned a number of tapestries and such from me. She's an honorable woman, one who would make a staunch friend."

Molly shook her head and shrugged. Then struggled to make her decision plain without sounding plaintive. It was harder to tell him than she had thought it would be. "It doesn't matter what the queen is like. I have nothing more to give you to work your magic."

He looked so upset she stepped near him and touched his shoulder. "It's all right, you know. You kept my father safe, sir. I cannot tell you how grateful I am."

Silence fell between them, but she left her hand where it was.

"What did you think," he said finally, "of the table-cloth I sent you?"

She was surprised at his choice of topic, but grateful that he wasn't arguing with her. "I thought it was the most remarkable piece I'd ever seen."

"It might do. There was a little magic in its making—something so that you would not miss the intent of the gift." He looked away. "If you tell me where it is, I will get it for you."

"No." She would not sacrifice his gift so that she could marry the king. Especially since she wasn't certain that death would not be preferable to the life of a miller's daughter married to the king.

"It was just a tablecloth," he said, though his eyes glittered with suspicious brightness.

She raised her chin, not letting tears fall for what might have been. "I will not sacrifice your work for his benefit—I would sooner sacrifice my firstborn child."

There was a long pause while he measured her words; then he gave an abrupt nod. "Accepted."

"What?" she gasped, but he was already speaking the words of his spelling.

This night she stayed awake, watching the golden straw give way to mounds of gold. As she watched, the realization came to her that he would not let her die, even though it meant she would marry the king. She also realized that she would rather this odd man raise her child than have it raised in the court with the king as its father.

When the last bit of straw was gone, she got stiffly to her feet and walked to him where he stood beside the spinning wheel. He'd pulled the hood of his cloak over his face and she pushed it down, kissing his cheek.

"Take care of my child for me," she whispered.

He started to say something, but the sound of a group of people approaching the door interrupted him. He took two steps back and vanished.

Molly said nothing when the king entered the room; she said nothing when he married her, nor did she speak a word that night.

*   *   *

In the morning, the king asked her to spin more straw into gold.

She shook her head. "I was given three gifts of magic. I have no more."

He slapped her face and stormed out of the lodge, leaving his retinue to follow. The queen visited her later and gave her a cold, wet cloth to hold against her cheek.

"I have reminded my son," she said, "that his word was given based on your past deeds, and that the gold you brought was more than the amount most of the heiresses in the kingdom could have amassed. He's leaving for the castle, and I doubt he'll be back. Can you read?"

Molly nodded.

"Good. I will send you letters once a week and you will reply. I'll see you set up comfortably here—Sir Thomas's wife will be here shortly. She's a sensible soul and can give you advice if you need it. I've arranged for several of the servants to stay here in addition to the normal staff. Your father may visit you, if you wish, but you are not to set foot outside the hunting lodge unless my son or I summon you to court."

Molly nodded again, as there didn't seem to be anything else to do.

The queen left, and Molly was alone.

The child was born nine months later with his father's dimples and his mother's warm smile. Molly named him Paderick, after her father. She sent no word to the court, but the queen arrived the evening after the baby did.

"I have persuaded my son to leave the baby here until he is weaned," she said. "After that, I will see that he is well brought up."

"Like your son?" said Molly, raising her eyebrow, for sometimes she forgot she was only a miller's daughter.

The queen flushed. "I am sorry for what his carelessness did to you. But I am not sorry to have a grandson. I doubt that my son would ever have married if he hadn't tricked himself into it." She took a closer look at the blanket that the baby was wrapped in. "Is that a tablecloth?"

Molly smiled serenely and kissed her son's cheek. "It was a gift."

Months passed, and Molly forgot that she had ever been lonely. Her father came to the lodge every evening to play with his grandson, and the servants all joined in. When Paderick cried, which was seldom, there were fifteen pairs of arms to hold him. The page, Kemlin, one of the servants the queen had left behind, would play nonsense games that left the baby crowing for more.

A year passed, and Paderick was weaned. None of the servants had the heart to send word to the queen—Molly certainly would not. If it had not been for the knowledge that the king would insist that her baby be sent to court and raised by servants, Molly would not have been able to give Paderick up to anyone, not even to her strange little weaver. As it was, she worried that he had forgotten.

The queen came at last, with an army of nursemaids— but Molly's servants kept them away from the baby. So it was that only the queen was sitting with Molly when the weaver came at last.

"It is time," he said softly.

Molly nodded and gathered her son up from his bed. "What is this?" asked the queen.

Molly cuddled Paderick against her shoulder, soothing him back to sleep. "Magic has its price, lady. This is the price of my dowry gold—the price of the king's whim."

"My grandson?" asked the queen. Molly noticed that she asked no other questions, and she wondered what magic the queen had asked for, and what its price had been.

The queen turned to the weaver. "Is there nothing that can be done?"

He looked at Molly's hands as they cradled her child. "I know of a way that you may keep the child." He spoke to Molly. "When I lost myself in the caverns, I lost my name as well. I was given one by my master—if you can tell me what it is, I will give you back the child and pay the price of the magic myself. You have three nights to do this—an hour each night."

"Heinrich," said the queen quickly. "Adam, Theodore."

"Molly must do the naming," he said. "But no, no, and no."

Molly stepped toward him. "Leonard, Thomas, David." She knew that it would be none of those.

He shook his head.

She continued until the hour was up. The clock in the corner chimed the hour, and he looked sad as he shook his head for the last time. He bowed to Molly, took two steps back, and vanished.

The dowager queen spent the next day gathering names from books in the library, writing great long lists for Molly to read. Molly spent her day in her suite, playing blocks with Paderick and Kemlin.

"It doesn't matter, does it?" said Kemlin. "If the little man doesn't take him away, the old queen will."

Molly nodded.

"I would rather," said Kemlin seriously, "go live with a weaver than return to court."

Molly read through the list the dowager had given her; then, in the queen's presence, she read it again to the weaver. He shook his head at each of the names.

The next day the old queen questioned the servants and sent them looking for odd names from nearby villages. Molly played with her son.

That afternoon a messenger came from the court with an urgent letter for the queen. She read it once, then turned as pale as milk. Molly took the letter from her.

After she had read it, she looked at the curious faces of the servants and said, "The king has suffered a fatal accident while hunting."

She left Paderick with his grieving grandmother and went to her study. Alone, she sat in front of her loom and began to weave while she thought.

Without the king, she could raise her son, could teach him kindness as she'd hoped the weaver could do. There was no reason to lose him now, if she could solve the riddle.

She knew that he didn't intend to take her child. He had given her a question that he thought she could answer.

It was a name given to him by his master, who had been a weaver and an outcast dwarf. It was a name that he himself was not fond of—perhaps even embarrassed about, for he hadn't told her what it was. Although the queen had done business with both him and his master, she hadn't the faintest idea of his name.

It was not his own name, he said. His master had named him, as she might name a stray cat. She thought of the pets she had—the pony, Patches; the mutt that had kept her company while she worked—Scruffy.

"He was named for his looks," she said out loud in a tone of revelation. "His master was a weaver and named him after something he looked like." She stared at the orange yarn on her loom, remembering the funny laugh he'd given when she told him how she had made it. She thought of the twisted orange-and-brown plant the dye came from—a plant any trained weaver would know if he had not been trained by a dwarf who lived in a cave. Brilliant colors, she thought, would be useless in a cave.

"Rumpelstiltskin," she said, very quietly.

That night, the little weaver looked at Molly, urging her silently to think.

"Drusselbart," she said, finishing the list the old queen had given her. "Rippenbeist, or Hammelswade?"

"No," he said, exasperated

"If I name you," she said softly, "you will pay the price of the magic and I will keep my son."

He nodded.

She wrapped the sleeping baby in the tablecloth that had been his first gift. She tucked Paderick into the weaver's arms, ignoring the queen's frightened question.

"I have no name for you," she said, leaning to kiss his soft lips. She would not have him pay a price for her rescue, since magic had already cost him too much. "No name, sir, but love."

The wood in the fireplace burst into flames, and the

lodge shook. In the hall, the servants who had been listening at the door cried out. The old queen screamed, either in fright or in fury.

In the weaver's arms, Paderick giggled and shook his fists.

When the lodge settled once more upon its foundation, the room quieted. Not even the servants breathed a sound.

"Oh, Molly," breathed the little weaver, though he now was taller than her by several inches. "Such a gift you have given me. Do you know what you have wrought?"

The hood fell back and she saw that the odd marks on his face were gone. Without them—well, he wasn't as handsome as the king—but joy is very beautiful to behold whatever face it wears. His hair was still red, but it covered his head in thick waves. When he moved forward, he moved as any man did, his stride straight and strong. He kissed her.

"Love," he said, pulling away only slightly, "can pay any price and never show the cost. Will you come with me?"

As he spoke, the hall clock chimed the end of the hour for naming.

"Oh, Rumpelstiltskin." She laughed, for the name did sound odd. "Oh, my love, yes."

The weaver shifted Paderick until he held him with one hand while his other held the miller's daughter. Smiling, he took two steps back and left the dowager queen alone in the room.

Search though she might, the old queen never found the miller's daughter or her son again. The throne passed in due time to a cousin who was a much better king than the last one. The old miller disappeared that night as well, leaving an empty mill behind.

When Kemlin told the story to his own children, he would smile and end it by saying, "And they traveled to a place that the weaver knew of, where no one might bother them again. There they lived happily from that day until this."

Glass Coffin

CAITLÍN R. KIERNAN

Caitlín R. Kiernan was born near Dublin, Ireland, but has lived most of her life in the southeastern United States. Her short stories have appeared in numerous anthologies, including Dark Terrors 2, Darkside: Horror for the Next Millennium, Love in Vein 2, Lethal Kisses, Noirotica 2, Dark of the Night, Sandman: Book of Dreams, Best New Horror, *and* The Year's Best Fantasy and Horror. *Her first novel,* Silk, *was published in 1998 and Meisha Merlin Press has recently released* Candles for Elizabeth, *a collection of her short fiction. She made her comic writing debut with "Souvenirs" for DC Comics' series* The Dreaming. *Kiernan currently lives in Athens, Georgia, where she divides her time between her writing and vertebrate paleontology.*

"Glass Coffin" is one of the few contemporary takes on fairy tales in this volume. According to Kiernan, her inspiration was the song "Hardly Wait," written by Polly Jean Harvey and sung by Juliette Lewis. Other elements that contributed to the story were the gift of a Whitman's candy sampler—a replica of one from a series of tins designed by Alphonse Mucha circa 1924, featuring a faerie-like woman he named Salmagundi—and Kiernan's

first trip to Manhattan in February 1996, which brought her to Newark Airport and a long bus ride "through this postindustrial New Jersey wasteland. It was beautiful, in a very terrible, empty sort of way."

Glass Coffin

1.

They built ships here. This forgotten place on the wide gray Hudson, past the sprawling rust crane and brick crumble wastes and quarry floods of Jersey. Manhattan like Heaven on the other side and it might as well be a thousand miles away, misty unreal thing of steel and sparkling glass as insubstantial as a matte painting of the Emerald City. The yard, once upon a time Desvernine Consolidated Shipyard, just "the yard" for twenty-five years now. All her ironclad children gone to wars or bellies full of oil, the cold and crushing bottom of the sea. One building dock empty and another clogged with still-birth scrap, unfinished tanker husk that will never be anything more, and the hammerhead cranes still standing speechless watch, counterbalanced midwives. Concrete and one hundred thousand shades of corrosion.

From one window of her room, once an office for engineers and blueprints, Salmagundi Desvernine watches the yard, has folded back the heavy plastic drape that keeps out the wind and snow and stares through broken panes across the corrugated rooftops toward front gates padlocked and chained against the world outside. Squints to see farther than she can, strains to steal a glimpse beyond the road that winds away through other abandoned industries, disappears, finally, between the high gneiss-and-granite bluffs, boulders pollution-scarred and spray-paint-tagged, wrapped in fog the color of rust.

"He'll be back soon," Ariadne Moreau whispers from the half-light and shadows behind Salmagundi, dust and the clutter of antique furniture, and she turns to see the girl, oldest of the seven, the children of the yard. The old wounds on her arms faded now, needle kisses, and it's been almost two months since the last time Ariadne came back herself; they all come back sooner or later, no matter the demons or angels that draw them away. Almost all the comfort left in the world, Salmagundi thinks, and she manages an unfinished smile for Ariadne.

"He should have been back Friday," should have come rumbling down that snaketwist road, all dust and exhaust in his battered snotgreen Lincoln Continental and the children rushing out to meet him, Jesus and Rat with their jangling keys, Wren and Joey anxious for the gifts he always brings, the emptiness where Glitch should be, and Jenny Haniver and Ariadne hanging back, cautious handholders, too lost in their own private urgencies and hungers to run to him or anyone else. And Salmagundi, standing alone a few minutes longer, waiting in the gravel at the foot of the stairs to her apartment, waiting for Jimmy DeSade.

"Sometimes he's late," Ariadne says and closes the book she's been reading for the last hour, her face close to the pages to see the words in the flat gray January afternoon leaking into the room. Something about Rosicrucians borrowed from Rat's pipe shop library, and she returns the smile, reflects the smile, brushes tangled black hair from her eyes. Salmagundi is the most beautiful woman, most beautiful thing, she's ever known; one-third of her trinity, but more beautiful by ten than either her lover or the smack; hair as gold as department-store Christmas tinsel, slenderlong hands and marble skin, if marble ever had the faint blush across Salmagundi's high cheekbones, the candy red in her lips. Everything Ariadne trusts, all the light she's ever seen, straight or stoned, and times like this she doesn't know why she ever needs the dope, why she ever needs anything but the certainty that she'll never be asked to leave the yard.

"He'll be here soon," and Ariadne hopes she sounds confident, reassuring, and Salmagundi sighs and turns back to her window, cold wind off the river fingering her hair, and she says, "When I close my eyes I can't find him," and she doesn't say anything else, and after a while, Ariadne goes back to her book.

Salmagundi's stingy fortune was exhausted long ago and now there's only the yard and what it gives up to the patient salvages of the children: dollars and more often pennies for wreck and ruin, copper wire and pipe, bits and warped pieces of presses and drills and sheet-metal cutters, sold off for scrap. And the money and food that Jimmy DeSade brings them, the white powder he brings back from Mexico and turns into cash in Baltimore and Philadelphia and Newark. So no one goes hungry and no one freezes in the winter and there are little comforts.

Rat and Jesus keep the keys and almost always find the best scrap. Rat, who doesn't look anyone in the eye anymore, his face a wormpink scar and hair oiled back smooth with industrial lubricants. Jesus all stringy hard muscle and Cuban-Chinese good looks, and today they're breaking down a gap press that Rat found hidden away in the subbasement of one of the pre-outfitting shops. Two treacherous days of block and tackle to get it up into the sun and their hands move sure as surgeons, or pathologists over a suspicious corpse, wrenches and acetylene fire for scalpels. Wren and Joey watch them, ready to help when they can, to bring water or roll cigarettes.

Wren hiding out here from the cops and juvie, sanctu-

ary after she finally got too tired of her stepfather's dick
between her legs, and she changed the rules with two
shots from a .38 she found in a garbage can on West
Forty-second Street. Joey, who just showed up at the gates
one day and maybe this'll be his last winter, endless diar-
rhea and losing so much weight, never mind the black-
market AZT that Jimmy brings.

Jesus shuts off his torch, squints and blinks behind
tinted goggles like fish eyes, "How 'bout a smoke, Wren
Bird?" and she reaches for the leather bag of tobacco
around her neck as Ariadne steps through a rotted jumble
of plywood pallets and pipe twisted like sections of
robot intestine.

"Hi," Rat says, not looking at her, and she hands his
book back, stands beside Wren and Joey and stares at the
gap press, what's left of it and the scatter of its dissection
spread across an oily dropcloth at their feet, motor still
one piece, grungy bits she can't identify. Wren finishes
rolling the cigarette, seals the paper expertly with one lick
and passes it to Jesus. Zippo from his pocket and he blows
smoke the hopeless color of the sky. "He'll be here soon,"
he says and she nods, shrugs and sits on the crate with
Wren and Joey.

"She's scared," and Ariadne realizes that she's scared,
too; wishes Jenny Haniver were with her now instead of
off digging mussels, hunting blue crabs along the mud-
flats at the old docks. "She's not eating," Ariadne says,
"Won't do anything but sit at the window watching the
road."

Same moment and same words from their mouths,
"Nobody fucks with Jimmy," and before Wren has a
chance, Joey says, "Jinx," and punches her in the arm.
"Jinx yourself, Joseph," but Ariadne sees how scared she
looks, too; all of them scared, like Salmagundi, all of them
waiting, watching the road, each in his or her own way
and in their own time. More scared because Salmagundi
is scared.

"Damn straight," Jesus says. "Not more'n once they
don't," and takes another drag off his cigarette before he
flicks the roach away and turns the oxyacetylene torch on

again and draws slicing fire down the gap press's steel skin.

Fading dusk, night already where the river winds away toward Hudson Bay, the sea beyond, and across the water Manhattan burns like a grounded slab of Milky Way, as distant, as unfathomable as the stars. Jenny Haniver sits over her bubbling hot-plate stew, big dinged and dented pot full of the things she found along the shore, and the other children sit around her; all eyes on the pot or the cement floor of the mostly empty warehouse where they sleep and eat and keep themselves from the wind. No light but stubby candles and she stirs the mussels and crabs, mud rinsed away and everything dropped in whole, lucky today so there's a small eel, too. Niggardly pinches of black pepper and salt, sage from her baby-food jars of spices, almost empty and there'll be no more until Jimmy comes back.

"It smells good," Wren says, and her voice just seems to make the silence that lies like ice over the yard that much heavier, hard blanket of unspoken fears, and Jesus says, "Yeah, it does," but Jenny only shrugs and the quiet rushes back to fill in even the tiniest unguarded space.

"Tell us a story," Joey says, looking at Ariadne Moreau where she sits on the floor next to Jenny. "Tell us about the city." Ariadne glances at Jenny Haniver, shakes her head. "You already know about the city, Joey. You know everything about the city you need to know."

"Then tell us about something else. Tell us about how the yard used to be when Salmagundi was a little kid."

And this is not so different from any other night, them asking her to talk to keep away the dark and all their ghosts, her complaining that they know all the stories, could recite them in their sleep: Silas Desvernine opening the yard a hundred years ago, longer than that, his ships built with rivets instead of welds, and the wars, then, and the fortunes handed down from Silas to his children, their children, grandchildren, Salmagundi's father. The bad times, finally, the yard closing, never a happy ending and she doesn't know why they want to hear. Same tired story, the clanging Desvernine empire of steel and smoke lost because its last emperor was a drunk and the empress a gambler and she bet away four generations on a spinning wheel and tiny black ball.

Same as ever, except for Salmagundi still sitting alone in her room, watching the road, and when Ariadne asked her if she was coming down for supper or wanted something brought up, she said no, I'm really not hungry, and her eyes never left the window. Same, except their minds are all somewhere else, waiting.

"Not tonight, Joey," Ariadne says softly, firm, and she shivers inside her raveling orange cardigan, holds Jenny's hand while dusk closes down and turns to barren darkness.

She fell asleep in the chair by the window, wrapped in quilts from her bed, her robes underneath, and now Salmagundi dreams that she's locked outside the gates of the yard. Chain-link and silver coils of razor wire, glinting blades in the moonlight and the lifeless or twitching bodies of rock doves and starlings trapped within the thorns. Fingers so cold they're numb, but she tries to free one of the birds, slices her thumb open, her blood and the starling's commingling painlessly and it doesn't matter how loud she calls out for Ariadne or the others. Shadows and dull shine off the cranes and tin roofs on the other side of the fence, span of jib cranes like the skeletons of dinosaurs sculpted in steel. Just blackness where the lights of New York City ought to be, and the bird dies in her bleeding hands.

"He's left you," her mother says, watching through the diamond weave of the fence. An old woman, which her mother never was; not the woman who died in a sanitarium upstate a long time before these wrinkles and crooked bones, this voice a dry place over naked gums. "There's always someone prettier," her mother says. "And very little you can do about it, in the end."

"No, Mother," and the old woman laughs, laugh too full of the night behind that withered face: *I see myself in your face,* she says. *Myself locked up in you like light coming off a mirror* . . . but Salmagundi is calling for Ariadne, for Rat or Jesus, drowning her out, or simply drowning.

"They won't hear you," the old woman says. "They're all asleep, heads full of dust and sand in their eyes. They know he isn't coming back this time."

And Salmagundi turns away from the old woman that her mother never became, and there's the road instead, broken asphalt crumble, potholes filled with oilsheen water, new cracks at her feet, as the razor wire grows around her like brambles, wriggles up from the dead soil and metal writhes across the tarmac. In the distance, just coming through the narrow cut in the bluff, she sees his headlights. Or the nighthungry eyes of something else altogether, but it doesn't matter which because the wire winds tighter around her, wraps her and slices her white skin, and the lights never get any closer.

"But what *is* it," Ariadne asks as Rat and Jesus set the bulky piece of machinery down, odd something like a stubby fan, hub and maybe twenty rubber straps where blades would be, heavy black rubber and the ends of the straps flattened and four round and pimpled metal disks attached to each, exotic coins or worthless slugs.

"Centrifugal flagellator," Rat says, and she shakes her head. "Fanciest words you come up with yet for a piece of junk," and so he pulls a small book from the back pocket of his coveralls, grease-stained and yellow pages and he flips to a diagram of the thing, almost an exact likeness, shows it to Ariadne without looking at her. "See," he says. "What I said. For cleaning metal, getting rid of loose mill scale or rust. Those things on the rotary flaps are tungsten shot."

"Tungsten. That oughta be worth a few bucks at least, eh, Ratboy?" Jesus smiling, sweating and filthy and tired, and almost enough to make her feel better, more like herself, less like the threatening sky overhead, indigo cumulonimbus underside of the frostbite sky, dead cold pressing down toward earth and there could be snow by afternoon.

Jesus sits on the ground, strong legs crossed, inspecting the device more closely, takes the book from Rat and makes a show of comparing the two. "Man, we need some sounds, Rat. Go get the box." And Rat comes back a few minutes later with the huge boom box Glitch left behind but now they all share when there are batteries. Pulls back strips of duct tape that hold the CD player's lid closed and slips in House of Pain. "Back from the Dead," and Jesus hums along.

None of them heard her coming up behind, but Ariadne knows it first, turns and there's Salmagundi dressed in velvet the color of smog and the long black leather overcoat Jimmy brought her last time. Sleepless bruisy red beneath those startling blue eyes and when she talks, Ariadne thinks it's more a ghost of Salmagundi and cringes inside where no one can see.

"Hello," a little slurred, and Ariadne wonders what she's on, Valium or Xanax or maybe she has needles of her own, and "What have you found, Jesus?" she says.

"I found it," Rat whispers and Jesus nods his head. "Yeah, true fact, Ratboy found it." And then Rat explains the peening wheel for Salmagundi, explains again, more nervous but more detail than before and the jittery hint of a stutter.

"It was in one of the painting sheds," Jesus adds, "buried under a whole buncha crap," and Salmagundi stoops down for a better look, velvet dragging in the mud, and Ariadne sees she's barefoot. "Has anyone seen Wren and Joey today?" absent flat tone, and Salmagundi runs the tips of her white fingers over the blunt ends of the straps, nails chewed ragged, raw cuticles.

"They were chasin' rats around the docks, went down there with Jenny," Jesus says and Salmagundi pulls her hand back, then jerks it away fast, and Ariadne sees the blood welling from the cut on her thumb, sees too the rust-brown sliver of steel like a stinger jutting from one of the rubber flaps. "Ah," and the thumb to her mouth, Ariadne bending to see. Salmagundi frowns and shakes her head, it's nothing, nothing serious, but when she takes her thumb out of her mouth Ariadne can see how deep the cut is, pad laid open, parted, and a little crimson left behind on Salmagundi's carnation lips.

"We should get some peroxide on it, at least, and a bandage," but no response from Salmagundi, and Rat's already run off for one of the first-aid boxes; there are no inconsequential cuts in the yard, no scratch so small that staph or lockjaw can't find its way in through the breach. Ariadne holds her hand, squeezes Salmagundi's thumb lightly so it will bleed away germs or filth, slow red drip to the gray earth, and Salmagundi watches each drop of herself grow too heavy to resist gravity, each red spat.

"Something's wrong, Ariadne," she says. "Something's happened to him."

"Shit, it might just be his fucking car broke down again," Jesus says and she turns on him, "Shut up," pulls free of Ariadne's grasp and something in her eyes now that they've never seen there before, something wild and frightened and mean, someone she could have been all along, if things were different. Desperation and whatever comes between faith and loss, the cold wind in her hair like it was taking sides.

"I'm sick of all of you pretending nothing's wrong, that it hasn't been days . . ." And she turns her back on them and her feet make hardly any sound at all in the mud and gravel as she goes. Ariadne thinks that maybe Jesus will cry and she doesn't want to see, so she looks at the ground and the small bloody place Salmagundi left behind.

2.

Here's the scene: Jimmy DeSade and his junkyard Lincoln rolling mercuric-smooth down the New Jersey Turnpike like asphalt was greased black glass, expert weave and tailgate and the other cars get out of his way. Thrash from the tape deck, this pale man behind the wheel and the glow from the dash on his face, ghost glow of deep-sea things, face past gaunt or hard and the sunglasses like his soul's windshield. Sleet for the past five miles and here's his exit; he lights another cigarette, last one from the pack on the seat beside him, and glides off the free-way into the night crouched past the streetlights.

Almost a week since he'd slipped across the border near Matamoros, untouchable, just one more desert shadow, and enough shit tucked away inside the car's secret places that his happy ass could stay put till spring. And then New Orleans and the Chartres Street deal gone bad—no, nothing so simple or sane as bad; skullfucking incendiary, to tell the truth, and a miracle he hadn't lost more than half the coke and a little skin besides. That the Haitians hadn't kept his teeth, hadn't kept his fucking balls for their gris-gris charms. The rest of the stuff dumped on his Philly connection, never mind that he'd almost had to give it away to unload that much that fast, a buyer's market, Jimmy, after all, and that Irish cocksucker grinning like a tetanus corpse as she split open a bag with her little pen knife, discreetest taste with the tongue-moist tip of one finger.

"What's got you makin' sucker deals, Jimmy?" And she had another taste while he counted her money, counted it twice just to piss her off, his money now, and the fucking blow isn't his problem anymore. Just this Jersey night, broken yellow line and the lights from Wee-hawken off that way, so he tries to forget New Orleans and Ciara Gallagher and let the road pull him smooth across the ruined marshes and divided stones, down the poisoned land to the river.

And, of course, the gates are locked. Jesus and Rat know it'd be both their asses if he came rolling up and found them any other way, and, of course, Jimmy DeSade has his keys. But the yard is still and cold as ash, every-thing turning silver oysterwhite from the sleet changing to snow, and he shifts into park and gets out, steps around into the space between the Lincoln's headlights and now he can see the new chains, new locks and sloppy loops of wire like barbed and bladed vines. "Hey," he shouts, and "Jesus," and nothing and no one answers, just the wind that ignores his trench-coat black leather and everything underneath, insubstantial, numbing teeth at his skin. There are bolt cutters in the trunk and proba-

bly nothing on the gate he can't get through in half an
hour or so, but no comfort there, nothing but affirmation,
dread freezing hard as the ice and slag beneath his boots.
So Jimmy DeSade stands in the gathering storm a minute
longer, calling Jesus and Rat and Ariadne Moreau until
his throat hurts, and Salmagundi, last of all.

There's still a little candlelight in the room and Jesus sits
in one corner, an arm around Wren and an arm around
Joey, holding them while they cry. Rat's been gone for
hours, and Jenny Haniver sits at Salmagundi's dressing
table, painting her face with white powder and cherry-
ripe rouge. Ariadne has started all over again, combing
Salmagundi's golden hair, when the door to the apartment opens, opens hard and bangs loud against the wall,
and there's Jimmy DeSade. Tall man of leather and studs
and chains, and what she sees on his face now, she's always known that was there. Wren tries to pull free, to
run to him, and Jesus holds her back.

"Ariadne?" he says, and "Jesus?" and his voice is raw
and colder than the wind flaying itself alive on the corners
of the building. "We did everything we knew how to do,
Jimmy," but three long strides and he's pushing her out
of the way, her ass bumps to the hard floor and the comb
tangles, pulls away a handful of Salmagundi's hair. "Fuck
this," he says, "Oh," and "Fuck this," and he shakes her,
shakes the hollow shell that was her, and Salmagundi's
head lolls rag-doll limp.

Most of the things they did to try and bring her back
are hidden beneath the gown that Ariadne has dressed
her in, silk the green-black color of avocado skin and lace.
And Jimmy just says the same thing, fuck me, oh, fuck
me, over and over and Wren is crying again. He kisses
Salmagundi hard, his living pale flesh against dead pale,
looks like maybe he's trying mouth-to-mouth or just kissing her harder than Ariadne's ever seen anyone kiss anyone or anything before.

"She just cut her finger," she says finally. "Cut her
thumb on a piece of junk," and Jimmy DeSade comes up
for air, looks at her, sunglass plastic where his eyes should

be. "What?" and she knew better than to repeat herself, stared down at the comb, the yellow strands of Salmagundi's hair in its teeth.

"You're saying she cut her fucking finger and now she's fucking *dead?!*" Ariadne nods then, because she's afraid not to, but just once.

He holds up her right hand, nothing there but lifeless fingers, and then her left and the ragged bandages, mummy fist and ugly stains like oil and strawberry jam. Unwinds the gauze and Salmagundi's thumb still so swollen, mutilated where they'd tried to get the poison out of her blood, and the sound starts way down inside him, makes Ariadne think of a subway train on its way into the station, not so much a sound as something you feel in every cell, subsonic, seismic. This isn't sorrow and it isn't rage, the sound of a soul tearing, and he's picking Ariadne up off the floor before she knows it, the comb dropped from her fingers and skittering away.

"You goddamn fucking *junkie,*" last word like a Roman's nail, and maybe that's what he means: nail her to this wall for their sin. "Haven't you ever fucking heard of a goddamn *hospital?*" No time for an answer, her feet dangling an inch above the floor, and he slams her into the wall so hard the world shimmers through her eyes.

"*Jimmy,*" and Jesus is trying to pull him off her, Wren and Joey both wailing in their corner, and she catches a glimpse of Jenny Haniver reversed in Salmagundi's mirror, mime face and smeared lips, before she falls, dazzled lump at the silver-tipped toes of his boots. The sound of his fist hitting Jesus is very loud, or just the sound of Jesus's nose breaking, either one or maybe both.

"You let her die," he says, and Jesus is cradling his face in his hands, blood between his fingers, shaking his head like he's forgotten how to talk, *no, Jimmy, no, we didn't* in his wide, dark eyes. "Yes, you *did,* Jesus. Yes, you fucking did. You *let* her die." Last thing he'll ever say to them, though Ariadne doesn't know that yet, all she can see is the gun that wasn't in his hands a minute ago, abracadabra and this huge fucking pistol black and perfect shiny even in the dim candlelight. He doesn't aim, just squeezes the trigger, and the world is too full of the sound of the gun for anything else, even breathing.

Then she's crawling toward Jesus, crawling past those boots, boots sharp and hard enough they could kill if they wanted to, crawling through the brittle, shell-shock deafness after the shot. Jesus curled fetal, and she thinks she can hear him whimpering, but that might just be the ringing in her ears. Nasty big gouge in the concrete floor, little crater and no sign of the slug. "Come on," she says, "get up," hears her voice more inside herself than coming out her mouth, and she forces Jesus up, on his knees at least, *just get them out of here, just get us out and maybe he won't kill us.*

Wren and Joey at her side without being called, neither of them crying now, scared past anything but wide-eyed, silent disbelief. And Jimmy sitting on Salmagundi's bed, leaning over her body, mother protective or threatful as a movie vampire, scarecrow fingers stroking her gray cheeks, black hair fallen forward and hiding his face. Ariadne goes to Jenny Haniver, tears streaking sloppy Robert Smith makeup now, kohl smudge around her eyes, holes and Jenny looking out at her through them.

"We were supposed to keep her safe," Jenny Haniver says. "That's all we had to do. Dig up junk and keep her safe . . ." And Ariadne sees where the mirror's broken, Jimmy DeSade's bullet ricocheted off the floor and buried somewhere behind the spiderwebbed looking glass. She jerks the girl up and off the stool, no cooperation but no resistance, either, lifeless zombie shuffle that pisses Ariadne off, makes her want to kick Jenny, let her sorrow and fear lash out and bite someone the way Jimmy's had. Instead, she pushes them forward, only Jesus looking back over his shoulder, pushes them into the narrow hallway cold as ice, dark as the memory of night, and closes the door behind her.

Two hours later, almost dawn, and Jimmy DeSade has found all the sheet metal he'll need in one of the cutting shops, that much and a hundred times more, and he's found Rat there, too, cringing alone in the rusting shadows. No words between them, nothing that can be said, but Rat helps him cut the steel plates down, carbon alloy steel shaped for hulls designed and never realized, flamesliced down into appropriate and manageable shapes, rough squares and rectangles from the blueprint in Jimmy's head and his sunglasses traded for smoky welder's goggles. Heavy pieces, still, and they carry them one at a time through the fresh snow and ice slick and Jimmy feels their eyes, watching, the eyes of the children of the yard hiding somewhere in the gloom. Trip after trip from the shop up the stairs to Salmagundi's apartment and back down to the shop and back to Salmagundi's apartment, her antiques, heirlooms for no one now, pushed aside, tipped over, as they lay the sections out on the floor.

"You're gonna need an outfit up here," Rat says finally, flinching bold stroke against the gelatin silence. And Jimmy nods his head, yeah, yeah, "And glass," he says. "Good, sturdy glass, Rat. Can you find me that, too?"

"Yeah. No problem," and Rat sounds grateful and relieved and afraid. "In the warehouses there's lots of good glass, if you know where to look." They leave her alone again, her cold body on the bed, and an hour later, the sun rising behind the clouds, black to gray to grayer, and they have the big tank of oxygen and a smaller blue tank of acetylene, lengths of hose and a torch, but there's still the glass and Rat, huffing, out of breath, propped against a hand truck and watching his feet when he says, "If Jesus helped, it'd be easier, go faster . . ." Jimmy wipes sweat off his face, shakes his head no and Rat doesn't bring it up again.

Rat leads him to the glass, neat rows a quarter inch thick and watery green under brown paper, shows him how to score it and tap hard enough to break along the groove without cracking or shattering the whole pane. And it's noon by the time they begin carrying the glass to Salmagundi's apartment, and the sky is almost the same color it was at dawn.

"Don't look directly at the flame," Rat says, and "You know that," apology, and he shows Jimmy how to stuff the legs of his black jeans down into his tall boots, some duct tape wrapped tight around to keep them in and the melting filler metal out. And no more words after that, no need, lifting the sections into place one after another and in between, the metal-on-metal scrape of the spark lighter and supernova white from the torch, flux and Rat keeping an eye on the four pressure gauges while Jimmy DeSade welds like he's done this all his life, or all his life has led to this moment of heat and light and he turns steel to molten drops and fleeting puddles as the flame travels the jagged length of each seam, solidifying again, strong new alloy of filler rod and steel left cooling behind.

Once, he pauses, sweatgrime face and the frame almost done; it makes Rat think of a giant's unfinished fish tank, blind and empty, no water or guppies or plastic seaweed inside. Jimmy glances back at Rat, Rat and the canisters of compressed gas, flare of his torch aimed careless and intentionally at the oxygen; Rat understands, thinks he *might* understand, and waits while Jimmy DeSade decides their futures, considers this other solution, eyes secret behind his goggles; a few seconds longer than long minutes and he turns back to his work and Rat feels no relief at all.

3.

Colder and it's getting dark again, and not one of them moves, hardly breathes as the Lincoln spins its tires and pulls away, suddenly nothing left of Jimmy DeSade but a cloud of exhaust rising up and coming apart in the wind, nothing but the fading sound of his wheels rolling away over scabby earth. And even then they wait, shivering together in the fresh dark until Ariadne moves first, first faltering step like she has to learn to walk all over again, and she doesn't think to let go of Jenny's hand, so she comes, too, and Jesus next, and Wren and Joey with him. Joey's been coughing hard the past couple of hours, and the sound makes Ariadne think of the river lapping, nibbling at the edges of the yard.

Their boots and tennis-shoe tatters quiet across the

snow, maybe two inches now, to the wide snowbare place
where Jimmy's car sat all day and they each walk around
that, to the stairs, rickety iron path up to Salmagundi's
apartment, and before she takes it, Ariadne Moreau looks
back at them. Four of the seven, small in the night and
the snow catching in their hair, on their clothes, and it
would kindly bury them if they only stood still long
enough to let it, by spring nothing left but clean bones
and empty rags to disappoint the gulls. Another thing
broken, she thinks, and remembering what Jenny Haniver
said before Salmagundi's shattered mirror, How'd we
ever believe we could keep anything safe? How'd we ever
believe . . . and she starts up the stairs, trying in vain not
to walk in Jimmy DeSade's footprints.

They follow her, not a word among them, slippery
steps and the railing too cold to hold on to; the stairs
creak and rustcry and sway a little from the wind and
their weight.

At the top, Ariadne opens the door before anyone can
stop her, before she can stop, and the room still has a
little candlelight, enough she can see by and stare sick at
all Salmagundi's threadbare fine furniture tossed about
careless like junk, like nobody ever loved it. Notices the
splintered leg on an overturned table before she even sees
Rat and the thing that Jimmy DeSade has made, and Salmagundi sealed inside. The straight, black lines that come
together in corners as sharp as the toes of Jimmy DeSade's
boots, Rat with one cheek squashed against the glass, and
the fat roll of bills in his hand; he's sobbing without a
sound and his tears run down and streak like the glass
has begun to melt from the heat of his face pressed too
long against it.

They push in around her, Jenny Haniver and Jesus,
Wren and Joey, and "Oh," Wren says, "oh," very softly;
Rat leaves a sticky print on the glass when he turns to
see, snot and salt water smudge, and he looks Ariadne in
the eye.

"He ain't comin' back," he says, "*never*," and now Ariadne looks away, at the gray face inside the cage of glass
and solder, those closed and sunken lids safer than this

boy's lost green eyes, "That's what he said, Jesus," and then Rat turns away from them again. And Ariadne Moreau walks past Salmagundi's glass coffin, waxlight shimmer, and she goes to the window. There's snow blown in under the plastic, a little drift on the floor, and she pushes back the drape. Outside, the yard is still and white, dulled beneath the snow like an old dog's teeth, and the road beyond is dark and nothing moves there, either.

The Vanishing Virgin

HARVEY JACOBS

Harvey Jacobs began his career with The Village Voice, *then published* East, *a weekly newspaper on New York's Lower East Side. He joined ABC-TV, where he became active in the early development of the global satellite system as an executive with ABC's Worldvision Network. For over twenty years, he lived as a freelancer based in New York City, publishing the novels* The Juror, Summer on a Mountain of Spices, Beautiful Soup, *and, most recently,* American Goliath, *a novel inspired by the true tale of the Cardiff Giant. His short stories have appeared in a wide variety of magazines, including* Omni *and* The Magazine of Fantasy and Science Fiction, *and in some forty anthologies. Some of them have been collected in* The Egg of the Glak. *He now lives in Sag Harbor, NY.*

"The Vanishing Virgin" is inspired by Hans Christian Andersen's "The Flea and the Professor." A relative of Harry Houdini once told Jacobs that, while the magician was the first to debunk any mystical power behind his "magic," family members strongly suspected that he was befuddled by some of his own escapes and illusions. Magic, even the most controlled, Jacobs asserts, "has a way of spinning out of control and creating magic of its own. 'The Vanishing Virgin' is a story about escape, about magic opening doors to rooms even the magician couldn't suspect. And that is the

source of surprise. When a fair maiden is disappeared, even in the most obvious vanishing act, where is she? And who returns to bear witness?"

The Vanishing Virgin

There was a failed magician who called himself Dr. Ohm, a short but massive man in his mid-thirties with a steamroller body, a bowling-ball head that flared patches of Brillo hair from behind ears that could have been bumblebee wings, a great, flaccid face that framed foglight eyes with caterpillar lashes, a doorknob nose with nostrils like bat caves, a slash of a mouth that dribbled spittle from between battered teeth, and a chin like an avocado pit.

After years of denial, he accepted the hard fact that he couldn't be called handsome in any traditional sense. But he did think of himself as impressive of aspect, certainly formidable, entirely charismatic and highly desirable to members of both sexes and even to animals both wild and domestic.

He also regarded himself as a gifted magician, which was something of a tragic flaw, since his bag of tricks was very limited even by the lowest standards and his technique was worse than cloddish.

Dr. Ohm came to "show business" quite by accident. Under another name he had long since forgotten, he once worked as a systems analyst for a major corporation. When the company downsized, he was left jobless, penniless, and without many prospects. The only work he could find was as a kind of billboard for a tattoo artist. The artist covered him with signs and symbols, New Age and mystical, which he wryly described as his "visible means of support." But along came the day when there was no space left to fill. Despite a diet of potatoes, corn and bananas designed to increase his surface, Dr. Ohm's pelt was insufficient to meet the artist's expanding needs. So he was fired again, this time without even unemployment insurance for comfort. And since his illustrator had used cheap, diluted inks, Dr. Ohm's tattoos faded day by day like an old man's memories of long-ago summers.

Thus, with a few dollars in a shabby pocket, he was cast back into the nervous world of the jobless. Covered as he was with drooping images of dragons and imps, gargoyles, dwarfs and pyramids, zodiac signs and hieroglyphs, Dr. Ohm resembled a secondhand sarcophagus. Human Resource managers gave him short shrift, deeming him overqualified or insufficiently motivated.

His only course was to go into business for himself. He browsed the classifieds looking for opportunity. Finally, after much searching, he found an ad placed by a dying wizard whose career dated back to the days of vaudeville. A deal was quickly struck for the old necromancer's store of ho-hum flimflammery, jaded feats of magic and a few pamphlets with titles like *How to Startle and Turn a Profit* and *Mastering the Truth About Deception.*

In exchange for his last money, Dr. Ohm bought the wizard's professional name, a deck of marked cards, a jacket with secret pockets, instruction manuals missing crucial pages, a decrepit rabbit called Pooper who had to be dragged by brute force from the ratty high hat that had become its only home, a moth-riddled cape with all the allure of a blanket from a cheap motel, a warped wand, a stuffed raven with a broken tape-recorded voice that could only croak *More! More!*, and a few other miscellaneous props and gizmos. The only item of any real value was an illusion called "The Vanishing Virgin," an ornately carved wooden desk that had once belonged to Harry Houdini, who had it cleverly built to disappear a petite assistant.

Dr. Ohm also got the petite assistant, a frail wisp of a lady called Ms. Molly, who had been part of the act for years. Her principal function as resident virgin, along with the usual posing and preening, was to climb into a cabinet in that ancient desk, seemingly vanish into thin air, then reappear, happily intact, inside a large drawer on the desk's far side.

It didn't take much imagination for Dr. Ohm to realize that the desk had a hidden compartment behind the cabinet and a crawl space that led to the drawer. Fortunately for the magician, the audiences he faced didn't have much imagination. Ms. Molly's magical act was the centerpiece of his show and the only reason he got bookings.

And tiny Ms. Molly proved to be a real bargain. Like Pooper, the exhausted rabbit, she was content with a few carrots and some lettuce for dinner. Occasionally Dr. Ohm gave her a dollar or two to cover the cost of what he called "indulgent female follies." These "follies" included buying detergent for washing their costumes, toothpaste for polishing their teeth, and thread she used to mend their ragged garments. Dr. Ohm quickly realized that Ms. Molly adored the stage, had a low opinion of her talents, and was happy to be exploited so long as her name appeared on Dr. Ohm's frayed posters, albeit in unreadable type the size of ant droppings.

To keep Ms. Molly from questioning her lot or complaining about her shabby treatment, Dr. Ohm was quick to remind her that she was lucky for the opportunity to orbit his rising star. He was also diabolically clever at finding engagements in cold places. Being so wispy and fragile, Ms. Molly was perpetually shivering in drafty theaters, so busy seeking a fragment of warmth that she had no time to think about distractions like a minimum wage.

To further ensure her essential loyalty, Dr. Ohm married her on a frigid Kansas afternoon. As a wedding gift, he gave her an icicle dipped in strawberry preserves, which she licked with relish and even shared with poor Pooper, who had been temporarily evicted from his high-hat home (which the pompous groom wore during the pathetic civil ceremony). Ms. Molly, whom Dr. Ohm called his little radiator, proved to be a pleasant source of warmth on long winter nights. He drained every thermal unit his bride had to give, leaving her on the verge of hypothermia.

All things considered, Dr. Ohm's itinerant lifestyle kept him reasonably comfortable if not content. He regarded his marriage as one of inconvenience forced on him by circumstance but far from painful. As for Ms. Molly, what affection she lacked from her husband was provided by the pleasure of hearing audiences gasp when she seemed to evaporate from inside the desk's deep cabinet, then applaud with relief when, after suitable chanting by Dr. Ohm, she was found alive, well and fully materialized in the desk's large drawer. She would look dazed at first, then leap gingerly into a bow, arms extended, glowing with approval while trying to raise her temperature with shards of heat from the hot white spotlight that punctuated "The Vanishing Virgin's" return from oblivion.

So it was that Dr. Ohm and his wife continued their endless string of one-night stands, eking out a living. While the magician grumbled and ground his teeth over fate's cruelty, his spouse read *Daily Variety*, did her chores, kept up appearances and cooked tasty meals for her mate. She took her own sparse meals with the balding, sullen rabbit. Her evenings were spent adding daubs of color to Dr. Ohm's pantheon of aging tattoos, preparing for their next performance, dismantling and packing their belongings for further travel and never uttering a negative word.

One night, in South Bend, Indiana, where they had gone to entertain a pep rally for senescent Notre Dame alumni, Ms. Molly was astonished when Pooper the rabbit spoke to her. She had no idea the sad creature could make any sound, much less structure entire coherent sentences. In a curiously strong voice, his pink nose twitching and his eyes blinking, Pooper said, "Did you see how the bastard pulled me out of my hat tonight? He yanked my ears so hard I nearly lost my scalp. My head is ringing like a bell tower."

"Dr. Ohm has decided to speed things along," Ms. Molly said. "He feels it takes too long to get you moving and there's some truth to that. You are dead weight and not very cooperative. As *impresario* and *artiste*, he's obsessed with bringing new life to the act."

"In more ways than you realize," Pooper said, rubbing his paws together with evident pleasure.

"Meaning what?" Molly said, folding her own paws around her breasts, which were turning blue in the merciless chill.

"Did you notice the little shamrock of a cheerleader sitting in the front row tonight? This afternoon I went for a hop around campus and I saw Dr. Ohm buttering up that brazen Irish biscuit. I couldn't help overhear their polite conversation. It seems the darling leprechaun, Mary Theresa Shannon O'Malley, Class of the Millennium, has theatrical aspirations."

"So what?" said Ms. Molly. "Dr. Ohm likes to encourage new talent. He worries often about the future of quality drama in America."

"Is that why he invited her on a tour of his classical tattoos? Take heed, Ms. Molly. If she was chubby or tall, I wouldn't bring this up to hurt you. But she's a wee thing. A slip of a girl entirely capable of slipping in and out of a desk drawer."

"Are you suggesting that Dr. Ohm would ever consider replacing me as 'The Vanishing Virgin'? No, I am an integral part of the act and his wife, remember?"

"I'm not suggesting anything. But if I were you, Ms. Molly, I would begin to look out for myself. You know how much you mean to me. You're my only friend in the world. If it wasn't for your kindness, I would have committed stewicide years ago. Into the pot and sweet dreams forever. So take my advice and accept that your partner has a roving eye and you've grown a bit thicker with time. Where will you be when your hips are substantial enough to get stuck in that drawer?"

"I am not going to let a bitter rabbit with sore ears stir snakes of suspicion in any bosom of mine," Ms. Molly said. But the expression on her face showed Pooper that those snakes were already wriggling and he smirked knowingly.

"I'm going to say this once, Ms. Molly. Tonight, when he stuffs you inside that cabinet and slams the door shut, instead of taking your usual route through the false panel and down the tunnel to the drawer, hook a sharp left. One more thing. Carry me with you."

"Turn left? Into solid oak an inch thick? Why would I slam into a wooden wall? And how could I possibly justify taking you into the cabinet? I suppose you're expecting to share my bow. Is that what this is about?"

Pooper munched the remnants of a radish rind, silent except for the chomping, his beady eyes focused on some inner realm. Ms. Molly scratched her confused head, wondering if she had imagined the whole silly conversation. It could be that she was being driven mad by the icy cold.

"Who were you talking to?" Dr. Ohm said, adjusting his flaking cape as he entered their dressing room.

"Nobody, dear," she said, blushing the color of Pooper's radish. "I was just thinking out loud."

"Well, think about my dinner," her husband snarled. "That miserable rabbit eats better than I do."

At the evening show, Ms. Molly fidgeted while she grinned and giggled on cue, assisting Dr. Ohm with his banal, predictable prestidigitations. Sure enough, in the very front row, cross-legged and wearing a revealing sequined frock, sat the very coed Pooper had mentioned. She was dew-fresh, wide-eyed and blessed with what Ms. Molly's mother called "a swift little body." Worse yet, she took notes on a laptop computer. There was evident chemistry between the girl and Dr. Ohm, who took pains to add flair and panache to his routines.

On sudden impulse, when it came time for "The Van-

ishing Virgin" to climax the night's entertainment, Ms.
Molly grabbed up the rabbit before she jumped into the
desk cabinet to be evaporated. Dr. Ohm was befuddled
and furious but would do nothing to break the magic
momentum. He glowered at Ms. Molly as he flapped his
cape and slammed the cabinet door shut. When he opened
it again, she and Pooper were gone and the audience
roared approval.

In the coffin-dark cabinet, Ms. Molly slid open the secret panel that led to the tunnel that would take her across
the desk to the drawer where she would be discovered.
Halfway through her dark journey, Pooper whispered, "I
told you, a left!" and despite her better judgment, she
made the turn.

To Ms. Molly's astonishment, instead of banging her
delicate head against wood, the back of the desk seemed
to melt away and she tumbled headlong through a lavender fog so thick she could feel its fuzz. During her tum-
bles and turns, Pooper leapt out of her grasp. She felt
abandoned and alone, facing unknown perils probably
much worse than the scolding she could expect from her
livid husband.

Ms. Molly came to rest in a huge, grassy field dotted
with daffodils, daisies and buttercups. A curious choir of
fleas, ticks, chiggers, crickets and ladybugs, all in splendid
silk robes, danced around her singing a cheerful song of
welcome. The field began to undulate like an ocean forming soft green waves. After some moments of vertigo, she
regained her equilibrium in time to watch a pair of turtles
in scarlet livery lumber toward her, pulling a coach carved
from a huge conch shell.

She boarded the coach and was carried toward a
snowcapped mountain whose peak seemed fulcrum for a
magnificent rainbow that arched across a silver sky. Ms.
Molly was certainly pleased by the landscape, but most
impressed by the climate. It was *warm, warm, warm*. The
air cuddled her like a fleece. She felt herself thaw after
years of glacial imprisonment. Her heart pumped fast and
her blood flowed like hot honey. She cracked out of an
ice cube like a young bird cracks out of its shell.

The trip ended at the door to a house fashioned from a shimmering bubble. There Pooper waited for her with a strange glint in his rolling eyes. "Where are we?" Ms. Molly asked him.

"Here And Now," Pooper said. "How do you like the place?"

"What's not to like?" Ms. Molly said as a swarm of wasps and hornets flew by in salute.

"Come down from your seat and tug at my ears," the rabbit said.

Obedient as ever, Ms. Molly got down from the conch coach and gave Pooper's ears a gentle yank, hardly hard enough to rouse him from Dr. Ohm's high hat. "No, show some spirit," Pooper said. Ms. Molly yanked again and stepped back in horror. The rabbit made a gurgling sound like a giant digesting a cherub. She heard an awful rip as Pooper split into two equal halves spilling rabbit parts in a pile.

A traumatized Ms. Molly barely had time to feel bad for her unraveled friend before a troupe of speckled spiders came sliding down glistening threads from a drifting cloud and began weaving his pieces together. Instead of a shabby rabbit, a man stood before her, naked and proud as a statue.

"I suppose some explanation is in order," he said. "Yes, I am the same Pooper with whom you shared friendship and vegetables. I rule as Supreme Beloved Monarch of this land. Many years ago I left here, cleverly disguised, in search of a soul mate. I sought a lovely woman of character who would love me for myself alone and not simply because of my status, wealth and stature. I have chosen you for my bride, Ms. Molly, if you will have me."

"I'm a married lady," Ms. Molly said. "With a career."

"Hardly a marriage to boast about," Pooper said, twitching his new aquiline nose in a way that made Ms. Molly smile. "As for your career, Dr. Ohm is about to desert you. Dear lady, I suspect that after a suitable court-ship, you will come to love me as much as I adore you. But please don't rush into rash action because you are seduced by a choir of bugs or evidence of my limitless power and affluence. That would defeat my whole purpose. I am patient. Go back and think things over."

"Oh, my lord," Ms. Molly said. "I forgot that my audience is waiting for Dr. Ohm to find me tucked in the drawer. How long have I been here?"

"Only seconds by outside time. Things move faster in my world. Look up at our sun. A year takes ninety-five thousand and three days. Dr. Ohm has hardly finished his silly abracadabras. You can be safely in place and ready to take your bows when he opens that drawer. Before you go, take what's left of my former pelt along with you. Just tell him Pooper got squished in transit. He'll accept that, give or take a few doubts. He had me marked for extinction anyhow."

The next thing Ms. Molly knew, she was back in South Bend, Indiana, jumping down out of the desk drawer to cheers from the assembled crowd of alumni, who began to sing the Notre Dame anthem.

Later, Dr. Ohm questioned her closely about Pooper's remains and the reason she took him into the cabinet in the first place.

"I don't know," Ms. Molly told him. "I thought it might spice things up. It was terribly cramped in the little tunnel and I guess I squashed the bunny."

"No wonder," Dr. Ohm said. "You are growing a bit balloonish. Outgrowing your role as 'The Vanishing Virgin.' I've been meaning to have a serious talk about your future. You might as well know I've hired an understudy, a certain Mary Theresa Shannon O'Malley, who is pert, perky and well versed in the Stanislavski method made famous by the Actors Studio in New York City. Of course, it will take me some time to train her to take your place. But in the meanwhile, put your spare time to productive use. Take that skimpy rabbit skin and make a scarf for the girl. And wipe that smile off your face. If there's one thing I cannot abide, it is a smiling wife."

In the weeks ahead, Ms. Molly made regular trips to the land of Here And Now, where she was treated with great elegance. King Pooper proved to be a witty and attentive companion. But just when Ms. Molly was ready to accept his proposal of marriage and assume the duties of his resident Queen, her decision was complicated by a torrent of guilt. Pooper was quick to sense some dilemma.

"What keeps you from leaving your frigid life of woe and coming to rule at my side?" he asked her. "I know you love me deeply. Is it that you will miss the adoration of your audience? Their kudos are transient at best."

"No, it's not that," Ms. Molly told him. "My problem is loyalty, a quality ingrained in my being. The truth is, my understudy has proved to be a terrible 'Vanishing Virgin.' She hates to navigate the tunnel and despises waiting for rescue in the drawer. She flops out of there in a lump and her bows look like a bad case of stomach cramps. Dr. Ohm is very disappointed. She would ruin the act."

"So much the worse for him," Pooper said. "He made his bed. Let him squirm in it. You owe him nothing."

"The man will be lost without 'The Vanishing Virgin.' He'll be lucky to get a gig in a Catskill Mountain motel. I could never pick up a copy of *Daily Variety* without feeling responsible. And even if I owe him nothing, I owe my audiences."

"There must be a solution," Pooper said. "I will ask my wisest counselor, the Octogenarian Octopus, for some guidance." Pooper led Ms. Molly to a room in the basement that held a huge tank filled to the brim with water from the Baltic Sea. Inside the tank floated a venerable octopus clutching eight fountain pens in its tentacles, using its own ink to author a book of poems, observations, and significant memoirs.

When the Octogenarian Octopus heard their problem, he waved his long arms and rocked his bulb body back and forth, dredging up wisdom from the furthest depths of the sea. After several hours, he turned his book to a blank page and wrote: FLEA!, then fell into a deep, sonorous sleep.

"Of course," Pooper said. "Yvonne is the answer."

"Yvonne?" Ms. Molly said. "Who is Yvonne and what has she got to do with any of this?"

"The great Octogenarian Octopus has, as usual, shown me the path. If you are to remain in Here And Now free from guilt or recrimination, we must send Yvonne to Dr. Ohm as your suitable replacement."

"Just a minute," Ms. Molly said. "I don't know that any Yvonne can satisfy the demands of 'The Vanishing Virgin.' It took me years of seasoning before . . ."

"Calm yourself," the former rabbit said. "Yvonne is no rival and would never be considered a suitable Virgin. Yvonne is, in fact, a flea possessing many special skills. Believe me, I would hate to part with such an amusing creature. But rest assured, she will be a huge asset to Dr. Ohm's career even after his rickety desk disintegrates to dust."

"A *flea*? You would send him a flea named Yvonne to replace me? I doubt he would be very happy about that."

"Oh, Dr. Ohm will never know. It will be an easy matter to cloud his mind. Alas, he never paid much attention to you, Ms. Molly, beyond your yeoman service. He will accept Yvonne as his working partner, and even as his spouse."

"What a depressing thought."

"One must face certain realities," Pooper said. "If you love me as much as I love you, agree, at least, to a trial. Next time Dr. Ohm opens his desk drawer, Yvonne will be waiting to jump out and bow. If the experiment fails, well, so be it. On the other hand, if Dr. Ohm is satisfied, you will remain with me forever and a day free of any recrimination or regret."

"I do adore you past calculation," Ms. Molly said. "And I love your delightful kingdom. Send your precious Yvonne and we'll see what we'll see, though I remain highly skeptical."

So it came to pass that when Dr. Ohm opened the desk drawer to show the audience that "The Vanishing Virgin" was safely home, instead of Ms. Molly it was Yvonne the flea who came leaping out into the spotlight. While a puff of Forgetful Vapor kept Dr. Ohm from detecting the major change in his assistant, the audience was completely puzzled and began to boo and hoot, stomp, howl, and demand a refund.

Dr. Ohm was quite alarmed at this insurrection. Yvonne immediately opened a small satchel which contained a cannon no bigger than a kernel of corn, a minuscule airplane, and a pin-sized trapeze. With a grand flourish, she marched in a circle like Napoleon and fired the cannon. It went off with a tremendous roar, numbing the crowd. Then she did acrobatics on the trapeze, such stunning swings and somersaults as to shame a playful dolphin. Finally, the frisky flea donned a pilot's hat and goggles, climbed into her airplane, took off, looped gracefully and flew over the orchestra seats, showering down a rain of violet petals as she went. The result was a standing ovation.

Dr. Ohm was delighted with the response and immediately booked to play in major palaces, concert halls and auditoriums around the world. His success escalated and he grew rich and famous. Yvonne proved a more demanding wife than had Ms. Molly, with a nasty tendency to bite at his most tender and private tattoos if he so much as looked at another female. Still, her endless talents continued to be the source of all blessings. Dr. Ohm quickly learned to treat his little woman with extreme respect and courtesy; he actually grew quite fond of his microscopic mate.

Far away, Ms. Molly and Pooper dwelt together in eternal harmony. As a special gift on their hundredth anniversary, Pooper gave her the very same desk she had once used as "The Vanishing Virgin." That part of her life was by then only a vague memory, but Ms. Molly still enjoyed hiding in the cabinet and emerging from the drawer for select gatherings of visiting diplomats, heads of state, and her many adorable children.

Occasional applause is necessary, even for the most radiant Queen.

Clad in Gossamer

NANCY KRESS

Nancy Kress lives in Silver Spring, Maryland. She is the author of more than fifteen books, including several fantasy and science fiction novels, two collections of short stories, and three books on writing fiction, most recently, Dynamic Characters. *Her most recent novels are* Maximum Light; Oaths and Miracles; *and its sequel,* Stinger. *Kress's short fiction has appeared regularly in* Omni, Asimov's Science Fiction Magazine, *and other major science fiction and fantasy magazines and anthologies. Her recent stories are collected in* Beaker's Dozen. *She has had a story in each volume of this series.*

"Clad in Gossamer" is about court life, its pressures and its intrigues. Kress asserts that she hates to shop and thinks that maybe the notion of people actually coming to a person to persuade him or her into new clothes is just congenial to her nature.

Clad in Gossamer

Of course I knew they were scoundrels. I knew the moment I set eyes on them. Florian, naturally, would not have believed it. He trusted the many travelers to court, trusted the pages and serving women, trusted his two-faced advisors, distrusted only me. Like all of them, he takes my looks for who I am. *You, distinguish a scoundrel?* he would have said, with that spew-making gentleness that conceals condescension. It is the condescension I cannot bear, and the patience. Let Florian be patient in hell, which was where these two rogues had come from. Fox-faced, quiet-voiced, elegant as ladies, sneaky as thieves. Or courtiers. Florian would not have known what they were, but I knew.

And I did not tell Florian.

Instead I gazed innocently at the two foreign tailors in their beautiful velvet breeches and silken tunics and woven sashes with strange foreign designs. "Tell me again," I said.

The shorter, older one said smoothly, "Garments in subtle colors like shaded sky, Your Highness. As finely spun and light to wear as spiderwebs. Yet warm, impervious to water, and impenetrable by stinging insects."

I nodded eagerly, as if I believed this nonsense. "And the magic . . ."

"Ah, the magic. Tell him again, Sorrel."

Sorrel, young and pasty-skinned, like one who never travels by day, recited, "I was raised in a distant land, Your Highness. Far, far from your beautiful kingdom." Indeed, he had an odd accent. So does my father's fool. "In my land, there are many old magics. Is that not so, Telliano? I learned but a humble one, that of cloaking the truth in fancy dress and the lie in nakedness. The cloth that my master taught me to weave can be seen only by the pure of heart, men and women honest and true and fit for their posts. To all others, it is invisible."

I let myself lean forward eagerly, like the credulous simpleton they think I am. "And if I had a coat of this clothing . . ."

"A whole suit," Telliano said.

"A court suit," Sorrel said.

"Or perhaps even a ceremonial robe . . ."

"For, perhaps, Crown Prince Florian's betrothal procession . . ."

"Most suitable—"

"*If* I had this clothing," I broke in, "then I could tell who among my brother's courtiers served him honestly and truly, and who conspired against him?"

"You could." Telliano, the more discreet. He dropped his eyes respectfully.

"And then," I said, with the air of a dimwit, "my royal brother the prince would admit me useful, and make me his viceroy!"

Sorrel could not hide his smile. Telliano nodded solemnly. I let myself despise them both, for despising me. There is no way Florian would ever admit me useful, or make me anything.

"I will pay what you ask," I said happily and wiped my nose on my sleeve like the stable louts whom I so

unfortunately resemble. Big and clumsy and grossly muscled. "And if I am made viceroy, I will double your fee."

The two scoundrels bowed low. We discussed fittings,
colors, secrecy. They bowed themselves out.

I sat in my chamber, thinking. Florian sent a page for
me, a golden-curled, tongue-tied child who had forgotten
his message before it reached me. I would have ignored
it anyway. If this scheme worked, Florian would not trouble me past his betrothal day. I had tried a bribed hunts-
man; the assassin had failed. I had tried poison; a royal
taster had died. I had tried turning our father against him;
he outtalked me to the old rattlepate. Now all the court
whispered of my failures. *Prince Jasper the Inept, Prince
Jasper the Butt, who looks like a stable lout and plots like a
dimwit.* But no longer.

Bow, arrow, poison, treason. All had failed.

I would try embroidery and silk.

My brother's bride arrived from across the sea ten days
before her betrothal procession. She arrived so robed and
veiled that she looked like a silken haystack. Such is apparently the custom in her country. But my father and
brother and I were to see her face after dinner, alone except for the guards thick around the king and his heir.
To protect them from the other heir.

I did not want to go. The dinner would be long. My
brother would talk brilliantly, reducing me to nothing. My
father's rheumy old eyes would rest on Florian with that
proud gleam that makes me wish to . . . to do what I
have been trying to do for a year now. My brother's bride
would be just the sort of sweet-faced, soft-voiced, loving
milksop to give him eternal devotion, popular approval,
and strong sons.

Only it did not turn out like that.

We sat over our wine after dinner, the long table
cleared, the hall empty of servants save for the sole musi-
cian hidden high in the gallery, playing a flute. The bride
was escorted in by her women. She was still heavily
veiled.

"Let us greet your face properly, my daughter," my

The viceroy's reply, whatever it was, was lost in a fit of dusty coughing.

But at the threshold of the chamber, he stopped coughing. His eyes ran over my two scoundrels: their intent concentration, their elegant foreign clothes, the strange nonsense symbols on Sorrel's sash. Then the viceroy slowly approached the loom, the cutting table, the baskets for ribbons and lace. He inspected everything, his wrinkled face blank as the loom. For a moment I doubted . . .

But no. "Incredible," Viceroy Madior murmured. "So subtle . . . View the cloth from one angle and it is one color, view it from another and the color shifts . . ."

I had him.

Over the next five days, I had them all. Chancellor of the Exchequer, Captain of the Guards, Minister of Justice, Chief Gentleman of the Bedchamber. Lying grovelers, all of them, afraid to admit they saw nothing. And Telliano bowed and smiled and explained, and Sorrel stitched, unsmiling, playing his part. While my brother's most trusted advisors, one by one and sworn to a secrecy they would of course violate, displayed before me their two-faced fear. Almost I was sorry when the day of the betrothal procession arrived and my private little mummery was over.

During the whole ten days, I saw my brother's betrothed only once. It was at night, when she should not have been away from the women's quarters at all. She and her women, heavily veiled, moved quietly along the walk from the Blue Garden. Had they merely been for a moonlit stroll? But there was a gate in the far wall of the Blue Garden, and beyond lay shrouded woods.

My brother's bride stopped on the stone path directly in front of me. She raised her veil. The black eyes, bluelidded this time, searched my face. Her lips were berry red, and her full, half-exposed breasts heaved.

She did not smile. It was better that way. I was the one to smile, from my much greater height, and move my body a fraction of a step closer to hers.

Immediately she lowered her veil. I had given away too much, in front of her ladies. She hurried away, leaving me on the moonlit path, still smiling.

She was the slut I had first thought her. And in another day, she would be mine.

The day of the betrothal procession, of course, dawned fine: even the sun wished to stay close to my brother. I could do nothing about the sun, but those advisors who would sell their souls to keep their posts beside him—they would soon be damned by their very loyalty.

The long walkway between castle and cathedral was hung with white flowers and thronged with courtiers, all eager for a first glimpse of their eventual queen. She would emerge from the cathedral, which in times long past had been a fort. Then, escorted by the prince's brother, His Royal Highness Prince Jasper, she would walk slowly toward the dais, where sat the king and his heir. And her escort would be quite naked.

I stood in the windowless, mirrorless secret chamber, letting the foreign rascals dress me in nothing. They draped and fussed and buttoned and tied, Telliano babbling like the practiced fraud he was: "How light and airy, Your Highness, how flattering to your broad shoulders, your lordly height . . ."

Beyond the walls, I heard the flutes and guitars begin to play.

I made my way through the secret passageway to my chamber, and from there by underground tunnel to the cathedral. I emerged in the unused and deserted guardroom, took a deep breath, and walked to the antechamber where the processional party waited.

A woman gasped. One of the bride's ladies. At the sound, the others—waiting women, pages, royal guards—turned and saw me.

The guards and pages had all been warned. I could picture the word running around court, loose as green-apple stools: *Magic clothes, he will wear them for the procession. If you wish to keep your post, you must be able to see . . .* They all pretended, except the foreign women, who had, of course, not been told. Their black eyes all widened in surprise. But they were women; they said nothing.

The men did. Guards, pages, the viceroy himself, all could not help showing the first shock on their faces, as Prince Jasper, second in line for the throne, stood before them naked. And all then covered their shock and murmured words of praise for the clothes I was not wearing: *extraordinary, beautiful, unsurpassed.* And from one inventive guard, who had undoubtedly spent time thinking up the compliment, *He outshines the bride.*

I walked up to my brother's betrothed and offered her my arm. She took it, her face stony. I understood. To walk to her betrothal on the arm of a naked man . . . but I would make it all up to her later. After Florian's courtiers were exposed as liars and fools, and Florian himself disgraced as a weakling served by lairs and fools. I would make it up to her when her red-lipped, green-nailed body was mine.

My manhood had come erect.

Well, so much the better. Let them see what a real man looked like, as he replaced the puny softling who was their crown prince. I held my shoulders back and my spine straight, and we started the processional walk from the cathedral and into the sunlight.

Gasps. Exclamations. Lies.

"Look at Prince Jasper—"

"Where did he get such robes?"

"Never have I seen—"

"The colors . . . the sash . . . the lightness . . ."

The lies.

We reached the dais. Florian looked stunned, my father displeased. I bowed. "Your Royal Highness my brother, I present your bride."

She moved from my arm and curtsied, very low, her ripe breasts bobbing. No one noticed. All eyes were still on me. Florian said, choking, "Brother . . ."

But before he could finish his condemnation—for Florian, as I had always known, would never pretend to see what he has not—another voice spoke loudly.

"But—the prince has no clothes on! He is naked!"

Everyone looked around. It was a child, the very youngest of the pages, standing in his velvets beside the dais. His golden curls shone in the sunlight, and his innocent face was turned upward to me.

Too innocent a face. Too blank, too vacant-eyed, the mouth a little agape . . .

"I told you!" someone hissed to my right. "Not fit to be a page, no matter whose son he is! An idiot child . . ." Other hands reached out, grabbed the little boy, led him away. He turned to look over his shoulder at me, his white, empty face as innocent as an infant's. And as unfit as an infant to serve a king.

I felt as if I had been kicked in the chest. My manhood abruptly wilted.

Finally Florian spoke. "A wonderful robe, my brother. No one has ever seen such clothing. You outshine us easily, and we are grateful for the trouble you have taken to array yourself so wonderfully to honor our beautiful bride."

There was a long exhalation from the crowd, a sigh of relief. The prince was not angry at having been outshone. Florian the generous-spirited, Florian the mild.

I looked down at my body. To my eyes it looked naked as the day I was born. Frantically I tried to pinch folds of my tunic between my fingers. I could feel nothing.

Florian continued graciously. "I confess we did not expect such honor from you. It is a wonderful surprise. On this most happy day, we are humbled to be reminded that things may not always be as they seem."

And what in all of damned hell did he mean by that? Had he somehow divined my scheme . . . had the two rogues told him? Was the whole court in on it, pretending to see clothing where there was none? Or was I indeed wearing a wonderful magic robe that only the honest could see . . . and I could not? Was I or was I not naked?

I had to pretend I was not. I had to sit naked on the dais while the king blessed this union. I had to dine naked in the Great Hall. I had to dance naked, my manhood flopping like limp turkey wattle, and see people glancing at me covertly: in displeasure, in amazement, in amusement. Was the displeasure because I was obscene, or because I had tried to upstage the bride? Was the amazement at my wonderful magic clothes, or at my effrontery? Was the amusement because I had failed to outshine the bride, or because I was flaccid, a prince dancing naked in front of his whole court, for the endless hours of the celebration?

Things may not always be as they seem.

The new princess smiled at me once as I danced with her, that bold smile from a painted face. But her eyes followed Florian, who treated her with gentle courtesy. She seemed, in her wordless way, to be charmed by him. And for the first time her ladies unveiled, and they all had bright red lips and low-cut dresses and thick eyelids painted green or violet or gold. They all glanced boldly, challengingly, at men. It is apparently the way of their country.

View the cloth from one angle and it is one color, view it from another and the color shifts . . .

Sorrel and Telliano have disappeared. I had paid them off—and who else did so as well? *Is* the new princess from the same country as they, some unimaginable country where the magic arts are sewn into the fabric of the world? Or were Sorrel and Telliano doubly scoundrels, who . . . I can no longer tell the fabric of truth from the lining of lies, not even my own. My head is dizzy. The flutes play, and I whirl—*am* I naked?—in the dance, the betrothal celebration, which goes on for hours and hours, as if it will never, ever end.

Precious

NALO HOPKINSON

Nalo Hopkinson was born in Jamaica, but has lived for the past twenty years in Toronto, Canada. As the daughter of a poet/playwright and a library technician, she's been surrounded all her life by words, stories, and the Dewey decimal system. She has had short fiction published in Black Swan, White Raven *and in* Sirens and Other Daemon Lovers. *Her first novel,* Brown Girl in the Ring, *was recently published.*

Hopkinson writes that "I've always hated the ending of the fairy tale about the good sister who has jewels and flowers fall from her lips when she speaks. Of course, the prince marries her, supposedly as her reward for being virtuous, but it's obvious that the prince sees her more as a boon to the royal coffers and a beautiful sex toy than as a person. 'Precious' takes up the thread after the marriage."

Precious

I stopped singing in the shower. I kept having to call the plumber to remove flakes of gold and rotted lilies from the clogged drain. On the phone I would say that I was calling for my poor darling cousin, the one struck dumb by a stroke at an early age. As I spoke, I would hold a cup to my chin to catch the pennies that rolled off my tongue. I would give my own address. If the plumber thought it odd that anyone could manage to spill her jewelry box into the bathtub, and not just once, he was too embarrassed to try to speak to the mute lady. I'm not sure what he thought about the lilies. When he was done, I would scribble my thanks onto a scrap of paper and tip him with a gold nugget.

I used to talk to myself when I was alone, until the day I slipped on an opal that had tumbled from my lips and fractured my elbow in the fall. At the impact, my cry of pain spat a diamond the size of an egg across the room, where it rolled under the couch. I pulled myself to my feet and called an ambulance. My sobs fell as bitter milkweed blossoms. I hated to let the flowers die. Holding my injured arm close to my body, I clumsily filled a drinking glass with water from the kitchen and stuck the pink clusters into it.

The pain in my elbow made me whimper. Quartz crystals formed on my tongue with each sound, soft as pudding in the first instance, but gems always hardened before I could spit them out. The facets abraded my gums as they slipped past my teeth. By the time the ambulance arrived, I had collected hundreds of agonized whimpers into a bowl I had fetched from the kitchen. During the jolting ride to the hospital, I nearly bit through my lip with the effort of making no sound. The few grunts that escaped me rolled onto the pillow as silver coins. "Ma'am," said a paramedic, "you've dropped your change. I'll just put it into your purse for you." The anesthetic in the emergency room was a greater mercy than the doctors could imagine. I went home as soon as they would allow.

My father often told me that a soft answer would turn away wrath. As a young woman I took his words to heart, tried to lull my stepmother with agreeableness, dull the edge of her taunts with a soft reply. I went cheerfully about my chores and smiled till my teeth ached when she had me do her daughter, Cass's, work too. I pretended that it didn't burn at my gut to see mother and daughter smirking as I scrubbed. I always tried to be pleasant, and so of course I was pleasant when Cass and I met the old woman while we were shopping that day. She was thirsty, she said, so I fetched her the drink of water, although she seemed spry enough to run her own errands. Cass told her as much, scorn in her voice as she derided my instant obedience.

Sometimes I wonder whether that old woman wasn't having a cruel game with both of us, my sister and me. I got a blessing in return for a kind word, Cassie a curse as payment for a harsh one. That's how it seemed then, but did the old lady know that I would come to fear attention almost as much as Cass feared slithering things? I believe I would rather taste the muscled length and cool scales of a snake in my mouth, sliding headfirst from my lips, than look once more into the greedy gaze of my banker when I bring him another shoebox crammed with jeweled phrases, silver sentences, and the rare pearl of laughter.

Jude used to make a game of surprising different sounds from me, to see what wealth would leap from my mouth. He was playful then, and kind, the husband who rescued me from my stepmother's greed and wrath. My father's eyes were sad when we drove away, but he only waved.

Jude could make me smile, but he preferred it when I laughed out loud, raining him with wealth. A game of tickle would summon strings of pearls that gleamed as they fell at our feet. Once, a pinch on my bottom rewarded him with a turquoise nugget. He had it strung on a leather thong, which he wore around his neck.

But it was the cries and groans of our lovemaking that he liked best. He would stroke and tongue me for hours, lick and kiss me where I enjoyed it most, thrust into me deeper with each wail of pleasure until, covered in the fragrance of crushed lily petals, we had no strength for more. Afterward he would collect sapphires and jade, silver love knots and gold doubloons, from the folds of the sheets. "I don't even need to bring you flowers," he would joke. "You speak better blossoms for yourself than I can ever buy."

Soon, however, my marriage began to sour. Jude's love-bites became painful nips that broke my skin and forced diamonds past my teeth. He often tried to scare me, hiding in the closet so that I shrieked when he leapt out, grains of white gold spilling from my mouth. One night he put a dead rat in the kitchen sink. I found it in the morning, and platinum rods clattered to the ground as I screamed. I begged him to be kind, but he only growled that we needed more money, that our investments weren't doing well. I could hear him on the phone late at night, pleading for more time to pay his debts. Often he came home with the smell of liquor on his breath. I grew nervous and quiet. Once he chided me for keeping silent, not holding up my part of the marriage, and I began to sob, withered tulips plummeting down.

"Bitch!" he shouted. "I need more gold, not your damned flowers!" The backhand across my mouth drew blood, but along with two cracked teeth, I spat out sapphires.

From then on, such beatings happened often. It was eight months later—when Jude broke my arm—that I left, taking nothing with me. I moved to a different city. My phone number is unlisted now. I pay all my bills at my bank, not through the mail. A high fence surrounds my house, and the gate is always locked.

Since I have no need to work, my time is my own. I search the folklore databases of libraries all over the world, looking for a spell that will reach the old woman. When I find her, I will beg her to take back her gift, her curse.

My stepmother will not say it, but Cassie is mad, driven to it by the bats and spiders wriggling from her mouth. It's good that her mother loves and cares for her out on that farm, because all she does is sit and rock and mutter curses, birthing an endless stream of lizards and greasy toads. "It keeps the snakes fed," my stepmother sighs when she calls with sour thanks for her monthly check. "That way they're not biting us." The mother and father who loved me are both long dead, but my stepmother still lives.

When the phone rang, I thought it was she, calling to complain about slugs in her lettuce.

"Hello?" I spat out a nasturtium.

"Precious. It *is* you." Jude's voice was honey dripped over steel. "Why have you been hiding, love?"

I clamped my lips together. I would not give him my words. I listened, though. I always listened to Jude.

"You don't have to answer, Princess. I can see you quite clearly from here. You must have wanted me to find you, leaving the back curtains open like that. And the lock on that gate wouldn't keep an imbecile out."

"Jude, go away, or I'll call the police." Deadly nightshade fell from my lips. I paused to spit out the poisonous sap. There was a crash in the living room as Jude came through the sliding back doors. He dropped the cell phone and the heavy mallet he carried when he stepped through the ruined glass. Petrified, struck dumb as a stone, I made it to the front door before he slammed me against the wall, wrenching my arm behind my back. From years of habitual silence, my only sound was a hiss of pain. A copper coin rolled over my tongue, a metallic taste of fear.

"You won't call anyone, my treasure. You know it would ruin your life if people found out. Think of the kidnapping attempts, the tabloid media following you everywhere. You'd have every bleeding-heart charity in the book breathing down your neck for donations. Let me protect you from all that, jewel. I'm your husband, and I love you, except when you anger me. I only want my fair share."

Pressed against mine, Jude's body was as tall as I remembered, cruelly thin, and driven by the strength of his rage. I thought perhaps I could talk my way out by being agreeable. "Let me go, Jude. I won't fight you anymore." I had to mouth the words around the petals of a dead rose. I carefully tongued the thorny stem past my teeth.

"You're sure?" He pushed my elbow higher up along my back until I whimpered, grinding my teeth on more dry thorns. I had almost fainted with relief from the pain, when he finally let me go. He grabbed my sore shoulder and pushed me ahead of him into the living room. Then he stopped and turned me to face him. "Okay, darling, you owe me. Left me in one hell of a financial mess back there. So come on, make the magic. Spit it out."

"Jude, I'm sorry I ran away like that, but I was frightened." Two silver coins rolled to the ground.

"You can do better than that, Precious." Jude raised his fist level with my face. My jaw still ached where he had dislocated it the first time he ever hit me. I forced a rush of words from my mouth:

"I mean, I love you, darling, and I hope that we can work this out, because I know you were the one who rescued me from my stepmother, and I'm grateful that you took care of me so I didn't have to worry about anything . . . " A rain of silver was piling up around Jude's feet: bars, sheets, rods, wire. He grinned, reaching down to touch the gleaming pile. I felt a little nudge of an emotion I didn't recognize. I kept talking.

"It was so wonderful living with you, not like at my stepmother's, where I had to do all the cooking and cleaning, and my father never spoke up for me . . . " Semiprecious stones started piling up with the silver: rose quartz, jade, hematite. The mound reached Jude's knees, and the delight on his face made him look like the playful man I had married. He sat on the hillock of treasure, shoveling it up over his lap. My words kept flowing:

"If Daddy were a fair man, if he really loved me, he could have said something, and wouldn't it have been easier if the four of us had split the chores?" I couldn't stop. All those years of resentment gouted forth: emeralds green with jealousy; seething red garnets; cold blue chunks of lapis. The stones were larger now, the size of plums. I ejected them from my mouth with the force of thrown rocks. They struck Jude's chest, his chin. He tried to stand, but the bounty piled up over his shoulders, slamming him back down to the floor. "Hey!" he cried. But my words flew even faster.

"So I fetched and I carried and I smiled and I simpered, while Daddy let it all wash over him and told me to be nicer, even nicer, and now he's dead and I can't tell him how much he hurt me, and the only thanks I got was that jealous, lazy hussy telling me it's *my* fault her daughter's spitting slugs, and then you come riding to my rescue so that I can spend the next year of my life trying to make you happy too, and you have the *gall* to lay hands on me, and to tell me that you have the right? Well, just listen to me, Jude: I am not your treasure trove, and I will not run anymore, and I shall be nice if and when

it pleases me, and stop calling me Precious; my *name* is
Isobel!"

As I shouted my name, a final stone formed on my
tongue, soft at first, as a hen's egg forms in her body. It
swelled, pushing my jaws apart until I gagged. I forced
it out. It flew from my mouth, a ruby as big as a human
heart that struck Jude sharply on the head, then fell onto
the pile of treasure. He collapsed unconscious amidst the
bounty, blood trickling from a dent in his temple. The red
ruby gleamed as though a coal lit its core. I felt light-
headed, exhilarated. Jude might still have been breathing,
but I didn't bother to check. I stepped around him to the
phone and dialed Emergency. "Police? There's an intruder
in my home."

It wasn't until I went outside to wait for the police
that I realized that nothing had fallen from my mouth
when I made the telephone call. I chuckled first, then I
laughed.

Just sounds, only sounds.

The Sea Hag

MELISSA LEE SHAW

*Melissa Lee Shaw is a graduate of the 1994
Clarion West Workshop and currently works at
a software company in the Pacific Northwest.
After receiving her B.S. in psychology, Shaw
spent three years training dolphins. Having
earned a master's degree in comparative cogni-
tion, she developed an intolerance for people
who refuse to believe that dolphins bite. She has
had fiction published in* The Writers of the
Future XI *and in* Sirens and Other Daemon
Lovers. *She is expanding her story in the former into a novel.*

*"The Sea Hag" originated as Shaw's rebel-
lion against the dearth of strong, sympathetic,
adult female characters in animated Disney
films. She noticed a disturbing trend for positive
female characters to be either adolescent heroines
or bumbling grandmothers, with women in between usually portrayed as villains. "The Sea
Hag" is meant to counteract that type of stereo-
typing.*

The Sea Hag

I felt the currents move to the rhythm of her tail long before she arrived. She was the loveliest of his daughters, and the most contemplative—as contemplative as vain creatures like mermaids can be. While her sisters asked me for creams for their milky skin, or polish for their lovely blue-green scales, or a lure to catch the most delectable fish, Coral had never come to me before. I thought perhaps she simply hated me more than the others did.

She swept into my prison—what he calls my "fortress," the broken carcass of a galleon in a deep ocean trench. Luminescent jellyfish floated nearby, trapped by my spells to light my work. I kept each only for a short time, releasing them before they wilted and died.

Coral must have thought I would not hear the mumbled incantation he had told them would protect them. But the currents brought me her whispers. Huddled over my cauldron, clad in barnacles and eel skins and loops of kelp, I kept my back stiff as a long iron nail while the soft words flayed my ears.

From balmy rollers to storm-tossed seas,
From tropical bath to arctic freeze,
From tidal waves to gentle swells . . .
Keep me safe from the Sea Hag's spells.

She cleared her throat.

I did not turn around. Age had not been kind to me. *He* had seen to that, with his stolen spells. My hair, once long and lush, had grown thin and ropy and gray as driftwood. My body was a jumble of sticks wrapped in rags of skin. I feared I would crumble like rotten wood if I looked in her eyes and saw her disgust.

She came around the side of the cauldron I was stirring, where I could not help but see her from the corner of my eye. "My father says you have power," she said, twining a lock of lustrous brown hair around one finger. Like her sisters before her, she tried to appear nonchalant.

"Oh?" *Is that all he says?* My mouth, like the thought, tasted bitter as bile.

"He says you can . . . transform things," she went on, a little more doggedly.

Going to change one of your sisters into a parrot fish? I wondered. *Did she steal your favorite whalebone comb?* With a piece of the galleon's smallest mast, I stirred the cauldron, a heavy cast-iron thing I'd found in the broken ship's galley. My spells heated it and kept its contents from commingling with the water. They also kept it from rusting.

"Can you?"

"You'll have to be more specific," I said, holding a ball of ice in my belly so the words would come out cold and dangerous. I did not like the flush on her face, the way she tapped restlessly at her arms. It was too familiar.

She glanced to the side and pursed her lips. "It was during a storm two days ago. He stood on a ship, and the sun sparkled in his black hair. His eyes were bluer than a tropical sea, his bare arms were a perfect golden brown—and the way he stood there, those amazing feet perfectly balanced against the swaying of the ship—it was as if he was attuned to the ocean's heartbeat. I . . . I cannot tell you how it moved me."

I understood in a flash. My hands gripped the cauldron's edge; the pain helped me hold on to my resolve.

"A storm shattered his ship—but instead of hopping into the lifeboat, he leapt overboard after a crewmate. He tried so valiantly, but the storm was too much for both of them. He started to drown. I . . . my father says we are not to interfere, but he was so brave, and it took so little from me. I pushed his face into the air and dragged him to the beach. I couldn't warm him—his blood is so hot compared to mine—and so I made three sea lions drape themselves around him and warm him with their fur. I lay near his head, though, and stroked his salt-crusted hair—and I shaded his face from the blistering sun all that day. He never woke."

Her voice warmed as she spoke. I tried to keep my spine frozen against her, but each word was like a gout of lava. I knew that I could refuse her nothing, and I hated myself in that moment.

She went on. "That night, under the light of half a moon, his eyes opened. The sea lions were grumbling that they were hungry, they wanted to hunt, but I held them fast. And he saw me in the moonlight, perched above his head. He reached up and touched my face, and he murmured something I could not hear. But his voice was music. I am not much of a singer myself, but I know music when I hear it—and without even holding a pitch, the timbre of his voice thrilled through me like the sweetest, saddest song.

"The next day—"

"Enough," I snapped. "What is it you want from me?"

"Three men chased away my sea lions and carried my sailor up the beach. I have to see what happened to him," Coral said, a little breathlessly. "I have to know he's all right. I . . . I must have him. He's all I think about. He needs me."

"And what am I supposed to do about this?" I braced

myself for what was coming: a spell to lure him back to the water, and then another to pull him into the ocean, to give him gills and fins and a mermaid's immortality.

"I must become a landswoman," Coral said. "I want to spend my life with him, in his world."

A cold shock burned through me like a jellyfish's stinging venom. I stared at her. Never had one of her sisters asked for such a thing.

"Will you help me?" she asked, her eyes wide and anxious now, all pretense gone. I could deny her nothing.

"No," I said. The word amazed me.

"But you must! You don't understand! The men who took my sailor—they may have hurt him. He may be a prisoner now."

"So?"

"I'll do anything. I'll give you anything. Do you want my hair? I've been told it's lovely." She held a long lock out to me. It was a light, luminous brown, like wood with sunlight shining on it. "It's yours."

"No," I said. "Nothing you have could make me do this thing. Go home to your father, to your sisters. Forget about this landsman. He is only a passing fancy."

She opened her mouth to object. Tears glistened in the corners of her eyes.

I held up a hand. "You're vain creatures, all of you, you mermaids. And fickle. You will soon find something else that tickles your thoughts. Go sing with the humpbacks, or hunt with the barracuda. Don't bother me with childish requests."

"It is true what he says," she whispered. "You have no heart. You have no idea what love is."

My mouth opened, but no words came out. I could not stand to look at her eyes, at the condemnation and the indifferent pity.

She turned to leave.

A word welled up from the pit of my stomach, trailing acid. "Coral . . ."

She swiveled toward me, her face cold and hard as the moon. "How do you know my name?"

"I know all your names," I said. "Yours and your sisters'.'' And before she read too much into that, I hastened to add, "I know all that goes on in the sea for hundreds of miles, in all directions. There's a reason your father sent you to me."

She looked down. "My father did not send me here. He has spoken of your power, of your . . . bargaining wiles. But he wouldn't have wanted me to come, not for this. When I mentioned my sailor to him, he flew into a rage."

"Coral, what you ask is no trifling spell. You can never be a landswoman, not really. You could assume the outer form of one, but—"

"Then you'll help me!"

And I would have died happy, right then, at the joy in her face, the excitement sparkling in her eyes. "I will tell you what is possible," I said. "Then you must decide for yourself."

"Go on." Her air was supremely confident.

"First, you must gather some things for me. A starfish, a man-o'-war jellyfish, a seagull, and a chunk of coral the size of your fist."

"What will you do with them?"

"Kill them. Any spell of transformation involves a certain amount of death."

Her eyes widened; mermaids love starfish and sea-birds, the former to wear like jewelry, the latter to watch wheel and dip in the sky. "What else?"

"I will concoct three potent brews for you. You must beach yourself at sunset, somewhere the landsmen won't find you till morning. Smear the first brew down the very center of your tail, where it will burn into your flesh until it cuts your tail in two. Then drink the second brew, which will cut your innards like knives sharp as eels' teeth. And when the first brew has finished its work, you must pour the third brew over every inch of your split tail. It will smooth away your scales and give your legs the appearance of human skin and feet."

Her eyes narrowed. "Only the appearance?"

I nodded. "You will have no bones in your legs. They'll be useless; you won't even be able to stand. The second potion will start nubs of bones growing down from your hips, but it will take months for the bones to reach your feet."

"I won't be able to walk? How am I to find him if I can't walk?"

I shrugged. "It's a fool's path. For that matter, there is no guarantee your sailor will even recognize you, much less fall in love with you."

"He *will* recognize me. And as for love—he loves me already, as I love him. You don't know the magic of that night, under the moon. The caress of his hand on my cheek was love so profound it could never fade."

"You don't know anything about the land! You don't know how to dress, how to behave—and if you do this thing, you will never be able to return to the sea. You will be trapped on the land, forever. And so if—*if*—something goes wrong with your sailor, you will be stranded. Alone. Permanently."

"You can't scare me," she said defiantly. "I won't be denied."

The words stung, so much like her father's. In desperation, I turned to lies. "It will kill you. Three days after you use the potions, you'll be dead."

She paled, but drew herself up like a princess. "Then I'll die. I will live a lifetime with him in those three days."

"Coral . . . "

"Is there anything else I need to bring you? Besides the starfish, man-o'-war, seagull, and coral?"

I slumped. "No."

She licked her lips slowly, covering her face with a blank expression. "And what price do you ask for these potions?"

The price? I thought. *My heart.* "You will lose everything," I whispered. "Your father, your sisters, your tail, your starfish, your sea lions. And, in becoming a landswoman, you will relinquish your immortality." Those were all things that would happen anyway. A price, something that I could keep and cherish . . . Something drastic that might change her mind. "Your voice."

"My voice?" She was startled; her voice was nowhere

near as lovely as her sisters'. I had watched them for years with my scrying glass; I had seen them laugh when she tried to sing.

"I will take that as my fee. Consider carefully what this will mean. You'll be a mute cripple, in a completely alien world, and you will have only three days to live. Is that what you really want?"

She lifted her chin and said, "I will return with the things you asked for by tonight."

It took very little time, really. She returned with everything but the seagull, then shot up to the surface and returned a few minutes later with a struggling, drowning bird. I took it from her and wrung its neck; there was no need for it to suffer.

She could not watch me tear the seagull apart and pull out its bones, nor could she bear to see me pull the tentacles off the jellyfish, one by one, and squeeze the venom from their stingers into my cauldron. And I saw her wince when I cracked open the starfish.

When the potions were ready, I picked up a battered old music box I had found in one of the rooms of my sunken galleon. "The price," I said ominously, rattling the box. It wasn't too late for her to change her mind.

She kept her mouth very tight. "What do I need to do?"

"Touch this to your lips."

She took the box from me and looked at it for a moment. Eyes on me, she set her lips against it.

I put my hand on the music box and chanted an incantation, then took the box. Her voice belonged to me.

"Take these," I said, handing her three stoppered jars. "This green one is the first. The brown one is the second. And this clear glass one is the third. Do you remember what you are to do?"

She nodded.

"Do you have any questions?"

A dozen lit her eyes, but she touched a hand to her silenced lips.

"You can still whisper," I said impatiently. "I only have your voice, not your teeth and lips and tongue."

Relief flooded her face. "Thank you," she whispered.

"For what?"

"For not taking everything."

My throat felt like it was filled with sand. "When you are done with the jars, toss them into the sea so they can find their way back to me."

"Why?"

"Because I require it." *Because I cannot afford to lose what little I still have.*

I watched through my scrying glass as Coral crawled up onto the beach at sundown, the three jars clutched tightly in her arms. She took a deep breath, unstoppered the green jar, and poured its thick liquid down the exact center of her tail. Her face clenched in pain. Smoke rose from the blackened line that marked where her legs would divide.

Then she drank down the contents of the brown jar and doubled over in agony. Hours passed while she hunched and gasped—my own gut wrenched in sympathy—but not once did she try to crawl back toward the sea. Finally her tail was seared into two long pieces that flopped around on the sand. She smoothed the thick unguent in the glass jar over both halves. It cooled the burning in her tail; relief lit her eyes. From where she lay, a few feet up the shore, she rolled the jars back into the water.

The next morning, her new body was complete. Her long brown hair stretched down to her new knees, covering all the areas human decency demanded. Before noon, a troop of fishermen spotted her while she slept. In great excitement, they ran up to her and prodded her awake. They tried to help her stand, but of course, her boneless legs would not take her weight. So they carried her, talking to each other in a lively chatter, up and over the sand dune that separated beach from fishing village.

It was done. I lifted the music box and opened its lid.

Her pure, sweet voice hummed at me, its tone without malice or suspicion.

I closed my eyes and listened to my daughter sing.

They came to me the next day, their eyes filled with accusation and dread.

I had spent the morning staring into my largest scrying glass, one I'd made from a silver-backed mirror. I watched Coral in that fishing village, a small, dirty town. She wore a patched green dress and sat in a chair, a gray woolen blanket tucked over her legs and another wrapped round her shoulders. Her hair had been brushed and coiled into a large bun, but strands of it rebelled and struggled free to frame her lovely face. Surrounded by fishwives with raw faces and salt-chapped hands, she shone like a pearl among lumps of sand.

Her eyes fluttered back and forth, evidence of her distraction. Women and a few men gathered close by to stroke her hair or pat her shoulder, as if she were a fool or an invalid. She looked up, her face like a child's, and tugged the sleeve of a woman who gently rested a reddened, scaly hand on her shoulder. The woman bent close and listened to her whispers, then smiled and shook her head.

"My poor dear, I am so sorry," the fishwife said. "I've told you, he's gone to the palace. He's royalty, you know. You're not the only girl to swoon for him. That won't bring him back."

Coral pulled her down again and whispered.

"Yes, of course, you poor moppet, we've sent word to the palace. It takes time, that's all. It's half a day's hard ride each way. He won't come before nightfall, if he's coming at all."

Poor Coral looked exhausted. Her cheeks were flushed, her eyes luminous and moist.

The currents whispered to me that someone was coming. No, not just someone, a whole swarm of someones. I tore my eyes from my glass in time to see them descend upon me, scales flashing, eyes bright, arms long and slender, tails graceful: Foam, eldest and most severe, with her white hair and ice-blue eyes; Pearl, second-born, vain as a cat, with shimmering eyes and tresses green as kelp; Sand, our bubbling child, full of mischief, hair of sunlight gold; Anemone, quieter and sometimes as sullen as her father, with a flashing temper and red locks; and Storm, penultimate daughter, given to fits of fury, hair black as the nighttime sky, eyes bright as stars.

Their soft chant came to me:

From balmy rollers to storm-tossed seas,
From tropical bath to arctic freeze,
From tidal waves to gentle swells . . .
Keep us safe from the Sea Hag's spells.

Foam pushed forward. "Coral is missing. The last time we saw her, she was swimming up toward the beach, with three of your jars clutched in her arms. What have you done?"

It was nearly more than my heart could stand. I said, "She came to me with a request, as all of you have done."

"What request?" Foam demanded

"Coral has fallen in love with a landsman. She asked me to transform her to a landswoman. I told her she shouldn't, but she wouldn't listen to me. None of you ever has."

Foam glared at me. "You didn't have to do it! Just because she asked . . ."

"She is as foolish as the rest of you! More foolish, perhaps. You come here when you want something from me, when *he* sends you to me. What do you want this time? More creams to polish your scales? More perfumes and lotions to smooth your skin?"

With a glance at the others, Foam said, "We want you to change her back."

"I can't."

"We will give you anything you ask. Please."

"You don't understand," I said frostily. "I would do it if I could. I can't. It isn't possible."

Foam stared at me. "Why not?"

Suddenly, the iceberg of my heart cracked and shattered into a million melting fragments. "Why not?" I cried. "You stupid, thoughtless creatures! What has he told you of me?"

The gathered mermaids rustled uneasily. Storm and Pearl glanced up.

"You are the Sea Hag," Foam said cautiously, selecting her words with care. "You have existed since time began. While he is a force of life, of good, you are a force . . . of death."

"And evil?"

She nodded, eyes locked on me. She believed what she said.

"And what has he told you of your mother?"

With a startled frown, Foam said, "I don't . . ."

"Has he told you that you, unlike every other creature in the world, have no mother? That he created you whole and perfect from his own body? *What has he told you?*"

Fear lit Foam's eyes. "Our mother is dead. She died when Coral was born."

Pearl piped up. "But he told me she was beached during a terrible storm. He scoured the oceans to find her, but he was too late. She died on the land, from the burning sun."

Defiantly, Anemone said, "No. She vanished one day, that's all. She could return."

I pushed the rage back down inside, away from my throat, so my words would come out calm. I had to pick my way carefully. "He has filled your heads with stories. Now *I* will tell you a story."

The mermaids all exchanged looks of trepidation. At last, at long last, I had them arranged in front of me, attentive, listening.

"Once, the Spirit of the Sea roamed the water freely, playing with the sharks, riding the bow waves of ships with the dolphins, watching the landsfolk fish and laugh and love. She hadn't a care in the world, until one day she chanced to spy a man fishing in the shallows near a village. She could take two forms: that of an enormous fish, or that of a woman. So enraptured was she by this man, with his low, crooning songs and the clean lines of his muscles as he cast his nets, that she transformed into a woman and crept closer.

"He saw her crouched underwater and was afraid. But curiosity soon overcame fear, and he beckoned her closer. 'I have never seen anything like you,' he said.

"The glint in his eye made her uneasy, but his face was handsome and lively, and she was lonely for someone to talk to.

" 'I am the Spirit of the Sea,' she said. 'I command the waters and all things that live in them.'

"His eyes grew greedy, yet she mistook it for desire. 'You command the fish?' he asked. 'And the porpoises, and the stinging anemones?'

" 'And everything else,' she said.

"He flashed a dazzling smile and murmured, 'And do you command me, because I am standing in the water?'

" 'No. You are not of the water. You command yourself.'

" 'And if I were to command you to come here and kiss me?' he asked.

" 'No man can command me,' she said, but she swam forward into his arms and laid her cold lips against his.

"He shrank back from her chilly embrace, but only for an instant, and then he returned it with all the fire of the sun. 'I have never seen any woman so beautiful,' he said, though he would not meet her eyes. 'I wish I could see your world, learn what you know. The ocean is enchanting—but not so enchanting as you.'

" 'I have cast no spells,' she said, puzzled.

" 'You have bespelled my heart,' he said, scooping her up into his arms. 'I am yours. I want to be with you forever. And I will not rest until I hear you tell me that you love me as I love you. I will not be denied.'

"The Spirit of the Sea knew nothing of trickery; no creature in her dominion had ever tried to deceive her. She made him a powerful potion of transformation, to give him the gills and tail of a fish. After he drank it, he dove into the water and said, 'Now I will always be by your side.'

"It seemed odd that he was so intent on learning her

spells and magics, but she loved him with a clear heart and was sure his love for her was as true, so she lent him more and more of her power. The more he learned, the more distracted he seemed, and the more distant. In an effort to regain his attention, she showed him ever more astounding spells, including, finally, the spells of transformation.

"After a few months, he told her that he was growing lonely for more companionship. He wanted a family, creatures brought to life by his union with her. While she didn't understand, she loved the earnestness in his face as he begged her for children. When she agreed, he told her that he wanted not just any children, but beautiful girls with fish's tails, so they would know they were his. And she, the Spirit of the Sea, could deny him nothing."

The mermaids' lips tightened. They exchanged angry glances, but I bore on.

"She brought them into life from her own body, one by one, spaced a few months apart. To her surprise, she loved them deeply, fiercely, within moments of their birth. The moment the sixth was born, he smiled and nodded and told her that he loved her, and now he was happy. And to show her how grateful he was, he had a surprise for her. He led her to a deep ocean trench that held the wreckage of a huge galleon. Fascinated, she swam down into the remains.

"He chanted a few words and sprang his trap. 'You stupid creature!' he crowed. 'You'd better get used to that broken old ship, because it will be your home forever. Now I am the King of the Sea. I am rich beyond measure! And you'—he pointed down at her, and she felt her body clutch and spasm—'you are a hag, an old Sea Hag! You have always been ugly, with your fish lips and your webbed hands. Now your body will reflect your spirit, your true soul.'

"Her body contorted and shriveled, and her hair turned gray and ragged. She tried to become a fish, to swim away, but her form was frozen. Trapped by his spell, she could not regain the power he had stolen, nor could she prevent him from drawing more at his whim.

'But my daughters!' she wailed. 'What about my daughters? I must see them!' She had never even held the youngest, her newborn infant, to her breast.

" 'They are *my* daughters, not yours. If you sit here quietly, I'll send them to you now and then. You can do little favors for them. But if you ever tell them that you are their mother, or try to escape, you will never see them again. If you think you suffer now, betray me and you will know suffering a thousand times worse. They belong to me, my mermaids.' "

The mermaids stared at me in shock and disbelief.

"You're lying," Foam hissed. "We should have known you would never help us."

I stared at her, my firstborn. Her hair was white as wavecaps. I remembered tangling it in my fingers when she was an infant. "I have never denied any of you anything," I said. "All this time, you gave me only your suspicion and your disgust, your caution and your fear. And I gave you everything you asked for." I could feel cold, gelid tears slide down my face. "You are my daughters," I said, spreading my arms wide to encompass all of them. "Mine and his. Did you never wonder why there were no other creatures like you in the whole of the sea? Why you looked part human and part fish? You are a blending of two worlds."

Foam stared at me, gathering her thoughts, calculating. Her father stared at me through her eyes. "We are not here to discuss our parentage," she said, maintaining an even voice with an effort. "We are here for Coral. You haven't explained why you can't change her back."

"She is out of my reach," I whispered. "I am trapped here."

"How?"

"By your father. There is only one way to break the spell."

Foam, watching me with her canny eyes, asked, "And what is that?"

"*You* must break it." The tears crawled down my throat and tried to stop my voice. "You must join hands and form a circle around me. With one voice, you must say, 'You are our beloved mother.' "

The blood trembled in my veins. He had laughed at me, on that day long ago, and told me that when he got through with his mermaids, not one would ever feel more than cold disgust for me. Not one.

They exchanged dark looks, some angry, some puzzled, some merely suspicious. But then Foam sighed and said, "It's clearly the only way she'll help us. What can it really cost?"

The others mumbled their protests, but they formed a circle around me and clasped hands. "You are our beloved mother," they said, their eyes impatient.

"Nothing happened," said Foam.

"I have rarely heard words spoken with such malice and disbelief," I said. "You must find a kernel of love in your hearts. Remember the trinkets I have given you. Remember the spells I have cast for you. Then try again."

Their faces softened, and they looked puzzled. The doubt creeping into their eyes gladdened me.

Once again, Foam led them. "You are our beloved mother."

Still nothing happened.

"Foam, come here," I said.

Foam detached herself from the circle and approached slowly.

I took her hands in my old, wrinkled ones. She shrank back. "You were almost two when Coral was born. When you were an infant, I used to hold you tight against me and sing to you. You played with my hair while you suckled. I sang:

From balmy rollers to storm-tossed seas,
From tropical bath to arctic freeze,
The sea protect you with this charm:
Keep my baby safe from harm."

Foam's mouth opened in a perfect circle that matched her widened eyes.

"You remember, don't you?" I asked.

She nodded. "The song—I remember the song." Her sisters stared at her in shock.

Softly, I said, "Join with your sisters and try again."

Tears slipped down Foam's cheeks and dissipated into the water. Trembling, she took her place. "Mother," she whispered.

Then, together, all of them. "You are our beloved mother."

The water around us quaked and shook. My heart swelled to hear them, and then I realized my body swelled too, filling out its wrinkles with smooth skin, straightening my spine. The ropes of my hair transformed to soft shining locks green as moss. The bonds that held me in my prison melted away, like ice under the hot sun, and my power, stolen for so many years, flowed back into me.

I was free.

"He will be very angry," I said. "But he has no power without mine, and he cannot harm you any longer. Now, we must see about Coral. There are things I will need— a seagull, a strand of kelp, a bag of coins, a young eel—"

"Wait a minute," Foam said. "Coral wasn't here. You said it would take all your daughters. But it still worked."

My heart squeezed. "It would have taken only one of you to break the spell," I admitted. "But I'd waited so long. I needed to hear it from all of you. For myself."

I counseled my daughters to flee to the far reaches of the ocean and hide until I returned and had time to deal with their father. With his magic gone, I did not know why I should fear his rage, and yet I worried that he might try to harm the mermaids for betraying him. But they insisted on staying in my old prison, the ship, so they could watch Coral, and me, through my scrying glass. I warned them to watch for their father, just in case. He would soon notice his missing power.

"I won't be long," I said. "I know where she is." I gathered up the new potions I had made for Coral and a few other things into a package wrapped in seaweed.

I transformed into a fish, held my supplies in my

mouth, and swam for the surface, feeling the delicious power of my muscular tail. I wanted to swim the whole ocean round and glory in it, but I had to move quickly, before he found out and tried to interfere.

With a last flick of my tail, I shot up onto the beach. Before I touched the sand, I transformed to my human shape and opened my seaweed package. I laid loops of kelp over my shoulders and chanted them into a lovely green velvet dress. My hair turned from moss green to black, and my skin lost its greenish hue and became rosy as any human girl's. I conjured shoes from the white gull feathers scattered on the beach.

I rewrapped the rest of the package in seaweed, and changed the seaweed into a canvas sack.

It was near sundown, but the village was only a ten-minute walk from the beach. I marched in and found the small marketplace, with only half a dozen stalls. Fish, fowl, and vegetables crowded the tables. Sacks of grain lay in neat piles.

I went to a vegetable vendor and said, "There was a cripple brought here yesterday, a young girl. Where is she?"

The fat old woman rubbed her chin. "Lady like you," she said, "could appreciate this fine exotic squash. Melt in your mouth." She lifted a stunted yellow-green vegetable. "For you, a special price."

My time with *him* had inured me to manipulation—but I understood that a purchase was the price of information, so I bought the squash. "Now, the cripple? She could speak only in whispers. Do you know where I can find her?"

With a jerk and a jiggle of her double chin, the vendor said, "The tavern there. She's been sleeping in the back, waiting for her handsome prince to whisk her away to a palace, where she will dine on pheasant and truffles, and sleep on satin sheets. You ask me, she'll be waiting a long, long time."

I tossed a small coin her way and headed for the tavern.

Inside, men gathered in small murmuring groups at

tables. I walked up to the kitchen door and rapped on it. "Who runs this place?"

An old, white-haired man with a thousand creases in his face poked his head through the door. "Who's asking?"

"I'm looking for a young girl, a cripple who was found on the beach yesterday. I must speak with her. Is she still here?"

He snorted. "Nowhere else. Come back and speak with her, if you like. Take her somewhere else to stay. Won't break my heart, and her eating all my food and paying nothing."

I pushed through the door and followed him to a small storeroom in the back. He rapped on the doorframe. "Coral? Coral, love, you awake?" His gruff voice softened. "Someone here to see you." He motioned me in. Sacks of flour and barrels of ale lined the walls.

With delirious expectation, Coral gazed up from a chair, hands on the chair's arms, pushing herself half up out of it. When she saw me, though, she deflated and fell back into the chair. "I'm sorry," she whispered. "I was waiting for someone else."

"I know, Coral," I said. She looked so haggard and sad. I could see that she had been crying.

"Did he send you?" she asked.

"No, he didn't send me." I moved inside, shut the door, and lowered my voice. "I was sent here by your sisters, to try to persuade you to return to the sea."

Her eyes grew huge. "Who are you?"

I didn't want to say the words, but they were the only ones she would recognize. "I am the Sea Hag."

"But you—you can't be. My father said you couldn't leave your old sunken ship. And besides, you look . . ."

I unwrapped the canvas package under my arm and held it out to her.

It was the music box that contained her voice.

I lifted the lid. Her own voice hummed a lullaby.

Her eyes filled; in annoyance, she wiped at them with the back of her hand. "I won't go! You can't make me—"

I held my hand out in a pacifying gesture. "Your sisters want you home again. They miss you." I looked around the dingy storeroom. It smelled musky, like rats. "He hasn't come yet, has he?"

She shook her head, glaring at me. "Not yet, but he will. I'm sure he will. And I will wait for him. Even if I die here, I will wait for him."

"You won't die tomorrow. I only said that to stop you from leaving. You'll live a natural lifespan for a human girl if you stay—but if you return to the sea with me, you'll live forever. What if he can't come? What if he doesn't know where to find you, or if"—I swallowed—"if he's already married? Love is not the only force that shapes human destiny."

"What do you care?" she snarled. "Just go away, leave me alone! He'll come! You're just trying to fill my head with doubts."

"I'm only trying to help."

"If you want to help me, then find him and bring him here! I must speak to him now, today!"

"But I just told you, you won't die tomorrow . . ."

"But I will, inside. Tomorrow, he's to be married. To a princess. It turns out he's a prince, and this is where he was sailing all along. They're to marry, and then he'll take her back to his mountain home, far from the ocean." She started crying. "I can't live without him."

How well I remembered that feeling. I knew, also, that nothing I could say would change her mind. I opened my mouth to tell her the truth, yet I could not bring myself to add to her turmoil. "Coral, you must come home. The sea is where you belong."

"Never."

"Not even if your sailor marries someone else?"

Her resolve started to crumble, but she shook her head.

The old man, the tavern proprietor, stuck his head in. "Coral! You won't believe it! It's the prince, your sailor! He's coming down the main street right now. He'll be here soon. Oh, Coral, you were right!"

I looked down at her, wasted little thing in that chair.

Mute, crippled—would he recognize her, or would he doubt his eyes? Was he a good man?

I left the tavern and glanced down the street, watching the procession of riders and tired horses. At its head rode a handsome black-haired man on a lathered buckskin horse. His face was flushed with concern and hope. He turned to speak to someone riding near him. His bright, ringing laugh told me all I needed to know.

Hastening back to the storeroom, I pondered my choices.

Coral struggled to raise herself upright in the chair. She ran her fingers through her hair.

"This is no way for you to greet him," I said, pulling the stopper from one of my jars. "Give me your hand."

Warily, she allowed me to take her hand.

I pulled a wriggling young eel from the jar.

Coral's eyes widened. "What are you doing?"

"Do you truly love him? Are you sure you want to spend your life with him, on the land, weighted down like an ox, instead of swimming freely in the ocean with your sisters?"

Through her tears, she nodded. "Yes."

I bit through the eel's neck. Coral gasped. I rubbed the dead creature's blood where our hands joined, then pulled back her lap blanket and touched our bloodied hands to her legs.

"What are you—"

I smeared the eel's blood on my own legs and started chanting. The power in my voice lulled her and glazed her eyes in trance. There was so little time; he would be here within moments.

I pulled Coral up out of her chair and seated myself, drawing her into my lap. Her face was lax as an infant's. To hold her, finally—I pressed my forehead to hers while I chanted. My legs began to burn and tremble, sagging beneath her slight weight.

Every transformation required a little death.

The last word of the spell rang out, and Coral came to herself with a start. She leapt from my lap.

"What—" she panted, reaching out a hand to steady

herself. Then she realized she was upright, standing on her own two feet. The eel blood was gone. She stared down at her clean legs, touched them in amazement. When she looked at me again, she had no words.

I had so much more now than when first she'd come to me. My daughters—most of them—had returned to me. "There is one more thing you will need," I said briskly, reaching for the music box. "Come here." I held the music box up and motioned to her mouth.

Staring at me, she pressed her lips against the music box. I closed my eyes and chanted, then put the empty box in my lap.

She touched a hand to her throat. "Can I . . ." she began, with full voice, and stopped because her question was answered.

"Have someone bring me down to the beach," I said, touching my useless legs. "And if it doesn't turn out as you expect with him—then come down to the beach yourself. I still have the potions."

From balmy rollers to storm-tossed seas . . .

"He and I will be together," she said softly. "Forever."

From tropical bath to arctic freeze . . .

I nodded; from her sailor's clean, joyful laugh, I believed they would.

The sea protect you with this charm . . .

Her eyes filled with questions. Mine filled with tears. I wanted to tell her everything; I would never have another chance. But I held up my hand to forestall her.

Keep my baby safe from harm.

I heard excited voices out in the hallway. "Go to him," I said, my voice breaking with the weight of words unspoken. "He's waiting."

The Frog Chauffeur

GARRY KILWORTH

Garry Kilworth lives in Essex, England. Since winning the Gollancz/Sunday Times *short-story competition in 1974, he has published sixteen novels, over one hundred short stories, six children's books, and some poetry. His most recent novels are* Archangel, House of Tribes, *the* Navigator Kings *series, consisting of* The Roof of Voyaging, The Princely Flower, *and* Land of Mists, Kings, *and* A Midsummer's Nightmare. *He and Robert Holdstock won the World Fantasy Award in 1992 for their novella, "The Ragthorn." Kilworth's most recent collection of stories is* In the Country of Tattooed Men.

Kilworth's inspiration came from wondering whether a traumatic experience like a frog becoming a human would have residual effects. After spending eighteen years in the military and seeing action in Aden, he still has the impulse to fling himself to the floor on hearing a loud bang and he still folds his clothes to precision before putting them away. So it seems logical to him that the prince would continue doing some froggy things. He saw tadpoles swarming in his pond one summer and wondered whether the sex drive of the prince while a frog would not have ensured the continuation of frog princes.

The Frog Chauffeur

Isabel Fairfax woke by the large pond in her garden to find a beautiful young man asleep beside her. He was dandelion-haired and handsome. He was also—she could not fail to notice—completely naked. She marveled at the way the droplets of water on his skin glistened with rainbow colors in the sunlight. Skin that was pale to the eye and firm to the touch. Beneath it were flat muscles, smooth as stepping-stones across a stream. He had small hips, a flat stomach, slim, strong shoulders and hard rounded buttocks with a shallow dimple in each.

Isabel wished she were twenty instead of forty as she carefully picked a piece of green pond weed from behind the youth's ear and threw it back where it belonged.

"Wake up, sleepyhead," she said to the drowsy youth. "You've wandered into the wrong garden. You're lying on my book of Tennyson's poems and making the pages damp."

It was surprising that the young man had decided to go swimming in her pond, in the nude, on this bright Sunday afternoon in June, but Isabel was broad-minded when it suited her. She was a spinster (a word she detested for its connotations of age) and almost a virgin (a word she rather liked for its undertones of youth), having only once yielded to a man who had loved her passionately for at least several minutes following a New Year's Eve party. That was a long time ago, twenty years, but remained a treasured souvenir from that other country of which L. P. Hartley spoke.

Despite her best efforts to wake him, the youth continued dozing in the late-afternoon sun. Isabel remained with him on the lawn, dressed in her old-fashioned shirtwaister and broad-brimmed hat. She tried studying the wide pond's yellow flags waving in the breeze, then her quite grand sixteenth-century cottage at the end of the sweeping lawns, restored to a former ambiguity now that the beams had been stripped of black paint, but each time her eyes were drawn back to the wonderful creature whose drying arm rested on her lap.

Finally he woke, and smiled at her, stretching his arms and legs, revealing membranes of skin between his fingers and toes. She rather liked this webby imperfection, which reached only as far as the first joints in any case. It made him more human to her, less of a sun god. His eyes, she noted, were of the deepest green, the color of a temperate ocean.

He reached out to touch her cheek and she drew back.

"Why, whatever is the matter?" he asked her. "Do you not want me now that you see me?"

"Want you?" she repeated faintly. "For what?"

"Why, for your lover, your man, your husband."

She looked around her then, suspecting a joke. Some of her friends were perhaps teasing her? Or some television program was happily making a fool out of an innocent woman in her own garden?

"Where are you from?" she asked, since she could think of nothing else to say. "Are you visiting the village?"

"From there"—he waved a hand generally over the garden—"and I want to live with you always."

"Do you have a name?" she said, smiling at this game.

"No, but you can give me one."

"We'll think of one later. In the meantime, why not come up to the house for tea?"

And so they went into the cottage. She found for him a pair of shorts which Special-Friend Frank had left there on one of his occasional visits, and a T-shirt with SAVE THE WHALES on the front. Then she made them Lapsang souchong tea, with scones, black currant jam and cream. Sometime before the flush of twilight had left the face of the sky, she found herself in bed with the marvelous youth.

His aromatic hair smelled of an afternoon left baking in the sun as he gently entered her. Gradually he eased his penis into the crevice in the soft mossy bank between her thighs. She kissed his shoulders, licked his textured skin, which tasted faintly muddy. Later he used his own tongue, that long, beautiful tongue, in a variety of wonderful ways which had her biting the pillow to prevent herself from screaming. Never had Isabel experienced such physical joy, and she cared not whether it lasted a few moments or an eternity.

Thereafter he remained at the house, seemingly happy just to be in her company. If they ever did go out, it was in her little green car, which she taught him to drive. They would simply cruise the byways of the countryside, staying clear of towns, with him perched happily behind the wheel. She sat in the back, navigating for him, giving him instructions. He became, as well as her lover, her most reliable chauffeur.

Special-Friend Frank, who had never shown the slightest sexual interest in Isabel, suddenly, after many years of sporadic forays to the house, began brushing against her in the greenhouse, and accidentally pressing his elbow against one of her breasts while he read Walter Scott's "Marmion" to her. True to the contrary nature of men, now that someone else wanted Isabel, Frank wanted her too.

She might have lived to be a hundred and Special-Friend Frank would still have been visiting the cottage only to prune her plum trees and do her accounts.

"Marry me?" Frank murmured one day. "I'm an accountant—I earn lots of money."

"No," she replied flatly.

"Why?" he asked angrily. "Because of him? Because of that *boy*? Who is he anyway? Where did he come from? He doesn't even have a name. I've been coming here for years, helping you with your tax returns, sorting out your plumbing, digging over the difficult bits of your garden. He's done nothing for you."

"I don't care," she said, lifting her chin defiantly. "He's lovely. He's loving. He's *love*. He spends too long in the bathroom, but nobody's perfect. I want *him*."

Thus Isabel married the golden youth, who smiled all the way through the ceremony. The wedding took place at the little eleventh-century minster, built by the Viking King Knut, on the hill above the river. The choir and altar boys wore scarlet cassocks, because it was a church connected with royalty. When it came to the part where the youth needed a name, he turned to Isabel.

"I shall take *your* name and be known as Fairfax!"

"And the given name?" asked the vicar with a little cough.

"Prince," said the youth without hesitation. "Prince Fairfax."

"No, that won't do at all," Isabel chided, this offending her sense of taste. "You're not a pop star, after all; you will be my husband. Some simple name would be best—John—John Fairfax."

And so they were wed in the season of the daffodils. Isabel was viciously happy, snatching at every precious moment with her young sun god and swallowing it whole. She had one, two, three children, just like that—two boys and a girl—and they were all very pretty babies. They sat in a row in the back of the car, while their father drove around the country lanes and their mother murmured instructions.

They lived, self-contained and blissfully happy, in the

Tudor cottage. She would read him poems under the lamplight and he would sit enrapt by her low voice, staring up at the standard lamp. When she asked him why he was always looking at the lamp, he told her that to him it was a kind of totem whose deistic duty it was to miraculously attract creatures like damselflies, or dragonflies, or even multihued moths.

"Why, what a lovely thought, dear," she said. "But would you like to see such creatures flying in your room?"

"Of course; they are the closest thing we have to pretty newts," he replied enigmatically, "swimming around one's head in the deepest part of the pond."

It was in their fifth year that Isabel first discovered things were going wrong. She entered the dining room of the cottage one day to find John with his face close to the bull's-eye windowpanes. She watched, fascinated, as he studied a fly while it buzzed, infuriated, in the corners of the window, wondering why there was this invisible wall in front of it. Then, to her horror, out shot John's tongue and the insect was gone, down his throat. Afterward he straightened and made a strange sound not unlike a burp.

"John?" she said faintly. "Whatever are you doing?"

"What?" He spun around, looking guilty. "Why, nothing, Isabel. Nothing at all. I was simply—peering through the glass, trying to see out into the garden."

"You ate that bluebottle!"

"No, no, you're mistaken, Isabel. Why should I do a thing like that?"

He sounded so sincere that she thought that perhaps she had been mistaken in what she had seen, that perhaps she had perceived something which had not actually taken place. It was in her nature to blame herself before others for any error of judgment or observation. She stopped taking the ginseng tea, believing it responsible.

Yet, three weeks later, as they were walking around the garden after a shower of rain and she was chatting about how lovely the lilac smelled, John absently reached out and picked a small snail from the leaf of a shrub. He popped it in his mouth, crunched and swallowed it, still lost in some reverie. She said nothing to him this time, but later, while sitting in the summerhouse on her own, she began to recall several strange habits of her husband.

There were those times when she had found him squatting in the corner of the room, apparently asleep. There was his obsession with cold baths. There was the eerie delight he took in drawing water lilies for their children, as if they were some kind of icon for future happiness. There was his dread of herons, his phobia of grass snakes, his intense dislike of French restaurants. Finally, there were those condemning webbed toes and fingers.

It was true he still liked to drive the car, but she was sure that came from some other hidden lake of his personality, some other well of his psyche.

Afraid, but wanting to know the truth, she found an encyclopedia and read all it had to say about frogs. Everything was there, even the snails, which formed a part of the common frog's diet. With increasing anxiety she decided to give John one last test. In order to put him off his guard one evening, she read him Andrew Marvell's "The Garden," knowing he loved the lines:

Annihilating all that's made
To a green thought in a green shade.

When he was safely locked in that dream world into which he slipped at times, she placed before him a dish of live garden slugs and earthworms. He ate them absently with apparent relish, not pausing to consider what kind of fare she had given him, and whether it was seemly for a youth to gobble such creatures. She knew then that he was from the pond, beside which she had first found him, damp and decorated with blanket weed.

Never mind, Isabel told herself. *He's my husband now and we can still live a good life.*

Nevertheless, she read a version of "The Frog Prince" from a red book of Grimms' tales published by Grosset & Dunlap of New York, one of a boxed set of two volumes, the other a green book of Andersen's stories.

It told how the frog changed into a prince, not with a

kiss, but when the princess threw the frog violently against her bedroom wall, and how the faithful servant Henry had his heart bound with three iron bands to stop it breaking when his master had become an amphibian, and how those bands snapped as his heart swelled with joy when the princess married the handsome returned prince.

Isabel looked up from her reading under the pale light of the lamp.

Not a kiss, then, as the romantics would have it, but a sudden sharp shock! What if the frog had been out of the pond that day, hopping by Isabel's sleeping form, when she suddenly thrashed in her dreams, struck out and hit the passing frog a blow, causing it to change into John?

But where would a frog have come from, in the first place, which had a human form locked inside it? There was certainly no accompanying Henry.

"No other heart but mine would break at John's demise," she murmured to herself, "and one would be sure to fill with gladness, to swell to bursting with joy."

She spoke, of course, of Special-Friend Frank.

Isabel was no slouch when it came to puzzles. She had intelligence, she had the patience. Slowly she unraveled the mystery to her own satisfaction.

What if the frog who turned into the prince, all those centuries ago, had been with another frog before his transfiguration? What if the female he had held in amplexus in the pond in the palace garden had spawned her three thousand eggs and he had fertilized them all? There would be, even after his elevation to kingship, thousands of frogs with the genetic code of a human being locked in their DNA, awaiting a sudden sharp shock to release it.

And those frogs would mate with other frogs, the females spawning, the males fertilizing, thus over the centuries laying millions of little hopping, swimming time bombs ready to burst into mortal form at any moment.

It was an amazing and breathtaking thought that all you had to do was go down to the pond in the garden, pick up a few dozen frogs and throw them at the nearest hard surface to produce a youth or a maiden. It would be like looking for pearls in oysters. Loneliness would become obsolete, for each Jack would find a Jill, and every Sheila a Bruce. Even better, collect a jar of tadpoles, put them in the blender and hand out children to childless couples, to be loved and cherished and grow into beautiful people.

Yet—that agonizing *yet*—Isabel had discovered that of course, after so many centuries, the frog and the human were too closely melded to ever separate completely. The man had been inside the frog, yet the frog would always be part of the man. It came out at the oddest times. Impossible to protect against. Perhaps a shock—a near-traffic miss crossing the street, stepping on the garden rake— might have the reverse effect, with the man changing back into the frog.

Isabel shuddered. *I must warn my John about what might happen to him,* she told herself, closing the book of fairy tales. *I must tell him what he is, where he came from, and caution him against any possible scare.*

That evening, in the privacy of their bedroom, while the children were asleep, she told him the dreadful news.

"But I will keep you safe, my darling," she said to him. "You have really nothing to fear."

He lay there in the dark, staring at the ceiling, and just before she fell asleep she heard him murmur, "So that's why I like water so much . . ."

The following morning, a bright spring day, she awoke to find the bed beside her empty. Fearing the worst, she put on her silk dressing gown and combed the house for her husband John. Not finding him there, she went out to the garage to see if he was sitting in the car. He was not. Finally, with a sinking heart, she ran down to the pond.

There he was, her dear heart, floating facedown in the water, the pond weed caressing his naked body, stroking it lovingly as if welcoming home a lost son. When she turned him over, on his face was a look of serenity, as if he had found the way to Marvell's green-shaded place, where he could think cool green thoughts forever.

The funeral was simple. She had him buried in the garden, by the pond. Special-Friend Frank came down to see her through her time of sorrow, but she didn't need him. She had her children, who were beginning to blossom in splendid ways. They still loved going out in the car and she was pleased to drive them.

It was while she was thus engaged that she realized why her husband had been fascinated by the car, felt comfortable inside it. Being in the car, looking through the glass at grass and overhead trees, was like being under a pond looking out through the watery surface at the green world beyond.

And two of her children are now famous.

You must remember Yvonne Fairfax, the Olympic long jumper, whose extraordinary standing-jump style won her the hearts and minds of the people of Munich. And Arthur Fairfax, who swam his way to a gold in the Games at Montreal. Two brilliant sporting children, who had inherited intrinsic skills passed on to them by their deceased father.

And the third child?

Why, he has a love of poetry that excels even that of his mother, whose traits he bears with vocal pride.

The Dybbuk in the Bottle

RUSSELL WILLIAM ASPLUND

Russell William Asplund lives in Pleasant Grove, Utah, with his wife and four children. He works as a multimedia programmer for a small software company he helped found. Asplund won first place in the quarterly Writers of the Future *contest and his short fiction has been published in* Writers of the Future XII, Marion Zimmer Bradley's Fantasy Magazine, *and* Realms of Fantasy.

The genie who grants wishes when released from its imprisonment in a lamp or bottle is well known from the tales of the Arabian nights. Usually, the genie is honorable. In this variation, the genie becomes the dybbuk, a demon from Jewish folklore. It, and wise Rabbi Meltzer, teach the protagonist a few lessons. The rabbi appeared in a story published last year in Alfred Hitchcock's Mystery Magazine *and is in the novel Asplund is writing.*

The Dybbuk in the Bottle

It was Avram Khaskle's curse to be born a farmer, and a poor one at that. He had inherited the land from his parents, and he worked it as was his duty, but he simply had no mind for the rhythms and seasons of the land, no gift for living things. As a result, his wheat was always a little shorter than his neighbor's, his chickens always a little skinnier.

Still, Avram did not waste time cursing his fate. While he was poor, at least he was not starving. And though it was true that he would never be a successful farmer, that had never been his dream anyway. Deep in his heart he wished to be a rabbi, and not just any rabbi, but a wonder-working rabbi like Rabbi Adam or the Ba'al Shem Tov. What little money he could put aside he spent on books, and he read them morning and night.

He read them while he plowed his fields, letting the horse set the path for the plow. His fields were the crookedest in the valley, but Avram learned of the deeds of the great Rabbi Mencham, who could call down the birds from the sky to fly him about. He read them while the eggs in his chicken coop sat ungathered. As a result, he missed market day, but he learned of the life of Rabbi Elimeyleck, who traveled to Paradise one Sabbath day, only to be sent back for speaking out of turn.

Sadly, Avram had no more talent for wonder working than for farming. No matter how hard he prayed, he could not call even a sparrow down from a tree. His Sabbaths were spent at a small synagogue in the town, and the rabbi there had no idea of the way to Paradise save the path of a good life. As for Avram's attempt to animate a golem, the less said about it the better.

Still Avram did not give up. After all, without his books there was only the farm, and the more he worked the farm, the more he wanted to work wonders instead. There was very little glory in cleaning a chicken coop.

And that is how Avram came upon the dybbuk in the bottle.

It was the height of summer, so while there was weeding to be done and the chickens to tend to, there was nothing so pressing on the farm that it couldn't be put off. Avram spent many an afternoon among the oaks and pines at the edge of his fields reading. One day, when he was reading about the Rabbi of Stolin, who brought rain to ease the drought that had plagued his city, a summer shower caught Avram unaware. As the first few drops spattered on the pages of his book, he realized that he could not make it back to the house in time. Out in the rain, his book would be ruined.

He looked about for a place to take shelter. The trees in this part of his field grew thick and tall, the last remainder of the vast forest that had once covered all the province. Nearby, Avram saw where some ancient fire had burned a small cavity at the base of a tall pine. It was just big enough for a man to fit in, so Avram crouched down and, drawing his knees to his chin, maneuvered himself inside the tree. The rain washed down in great gray sheets, blocking out most of the sun. Avram clutched his book protectively and pressed back as far into the tree as he could. It was then that his hand found the bottle.

He couldn't see it in the dim light, but he could feel the cold, smooth glass and faceted shape. There was a stopper in the top, a little round ball of glass that gleamed even in the near darkness, reflecting back again and again what little light there was. He clutched the bottle tightly, his mind racing with possibilities. Was it a magic potion? A good-luck charm? When the storm broke, he rushed home with his book in one hand and the bottle in the other.

There, sitting on his kitchen table, the bottle looked even more magical. The glass was the deepest blue he had ever seen, and the bottle itself, while small, was ornately crafted. Compared to the rough wooden furniture and plain, homely decoration of his house, the bottle fairly glowed with magic. Avram realized that this was the whole reason he had been out that day, just to be led to this bottle. Perhaps that was the whole reason he had been given the farm. Certainly it boded well for his future as a wonder worker.

He weighed it in his hand for a moment, nearly shaking with excitement. Then he put the other hand on the stopper and began to pull. The bottle had obviously been closed for some time, and at first the stopper would not budge. Avram pulled, and he tugged; he stood up to get better leverage, but it would not budge. He tapped the top of the bottle lightly against the table, but it didn't loosen. He almost considered simply smashing the bottle, but who knew what that would do to whatever was inside?

Finally he sat back down to think. "Now, what would Rabbi Adam do?" he said quietly to himself. At the sound of his words there was a pop from the bottle, and the stopper flew off. A cloud of thick, evil-smelling smoke poured out of the bottle, and before Avram had time to even call out, a dybbuk shot from the bottle, grabbed him by the throat and had him pinned to the wall.

The demon was bright red; its clawed hands seemed

to burn where they held Avram by the throat. It let out a yowl of pure anger, then suddenly stopped. It took a good look at Avram, blinked twice and let him drop.

"You're not Rabbi Adam." The demon's voice was low and rough. Avram fell to his knees, still trying to catch his breath. "Are you?"

"No," Avram said. "No, I'm not."

The Dybbuk seemed disappointed and actually seemed to shrink a bit. It looked around the room. "No, I don't suppose you are. Rabbi Adam and I were having a little contest before he tricked me into that bottle. You don't know where I could find him, do you?"

The dybbuk's voice had changed; now it was smooth and melodic, friendly even. If anything, this made Avram more nervous. He thought hard, trying to remember if he had ever read how to handle a dybbuk. "Rabbi Adam is dead."

"Dead? When did that happen? I thought that one would live forever."

"He's been dead for over a hundred years." Yes, Avram thought as he spoke, plenty of rabbis had made their names outwitting dybbuks. Certainly he should be able to—

"A hundred years!" the demon roared. It turned on Avram, backing him into the wall again. "A hundred years he left me to rot in that bottle. What did he do, hide it in a tree or something?"

"Well, yes," Avram said quietly. "That is where I found the bottle."

The demon turned its back and walked across the room, shaking its head. "I should have known. A hundred years. Who would have thought?"

Avram dusted himself off. He was tired of being pushed around in his own house. He was a little wary of the demon, but after all, the dybbuk had allowed itself to be tricked into the bottle in the first place—how bright could it be? Besides, this was the chance he had been waiting for all his life.

"Excuse me, mister demon, sir?" The dybbuk ignored him, and instantly Avram felt foolish. Calling a demon "sir?" Would any of the wonder rabbis have stooped so low? He cleared his throat and tried again in his most commanding voice. "Demon, come to me."

The demon turned to face him then, and the glint in its eye almost made Avram wish he hadn't spoken at all. "What do you want, little man?"

Avram swallowed hard, but pressed on. "I freed you from the bottle. That puts you in my service, doesn't it?"

"IN YOUR SERVICE?" the demon bellowed. Avram backed up into the wall, wincing at the thought of the sharp claws once again wrapped around his throat, but the demon stopped in mid-stride, and a smile spread slowly across its face. "In your service. Well—why, yes, I suppose it does."

Avram smiled; this was easier than he had thought. "Good, then . . ."

"Of course, I'll need a place to stay."

"Fine," said Avram. "You may stay out in the chicken coop."

"The chicken coop?" The demon looked hurt. "You want me to stay in a chicken coop? No, thanks, I'll just get right back in the bottle and take my chances on being found by someone a little less stingy."

The dybbuk actually moved toward the bottle, but Avram stepped in its way. "No, no, of course you can't stay in the chicken coop. You would just frighten the chickens anyway, and they produce little enough." Avram paced for a moment, thinking. "You will stay here with me, in my house. That way I can keep an eye on you." Yes, he thought, that should work. After all, who knew what the demon would do left on its own? Better to keep it here.

"Fine, then. I will stay here with you. Now, why don't you get some sleep, and tomorrow you can set me to my tasks."

"Yes," Avram said. The dybbuk seemed friendly enough, but there was something in its smile that made Avram's knees quake. He did not think he would sleep well that night at all.

*　　*　　*

Indeed, Avram was right. He tossed and turned in his bed all night, shifting through the stories he'd read about dybbuks. Try as he might, he could not get comfortable in his bed; still, he drifted off to sleep sometime during the night.

When he woke in the morning it was obvious why he'd had trouble getting comfortable. His bed had shrunk and was now no bigger than a child's. His feet hung over the foot of the bed, almost from his knees. He jumped up quickly in surprise, only to smack his head against the ceiling.

He looked around the room. Everything was smaller, or else he was bigger. His little wooden chest looked more like a shoebox; the large mirror in the corner he could easily pick up with one hand. And even as he looked, things seemed to be getting smaller.

"Demon, come to me," he yelled. He was pleased that he managed to keep the quaver out of his voice. He was starting to get the hang of this; certainly no dybbuk was going to get the better of him.

The dybbuk appeared quickly, poking its head through the door. It was the same size as the furniture. Avram picked the demon up by the shoulders as he would a small child. It looked up at him innocently. "Is something wrong?"

"Of course there's something wrong. Look at me, what have you done?"

"To you, nothing, but I thought since I was staying here, you wouldn't mind if I made a few changes." The demon shrugged amiably.

"A few changes? Why, I can hardly fit in my room." Avram set the demon down. In fact, the room had gotten smaller while they argued, and now Avram had to stoop noticeably just to keep from hitting the ceiling.

"Well, you see, I'm used to living in a bottle. I feel a lot more at home with things at a slightly smaller scale—"

"Put it back the way it was." Avram was through arguing with the demon. After all, who was the servant? He put a large finger to the demon's chest. "And do it now."

The demon shrugged again, still smiling. "As you wish."

Instantly the room was as it had been before. Avram straightened up gratefully, his back aching from bending over. The demon was back to its original size as well, almost as tall as Avram himself.

"That's much better," Avram said, reaching for his clothes. "Now let's get going—there's much work to be done."

"Work?" The demon looked surprised.

"Yes, work." Avram was beginning to lose patience. "You are my servant, remember? I freed you from the bottle and now you must do my bidding."

"Oh, that," said the demon. "Well, yes, but as I'm sure a wise man like you must know, you may command me only once a day. And since you have already asked me to put the house back as it was, well, then, the rest of the day is mine."

The demon turned and walked out of the room. Avram opened his mouth to argue, but shut it again. Maybe the demon was right. Obviously the dybbuk thought that Avram knew more about the situation than he did. It would be foolish to show his ignorance. He would read up on the subject, and then, if the demon had lied to him, he would make it pay.

Avram did not see the demon again that day. He did what chores he could not postpone—very few, to his mind. After all, what did not get done today he could set the demon to do tomorrow. He went over and over again in his mind how he had been tricked that morning, determined it would not happen again. All afternoon he read everything he could on the subject of dybbuks, but he learned very little. Still, he thought, a little common sense, a little luck, and he would yet come out ahead.

He dreamed that night that he was taken up to heaven, where he sat talking and swapping stories with the prophets and wise old men of Israel. When darkness came, he lay down on a cloud to sleep. The cloud was soft and bore him gently, but he was troubled. From below he could hear the sound of demons laughing, reveling, and making merry. In his dream he was about to go and complain, when he awoke with a start.

It took him a moment to realize he was awake. The sound of laughter continued, and he thought at first he was still sleeping on a cloud—until he realized it was just his feather bed, now enormous in size. He made his way to the edge of the bed, his feet sinking down into the mattress with each step. It was like traveling through deep snow. "Demon," he cried, shaking his fist, "come to me."

When he reached the edge of the bed, the dybbuk was waiting for him. It was huge, its red eyes as big as windows. It stood between Avram and the chest of drawers, a space as vast as a canyon. The dybbuk clapped its hands together. "What can I do for you today, master?"

"What have you done?" The giant demon was an imposing sight, but Avram was too angry to care. He walked as close to the edge of his bed as he dared. At the door, other demons looked on, laughing. It was this that had woken him from his dream.

"Ah, well, you see, some friends came to visit. Being locked up for a hundred years, there was a lot to catch up on. The house seemed a little crowded, so I made it bigger."

"Have you forgotten what I told you yesterday? I do not want my house changed."

The dybbuk looked apologetic, as those behind him laughed. "Well, I know you do not want it smaller, and I could understand that. But most men dream of owning a larger home. Why, right now you have the largest home in the province."

"I don't care, just put it—" Avram stopped abruptly, seeing the demon's smile.

"Yes," said the dybbuk, "what is it you want?"

"Nothing," said Avram, calming himself. The demon must think him a fool to fall for the same trick twice. "Come see me after breakfast and I will set you to your task."

"As you wish." The dybbuk turned and left, leaving

Avram standing alone on his enlarged bed. He looked down, and wished he hadn't—it was like standing on top of a tall house. It took him a few minutes to work up his courage to climb down the sheet to the floor.

He made his way through the strange landscape of oversized shoes and giant furniture. He had to hop over the cracks between the floorboards, which lay as rough as new-plowed fields and smelled of dust and chicken droppings. Just like yesterday, things seemed to be getting worse as time went on, but he set his jaw resolutely and made for the kitchen.

The trek took most of the morning. By the time he reached the kitchen, he was hungry and sore. He spent nearly half an hour hiding from a hairy spider almost as large as he. The dybbuk sat at the table, surrounded by his friends. Avram tried to climb up the bench beside him, but it was too tall and he didn't have the strength. A large blue demon almost stepped on him on the way to the cupboards. Avram hopped aside just in time.

The demons were feasting on his food, and Avram's stomach growled. He tried a few more times to approach the table, but the danger was too great.

Avram sat down and leaned against the wall. "Demon," he said wearily. Somehow, even above the noise of the revelry, the dybbuk heard him.

"Yes," it said, turning around at the table. "Who said that? I thought I heard a voice." The other demons roared with laughter.

"You win, demon." Avram did not look up; he knew the dybbuk could hear him. "Put things back as they were. Or perhaps I should speak more clearly from now on. Make the house its normal size and send your friends home, then leave me till tomorrow."

Avram finally looked up, scowling. "And come early tomorrow. I will have work for you."

The demon nodded silently, and all was as it had been before. Avram sat alone in his kitchen. He got wearily to his feet and walked to the cupboards, but there was no food left. He sat down at the table and picked at what was left of the demons' feast.

*   *   *

All day Avram read and planned, ignoring his farm completely. Obviously the demon would try to trick him again tomorrow, but this time he would be prepared. He slept most of the afternoon in relative peace, knowing he had sent the dybbuk away for the rest of the day.

By the time night fell, Avram was ready. He lit a large fire in the hearth, his mind racing with plans of what he would ask the dybbuk in the morning. He lit a candle and set it on the table and prepared to wait out the night. When the lazy smoke and crackling flames began to lull him to sleep, he simply remembered the tricks the dybbuk had played on him the past two nights, and the anger kept him awake.

It was a long night, but Avram kept his vigil. Very early in the morning, his patience was rewarded. Sometime before sunrise he heard a sound like the rushing of wind, and the demon stood before him.

Avram leapt to his feet. "Aha, I have you this time. None of your mischief this morning, demon. Today you will do as I say."

"Of course," the demon said. It hid its disappointment with a smile, but Avram knew better. It had expected Avram to continue playing the fool.

"Fine." In truth, Avram had been expecting more of a fight. He paced the room as he thought of how to word his request. "I command you to . . ."

"You know, maybe you shouldn't rush into things. Maybe you should have some breakfast first. I'm a good cook; just say the word and I'll make something up."

"Silence," Avram said. "I know your tricks. I ask you to get breakfast, and that's all I get—other than chased out of my home. No, you will do as I command. All my life I have wanted to be able to work wonders, like the great rabbis. Make me a wonder worker. That is my command."

The dybbuk stared at him in silence for a while. "A wonder worker?"

"Yes, you know. Like Rabbi Mencham, who could call the birds down from the sky. Like Rabbi—"

"Oh. I see. Why didn't you say so in the first place? There, it is done. Now I'm off to breakfast. By the way, you're a little low on bread." The dybbuk walked toward the kitchen. Avram ran after it.

"What do you mean it's done?"

"Just call the birds; you'll see," the dybbuk called over its shoulder. Avram stopped and watched the demon go into the kitchen. He didn't feel any different; still, it would be easy enough to tell if the dybbuk was lying.

The sun was just beginning to rise as Avram stepped out of his house and looked out on his farm. This early in the morning it looked peaceful and calm—a slight mist hung over the fields as the first rays of the sun shone greenly through the leaves of the surrounding trees. A few birds called high above, and Avram felt his heart lift with excitement.

"Come, birds," he called. "Come to me."

He waited for the sound of beating wings, or the call of songs. Instead he heard a flurry of clucking and a rush of feathers from the chicken coop. He turned just in time to see them bearing down upon him. The big rooster landed on his shoulder as the hens gathered around his feet. He tried to move, but there were chickens everywhere.

"Demon," he called out, and instantly the demon was there.

"And what might I do for you, O wonder worker?"

"I said birds, not chickens." Avram waded through the chickens to stand beside the demon. "What kind of wonder is it to be able to call chickens?"

"Chickens are birds, you have to admit. Still, I can see your point; go ahead—call any birds you like."

Avram turned his back to the demon, and shaking the rooster from his shoulder, he called. Sure enough, the birds in the trees answered, alighting on Avram's shoulders and arms. There were tiny gray sparrows and black-capped chickadees. There were brightly colored jays and noisy crows. Soon Avram could barely see, let alone move.

"Shoo," he said. "Go away." But the birds stayed put. He tried flapping his arms and shouting, but the birds just retreated a bit, only to come to rest again when he stopped.

"Demon, how do I call them off?" Avram asked.

"Oh, no, I've already done you one favor today. You asked to be able to call birds; now you can call birds. If you'll excuse me, you're interrupting my breakfast."

With that the dybbuk headed back into the house. Avram followed, slowly making his way through the birds and chickens. When he reached the door he could hear demons laughing. Avram stood at the door for a while, listening to the unholy revelry, then hung his head in shame and defeat.

He turned his back on his home and started walking for town. He needed help. His home was overrun with demons and the only wonder he could perform was less than useless. He hoped the rabbi would have more wisdom than he had shown. A cloud of birds followed him along the road, chirping and clucking noisily. By the time he reached the town, quite a crowd had gathered to watch his journey. They laughed and pointed, and Avram's ears burned with shame.

He made his way to the rabbi's house and knocked on the door. The village rabbi answered it. He was an old man, his hair thinning and his beard white. He jumped back as the birds flitted past his face and around his door.

"Ah, Avram, I knew you would be coming."

Avram blushed even deeper. "Gossip must travel fast. I came to your home as soon as I reached town, but already news of my shame has spread."

"Gossip?" The village rabbi swatted at a thrush that was trying to fly through the open door. "What gossip? I was visited by a holy man named Rabbi Meltzer. He said that you would be coming to seek his help. Come around back; I left him there tending to his horse."

The rabbi shut the door and walked to the rear of the house; Avram followed behind, leaving a trail of feathers. Out back, a small man in dark robes was watering a fine white horse. He had dark hair and a long beard that hung down to his chest. At the sound of Avram's flock, he lifted his head and smiled as Avram came forward.

"You must be Avram," he said, stepping up to meet the farmer. The birds parted before him. Avram must have been a head taller than the small man. "My name is Rabbi Meltzer, and I am here to help you. Tell me how this came about."

Something in the way he smiled set Avram at ease. The holy man was not here to mock him or shame him; he seemed genuinely concerned as Avram told him everything—his discovery of the bottle, the attempt to put the demon in his service, the demon's trickery. Rabbi Meltzer listened to it all. When Avram was finished, the small man was quiet for a moment.

"You say he mentioned Rabbi Adam?"

"Yes," Avram said. "At the beginning, he seemed to think that I would be him."

"Yes," Rabbi Meltzer said, turning to the town rabbi. "It is as we thought: there is no time to lose. Would you be so kind as to lend Avram a horse?"

The rabbi agreed, and Rabbi Meltzer turned back to Avram. "Do not feel bad. Even Rabbi Adam had to struggle with this demon before he overcame it. But listen closely—by bargaining with the dybbuk, you have given it some level of control. You will have to follow me carefully, and do everything I tell you to do, but if you do, you will be saved. Do you agree?"

Although he was small, Avram could feel the strength in Rabbi Meltzer's words. He nodded in agreement.

"Good. The first thing you need to do is sell me your house."

"What?" asked Avram.

"Everything I say. First you must sell me your house— here are five kopecks to seal the deal. Do you agree?"

Avram nodded dumbly as he took the five coins from Rabbi Meltzer, who looked pleased, as well he should. Avram knew his farm was not worth much, but certainly far more than this. Just then the rooster alighted on his shoulder and crowed loudly. Avram winced and pocketed the coins. If the dybbuk stayed, his farm was worth nothing. He had no choice but to trust Rabbi Meltzer.

"Good man," Rabbi Meltzer said, patting him on the arm. "Ah, look, here is the good rabbi with your horse."

The town rabbi came around the house leading his own brown mare. He helped Avram into the saddle, wishing him God's blessing. Rabbi Meltzer mounted his own horse and started off toward Avram's farm without asking directions. Avram tried to ask the rabbi how he knew, but his horse always seemed one step behind the fine white stallion, and Avram was not much of a rider. Finally he gave up and concentrated on not falling off the mare.

They were almost a quarter of a mile from his farm when they began to hear the demons' revelry. The sound grew louder as they approached—harsh and joyless for all its mirth. Rabbi Meltzer stopped and said a little prayer, then rode right to the front door and got off his horse.

"Now, then," he said as Avram dismounted, "you have agreed to do whatever I command. That makes you my servant, am I correct?"

Avram could hear glass breaking in the kitchen. Rabbi Meltzer awaited his reply. "I suppose."

"Good." Rabbi Meltzer turned and rapped sharply on the door. "Come out, foul demon. Leave off your violence to my house."

The dybbuk appeared at the door. It smiled broadly when it saw Avram. "Ah, you will have to wait for tomorrow before I can help you some more."

The other demons laughed, hooting and shouting names. Rabbi Meltzer took a step closer to the demon. "I ask you again, creature of sin, remove yourself from my house."

Rabbi Meltzer came barely to the demon's shoulders, yet he did not seem at all frightened. It was the demon who took a step back. "What do you mean, your house? I have the right to live here. I made a deal with Avram Khaskle, whose house this is."

"This house is mine," Rabbi Meltzer said again. "Purchased fairly and legally, and this man is my servant. Now be off with you."

"I will not." The dybbuk bared its teeth. "I have given service to this pitiful excuse for a man, and I demand the payment agreed. Which was permission to reside in this house."

This time it was Rabbi Meltzer who took a step back. "Hmm, I see your point. You believed you were dealing with the owner of the house. Certainly it would be a poor master who did not honor deals made by his servant. You may stay in the house."

Again the demons roared with laughter. Rabbi Meltzer had to yell to be heard over the noise. "I will see you here tomorrow, then, to assign you your task."

The dybbuk had turned its back on the rabbi, thinking him defeated. It turned back quickly. "What was that you said?"

"I said that I will see you here tomorrow to assign you your task. That was the deal, was it not?"

"I agreed to serve him." The demon pointed a claw at Avram.

"You have demanded that I honor an agreement made by my servant, and I have agreed. And yet if I am bound to honor his part in the agreement, surely you must agree that I have now taken his place in the bargain. After all, he is my servant. What does it matter if I give the orders, or if I merely order him to order you? Of course, if you prefer, we could simply call the whole thing off."

The other demons were quiet now, as the dybbuk bared its teeth in a feral smile. "No, no, I suppose you're right. I will serve you every bit as well as I did Avram."

"Fine," said the rabbi, his smile as wide and innocent as the demon's was savage. "Come, Avram, let's go in."

Avram hesitated. "But, Rabbi, what about the birds?"

They were all around him still, fluttering and pecking at one another. The noise and mess they made were frightening. Avram shuddered to think what they would do inside the house.

"I see your point." Rabbi Meltzer reached up and scratched his beard. "The birds must be terribly hungry after following you all day. Go to the chicken coop and feed them, then come back to the house."

Avram began to protest, but Rabbi Meltzer lifted a hand in warning. "Everything, remember?"

So Avram trudged to the coop and scattered grain upon the ground. The birds dove at it hungrily, jostling for position. Avram sat at the door to the coop and watched. The chickens took the lion's share, with the smaller birds darting in and out beneath them to grab a seed here and there. Avram watched one small magpie, barely older than a fledgling, get chased away first by the chickens, then by a robin. Avram felt sorry for the little bird—one day it would be a robber, like most magpies, eating his grain seed before it had time to grow. But right now it looked nothing so much like a frightened child. Avram scooped up a handful of seed and carried it to the little bird, smiling as it ate from his hand.

When the birds had their fill, Avram walked back to the house. He hesitated at the door, then shrugged. He was not going to sleep outside. He opened the door and walked through. Amazingly, the birds did not follow; they arranged themselves around the door stoop, perching and sitting on the steps, the windows and the roof.

The house itself was quiet and dark in the evening light. Avram found Rabbi Meltzer alone in the kitchen reading one of Avram's books. He looked up when Avram walked in. "So that's where you got the idea for the birds."

Avram looked around the kitchen warily. "Where are the demons?"

"Apparently they didn't like the company." The rabbi managed to sound almost disappointed. "Don't worry, our dybbuk will be back tomorrow."

Avram sat on the bench across from Rabbi Meltzer. "And what will you do then?"

"Watch and see, my loyal servant." Rabbi Meltzer patted his arm and smiled broadly. "Perhaps you will learn that there is more to life than what is in these books."

With that the rabbi rose and went to lie down in Avram's bed. Avram no longer even thought to complain;

he was weary to the bone. He made himself a bed outside the door to the bedroom, as was fitting for a servant, and lay down to sleep.

He awoke to a hand on his shoulder. He looked up groggily to see Rabbi Meltzer leaning over him, gesturing for silence. The house was dark, but Avram could see through the windows the horizon just beginning to lighten with the promise of dawn. He rose quietly and followed the rabbi into his living room.

They paused at the door, and the rabbi pointed. In the room, the dybbuk stood with its back to them. It was gesturing broadly with its hands and chanting strange words softly to itself. Rabbi Meltzer smiled and winked at Avram, then walked boldly into the room.

"Good, I like to see my servants get off to an early start, but I'm afraid I need no spells today. Still, if you are that anxious to get started, I see no reason we cannot begin."

The demon turned in surprise to find Rabbi Meltzer bearing down upon it. It growled low in its throat, the spell dying on its lips. Avram inched slowly into the room, behind the rabbi.

"Fine." The dybbuk's smile showed all its teeth. "What do you command, master?"

"It is a simple thing, and the same for both of you." The rabbi turned so he was facing both Avram and the dybbuk. "Just do as you see me do, nothing more, nothing less."

"What?" said the dybbuk and Avram simultaneously.

"Just do what I do. Come on now, or the day will be gone before we are even started." Rabbi Meltzer walked toward the door. The dybbuk looked at Avram, who shrugged and turned to follow. He could hear the footsteps of the demon as it followed.

Outside, the birds were waiting. They chirped joyfully when Avram stuck his head out the door. The rooster crowed, and there was a rush of wings from all around. Avram smiled despite himself as the birds looped around him. The young magpie landed on his shoulder, and Avram stroked its neck.

Rabbi Meltzer stood for a moment surveying the farm. Avram looked too, embarrassed by what he saw. The fields were full of weeds, the fences falling down, and the chicken coop ramshackle and in need of cleaning. The rabbi pointed at the chicken coop. "There, that's where we'll start."

"The chicken coop?" The demon stood just inside the door, staring at the rabbi in disbelief.

"Yes, it looks like it hasn't been cleaned in months. That will do for a start."

"You want me to clean a chicken coop? Do you realize the powers I have? I could give you armies, riches, whatever you desire."

"What I desire is a nice home for the chickens. Now come." Rabbi Meltzer turned and walked toward the coop. The demon muttered under its breath and took a step out of the door.

As soon as it appeared, the birds began to chirp loudly. First one, then another would dive toward the dybbuk, pulling up only at the last second. The demon was forced to duck and dodge as starlings and sparrows flew angrily around it.

"Call them off, would you?" The demon glared at Avram.

"I have only the power to call birds, not command them, remember?" Avram had to smile. The demon swore and tried to swipe at one of the birds. It dodged easily.

Rabbi Meltzer turned and called to them. "Hurry up, you two. Don't be all day."

Rabbi Meltzer sent Avram for shovels; then they cleaned out the coop and put in fresh hay. They hammered nails into loose boards, and when all was done, they raked clean the ground around the coop and spread grain out for the birds to eat. Rabbi Meltzer sat for a moment watching the birds.

The demon stayed just far enough away from Avram and the birds. "Fine, I've cleaned your chicken coop. I will return tomorrow to see what other imaginative task you have in store."

"Stay," Rabbi Meltzer said sharply as the demon made

to leave. "We are not finished yet. Next, I believe the fences need to be repaired."

The dybbuk turned, snarling viciously. "I will not be your farmhand, no matter what our bargain."

"You said you would follow my commands. Certainly I would think a powerful dybbuk could do anything a poor, simple rabbi could do, but I suppose I was wrong. If you wish to admit you cannot live up to our bargain, we can call the whole thing off."

The demon stared for a moment, then chuckled softly. "So that's your game. Well, I cannot be chased off as easily as that; lead on."

And so they spent the day working on the farm. By noon Avram's arms were sore and tired, and by evening he felt he could barely walk. Rabbi Meltzer asked nothing of them that he would not do himself—he worked throughout the day, always smiling and often singing softly to himself.

Finally, as the sun began to set, Rabbi Meltzer led them again to the house. He looked briefly over what they had done, and Avram had to admit he was impressed. Already the farm appeared cleaner, better cared for, even more prosperous. His arms burned from the effort, but it felt good in a way.

"You may go now," Rabbi Meltzer told the demon. "I release you for the day. But be back tomorrow."

The dybbuk said nothing, just disappeared in a puff of smoke.

"Come," said the rabbi to Avram, "let's get our rest. There is much more to be done tomorrow."

The next day went much like the first. Again the rabbi woke Avram early and caught the dybbuk attempting to work some mischief. Again Rabbi Meltzer's only command was to do as he did. This time the demon did not argue, and soon they were out weeding the fields.

Avram's arms were stiff and sore from yesterday's efforts, but they soon loosened up, and he found himself almost enjoying the feel of his hoe slicing into the earth.

The birds sang to him as he worked his way down the rows of grain.

The dybbuk grumbled loudly at first; then about half-way through the morning it began to smile. It lifted its hoe and walked through the field past Avram to where Rabbi Meltzer was weeding.

"Have you tired of the work already?" the rabbi asked.

"Oh, no," the demon said. "I just wanted to make things clear. I am to do whatever you do, correct?"

"That is so." Rabbi Meltzer went back to working the soil carefully around the young plants. The dybbuk stood by until Rabbi Meltzer took a step down the row, then hoed the same spot in exactly the same way Rabbi Meltzer had done.

Rabbi Meltzer stopped and looked at the demon.

"Is there a problem?" The dybbuk grinned. "I am just doing exactly what I see you do."

"No," Rabbi Meltzer said. "No problem."

Avram watched as the rabbi continued his work. The small man hoed as before, but this time he took care not to sever the weeds completely. The dybbuk, mirroring his actions, would cut the weeds the rest of the way when it followed behind. The demon growled when it realized it was being tricked into doing useful labor.

Avram stopped his own labors completely to watch the drama playing out before him. The demon began to cut softly as well, leaving the weeds standing. The rabbi shrugged and went back to hoeing as before, severing the weeds completely, but this time he began to hop from one side of the row to the other. The demon, following behind, did the same. Then the rabbi began hopping on one foot as he hoed.

Avram laughed as Rabbi Meltzer led the dybbuk in a merry dance. The sight of the red-faced demon skipping down the row behind Rabbi Meltzer was too much to take. Rabbi Meltzer hopped and spun like a young man at a wedding; finally the demon stopped and threw down its hoe.

Rabbi Meltzer stopped too. "Perhaps it's best not to take things too literally. Just hoe."

The dybbuk picked up the hoe and walked slowly back to the row it had been working on before. It glared at Avram, who still laughed as he himself went back to weeding the field.

There was no more trouble from the demon that day. Again they labored until the sun set. By the end of the day, the farm looked as good as Avram could remember seeing it. After the dybbuk disappeared in a sullen puff of smoke, Avram sat for a long time just gazing out at the well-tended fields. The chickens wandered off to their freshly cleaned coop, and the birds found perches among the eaves of the house, all but the little magpie, who stayed on Avram's shoulder.

Rabbi Meltzer sat down beside him. "We plant the seeds, but we cannot make them grow. It is a wonder, when you think about it, that the seeds grow, that the chickens lay their eggs; even the sky on a night like tonight is a wonder."

Avram nodded, looking up at the first few stars now gleaming in the sky.

"Remember," Rabbi Meltzer said softly. "If you want to work wonders, you must first learn to see them, and to remember that no work of man will ever match the wonders of God."

With that the rabbi rose and went into the house. Avram sat for a long time on the porch, watching the night fall over his farm.

The next day was the Sabbath, but Rabbi Meltzer again woke Avram early. This time the demon was merely sitting in a chair waiting for them.

"Well, back to the fields?" the dybbuk asked, rising from the chair.

"Not today; today is the Sabbath," Rabbi Meltzer said. "Today is a day of rest. Still, my orders are the same: do as you see me do."

With that the rabbi walked to the kitchen to prepare breakfast. He beckoned Avram and the dybbuk to sit, then set food before them. As they began to eat, Rabbi Meltzer left the room and came back carrying Avram's copy of the holy books. The dybbuk looked nervous, and when Rabbi Meltzer began to read from the book of Moses, it stood up noisily.

"I did not come here to eat. Tell me what you would have me do, or I will take my leave."

"Why, just what I said." The rabbi turned the book around and pushed it across the table to the dybbuk. "Do as I have done; read us a passage of the holy word."

The dybbuk went pale. "You know I cannot."

"You have the book, you have eyes." Rabbi Meltzer's eyes never left the demon's. "Read."

The dybbuk took a step back from the book. "You cannot make me—it would be my undoing."

"I can make you do nothing." Rabbi Meltzer's eyes were hard and dark as flints. "It is the power of your bargain that compels you. Now read."

The dybbuk was pressed up against the wall. "I cannot," it said softly.

"I tell you, you must read, or else declare our bargain invalid. Which will it be?"

The demon hung its head. "You have won. I release you from the bargain. I will leave."

The demon began to fade when Rabbi Meltzer called, "Hold! I believe the bargain was in exchange for your release from the bottle." Rabbi Meltzer walked over to face the demon. "If you will not honor your end, then you must go back from where you came. Avram, bring the bottle."

"You can't be serious," the dybbuk said, its eyes never leaving Rabbi Meltzer. Avram walked around the table and took the blue bottle from the cupboard. Rabbi Meltzer took it from him and set it on the table, removing the stopper.

"It was your bargain," Rabbi Meltzer said, "and your own law that condemn you."

The demon looked from the bottle to Rabbi Meltzer. Then, with its eyes downcast, it moved toward the bottle. Avram breathed a sigh of relief.

The demon reached for the bottle, then stopped. "I WILL NOT!" the dybbuk roared, throwing the bottle across the room. It turned on Rabbi Meltzer, grabbing him by the throat and pinning him to the wall. "I will destroy you!"

The bottle bounced off the far wall of the room, but did not break. Avram jumped on the demon's back, trying to pull it off the smaller rabbi. The demon shook him off, sending Avram crashing against the window.

Avram heard scratching against the window, and looked up to see his small magpie trying to get in, surrounded by a multitude of other birds. Avram threw open the window, shouting, "Come to me!"

The birds came, seemingly thousands of them pouring through the window, screeching and flapping furiously. They flew directly at the demon and pecked at it viciously. It tried to shake them off, but there were too many. It had to drop the rabbi to protect its eyes.

Rabbi Meltzer picked himself up off the floor. He seemed somehow larger. Not physically, but he radiated power. "Hold," he cried, and his voice was deep and resonant. Instantly the birds stopped their attack and perched around the room. The demon, too, stopped and turned to look at Rabbi Meltzer.

"There are laws that govern even you, laws that cannot be disobeyed. You sought to destroy a poor fool because of his words and his pride, and yet when your word and your pride were turned against you, you scream betrayal. Nevertheless, they are your words, and you must obey."

The dybbuk screamed in rage, yet even as it screamed, it began to shrink. The room filled with foul, evil-smelling smoke. When it cleared, Rabbi Meltzer ran to where the bottle lay and stuffed the stopper in.

He brought it to the table and sat down wearily. "That was far too much work for the Sabbath," he said, wiping his brow. "But perhaps the Lord will understand. Come, let's go to the synagogue and thank Him for His help this day."

*   *   *

Rabbi Meltzer again stayed that night with Avram. He begged Avram to take the bed, but the farmer refused, preferring to sleep on the floor. In the morning Rabbi Meltzer arose and sold Avram back his house for five kopecks, then prepared to leave.

Avram followed him as he saddled and packed his horse for the journey.

"Was I really such a fool?"

Rabbi Meltzer turned from his saddlebags. "We are all fools in the sight of God."

Avram laughed. "A diplomatic answer, if not a full one."

"A fool is someone who doesn't know who he is. It's never too late to learn." Rabbi Meltzer mounted his horse.

Avram gazed around at his farm. "I think I can learn. But, Rabbi, what about the birds?" He had gotten so used to them, he had almost forgotten they were there, but it did not seem fair to keep them like this.

"Oh, yes," Rabbi Meltzer said, and waved his hand at the birds. They took to the air, flying up over the farm. The chickens wandered back to their coop, scratching at the ground for food. Avram watched the birds go and was almost sorry. It was the closest he'd ever come to working a wonder.

"Goodbye, Avram the farmer." Rabbi Meltzer urged his horse forward onto the road. Avram waved until he lost sight of the man who had saved his farm.

Avram felt a tug on his shoulder and turned to see the little magpie alighted there. He scratched it under the chin. "You are free to go now," he said, but the bird only rubbed its head against his cheek.

Avram laughed. "Okay, then, you can stay."

He picked up a hoe and walked out into his field.

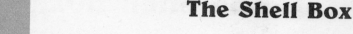

The Shell Box

KARAWYNN LONG

Karawynn Long currently lives in Seattle, where she works as a web designer. Her first story was published in the Writers of the Future IX. *Other stories have been published in the magazine* Century *and in the anthologies* Full Spectrum 5, Enchanted Forests, Alternate Tyrants, *and* Sorceries.

Long's story is a conflation of various Selkie and Roane stories, some "Bluebeard" tales, with a bit of "The Little Mermaid." She also took several elements from a Welsh tale called "The Lady of Llyn y Fan Fach," including the idea that the husband loses his wife after striking her three times. Adding her own spin and her own voice to this material, Long has created "The Shell Box."

The Shell Box

Merwen lived alone in the cottage her father had built for her mother just beyond sight of the sea.

Her father had been a fisherman, his name known in villages far up and down the coast, as much for his wild daring as for his strength and the skill of his spear. It was a matter of pride with him to take his small boat out in the worst of storms, when every other fisherman wisely stayed at home and whittled wood in front of a hearth-fire. And in truth, the fish he brought back on those dark days were bigger and finer than any other, and his boat always rode low in the water with the weight of them.

Only once, in his youth, had he rowed out into a storm and returned with no fish at all. That was the story told at the town's one inn—how the flash of pale skin glimpsed under the water made him hold back his spear, how he plunged both hands into the savage sea and pulled forth a body with neither scales nor fins. He blew the water from the drowning woman's lungs and filled them with his own breath, so that she was bound to love him forever after.

Merwen's father built her shipwrecked mother a cottage far back on the cliffs above the narrow beach so she would not be frightened by the sight of the sea. But Merwen always remembered the way her mother would stand very still, listening, as if caught by the hiss and sigh the waves made upon the sand. She could not have said what the expression on her mother's face might have meant, only that it had never seemed quite like fear.

And now Merwen lived alone, because her mother had left the cottage, and her husband and her two children, when Merwen was only thirteen. After that the girl watched her father turn sullen and snappish, and her older brother accusing and defiant, until their blows and nightly shouting drowned out the low, ceaseless sound of the sea. Within a year her brother joined a caravan traveling east over the mountains, and she did not hear from him again.

Then some measure of peace came back to the house, though none of affection. Her father seldom spoke to her, and spent most of his time out at sea. One winter day after Merwen had turned fifteen, her father rowed out into a wild and raging storm and never returned. She found his boat washed up on shore the next morning like a gigantic, improbable piece of driftwood.

Merwen liked to walk along the edge of the waves at sunrise, smelling the salt air, with the cries of seagulls overhead and the squishy, gritty feel of wet sand between her bare toes. She dug for clams, or walked up the path toward the woods and picked wild berries and mushrooms. Sometimes, when she had more than she needed, she would trade the rest in town for things like flour and candles.

The townspeople thought her strange and fey, when they thought about her at all. No one was unkind to her, but neither did they come to visit or invite her over for supper, and no one had ever courted her. Mostly she stayed at home, talking to the orange cat she'd taken in, or wandered along the beach singing to herself, pausing to listen for an answer that never came. During the worst storms she left her cottage to stand at the edge of the cliff, cold rain plastering her blouse to her skin, watching the dark, heaving ocean in silence.

Two winters after Merwen's father died a stranger came to town, a man from far inland, beyond the mountains. He had some gold, though no craft or trade that anyone could discover. He took up residence at the town's inn, and let it be known that he might want to buy some property with a house and settle down here. His name was Donavan.

Eventually someone mentioned the girl who lived alone in a cottage near the ocean. Donavan asked a few more questions. Did she have any family? What had been her father's trade? What happened to the man's boat when he died? When the answers he got satisfied him, he went to see her for himself.

He found the girl walking along the beach as the sun rose over the mountains. As he drew closer he could hear her singing, a cheerful round that he recognized from his childhood. Something about the timbre of the girl's voice made a shiver run up his spine.

When she came again to the beginning of the verse, he took a deep breath, tapped four beats out on his thigh, and began singing after her in his own rough voice. The girl's voice faltered and she whirled to face him. He continued walking toward her, slowly, as he finished out the song.

The wind off the ocean whipped her long brown hair, and she raised a hand to pull it from her eyes. Her features were plain, her nose a little too large, but he thought she was pretty enough for all of that. Her eyes were a remarkable shade of pale green, and there had been a sort of grace to her walk. He smiled at her then, and complimented her singing voice, and walked along the beach at her side.

She seemed nervous under his attentions, but easily pleased, with a charming smile. Donavan thought it sweet the way she blushed whenever he caught her watching him from the corner of her eye. Soon they came to her cottage, which Donavan could see was sturdily built and well kept, if small. She stood in the doorway, flustered, until he rescued her by asking if he might see her again. She agreed, and he walked back to the inn, well pleased.

The stranger brought her a pretty spray of blue flowers the next day while she was out digging clams. Merwen heard him from a long way off, scrambling down the place where the cliff was no more than a steep hill, and she really ought to have had time to think of something to say. But there he was, standing near the high sun so that she had to squint up at him, and she couldn't remember how to form any words at all.

"I thought you might like these," he said, squatting across from her and holding out the flowers. She took hold of them by the stems, shivering as her fingers touched his. "Though they're not half so pretty a color as your eyes."

Heat flooded her cheeks, and she stared down at the flowers so she wouldn't have to meet his gaze. They were a sort that grew among the dunes farther down the beach, with five pointed petals like stars.

"What happened to that lovely voice I heard yesterday? Did a cat come and steal it away?"

"No," she managed, with only a slight quaver. She stole a glance at his face, broad and swarthy with a thick, dark beard.

"Ah," said Donavan. He was smiling at her. "Good."

The next time he came, he brought a fat chicken. Merwen didn't have the faintest idea what to do with it; she'd never learned to cook anything that didn't come from the sea. Still, she thanked him, and—because he seemed to expect it—invited him for supper that evening. She watched him walking back toward the village, until his broad back was lost in the last of the morning fog, and then went running east up the path toward the woods.

The door to the beekeeper's cottage stood open; to one

side, his dark-haired sister was shaking dust from a rug. Unlike most of the women in town, Sarina tended to smile at Merwen when they passed, though they'd never spoken. She smiled again now, and gestured for Merwen to follow her inside.

"Can you tell me how to cook a chicken?" Merwen blurted, standing in the doorway. The woman frowned and tilted her head to the side like a bird, and Merwen felt her face flush hot in embarrassment. "I'm sorry; you don't even know who I am. I'm Merwen, I've seen you in town, and this man brought me a chicken just now and I'm supposed to cook him supper, but I don't know how I . . ." She trailed off, heart dropping in disappointment, as the other woman shook her head.

Sarina reached out and took one of Merwen's hands in her own and placed it on her throat. She opened her mouth as if to speak, but no sound came out.

"Oh," Merwen said, startled. "You've lost your voice." That happened to her sometimes, when she was sick or had been singing too much.

Sarina nodded once, then placed one hand flat over each ear. Merwen stared. "You've . . . lost your ears?" She had never heard of such a thing. Sarina nodded again.

"You can't hear, or speak?"

Sarina shook her head.

"But then how do you understand what I am saying?" Merwen asked, confused. Sarina reached over and touched her fingertips to Merwen's mouth. It felt like a soft kiss.

"Oh," Merwen said when Sarina withdrew her hand. "For how long?" she whispered, suddenly horrified.

Sarina shrugged.

"Forever?"

Sarina gave a small, sad smile.

"Oh," said Merwen, at a loss. It was nearly the most horrible thing she could imagine, to be unable to sing a song or hear the cries of birds or the sighing of the sea. "I guess you can't help me, then, after all."

Sarina's brow furrowed. Merwen wondered if she'd been talking too fast. "With the chicken," she explained, and flapped her arms a little. Then she felt silly, and grinned in embarrassment.

Sarina nodded and, taking Merwen's hand, led her out the door and down the path back to her own cottage. Quick and deft, she held the chicken and showed Merwen how to pluck the feathers, where to cut it and how to scoop out the organs inside, how to rub fat over the skin and which herbs to put into the cavity.

When they put the finished bird into the oven, Merwen gave Sarina an impulsive hug, squeezing hard to show how grateful she was. Sarina returned the hug and then bent down to stroke the orange cat, who had been rubbing its head against her shins. It sniffed her fingertips and then licked them, because they smelled of chicken. Merwen laughed.

That night Donavan licked the chicken juices off his fingers and then, kneeling in front of her, took one of her hands in both of his and asked her to marry him. Merwen nodded, heart racing. Donavan nodded once in return, solemnly, and got to his feet. In the doorway before he left, he kissed her cheek.

Merwen shut the door and held one hand to the place his lips had touched. No one had ever paid so much attention to her. She felt the way her heart thudded fast and hard in her chest, and thought, I must love him.

The next week, after the priest had come and married them and taken away some of Donavan's gold, Merwen lay beside her new husband on the wide straw mattress that had been her parents', and thought again, I must love him. It was a hard thought to hold to just then, because of the way she hurt. The pain was more frightening for being deep inside where she couldn't touch.

Merwen placed one hand flat on the broad back of the man sleeping beside her, and then withdrew it. She mustn't let him know that anything was wrong. She had been so happy that someone had finally wanted her; she didn't think she could bear it if Donavan came to despise her. If he, too, went away, leaving her alone.

*   *   *

The next month went hard. The fishing season had begun; Donavan took her father's boat out every day, but he brought home no fish, and when she suggested hiring a boy to help, he shouted at her. Did she think some beardless stripling could do a better job than he? When she persisted, he struck her, one sharp clout across the cheek with the back of his hand.

Merwen could see how Donavan's failure made him hate himself, and so tried not to hold the blow against him, seeking instead a way she might help. Every spare moment she had during the day, Merwen worked to mend her father's old nets, until her fingers bled from the rough cords. She kept her mending a secret, intending to surprise him, and though she worried that he might notice her raw fingers and ask, he never did.

It took two people to use the nets instead of a spear; her father and brother had pulled them in together. Merwen thought perhaps Donavan would accept her help if no one else's; he did after all eat the clams she dug, though without any pleasure. She was as strong now as her brother had been at fourteen.

"No," he said firmly when she finally showed him the nets and broached the idea. "That is not woman's work." He did not yell at her for the time wasted, though, only chewed his lip as he stared at the nets. He took them with him the next morning, kissing her cheek as he left, which he had not done in a long time, and though she knew how impossible it was that he might manage the water-laden nets alone, still she hoped.

She could tell from the set of his shoulders even before the boat touched the beach that it had gone no better. If anything, his mood was worse than before. He did not even taste the soup she'd prepared, but strode past without a word. From the other room she heard the clink of a few coins, and then he walked out again, and down the path toward town.

She woke up when he came home, smelling of liquor and mumbling to himself. He seemed to desire her, and she steeled herself against the pain, but he had scarcely begun to touch her before he fell asleep.

Merwen lay in the dark, hugging her arms around her ribs and feeling more strongly than ever that this man in her bed was a stranger. She thought of the sweet things he had said to her on their first meeting, and then made up other things he'd never said, until at last she too could sleep.

Merwen woke while the sky was still dark and the only sound was that of the waves rushing up the sand and away again. She slipped out from under Donavan's arm and crept out into the other room, shivering a little in the cold.

She bent and lit a candle from the embers in the stove, and set it into an iron holder on the table. Then from a nook in the wall Merwen drew out a small box that had been her grandmother's. It sat lightly in her palm, oval and polished to a smooth shine, but as Merwen ran her fingers over the top she could feel the faint ridges. When she tilted it, the seashell ripples of green and gold and blue caught fire in the candlelight. The lid was cunningly hinged, not with metal but with part of the shell itself. Merwen opened it, carefully, and gazed at what lay inside.

Her mother had given her the box when Merwen turned thirteen. "My mother gave this to me," she had said, "and I want you to have it now."

Merwen had immediately opened it and looked inside, causing her mother to laugh. "No, it's empty," her mother said. "The box itself is the gift."

Merwen looked up. "Oh," she said doubtfully, not wishing to be rude. It didn't seem very useful. "Thank you. It's very pretty."

"It is a special sort of box," her mother told her. "It will hold anything you put into it. Anything at all." When Merwen still seemed unimpressed, she said, "Well, put it away for now. You'll find a use for it someday."

The next morning when Merwen woke up, her mother was gone. Not to the market or to a neighbor's, just gone. Merwen walked down to the beach and spent the whole day staring out at the sea. Neither her father nor her brother came to get her. When the last red sliver of sun sank beneath the dark ocean, Merwen stood up and walked over the hill and up the path to the cottage. She pulled the little shell box from under her mattress and put into it everything of her mother's she could find: a twist of tangled hair from her hairbrush, a scrap of blue cloth from her favorite dress, and the two large iridescent scales Merwen had found lying on the beach that morning.

Nothing happened, however. Perhaps the box could hold anything she put into it, but it could not hold her mother, because her mother was already gone.

Carefully now, Merwen removed the tangle of hair, the scrap of blue cloth, and the two pearly-green scales and tucked them back into the nook. Then, a little self-consciously, she brought the box up near her mouth, took a deep breath, and sang. A fishing song that her father used to chant was the first thing that came to mind; she didn't know many songs with words beyond simple children's rhymes. Her mother had sung often, Merwen remembered, but the words had been foreign and the melodies strange.

When the song was finished, she closed the box and held it. The orange cat lay curled in front of the stove, and she opened her mouth to talk to it as she always did. Nothing came out. She could form words with teeth and tongue, but there was no voice behind them, not even breath for whispering. She remembered Sarina holding her hand to her throat, and shivered. It's true, then, she thought, and stared down at the green and blue ripples in her hand. Anything I put into it.

She wrapped the box carefully in a cloth and nestled it in the bottom of the bag with the bread and cheese Donavan would take for lunch. That day, when she missed being able to sing as she worked, or to talk to the orange cat, she thought of her voice keeping Donavan company in the lonely boat, and smiled to herself.

*   *   *

Donavan had spent most of the morning wrestling the boat against a difficult wind, and the rest of it stabbing the spear uselessly into the water. He decided to try again with the net, though it had almost ripped his arms from their sockets to get it into the boat yesterday, empty as it had been. But first he dropped anchor and sat down for lunch.

When he found the small, smooth shell box, he was puzzled; when he opened it and Merwen's voice came pouring out, high and sweet, he was so startled that he dropped it. It closed as it hit the bottom of the boat, cutting the sound off abruptly. Donavan swallowed the lump of bread in his mouth and cautiously bent to pick it up again.

The box was brilliant in the sunlight, ripples of green and bright blue edged with pink and gold. He opened it again, and again he heard his wife's voice pour forth. The song was something about fish, not one he knew. Donavan peered inside, frowning, then shut it and thrust it back into the leather sack.

It was only after he finished his lunch and stood up that he saw the fish crowding around his anchored boat, silver backs as thick as his arm glinting just under the surface, and crowded so close together he could almost walk out across them, all the way back to land.

When Donavan flung open the door of the cottage that evening, it rebounded with a bang that made Merwen jump. When she turned, though, she could see immediately that he wasn't angry.

"Hold out your hands," he instructed. His mustache twitched as he suppressed a smile.

Merwen put out both hands, palms up. Donavan reached into the bag slung over his back, pulled out a tremendous silver fish, and laid it across her palms. She could see the pair of holes angling through the side where the spear had pierced it. The fish weighed more than the orange cat; it was all Merwen could do to keep from dropping it on the floor.

Now Donavan was grinning. "There's twenty more

like that one," he told her. "And twice that many tomorrow, and the day after that. We're going to be rich, Merwen," he said, and laughed out loud, a great booming sound.

She smiled up at him, still holding the fish, though the muscles in her arms were beginning to ache. After a moment, his laughter trailed off. "Don't you have anything to say, girl? I'm going to make us rich, I said."

Merwen's smile faltered, and she turned to lay the fish down on the table. When she turned back he was frowning at her, and her heart skipped a beat. He hadn't said anything about her gift—what if it had displeased him?

Smiling up at him in what she hoped was a reassuring way, Merwen pulled at the strap of his pack. He shrugged it off and watched her with narrowed eyes. Merwen dug inside the bag for the smaller lunch sack, drew it out, and felt around inside. When her hand found nothing but crumbs, she looked up at Donavan, stricken.

He nodded once, apparently satisfied. Then he undid the laces of the leather coin purse at his waist and removed the shell box from it. "So you've got no voice, is that it?" he asked, handing it to her. "You put it inside that box somehow, and you've got no voice anymore." Fortunately, he didn't seem to expect an answer.

Merwen stroked the rippled surface of the box once, then opened it. For a second there was a hint of song, one note so faint it was like an indrawn breath, and then there was a warm feeling in Merwen's throat, as though she'd just swallowed strong wine.

"Ah," she said experimentally, and closed her eyes in relief. Turning to her husband, she explained, "I wanted you to have my voice to keep you company." When he said nothing, she added shyly, "When we met on the beach that day, you told me"—she faltered—"you told me I had a . . . a nice voice." Beautiful, he'd said, but somehow the word wouldn't leave her lips.

Still he didn't answer, only stared at the box, deep in thought. Merwen's heart thudded once, hard, in her chest. "This is wonderful, Donavan," she said, gesturing to the fish. "You must have a natural talent for it. Twenty of these! My father fished all his life and never brought in a catch so fine."

That made him look at her. For a moment their eyes met, and then Donavan's slid away. "Yes," he said. "There's a trick to it that took me a while to learn, but I think I understand how it's done now."

Without looking at her again, he went to haul in the rest of the fish.

The next morning, Merwen was surprised and pleased when Donavan came to her with the shell box cupped in the palm of his large hand, and asked her to sing into it again. She hadn't thought he'd particularly cared about her gift. "To keep me company," he said, watching her. She smiled at him, and put her voice in the box for him to carry out to sea.

During that day, when she missed being able to talk to the orange cat, or sing, she thought of her husband cheered by the sound of her voice as he worked, and set her loss aside. But on the day after that she began to feel restless and a little lonely, without even the sound of her own voice for company.

In the middle of the day it occurred to her that there was someone she might talk to, even without a voice. She felt her face heat up with guilt. Sarina had been good to her and Merwen had hardly thought of her for weeks.

She scaled and cleaned one of the big fish to take to Sarina as gift and apology, then hurried off down the east path toward the beekeeper's cottage.

Sarina gave Merwen an enthusiastic hug, and her eyes grew huge and round when Merwen laid her bundle on the table and unfolded the cloth to reveal the huge fish.

Then Merwen took one of Sarina's hands in hers and placed it on her throat, and tried to say Sarina's name. Her lips moved, but under Sarina's fingers and her own there was no vibration, not even breath.

Sarina raised her eyebrows and pulled back her hand. Tilting her head to the side like a seagull eyeing a clam, she blinked at her friend. Merwen could see she was curious, and knew that Sarina could watch her lips and understand. But the story was too large for that. She couldn't explain about her voice without telling Sarina about her husband, about her mother—and the thought of struggling with those words, speaking soundlessly in the dead silence, was too much. Something in her chest was too close to breaking. With her eyes and expression she pleaded with Sarina to understand what she needed.

Sarina watched, then smiled her reassurance, reaching out and touching Merwen's cheek for just a moment before she turned away. Merwen's heart lurched, and she swallowed hard. Sarina had picked up a bright red apple from the straw basket on the table. Her other hand she closed in a fist, then put it to her cheek and turned her wrist, just so. Holding the apple up, she made the gesture again.

Awkwardly, Merwen tried to copy her. Twice Sarina frowned and shook her head, taking Merwen's hand and adjusting its position. The third time she smiled and nodded, and tossed the apple at Merwen, who was startled but caught it out of reflex.

Sarina was grinning at her. Merwen grinned back, and took a ferocious bite out of the apple.

The two women visited each other almost every day, in one cottage or the other. They would do the chores together, and then Sarina would give Merwen lessons in the hand talk. Sometimes her brother, Galen, would come in and sit with them, and though Merwen was shy of him at first, she grew used to him quickly. He was hardly taller than Sarina, about an inch shorter than Merwen herself, and he had a soft voice, so soft she sometimes had to strain to hear it. Like Sarina, he could speak with his hands, so that as Merwen got better at it, the three of them would sometimes sit around the table and talk together, the silence punctuated by intermittent laughter.

Meanwhile, Donavan continued to bring in fish in prodigious quantities. One evening Merwen joked with him that the sea would soon run empty if he didn't slow down—and then caught her breath at her daring. Donavan only laughed, though, a loud booming laugh, and continued tossing fish out of the boat.

Donavan traded with someone in town for a horse and paid to stable it at the inn, since there was no good grazing near the cottage. Once a month he would pack up the surplus of smoked fish and ride to the market. He would be gone two nights, and when he returned, the leather purse at his belt would be bulging full and heavy. After each market day would come a spate of evenings spent in town at the inn's tavern. Now and then Donavan would not return home at all until after dawn, and Merwen would wonder if he'd gotten so drunk he'd fallen asleep at a tavern table, or if he had been bedding a whore in a room upstairs.

Merwen found that for all she disliked the way Donavan thrust and grunted on top of her at night, she missed curling up in bed next to his warm, solid bulk. The days were less lonely, because she had Sarina and Galen for company. She particularly liked to visit them in the early mornings, when Galen and his sister tended the bees. Merwen was surprised to learn that, while Galen kept all the records—of how much honey each hive had produced, and when each had swarmed, and so on—it was usually Sarina who handled the bees.

One chilly morning Merwen watched in fascination as Sarina lifted a sheet of honeycomb from one of the hive baskets and gently brushed off with a bare hand the few bees still clinging to it. Galen stood beside Merwen, talking in his quiet voice. "Sarina has always been good with the bees. They like the way she smells," he explained. "And, of course, the sound of them never frightens her the way it does some people. She's very calm. They like that."

Merwen looked at Galen then, studying the fine bones of his face, the arch of his thin brows, the faint fan of lines at the corners of his hazel eyes. Calm, yes. He was so unlike any man she had ever known. She couldn't imagine him ever shouting in anger the way her father had, or her brother, or Donavan.

Galen endured her scrutiny, unruffled and slightly

amused. She wanted to tell him how comfortable he made her feel, and how much she appreciated that, but Merwen didn't yet know the right words in the hand language to explain something so abstract. She merely shrugged in response to the query in his raised brows, and smiled. Galen returned the smile, putting a brotherly arm around her shoulders, and Merwen leaned into the embrace, content.

One night near Midsummer, Donavan staggered through the front door of the cottage with a split lip and a blackening eye. "They're jealous," he muttered as Merwen cleaned him up. "All of them. Jealous bastards. Just can't stand to see someone doing better than they are. I work just as hard as any of them. Harder! How dare they. Accuse me!" One thumb stabbed at his chest. "Jealous sons-of-bitches."

Merwen helped him onto the mattress, where he fell instantly asleep, mouth open in a raucous snore. She never did find out exactly what the villagers had accused him of; he never spoke of the incident again. After that, though, he stayed home in the evenings, and his temper grew shorter.

The next week, on a day when Donavan stayed home to smoke the fish he would later take to the market, Merwen sat inside the cottage and fretted, bored and restless. She wanted to visit Sarina, but she was reluctant to broach the subject with Donavan. You're being silly, she told herself sternly. The chores were done; why should her husband care if she visited a friend? Yet still she was uneasy. Finally she stepped out and waved at Donavan where he was bent over the fire. "I'm going up into the woods for a while, where the beekeeper lives. I'll be back soon." She was already out of sight around the cottage before his voice stopped her.

"What business do you have with the beekeeper?"

She walked back, flushing at the insinuation. "None. I mean, I go to see his sister. We talk sometimes." Then, afraid that simple friendship wouldn't be reason enough, she said, "I thought I could get a little honey from her to sweeten our bread tonight." She held her breath while he considered.

"All right. Hurry back, then," he growled.

"I will," she said, and fled up the path before he could change his mind.

Late that afternoon, Merwen looked at the angle of sunlight slanting through the open door, and her hands flew to her mouth. "I must go," she signed to a startled Sarina and Galen. "I am late; my husband will be furious." Merwen ran the whole way home, only remembering as she laid her hand on the door of her own cottage that she had forgotten to bring home any honey.

Donavan said nothing to her when she entered, nothing as she prepared their dinner, nothing as he ate it. When she handed him a slice of unsweetened bread, he stared at it for a long, meaningful moment while Merwen flushed. She found herself wishing he would rage at her, yell, even hit her. Anything to break the terrible silence. He said nothing as she extinguished the candles and lanterns, nothing as she removed her outer clothes and lay upon the straw mattress, nothing as he climbed on top of her in the dark. For a while he grunted rhythmically, the only noise he had made all evening. Merwen found it almost comforting despite the pain, which anyway was not nearly so great as it had been in the beginning.

At last all his muscles tightened and spasmed at once, and he cried out wordlessly and collapsed, his sweaty hair brushing her cheek. He lay there for a moment, panting, before he rolled off. Only then did he speak. "You won't go up there again," he said.

"Yes," she agreed, and cried silent tears while he slept.

To her surprise, Donavan seemed almost cheerful the next morning. He smiled at her when she handed him the shell box with her voice in it, and touched her cheek tenderly as he left. Her heart fluttered.

She stood at the cliff edge and watched his boat out of sight. When he had gone, she walked back to the cottage. Merwen sat down in a chair and coaxed the orange cat into her lap; it had learned to come when she snapped her fingers. She began combing her fingers through its coat, pulling out the tiny grass burrs. She couldn't think that she would never see Sarina again; it made her hands shake. Donavan had been kind to her that morning; surely he would relent, if she was dutiful and pleased him.

She buried her face in the cat's fur, soothed by the rumble of its purr under her fingertips, and held to the memory of Donavan's smile, his touch upon her cheek. A few days, a week at most, and all would be fine.

That afternoon Donavan returned from fishing empty-handed. Merwen watched him anxiously, but he didn't seem angry. He took both of her hands in his own large ones, holding them gently.

"I have something to tell you, some bad news," he said. His face was solemn, but there was a light behind his eyes. "Today I speared the largest fish I have ever seen. I held it, though it fought with the strength of three men—" He shook his head. "I should have let it go. It turned and swam under the boat, pulling me overboard, and my legs catching the side of the boat as the fish passed beneath turned it over." He spread his hands. "I am sorry, my dear. Everything was lost. It was all I could do to right the boat again and get it home." Donavan looked at her in sorrow.

Merwen's grin faded and she frowned, shrugging a little. The spear had been her father's, but it held no particular meaning for her. It was a shame to lose the nice leather pack, but they had plenty of money to buy another one. The boat was the important thing, and it hadn't been lost. She didn't understand why Donavan was looking at her that way.

He saw her confusion. "The box," he explained, his voice as soft as she'd ever heard it. "The shell box that you gave me, that held your voice. It was in my bag that fell overboard into the sea."

She stared at him in slowly dawning horror. Her voice. He had lost her voice. Her hands crept to her throat, clutched there as her mouth opened on its own and tried in vain to shout, to scream, to make any sound at all. Far away, the waves hissed and sighed.

Slowly her hands dropped to her sides and she turned away from her husband. She knew she shouldn't blame him, and she tried, but she couldn't bear to receive his comfort, or to watch the pity on his face or the shining behind his eyes.

She crawled into bed and lay there, burying her face in her arm to shut out the light. Donavan came in and lay down beside her but didn't try to touch her, not that whole night while she lay there awake with a sorrow too deep for tears.

Merwen was not surprised by the rap at her door late the next morning; she had known Sarina would soon wonder what had become of her. But she surprised herself with how desperately glad she was to see her friend. She had dutifully tried to banish all thoughts of Sarina and her brother and concentrate on her work, on trying to please her husband. But at the first sight of Sarina standing outside her door, dark brows furrowed in concern, Merwen threw herself unthinking into her friend's arms.

After a moment, Merwen pulled back so Sarina could see her hands. "I missed you." She blinked back tears. "I cannot come up to your cottage anymore," she said, her gestures heavy with regret. "My husband forbids it."

Sarina cocked her head, a motion so characteristic that Merwen's heart turned over. "Then I will visit you here," she signed, her expression matter-of-fact.

Merwen stared at her, despairing. "No," she signed. It was true, Donavan had only forbidden her to go up to the beekeeper's cottage, but she knew he would be just as enraged to find visitors here. "No," she gestured again, firmly.

Sarina looked as though she would argue. "Go, go," signed Merwen. "I am hoping he will change his mind, but if he finds you here—go, please." She looked anxiously in the direction of the village; Donavan had only gone to buy a new spear, and could be back at any time.

Sarina caught her hand, her dark eyes staring hard

into Merwen's. Then she squeezed it, once, and turned away. Merwen shut the door and hugged her arms to herself, biting her lip while her heart beat fast and hard.

She took it as a good omen when Donavan returned the following day with a catch as large as ever. He was in a merry mood that evening, complimenting her cooking, laughing and teasing her until she blushed and trembled. "Come," he coaxed, "show me how you work the dough to make it rise."

Her silent embarrassment seemed to inspire him to new heights of ribaldry. Merwen bore it all with a light heart, certain he could not refuse her wish tonight.

She waited until he had sated his desire and lay beside her, content and generous. And only then, in the silent dark, did the full impact of her loss dawn upon her: she had no voice with which to ask.

She stifled her panic. Tomorrow, in the daylight, she would find a way to show him what she wanted.

Merwen produced the empty jar which had once held honey, pointed in the direction of the beekeeper's, pantomimed bringing more. Donavan refused to understand. She took his hand and tried to lead him down the path to the woods, but he shrugged her off. "No," he told her, his voice sharp with irritation, "I'm going to town. I don't want to go into the forest." Dismayed, she watched him leave.

A week passed, long and lonely. Merwen told herself that she didn't need her voice, that it didn't matter. And then she would catch herself trying to hum as she baked or sewed, her throat straining until it hurt. The silence pressed upon her ears like hands.

Merwen went walking along the beach as she had not done for months. The sand burned her bare feet, and she angled toward the damp, cooler sand nearest the ocean. Crabs scuttled sideways at her approach and disappeared down narrow holes, and sandpipers darted along the edge of the water. Merwen stood for a while, breathing the salty air and listening to the waves. There was music in their sighing, but it mocked rather than comforted her.

She returned to the cottage and hunted in vain for the orange cat, wanting something to hold, but the beast had ranged beyond the sound of her snapping fingers. She sat and combed her hair instead, and tried to console herself with the old daydreams in which Donavan charmed and courted her, his brown eyes attentive and adoring.

But the pictures twisted in her head, and the brown eyes she saw weren't his at all.

The sight of his wife filled Donavan with such guilt that he could hardly bear to be in the room with her. Sometimes he imagined that she guessed his lie, that there was accusation in her pale, silent stare.

Donavan held the shell box in his palm and stared at it in disgust. Each day the voice emanating from it seemed thinner, fainter, even sadder. The fish still came to the boat when he opened it, but in fewer and fewer numbers.

He'd thought at first it was just the changing season, the fish running elsewhere as the weather turned colder. But when he arrived at the next market it was obvious— he was no longer bringing in the biggest catch in the region, or even in their small village.

It baffled and enraged him, everything slipping away from him while he watched, powerless to stop it.

He sold his meager surplus in but a single day, and started home that same evening rather than waste coin on another night's lodging.

In the late afternoon, while Donavan was gone to market, Merwen went gathering mushrooms in the woods. After kneeling to harvest a clump of flat white ones from where they poked through the damp leaves, she rose and saw the round humps of beehives at the edge of the clearing, and the cottage beyond them.

Merwen stood motionless for a long moment. Donavan would be gone until midday tomorrow. He would never know.

She took a step forward. By the time she reached the

cottage, she was nearly running. Merwen flung open the door—knocking would go unnoticed if Sarina were alone—and stamped on the floor.

Sarina glanced up from her seat at the table. Her face lit up and she rose, oblivious to the chair falling behind her, and caught Merwen in a hug that sent her basket of mushrooms tumbling and scattering. Before she could catch her breath, Galen swooped her out of his sister's arms and swung her around until her feet left the floor, though between them she was easily the taller. She laughed in startlement and delight.

"I'm so glad I was wrong," signed Sarina when Merwen had managed to persuade Galen to set her down. "I told Galen your husband would never let you see us again. But here you are." She smiled up at her friend.

Merwen dropped her gaze. When she raised it again, Sarina was looking at her with sympathy and sorrow.

"He's a beast," Galen said with sudden fervor. "It wouldn't hurt a thing for you to visit us—it's not as though I'm likely to be cuckolding him, with my own sister as chaperone." He gestured in exasperation.

Merwen frowned, feeling that she ought to defend Donavan but unable to think how. "He's not a beast," she said.

Galen and Sarina exchanged a glance. "Merwen, he's not kind to you," Sarina said.

"He is sometimes," she argued.

"Not often enough," growled Galen.

Merwen shook her head. How could she explain what she felt? "He's my husband." He had come to her when she was alone. He had wanted her when no one else had. "And I love him."

Sarina gazed at her, eyes wide and dark as a deer's, and said nothing. Merwen felt herself flush, but she refused to look away.

Finally Galen shifted uncomfortably, breaking the stillness. Both women turned to look at him. "Will you have supper with us?" he asked.

Merwen nodded, and the three of them relaxed then into more ordinary conversation. She helped Sarina cook, and lingered long after the meal was done, talking. No one spoke of her husband.

Once Sarina rose, bending to tend the fire in the hearth, and then straightened and gave her brother a pointed look.

Galen smacked his forehead with the palm of his hand. "Gah," he said. "I forgot all about it." To Merwen he explained, "Sarina was just sending me out to chop some more wood when you arrived and drove all other thoughts out of my head." He grinned at her.

"I'm sorry," she said, nonplussed and pleased together.

He laughed. "I'm afraid this sort of thing happens far too often for me to blame my muddleheadedness on you. I'll take the lantern out and hunt enough deadwood to keep us until the morning. Though I'll have the devil's own time of it in the dark."

Her distress caused him to chuckle again. He laid a hand against her cheek as he passed. "Don't worry about it. Really. I'm glad you came."

It was well after dark when Donavan arrived at the inn; he had to roust the stable boy from his bed to tend to the horse. From there he approached the cottage on foot.

He was not particularly surprised to find the bed empty and the cottage vacant, nor did he have any doubt about where his wife could be found. It was with something close to satisfaction that Donavan strode up the path toward the woods. They took him for a fool, but he wasn't blind; he'd guessed her purpose the moment Merwen had mentioned visiting the beekeeper. The look on her face—Donavan growled to himself, remembering. *He* was her husband—why did she never look at him with such devotion? Well, he'd not be cuckolded, especially not by the likes of that scrawny beekeeper.

Upon reaching the cottage, he threw open the door and looked around. Merwen was there, as he'd expected, but she was sitting at the table with another woman. The beekeeper was nowhere in sight. Donavan hesitated, his gaze traveling around the room and then returning to the two women, who stared at him in frozen horror. Without speaking, he crossed the room, grabbed his wife's wrist, and dragged her to her feet. They had gone only a couple of steps when the other woman caught up and stepped in front of him, barring his way to the door.

Donavan stared down at her in disbelief. "What is the matter with you? This is my wife. Get out of my way." Beside him, Merwen made some rapid motion with her free hand. The woman watched, then looked back at Donavan. Slowly she stepped aside, still never saying a word. The hate blazing from her eyes was unmistakable. It made Donavan want to slap her, but he held his hand. Let her brother handle her, if he could; he had his own woman to take care of. He dug his fingers into the flesh of Merwen's arm and pulled her along after him out of the cottage.

The path through the woods was too narrow in most places for two people to walk abreast. Donavan let go of Merwen's arm, but made her walk ahead of him where he could watch her.

One part of his mind was still puzzling over the bee-keeper's absence. He might have been hiding in the other room; when he thought of that, Donavan cursed himself for not checking. The fellow must be a coward indeed if that were the case. Donavan sneered.

But that still didn't explain why the woman had been there, the beekeeper's sister. Crazy, she was—he'd heard it said in town. Merwen had said something about the sister before. That they were friends, perhaps. He frowned at Merwen's back.

When they arrived at their cottage, Merwen moved to light candles. Donavan saw the way she glanced at him every few seconds like a nervous rabbit. "Stop looking at me like that," he snapped. She started at the sound of his voice, nearly knocking the candle from its holder.

Suddenly he was more weary than furious. He realized that he no longer really believed she'd taken the other man as a lover. "I'm not going to beat you," he said.

She paused and looked at him, pale eyes holding each of his own in turn. Whatever they saw there made her relax, her shoulders dropping fractionally. Perversely, this fanned his anger once more. "Though I should," he added. Lover or no, she'd gone where he had forbidden. He caught her arm as she passed. "And I will, if you *ever* disobey me again." He said the words calmly, spacing them out.

Merwen nodded, biting her lip where it quivered. Donavan let her go, satisfied. She wouldn't dare visit the crazy woman again, and no one else would pay attention to a girl who never spoke.

The next day Donavan took the boat out again as usual. It was only late morning, while Merwen was kneading dough to bake for the evening's bread, when Donavan burst through the door. "You thieving slut!" he roared as she whirled around. "I'll teach you to take what doesn't belong to you!"

In two strides he was across the room and hitting her. At the first blow she stumbled; the second knocked her to the floor. Still he struck her, again and again without respite. She warded off the blows as best she could and tried to plead, to beg with her posture, even voiceless as she was. He'll kill me, she thought in a sudden moment of clarity. He'll kill me without meaning to, because I can't tell him to stop.

Then he grabbed her by the shoulders and lifted her, slammed her up against the wall. "Where is it?" he demanded.

She stared at him, desperately trying to understand what he wanted. Donavan shook her and the room danced and swam, her head bobbing on her neck like a dead chicken's. Tears blurred her vision and she blinked, frantic to see his face but too frightened to raise a hand.

"Where did you put it?"

What, what, what, what, she tried to say, mouthing the word over and over. She could feel her lips stretched and distorted with her crying, and despaired.

He slapped her once across the cheek, and she stopped, eyes closed, breathing raggedly through her mouth. She waited for the next blow, ears anticipating the rush of air, eyes seeking the shift in shadows on her lids.

Nothing happened.

When she dared to look, she saw that Donavan was staring at her, a small frown between his brows. "It wasn't you, was it?" His voice had turned calm and wondering. Merwen shook her head mutely, more in denial of what was happening to her, in denial of the pain, than of words which scarcely made sense.

"No," he said, and the rage was in his voice again, low and threatening. "It must have been one of those other jealous sots in town." He spoke through clenched teeth, making Merwen's skin prickle. "I'll find the thieving son-of-a-bitch and kill him." He let go of her shoulders. The door stood wide open after he had gone.

Merwen took an unsteady step away from the wall. She waited out the wave of nausea and then walked back into the kitchen, where the bread dough was drying into a hard lump, and began working it again. Her ears were ringing, and she lacked the strength in her hands to squeeze the dough. Her head felt like it was stuffed with wool. Sounds came slow and faint.

She stared down at a dark stain on the pale dough for some time, unmoving, before she recognized that it was her own blood. Her hands began to shake. She left the dough on the table and started to wander around the room, shivering and looking for something she couldn't name.

Some time later, her head cleared enough for one thought to surface: Sarina. She needed Sarina. Merwen stumbled out of the cottage and up the long path, scarcely feeling the stones and twigs under her bare feet.

Somewhere deep in the woods Merwen became aware of a sound. She raised her head. There it was—a faint thread of song. Merwen stopped to hear it better. The melody faded in and out, but the voice . . . the voice was high and sweet and unmistakable. It had sung her to sleep as a child, and led her through her dreams all the days of her life.

Mama. Her lips moved, no sound behind them and all

of her soul. She turned and began to run back toward the
sea. The trees spun around her at odd angles, catching
thin fingers in her hair. Merwen stumbled and pitched
forward, clutching at dead pine needles. Silence. She
crouched motionless, willing her pounding heart to quiet.
Nothing. Not even the constant roar of the ocean pene-
trated this far into the woods. Her throat tightened as she
pushed herself to her feet and turned back toward Sarina's cottage. It had been an illusion, her own mind making manifest the wish of her heart.

When she heard the music again, Merwen put her
hands over her ears to shut out the false sound and kept
walking. She let the tears slip down her cheeks unhin-
dered, and lowered her hands at last only to push open
the cottage door.

The music struck her like a gust of wind off the sea.
She had a moment's clear glimpse of Sarina glancing up,
her mouth dropping open in shock. Merwen ignored her,
all her attention focused upon the music. She scanned the
room, listening—there. On a small table against the wall
sat the shell box, its lid cracked open on stiff hinges.

Not her mother's voice at all, but her own.

Merwen walked toward it, holding her eyes open and
steady as though if she blinked it would disappear. She
touched the edge of the lid—solid, yes—and picked it up.
The song faded to a sigh and then silence. Merwen's
throat burned and she doubled over, coughing. The sound
rang in her ears, harsh and beautiful.

When the spasms subsided, Merwen straightened, lifting her hand and uncurling her fingers. The oval box
rested on her palm, a bit of innocuous bric-a-brac, polished whorls and ripples of green. Sarina touched her
arm, guiding her toward a chair, but Merwen pulled away
from her hand. She held the box out, her question plain.

Sarina stopped and looked embarrassed. "Last night,"
she explained, her hands hesitant, "after you left, I went
down to the beach and . . . searched your husband's boat.
I'm sorry. I was angry at him," she pleaded, "for hurting you.

"I found that"—she pointed at the shell box—

"wrapped in a cloth, hidden under the pile of nets. It looked valuable, and I thought its loss might pain him." She paused, looking down at the box and up again into Merwen's face. "Is it yours?"

Merwen felt she'd been turned to stone. She could move neither her lips nor her hands to answer. Hidden under the nets. Her husband's boat. Perhaps a fish had swallowed it, and Donavan had found the box when he gutted his catch. But even as she thought this, she remembered the way his eyes had shone when he told her, belying his sorrowful expression.

He had stolen her voice.

Merwen groped for the chair and sank into it. A huge and terrible wave was building in her chest.

Sarina left the room and returned holding a folded cloth damp with water. She lifted Merwen's chin and dabbed gently at her forehead. Merwen closed her eyes. The whole left side of her face ached to the touch, but the cloth was cool, and Sarina's fingers as she smoothed Merwen's hair away from her forehead and cheek were gentle. They lingered, following the line of her cheekbone. Merwen shivered with sudden goose bumps and opened her eyes.

Sarina's face was stiff with anger, but her expression softened when she met Merwen's gaze. "Tell me," she signed.

Merwen glanced away, around the room, reluctant. She suddenly thought to wonder where Galen was, and asked.

"In town. He took beeswax to the chandler's, and some other errands." Sarina waited, patient and still.

When Merwen raised her hands at last, it wasn't to tell of Donavan, or the loss of her voice, or even the shell box. Instead, she told Sarina about her mother. Her hands drew the woman in the air, tall to the eyes of the child she had been, hair so black it looked blue in sunlight, like a crow's wing. Pale eyes that changed color with her mood, gray to green to blue. Just a glance from those eyes, and her father's wrath would dissipate like storm clouds fleeing before the sun. Her hands, chapped rough but gentle in their touch.

And woven through everything, the sound of her mother's voice. Her older brother, who even as a small child had been full of independence and indignant pride, would nevertheless allow that voice to tease him out of his pique. It was musical in speech, low and sweet. It was soft and husky at night, singing Merwen and her brother to sleep. But other times, when her mother was working and thought she was alone, her voice would skirl up, high and eerie. Plaintive, like the cry of gulls over the ocean, and shivering.

Merwen dropped her hands into her lap. So much she knew of her mother, and so little. She picked up the shell box and rubbed her thumb rhythmically across its lid. Finally she set it down again and told Sarina of the day her mother had given the box to her, and then of the day after, when she had disappeared. She bit her lip to keep from crying. After that she talked of Donavan.

When Merwen told how he had beaten her, Sarina moved at last, putting her hands up to her mouth, and then higher, covering her eyes. Merwen stopped, then reached out and gently tugged at one of her wrists. Sarina lowered her hands then, and Merwen saw she was crying. "I'm sorry," Sarina said. Her fingers trembled. "It's my fault; I shouldn't have taken the box. I never thought he'd blame you for it. I'm sorry."

"No, no," Merwen said. "Without you, I would never have gotten my voice back. I would have stayed with him forever, and never—" She broke off, staring at nothing, her hands frozen in midair.

"What?" asked Sarina. "Merwen, what?"

Merwen blinked and brought her focus back to Sarina's face. "Come with me," she said, standing. She slipped the shell box into a pocket of her apron. "There is something I need to do, quickly, before he comes home, before I must face him again."

The sun was setting beyond the sea. Merwen led her friend down the path in the deepening dusk, not daring to bring a lantern, which could be seen from a distance. At the edge of the woods she bore left, away from her cottage. As they walked Merwen peered far ahead, worried that they might meet her husband returning from town. Gradually the cliff they walked along grew shorter, until it met the narrow beach below in a sloping hill of sand. Merwen turned off the path and climbed down the dune, holding on to clumps of grass to keep her balance. Sarina scrambled after.

The moon was half full and high at her back, and limned the waves with white. Merwen walked forward to where the sand was flat and damp and stood looking out across the shifting water. A wave rushed forward and lapped over her feet, cold and tickling like a cat batting at her ankles. She drew the shell box from her pocket. Sarina stood to one side, arms hugged to herself against the cold.

Merwen held the shell box and thought of her love for Donavan, or the thing she had believed was love, having nothing greater to compare it to. She knew it now for what it was, a twisted tangle of innocence and loneliness and need and hope. She gathered all of it—the gentle touch and the rough, the sounds he made above her at night, the feel of him solid in bed by her side. A smile, a scowl. Blue flowers, five-petaled like stars. She pulled all the feeling she had for him, from all the corners of her soul, and thrust it forward, out of herself toward the box cupped in her hands. For a moment she seemed to see something hanging in the air, pale and distorted and forlorn.

And then she was free of it. The pressure in her chest broke like a wave upon the beach and receded, leaving her smooth and empty. Merwen lowered the lid and glanced at Sarina. The other woman was staring at the box with a thoughtful frown.

Merwen drew back her hand and hurled the box as far as she could. It caught the moonlight in a flash of silver as it arced out over the water, and she heard the plunk like a jumping fish as it sank into the sea.

From far out across the ocean, thunder rumbled as if in answer.

The rain was falling hard enough to sting by the time the two women reached Merwen's cottage. Merwen lit candles and poked the embers in the stove to life, and the two of them argued about what to do next.

"You should come stay with us," Sarina insisted. The orange cat bumped its head against her shins and meowed for attention. "Both of you," she amended, a grin twitching the corners of her mouth.

Merwen shook her head. "No. Thank you, but no."

"You will stay here with him, then?" Sarina put her hands on her hips.

"No." Even the thought made her skin crawl. How could I have believed I loved him? she wondered. She saw again the box arcing into the ocean. "I'll make him go."

"How? He'll hurt you, Merwen, if you cross him. You have to come stay with us."

"Sarina, I can't. I can't leave—" The sea, she thought, and shook her head. She waved a hand around the room. "This is my home. It's all I have. I won't leave it."

"You can't stay. Merwen, he could kill you!"

"Sarina—" Exasperated, Merwen turned her back, effectively preventing her friend from saying anything more. She busied herself with cleaning up the mess of dried bread dough in the kitchen while she tried to think of a way to explain. Donavan couldn't hurt her now; she knew that like she knew her own name. It was why she had thrown the box into the sea. Her own feelings for him, her own need, had made her vulnerable.

Behind her the door opened, letting in a great gust of damp wind, and Merwen spun around. Could she have made Sarina angry enough that she'd just leave?

But it was her husband who stood in the doorway, one hand still on the knob. His size alone made him a menacing figure; his thick, dripping beard hid all expression. Merwen could see Sarina half hidden in the shadows behind the door, staring at her in obvious fear and indecision.

"Hello, Donavan," Merwen said.

He nodded in return, stepped into the room, and shut the door behind him without looking. Merwen waited with some amusement for the realization to hit him. When it did, his face fell into a perfect mask of surprise. Then, slowly, his eyes narrowed and his expression darkened into rage.

"You lying bitch," he said. "You had it all along, didn't you?" Merwen only looked at him, half smiling. He snarled and moved toward her. Thunder crackled sharply nearby.

"No," she said, serious now, and firm. "Stop."

He paused for a moment, visibly wondering, and then continued his advance. Merwen backed up and put the table between them, marveling at her own calm. "Donavan, stop," she warned again. *I will not let you hurt me.* Once, the mere fact of his anger would have flayed her to the bone, but no longer.

He kept coming, relentlessly, around the table. Merwen backed away, keeping the same distance between them. Then her calf bumped into a chair pulled out from the table, and everything slowed and stretched. Merwen teetered for what seemed like minutes, trying to keep her balance. Slowly, though, inevitably, she fell backward into the chair. Donavan's eyes lit up as he closed the distance between them. His breath had the sharp smell of ale.

Merwen had one long moment to realize that she had been wrong, and foolish—that this man could hurt her very badly indeed. All she could do, then, was to keep his attention focused on herself long enough for Sarina to escape unnoticed. With an odd sense of detachment, Merwen watched Donavan draw back his hand. She couldn't see Sarina, but it occurred to her that she should make as much noise as possible to cover whatever sounds Sarina might make. With Donavan's palm inches from her face, Merwen opened her mouth to yell.

The sound she made was half scream and half song, piercing and wild. Donavan clapped both hands over his ears in mid-swing. His face contorted and he backed away.

Merwen stood. The high, ululating cry continued, sounding terrible and far-off to her own ears, as if it issued from somewhere else. Donavan stumbled and fell to the floor. Merwen looked at the man in front of her, curled into himself in obvious pain, and felt nothing, neither triumph nor sorrow. His mouth was open and moving, but if he made any sound it was entirely drowned out by her own. Blood began to seep from beneath his fingers; she watched one perfect red line trickle across his cheek above his beard, and then his hands relaxed and slipped away from his head, smearing it. His brown eyes stared forward, unblinking.

The terrible song died away, leaving an odd echo ringing in her ears. She looked up at Sarina, standing next to the stove, the iron poker dangling forgotten in her hand as she gaped at the man on the floor in open wonder.

Merwen retreated around the table the other way, pushing the chair in as she passed. The emptiness in her heart disturbed her. How could she kill a man who had been her husband and feel nothing?

Then she saw the orange cat where it lay crumpled on the floor.

"Oh, *no*," Merwen breathed, falling to her knees beside the animal. The cat's mouth was open, its lips pulled back from its teeth. Blood darkened and matted the thin fur in front of its ear. She held out a trembling hand, brushed it lightly along the fur of its side. So soft.

Merwen's hands crept up to cover her face and she began to sob, rocking back and forth. Sarina knelt beside her, put her arms around Merwen's shoulders, and held her while she cried. She turned in the embrace and buried her face in the curve of Sarina's neck. Sarina rocked her and stroked her hair.

Sarina, who lived only because she could not hear.

When she had no tears left, Merwen pulled back, sniffling and wiping at the salt drying on her cheeks. She glanced down at the orange cat and away again. "We'll have to bury it," she said. Her words sounded overloud, and she realized the rain had stopped. "And . . . him." She did not look at Donavan's body. "I'll get a cloth to wrap it in." But she did not move.

Behind her the door opened, and Merwen whirled around, heart pounding.

A woman stood in the open doorway. Her black hair hung in dozens of tiny braids, and she wore a length of vivid turquoise cloth draped around her hips and across one shoulder, clinging damply to her breasts and belly and thighs.

Merwen's mouth moved as soundlessly as when she had had no voice, and then she ran forward into her mother's arms. She smelled of seawater and fish, but Merwen didn't care. "You came back," she said, and hugged her tighter.

Her mother held her for a time, then gently pushed her away. All Merwen's anger and hurt at her abandonment came flooding forward with that gesture.

"Where have you been?" she exploded. "Why did you leave us?" *Why didn't you take me with you?*

Her mother's eyebrows lifted in puzzlement at the question. "I missed my home," she said.

Merwen's throat tightened painfully. I missed *you*, she thought. "Why did you ever come in the first place, then," she demanded, "if you weren't going to stay?"

Her mother frowned. "I was . . . charmed, I think," she said, "though there was more to it than that." She sighed and looked away. "I can't explain what I never understood myself. I often wondered, later, why I had come, why I had agreed to stay. But by the time I knew enough to wonder—there was your brother, and then you. I couldn't just leave you, not until you were old enough to take care of yourselves." She looked back at her daughter, pleading. "I waited," she said. "I stayed as long as you needed me."

Merwen stared at her. "I never stopped needing you," she whispered. Her mother held her gaze, but her head moved as if struck.

"Do you have any idea what happened to us after you left?" Merwen demanded. "Do you even care? Papa and Bevin fought all the time. I thought one of them would kill the other, I truly did. But first Bevin stole all of Papa's money and ran off with a band of traders who probably knifed him for his purse before they got halfway to the mountains. And Papa scarcely knew I was alive. He went out every day, looking for you, until finally his boat came back without him." She stopped, suddenly unable to ask the question she'd carried unspoken for so long.

"No," her mother answered gently. "He died. His body came down to us, after the storm."

Merwen shut her eyes. "I always imagined that he'd found you," she said. It seemed she had some tears left after all. "That the two of you were living together somewhere, happy, and someday you'd come for me. Oh, Mama, how I hoped. I used to walk beside the waves every day, listening for your voice." She laughed, bitterly, and opened her eyes. "When I finally did hear it, it turned out to be my own instead."

Her mother nodded as if she understood that, too. "Your father sang the fish to his spear almost as well as one of us, well enough that I knew he must have some of the sea in his blood. A grandmother, perhaps, lured to shore for a time just as I was." *Sang the fish to his spear.* Merwen blinked, understanding something of her husband at last.

Her mother gestured at Donavan's body sprawled on the floor, the only time she had acknowledged it since entering the cottage. "But your father never had this kind of power. And your brother belonged to the land, or he would not have traveled away from the ocean as willingly as he did.

"But you, Merwen—you are a true daughter of the sea." She touched Merwen's cheek with the back of one finger, a gesture of pride and wonder. "Come with me," she said. "This is no place for you. Those of the land can only cause you grief and pain." She held out her hand. "Come home."

It was the wish of her heart. Merwen drank in the words like water. She stepped forward and took her mother's hand.

From the corner of her eye she caught a slight motion.

Merwen paused, then pulled back her hand and turned to Sarina. "She wants me to go with her," she signed.

Sarina's face was calm and unreadable. "Galen would miss you," she pointed out.

Merwen nodded, glancing down while she gathered courage. "And you?" she asked at last, holding her breath.

Something flared up in Sarina's eyes. "Would I miss my life if it were to walk into the sea without me?"

Merwen felt her blood roaring in her ears. She closed her eyes briefly, then turned back to her mother. "I will stay here," she said.

Her mother looked from one to the other and nodded, but her smile was small and sad. "Then you have stopped needing me after all."

Merwen met her gaze and said nothing. Her mother nodded once more. "I hope you will be happy, Merwen. Truly." She reached into a fold of her garment and held out the shell box. Merwen recoiled, but her mother shook her head. "No, it is empty again. Take it. You may find another use for it, someday."

"I don't want it. You may keep it, if you like," she said haughtily, "to remind you of me."

"Take it," her mother said gently, and Merwen did, suddenly ashamed. Mother and daughter looked at each other, equally awkward, and then her mother turned in the doorway and was gone.

Merwen ran out after her, but clouds hid the moon and she could see nothing in the darkness. "Why won't you ever say goodbye?" she asked softly. There was no response but the low, ceaseless sound of the sea.

She felt Sarina come up beside her, and dropped one hand to her side. With the other she clutched the shell box to her chest. Sarina's fingers slid into hers, and Merwen smiled, feeling something in her heart take wing at last.

Ivory Bones

SUSAN WADE

Susan Wade's short fiction has appeared in The
Magazine of Fantasy and Science Fiction;
Realms of Fantasy; Snow White, Blood Red;
Black Thorn, White Rose; Ruby Slippers,
Golden Tears; Off Limits; Twists of the
Tale; *and* Tarot Fantastic. *Her first novel,*
Walking Rain, *was chosen by* The Purloined
Letter *as the best paperback original mystery
of 1996 and nominated for an Edgar Award by
the Mystery Writers of America. She is finish-
ing her second suspense novel. She lives in Aus-
tin, Texas.*

*Wade admits that as a child she imprinted
on Hans Christian Andersen's stories—she
thinks it may be because they're such a blend
of sweet fantasy and a bleak view of human
cruelties. Of "Ivory Bones," she says, "The first
two lines of this story just came to me, and I
knew it was 'Thumbelina.' I loved the image of
the pearlized bones and the menace of the
voice."*

Ivory Bones

I have a pearl shaped like a skull. I wear it on my thumb, and it winks at me.

As you see, the pearl is set in a band of hammered gold, but is otherwise unadorned. For a time, I considered having the eye sockets set with emeralds. It would have made for a pretty trinket. In the end, I did not do it. My choice is to keep the pearl just as I found it. I do this in memory of her.

You are curious about its history? I have gone to great trouble to learn it, and shall be glad to tell you. You are my guest, after all.

She came to me when she was full-grown, though I understand she had been born only three seasons before. She was no taller than my hand, and as beautifully made as a porcelain figure. Her hair was fair, with a sheen of silver, and her voice—ah, her voice! The memory of its fineness pains me.

She had an elaborate home when she was with me, everything of the finest, and crafted to her proportions. She wanted for nothing. Nothing, I tell you. I gave her everything her heart desired and many things beyond. She was my greatest treasure, and when she sang, strong men wept for joy.

Oh, as to her origins . . . She was not conceived in the ordinary way. Her mother had longed to have a child for many years, but was barren, and so I understand she indulged in witchery. For this, she took a silver disk that had come down to her from her mother's mother's mother, who was renowned as an enchantress. It is said this disk was formed from one of the tears of the moon, and would never tarnish, but remain always pure and shining.

I have long sought for such a disk, like a coin imprinted with the aspects of the moon, and always shining. Sadly, my efforts have thus far proved fruitless . . .

The witch took this disk and laid it in the emptied polished shell of a large black walnut, which she had lined with richest velvet. She fastened it with a loop of golden thread. This charm she took to a place she knew in the wood, where stood an ancient oak, in a grove that was sacred to the goddess who lives in the moon.

There the witch surrendered her treasure with a special incantation, with tinctures of herbs and many fragrant blossoms. In exchange, she pled for a pearl beyond price: a life. She petitioned the goddess for a new-formed life, to be her child and her comfort, a daughter to carry on her witch's line. You can see by this that the witch was very clever, for she knew a life transformed is likely to return to its true nature in time, while a life shaped anew by a god is an entirely different thing. Still, she dared greatly to ask it.

She sang her chant from the time the full moon rose until it set. At moonset, she cut her thumb with a silver knife and spilled her blood at the base of the tree to seal the compact. Then she made her way home to wait.

At moonrise on the third day, when she returned to the grove, the walnut still lay where she had placed it. With a cry of rage, the witch struck out at the great tree, giving it such a blow with her knife that the sap bled freely; its face still wears the scar. Then she caught up her rejected treasure and bore it home.

But when she arrived and opened the walnut shell to retrieve the sacred disk, what should she find but a tiny, perfect baby girl, sleeping sweetly among the folds of velvet, her skin like milk and her lips like roses. The witch-mother gave a cry of astonished joy, and the babe stretched and yawned and blinked open her eyes, which were purest green, like a new leaf in the sun.

And at the sight of those eyes, the witch's heart misgave her, for she understood then the gravity of her transgression in the grove. Still, her joy in her new daughter was very great, and she resolved to make offerings at every moon, until she should be forgiven and regain the goddess's favor for herself and her child.

She named the child Felicia, which means "joy"; and never doubted that her daughter would grow as tall as other children (though doubtless twice as lovely). Meantime, the witch fashioned many clever things for the babe: a willow-twig stand for the walnut cradle, a coverlet of lamb's wool for warmth, a dried juniper berry for a rattle. She nursed the child on milk sweetened with flower nectar and herbs and fed her only the finest grains and sweetest fruits.

It is true the child grew quickly, though not as quickly as the witch-mother had hoped. At seven months, she appeared as a seven-year-old child, but was no taller than a man's thumb. And even as a woman grown, she was not a great deal taller. For this is the way of gifts from the gods: they may dazzle with their magnificence, and are never ordinary.

In the beginning, the witch-mother was delighted with the novelty of this diminutive woman-child, who could tat a lace as small and fine as a lacewing's wing and sing with a voice as clear and bright as a nightingale's. So fine was her lace that the spiders all spoke of her with envy; so sweet was her song that the birds gathered round her window to listen in admiration. Felicia fed and stroked them, and the birds became her loyal friends, singing chorus to her melodies. One swallow became her particular confidant, and would fly many miles carrying messages to her other friends.

But come spring, the witch-mother grew impatient of her tiny daughter's limitations. The girl could not so much as gather herbs from the wood, for her size made her vulnerable to the smallest predators.

"A rat or a hawk could swallow her whole," the witch was heard to mumble. "They are large as a cow compared to her. And the venom of an insect would be to her as deadly as the venom of a snake. Why, the very household is fraught with mortal dangers—a drawer shut or an ill-timed step taken! Quite insupportable."

The witch redoubled her propitiations to the goddess, with grim sacrifices at the dark and full of every moon, in hopes that Felicia would yet grow. But once the gods turn their face from you, they are slow to forgive. When the witch's offerings had no effect on her daughter's size, she began to plot another way to profit from the situation. If she were not to have the daughter-apprentice she had longed for, she would at least have some recompense for her moon-disk. Not to mention all her trouble in rearing such a tiny, fragile thing.

She cast about for a gainful bargain, whilst Felicia grew more lovely—and more beloved of all who saw her—singing and spinning lace on her mother's window-sill, day in and day out.

This is where I enter the story. For I am something of a collector, you see, and one must have one's sources. I shan't reveal them to you; naturally not, for they are of great value to me. Suffice it to say that word came to me of the witch's tiny treasure and of her willingness to part with it for a price; also of Felicia's beauty and grace, and of her lovely voice.

You yourself have remarked on my appearance—you

likened me to a mole, I believe? Yes, yes, I quite accept your valuation; I am not an attractive man. And it is true I am quite shortsighted. But however unlovely and blind I may be, I have a fine appreciation of beauty. You have only to look around you to see the truth of that. I knew at once Felicia belonged here, among objects that could not rival her beauty but would certainly serve as an appropriate setting for it. She was to be my priceless pearl, the crown jewel of my collection.

The old witch drove a hard bargain, I'll say that for her. But the cost was nothing to me, not when it won my lovely Felicia.

I made everything ready for her here, with the finest of craftsmen turned to the task instantly, I assure you. A tiny house, most cunningly made, with every convenience and everything of the finest.

And when the day we had agreed upon arrived, so did my lovely Felicia; brought on the back of her mother's cat (a handsome creature, if too knowing for my taste). Felicia was frightened of me at the first—my lamentable ugliness startled her—but I flatter myself that she became accustomed to my appearance in time, and grew quite happy here. She could want for nothing in my care, after all, and could never doubt my adoration.

We were happy enough in that winter, it seems to me. She quite loved the warmth and coziness of her new home, and came to enjoy my company, I believe. True, she missed the companionship of her friends, the birds, who had flown south to warmer climes. But we were content here together. We conversed on many topics; I taught her to read and provided her with all the books she wished, copied over in miniature for her comfort. We shared our evening meal, mine here before the fire, hers in the dining hall of her own house, set there on that table. Her little house is exquisite, is it not? All of rare woods, and the floors inlaid with ivory and jet.

She sang to me every evening, and I have never been happier. Her voice was as sweet and pure as a mountain stream.

It is a constant anguish to me, pondering the question

of why she should have been less content than I. Could I have given her more? I do not think so. It must be the nature of woman; such inconstancy and acts of ingratitude could have no foundation in my treatment of her.

Yes, of course, the story. My apologies.

The seasons turned, as they always do, and Felicia's birds returned with the spring. She was so elated by their company that I was delighted as well. I even caused that large stone ledge and pediment to be constructed at her window so her avian friends might roost comfortably near her, and visit freely. I can imagine nothing more that I might have done to make her happy; it is most distressing to me to think I might have overlooked a single thing.

It was most unfortunate that the birds should be such filthy creatures; the servants complained bitterly about their dirt. Eventually, I was forced to have the windows shut, and Felicia's house drawn a little away from them, to keep it from becoming soiled.

As summer drew to a close, I saw that she was pale and less animated. She no longer wished to sing of an evening, and when I pressed her, said, "I cannot sing. I have no voice for sadness and there is no joy in me now."

She said it was because her friends would fly away again soon with the cold weather and leave her alone. I assured her I should not desert her, but it made no improvement in her state of mind. Of course not. Who am I to compare with a flock of foolish birds?

Without her songs, my evenings were sad and dark. I was quite desperate to restore her to happiness and voice. Was there anything I might not have done? She was pining away, and I was mad with fear that she would die, for I could not bear to lose her.

It came to me that a companion would cheer her, and that was when I brought her the songbird whose cage stands there beside her house. A sweet-voiced canary, as tame and cheerful as can be. But he seemed only to make her sadder, and when I asked, she said it was because he was not free.

She released him before she went. Most doubtful that

he survived a single day of his cruel freedom; he had no experience with the harshness of the natural world.

Oh, yes, she left me. She—

I beg your pardon; it grieves me still.

It was in the spring, when the birds returned. She had grown so melancholy that I had her window opened again so she could consort with them. A sad mistake, to trust her so—though the fault belongs in truth to the birds. They filled her head with nonsense, chattering always about the beautiful south, and a particular race of small folk who lived there. The foolish things told her their king had fallen in love with her from their fond descriptions.

Do you know of the Flower Folk? No? Well, a flower-spirit is a winged sprite, no taller than its flower's stalk, with a spun-silk hair of palest green, and silver eyes. They are a fair people, their king fairest of all. I understand he was quite magnificent with his gold crown, and his fine cloak as soft and purple as the petal of the foxglove that was his life-root. He is dead now. So tragic.

But she could never have been happy with the Flower Folk; how could she have thought it? They are winged, and wild, and would doubtless have rejected her most cruelly. As lovely as she was to me, they are the Fair Folk, and would see nothing to praise in her. But she knew little enough of the world, and no doubt believed the birds and all their foolishness.

Felicia took very little with her, in the end, which sometimes grieves me most of all. Did she value so little all that I had lavished on her? But no matter; I am losing the thread of my story again. She took with her only the dowry lace she had herself tatted, an ivory fan given her by her mother, and a tiny silver ring. I do not know how she came by that; I had not seen it before. Perhaps that accursed swallow brought it to her when he came from the south.

It was he who carried her away; he urged her to tie herself to his back with a ribbon, and this she did. My dear, foolish Felicia!

I came into this room and saw them flee into the bright

sky. In my horror and fear for her, I cried out to the guards to capture them.

The fools. Utter, detestable fools! Instead of netting the bird, or following it until it must rest, they notched arrow to bow and shot it from the heavens.

My Felicia fell into the river and was drowned.

Forgive me. To speak of it is still harrowing. I watched it all from this very window, you see.

I had the archer and the captain of the guard hanged, though it were precious little solace for the loss of my beloved Felicia.

The river flows, like words and tears; just as swallows fall and memories fade.

Felicia's small body was carried out to sea on the river's back and, in the waves, her bones separated. By purest chance, they came to rest in a bed of oysters, which swallowed them. And there they lay for many years, glazed with layer after layer of ivory luster.

Beautiful things, are they not? The tiny humerus, the delicate navicular, this fragile cage of ribs. The exquisite shape of her skull, here on my thumb. There is a hint of pink in the iridescence, I believe. Quite an extraordinary luster. I was told it comes from certain minerals unique to the oyster beds where the pearls were formed.

I keep the bones here beside her little house, in an ebony box inlaid with gold. Having them near is something of a comfort to me.

Do not be absurd; how could I have caused her to be fed to the oysters? My beloved Felicia? No, no, I merely located the bones through my usual sources. I assure you, identifying the exact locality took enormous effort. Once found, it was fortunately not so great a task to have them retrieved.

The fate of the pearl-divers? Why should you ask? Their deaths were merest accident, I promise you. The natural result of a rather hazardous profession. I see you are very nervous of doing business with me. But there is no need, my dear. None at all.

Well, there are many variations of the tale; it does not

surprise me that you might have heard another. Believe me, this one is quite accurate. Other endings? Why, none that is any happier, my dear.

One version has it that at the dark of her monthly journey, the moon-goddess visits her uncle in his great hall under the sea. It is said she sits at his right hand and weeps for her lost child, and that by now the ocean bed is paved with silver from her tears.

But we should be quite foolish to believe such a tale as that, should we not, my dear? The gods are not so sentimental.

The Wild Heart

ANNE BISHOP

Anne Bishop lives in western New York and enjoys gardening, a variety of arts and crafts, storytelling, and music, especially playing Celtic folk music on the hammered dulcimer. Her stories have been published in Ruby Slippers, Golden Tears *and* Black Swan, White Raven. *She is also the author of two dark fantasy novels,* Daughter of the Moon *and* Heir to the Shadows.

"The Wild Heart" blends Bishop's interest in psychology, women's studies, and archetypes with her love of fairy tales and fantasy.

The Wild Heart

Nothing hobbles a good story as much as the truth.

So I saved my breath to cool the bowl of stew and swallowed the words along with the ale. Besides, I've heard this story in every village I've passed through.

Satisfied that she'd have an audience at least until the bowl was empty, the plump wife of the tavern owner wiped one end of my table with a damp, dirty rag.

"There was this magical frog," said the tavern wife, "and he jumped right out of the pond where the Queen was doing her washing up, and he told her she'd be having a babe right quick. Well, the King and Queen were that happy because they'd wanted a babe for ever so long."

I finished my stew while she told me about the fairy's curse and how the princess fell into a deep sleep after she pricked herself with a spindle, and how a briar hedge grew up suddenly and surrounded the old tower that stands next to the castle. When she told me the terrible fate of the brave, handsome princes who had come to rescue the princess, she dabbled at her eyes with an apron that was as dirty as the rag she'd used to wipe the table.

"So the princess still sleeps in the tower?" I asked, straightening the leather cap that covered my head from crown to neck.

She nodded. "It's been fifteen . . . ah, no, it's been ten years now." She smiled slyly. "I remember because that was the year all the young men were courting me."

I drained the tankard and opened my coin pouch.

All business now, the woman looked me over more carefully. My clothes were worn, but the quality was as good as her husband might buy. And I'm sure mine were much cleaner.

"What brings you to these parts?" she asked.

I smiled at her. "You tell the tale well, but I've heard it before. I thought I'd see if I could wake the sleeping beauty."

She laughed so hard she almost fell over. "You?" she gasped, clutching her sides. "You? You're not a prince."

My smile faded.

Her laughter died.

I carefully laid the coins on the table. "No, I'm not."

The castle's just over the next rise. To pass the time, let me tell you a story.

Once upon a time, there was a lovely queen who was married to a king almost twice her age. One day, while bathing in a secluded pool near the castle, she was joined by a companion who promised her a child. Only the queen knows for sure, but it's doubtful her companion was a talking frog. Which might explain why, a few years later when a guest at the castle teasingly said the little princess must have a bit of Gypsy blood, the king looked furious and the queen looked very pale.

Despite what you may have heard, the princess wasn't beautiful, and she wasn't plain. Like most people, she was somewhere in between. But what made people notice her was the inner light burning so brightly she seemed to glow. She embraced life joyously. Yes, she was polite. Yes, she was kind. Yes, she was gentle and caring. She also had curiosity and courage and an adventurous spirit. She laughed and jumped and ran. She skinned her elbows and skinned her knees. She climbed the trees in the orchard better than the boys. If her eyes swam in tears when she was scolded for tearing her gowns, it didn't stop her from embracing the next adventure, the next challenge.

Twelve of the nurses responsible for the princess's care would cluck their tongues, shake their heads, and talk among themselves about this stubborn, unladylike streak in their otherwise delightful charge. The thirteenth nurse, who, it was rumored, had a few drops of Gypsy blood and had been hired by the queen despite the king's objections, merely smiled and said only gentleness could tame the wild heart.

The other nurses didn't like the Gypsy nurse, probably because the princess liked her best. She was the only one willing to take long rambles or go riding. She was the only one willing to hitch up her skirts and wade in a stream. She was the only one who understood that the Wild Heart and the Gentle Heart were two halves of a whole, and both were as necessary as air and water, food and sleep.

Sometimes the other nurses would talk as they stitched and mended. Sometimes, if the princess was working quietly on the other side of the room, they would talk woman talk, forgetting how well voices can carry.

"The kitchen maid's belly is swelling," one of them would say, sniffing in disapproval. "She pricked herself with a spindle."

That's what they said when one of the lower serving girls was dismissed. "She pricked herself with a spindle."

But sometimes, when one of *them* came to the sewing room looking smugly pleased, the others would just as smugly tease, "Oh, did you sit on a spindle last night? Was it a *big* spindle?" And they'd laugh.

"Why would anyone want to sit on a spindle?" the princess asked the Gypsy nurse one time. "Wouldn't it hurt?"

The Gypsy nurse's lips tightened. She looked nervously at the other women. "There are spindles and there are spindles. Now hush. I've already said too much."

Not enough, not near enough, but still too much, because the next day there were only twelve nurses looking after the princess.

The day the princess turned fifteen, a great feast was planned. Since the king was out for the day doing something kingly, the princess went up to the queen's rooms to visit. The queen wasn't in her sitting room, but a handsome stranger was. Believing he was a guest who had come for the feast, she brushed off her manners and greeted him as a proper young lady should.

Instead of conversing politely, he circled around her, blocking the door. "Do you like spinning?" he asked.

"Not really," she said, backing away from him.

He licked his lips. "Maybe you haven't used the right spindle."

She didn't like the strange look in his eyes. She didn't like the way he kept smiling as he walked toward her.

She ran for the queen's bedchamber, hoping her mother was there, hoping she could reach the door and lock him out.

Her legs tangled in her skirt.

Do I need to tell you what happened next? Let's just say that she fought with all her strength and courage, but it wasn't enough. Not nearly enough.

After he left the room, she heard voices murmuring, then turning harsh. When the queen flew into the bedchamber, she drew some courage from her mother's fury until the first hard slap.

"You little bitch," the queen hissed. "You've ruined everything. *Everything.* How dare you come here, to *my* rooms, and tease him, entice him, spread your legs for him in *my* bed. He was *my* lover. *Mine!* You think this makes up for all the other ways you don't act like a proper woman? You think your husband's not going to know what a little slut you are when he mounts you on your wedding night? And your father's going to blame *me* for this when your noble bridegroom complains." She raked her hands through her hair. "And if your belly swells . . . Isn't it enough that you ruined the pleasure I've been looking forward to for *weeks* without me having to worry about that, too?" Her eyes glittered. She bared her teeth. "Damn your wild ways. Damn your wild heart. I've endured enough from you. No more, do you hear me? *No more.*"

The queen swept out of the room, locking the door behind her.

Caged by the Gentle Heart's fear, the Wild Heart raged in silence.

A short while later, the queen swept into the room again. She set a basin of warm water and a sponge on the wash table, and dropped a towel and an old skirt and top on the chest at the end of the bed. Yanking the torn gown and undergarments off the princess, she snapped, "Wash yourself, and do a good job."

While the queen bundled up the bloody sheets and ruined clothes, the princess washed herself. And washed herself. And washed.

Even though it, too, was afraid, the Wild Heart howled to be free to move, to act. But the Gentle Heart clung to it desperately.

Things blurred after that. The basin with the sponge and blood-tinted water disappeared. So did the dirty towel. The queen helped the princess dress. With one hand wrapped around the girl's wrist and the other arm hugging a lidded clay pot, the queen hurried them through the servants' corridors and out of the castle to the old tower.

They climbed the narrow, winding staircase until they reached the room at the top. Inside was a bed, a piece of polished metal that was used as a mirror, a small table with uneven legs, a candleholder with a partially burned candle, and steel and flint.

"We have to hurry," the queen muttered. "The king will be back soon, and this must be done before he returns." She took the lid off the clay pot, which was filled with earth. She lit the candle and tried to smile. "In a way, what happened today was partly my fault. I should have done this sooner. Right after the first time you bled. That's when my mother did it to me. For me. It hurts a little, but it's better this way. In a few days you won't even notice. Now more than ever, it's important for you to act like a modest young woman. You'll never do it while the wildness is in your heart."

Too frightened to move, the princess watched while the queen mumbled strange words and moved her hands over the clay pot.

The princess felt a queer tugging inside her, as if something was being pulled out of her and into the strange words and patterns the queen was forming. As her inner light grew weaker and weaker, her right hand felt heavier and heavier. It pulsed.

The Wild Heart howled in fierce desperation.

"It's ready," the queen said. Taking a little knife out of her skirt pocket, she pulled the princess's right hand over the clay pot, jabbed the girl's fingers several times, and then squeezed to draw the blood. "This will get the wildness out. All it takes is a few drops of blood on the spelled earth and the wildness will be trapped inside the pot." She smiled grimly. "Don't worry. Some of it has to remain with you. Otherwise, you'll give your husband no pleasure when he comes to your bed."

The princess shivered. A husband. A bed. Another man wanting to use his spindle like the stranger had. And the Wild Heart gone.

It's hard to say whether it was fear or rage that reacted when the first drops of blood fell onto the earth in the clay pot.

The princess yanked her hand out of the queen's grasp. Unbalanced, she hit the table as she fell. The uneven legs rocked hard enough to pitch the clay pot onto the floor, shattering it.

Blood dripped from her fingers.

Air claimed some drops.

Her tears claimed some.

The candle flame claimed a few before it went out.

The earth, freed of both pot and spell, claimed more.

And from those things, an older, wilder magic gave birth.

Thunder shook the tower. When it faded, there were three people in the room where there had been two.

The third, with its savage eyes and bared teeth . . . it was more than a shadow and less than a soul.

It was the Wild Heart, unchained.

"Go," the princess whispered as she struggled to sit up. "Go before she finds a way to trap you."

It didn't question, didn't hesitate. It was out the door and down the stairs before the queen could gather her wits.

When it left the tower and ran into the woods, the princess collapsed, still living but no longer alive.

Once the queen realized she couldn't wake the girl, she dragged her over to the bed. Then, weeping hysterically, she made her way back to the castle just as the king returned.

The queen wept out a pathetic story about the Gypsy nurse returning and casting a wicked spell on their precious daughter, and how she, realizing the princess was missing and seeing the woman sneaking out of the old tower, had rushed to her daughter's defense while one of the guests—did the king see the scratches on the poor man's face?—had chased the woman, catching her long enough to discover that the spell could be broken by a prince's kiss. But she had used more of her wicked magic and escaped into the woods.

As you can imagine, the castle was in an uproar. So it was easy for the Wild Heart to sneak back in and steal clothing from the male servants' quarters.

The Wild Heart knew two things: it had to grow older and stronger before it returned to the Gentle Heart, and the Gentle Heart had to be protected until that time.

It waited long into the night, until everyone had wearily gone to bed. Then it called the old magic that had given it birth, and crying softly for the one who lay within, it circled the tower three times.

By the time it finished the third circle, the briar hedge

had begun to grow. By the time the sun rose, a thick, tangled, thorny mass surrounded the tower.

Before the first servant stirred, the Wild Heart was gone.

You wonder about the princes? Oh, they came, and they did look splendid as they rode to the castle on their fine horses. But they didn't come out of love. They came for the prize hidden in the old tower. They came for a chance to rule a kingdom.

They didn't understand the nature of the briar hedge.

So they drew their swords and battled the thorns that were as long and as sharp as daggers. They hacked and slashed, slashed and hacked, and the more they cut, the faster and thicker and more tangled the briar hedge grew. Sometimes it grew so fast it surrounded one of them between one sword stroke and the next.

But they didn't remain caught there. As long as no one tried to push forward into the tower, a prince's companions were always able to cut away enough of the hedge to pull him free.

There were a couple of them who almost understood the magic. They kept their swords sheathed and used poetry and songs for their weapons. Moving gently, speaking softly, they coaxed their way through the thorns and tangles, all the way up to the room at the top of the tower. Once there, they discovered that the hedge had broken through the shutters of the window near the bed and filled half the room, arching over the bed like a canopy.

Being able to see the prize, they became frustrated and drew their swords to slash and hack their way through those final few feet. Violated so close to the Gentle Heart, the thorns retaliated.

They did cut. They did wound. But even then they didn't kill.

Finally admitting defeat, the princes who had understood enough to reach the room but not enough to win the prize were allowed to pass back through the hedge and rejoin their companions.

After a while, they all decided the prize wasn't worth the pain, and they returned home.

Nothing died among the thorns except greed and ambition.

Ah, there's the castle. That dark, tangled mass beside it is the old tower.

The princess is still up there, living but not alive.

The king died a few years ago. After the year of mourning ended, the queen married one of the handsome princes who had come to claim the prize. She lives in another castle now, a long ways from here, but when the royal procession passes through this part of the land, she and her prince-husband spend a few days at the castle.

No one talks about the tower or the one who lies within. No one tries to understand the nature of the briar hedge.

The princess is neither mourned nor missed by anyone except the Wild Heart.

It's better that way.

You like the other tale better?

Well, nothing hobbles a good story as much as the truth.

I left my traveling pack at the edge of the woods and walked toward the old tower, wondering if I would be welcome.

It was easy to find the starting point. The briar hedge was thicker and more tangled near the tower door.

I pricked my finger on one of the thorns. Let it taste me. It quivered. Inside the tower, something else stirred.

I slowly circled the tower, walking widdershins to unmake what had been made. As I walked, I touched the hedge gently, sang to it softly.

By the time I completed the first circle, the hedge was covered with green leaves. By the time I completed the second, buds were swelling. By the time I completed the last circle, the tower was covered with beautiful, blood-red flowers nestled among the thorns.

I stood before the hedge, waiting.

It stirred, untangled, formed an archway leading straight to the tower door.

I climbed the narrow, winding staircase and entered

the room. The hedge parted. I walked into the thorny, blooming bower, leaned over the bed, and gently kissed her lips.

She sighed, stirred, opened her eyes.

"It's time to go," I said softly.

I helped her stand, supported her as we passed through the hedge. By the time we reached the other side of the room, she was able to stand on her own.

I stepped back and studied her while I waited.

Protected by the thorns, she, too, had grown in her own way.

She took a deep breath. Took another.

I pulled off the leather cap that covered my head from crown to neck. My hair tumbled down my back.

"I've missed you," I said quietly. "I've needed you."

She stared at me. "You're—"

"More than a shadow and less than a soul."

Her eyes filled with tears, but she smiled. "I've dreamed of you."

"And I of you."

We studied each other for another minute before shyly opening our arms and stepping into an embrace.

The wind sighed. The hedge stirred.

When the sounds faded, there was one person hugging herself where there had been two.

We wore my leather jerkin and shirt over her skirt. We wore my boots instead of her slippers.

We made a neat bundle of the leftover clothes and left the tower.

Stopping just beyond the hedge, she broke off one of the thorns and slipped it into our skirt pocket. I picked one of the flowers and tucked it into the jerkin's ties.

We wanted to jump and run. We wanted to cry healing tears.

Instead, we sneaked into the kitchen, snitched a carry sack, and filled it with bread, cheese, and joints of cooked meat. Finding a litter of newly weaned kittens in one of the storage rooms, we were tempted to take one.

Nuzzling the small bundle of fur, I offered to find a quiet village where we could settle down.

Gently returning the kitten to its littermates, she said she wanted to see a bit of the world first.

We had to slip out of the kitchen quickly before our muffled laughter woke the servants.

Gathering up our traveling pack on the way, we stopped at the orchard, climbed a tree, and picked all the apples we could carry.

Laughing quietly, we feasted on our stolen bounty. Alive and once more whole, we slept in the orchard for a little while.

By the time the sun rose and the servants began to stir, the briar hedge was sinking back into the earth, and the Gentle Heart and the Wild Heart were gone.

You Wandered Off Like a Foolish Child to Break Your Heart and Mine

PAT YORK

Pat York was born in Kalamazoo, Michigan, and now lives outside Buffalo, New York, with her husband and two children. Her stories have been published in Full Spectrum V, New Altars, Realms of Fantasy, *and elsewhere. She is currently working on a book about family values set in a far future Chautauqua County, where the families are polygynous.*

York has always been interested in what might be called the "back" story of the traditional fairy tale—the incidental folk—the princes who tried and failed and their families. When reading Anne Bishop's "The Wild Heart" in manuscript, York asked her how the princes in the thorns could be killed, as even big thorns probably wouldn't kill a person very quickly. Bishop apparently responded with equanimity that "an early version of the story says they died a slow, terrible death." York took her cue from that comment.

You Wandered Off Like a Foolish Child to Break Your Heart and Mine

The thorns had grown in again during the night.

Queen Rose Mary examined with a critical eye what the dark, magical briar hedge had done to her son. A thick branch—the one that grew from between the prince's legs and branched up to surround his lower torso and push his back into a painful arch—had sprouted an evil tendril. The new, small thorns were eating a path into the skin of John's right hip. A thinner branch that encircled his neck had begun to grow a sucker deep in the foliage, far deeper than she could reach, even with her long-handled pruning knife. This morning it was twined around John's forehead so tightly his face was red. He hung in the hedge like a wren in a net; one leg pulled off the ground, an arm surrounded and flung out from his side, the other arm more or less free.

She wiped her hands on her leather apron. "Mariah, please bring me the small pole nippers and my gloves.

I'll need young Jacob and the smallest saw for that far twig." The maid nodded and went to the toolshed. It was a morning drill as old as her son's imprisonment in the hedge, and so the tools and those who would use them were at work almost before the words had left Rose Mary's lips.

"I am ready, ma'am." Loyal Jacob spoke from behind her. Jacob. Dressed in thick leather that covered even his face, Jacob crouched through the growth, carefully working his way along until he was, perhaps, eight feet in. He reached up past John's shoulder with the saw.

"Move the blade slightly to your left, Jacob. Now up. Good. Now saw." Jacob was one of the smallest, lithest men in her kingdom and unparalleled for the painstaking work of squirming into the thorns and nipping out those pieces that the great snarl would allow to be taken without reprisals. It took courage to crawl in as far as he did, and courage to cut. Others who had been too greedy— who had tried to free their sons and brothers from the magical thorns—had become as entangled as the young noblemen themselves. But, of course, most were dead, princes and commoners alike.

When the small branch was cut and John's forehead freed, Jacob worked his way back out. Rose Mary berated herself silently for not sending some salve in with him for John's back, but she said only, "Good. I can reach these new thorns myself with the pole nips. Hold fast, John; I must drag them across your skin a little."

"Do what you must, Mother."

That was his answer every morning. And she did do what she must, without fanfare or tremor. She had to smile when she thought of those first days and weeks when to simply look at John's plight was almost past her strength. She had been soft and gentle then, happy to let the King guide her in everything. Time and the thorn hedge had changed that. She was not soft anymore and she could not always be as gentle as she would have wished.

Dearest love, the note in her bosom read, *I cherish our son as much as you, perhaps more because he is my kingdom's*

*future, but I cannot go on living a shadow life. You stand vigil
at that cursed castle while I rule far away without your love
or help. I can tolerate no more. Come home. The servants are
loyal and clever. They will protect John; you must know that
in your heart. Come home to me, for with the troubles in the
east, I dare not come to you. Please, my beautiful Rose, come
back to the one who adores you. I am no longer young. All I
can think of is you.*

But servants could not be trusted. She had tried that
once last year. A few days' respite and she had returned
to find John close to death, cold and wet, his back bent
halfway over by the weight of new growth. It had taken
her weeks to re-coax the enchanted thorns into a shape
that would not kill him.

She teased the tendrils forward. It made an evil dragging sound across John's face and through his short beard.
Dark blood welled up on the bridge of his nose. Rose
Mary's stomach clutched and then clutched harder. But if
she did not do this, no one else would. No one else had
the courage to hurt his prince. She swallowed hard and
yanked, finishing the job. "There. I have it." She finally
held in her hand the bloodstained snarl. It was at least
the length of her arm, and all grown overnight. Such was
the magic of the brambles.

Mariah handed her the morning basket and the long
spoon and pole cup. She then went to build up the fire
under the washtub. The night had been cool, but not too
cool, thank God. John would want a hot scrub over those
parts of him they could reach.

The Queen lifted the water jar from the basket and
poured a long drink. She reached the cup through the
thorns to her son. He drank deeply.

"Thank you, Mother. Would you turn, please?"

"Yes, dear. But let me move your robe out of the way
a little."

"I worked my leg a little freer last night. I think we'll
be able to get the robe a little further on this morning,"
he said.

Rose Mary bit her tongue to keep the oath from her
lips. Idiot child! When he struggled with the thorns, they

always paid him back with some new malevolence. When would he learn? She breathed deeply and breathed again to calm her anger.

She pulled away John's robe with the jug handle, catching it lightly on a familiar thorn that she often used for a hanger. She turned her back and listened with satisfaction to the sound of her son pissing into a jar. A man who can pass water is not so weak, she thought. He will last another day.

Rose Mary had Jacob and one of the other men shift the boards around on the soggy ground on the verge of the hedge until she could walk again without muddying her skirts much. He and Mariah washed John in as many places as they could reach with their specially designed scrubbers. The modesty the prince maintained for his bodily functions did not extend to his bath. He was not a fool. When they were done, Rose Mary tucked fresh lamb's wool between her son's back and the branch over which he was bent.

"Mother, you're poking again! Have a care." John used his free hand to help where he could. They were never able to settle the soft stuff in a position comfortable enough for him and tidy enough for her.

Finally she used a hooked pole to pull on fresh stockings and again tucked the warm robe around her son's body and the branches that surrounded him.

"I dreamed of the sleeping princess last night," John said as she stretched the spoon in to put oil-soaked bread into his mouth.

"Oh?"

"She was singing to me, telling me not to despair."

Rose Mary had once seen a picture of the legendary princess at a festival. John had never seen it, but he had loved the stories the travelers brought to the castle of a lovely girl, asleep, enshrined within a forest of vicious thorns, to be freed only by a hero who would give her true love's first kiss.

I gave John true love's first kiss she thought, *when they laid him on my stomach on the bright winter day he was born. He had looked about himself curiously with sapphire eyes and*

*a shock of gummy black hair on his head. He had cried once—
a sound of surprise and curiosity rather than pain—and then
he had been quiet.*

"Mother?" John said.

"I was thinking about the day you were born," she
said softly.

"I was trying to tell you my dream." The edge of impatience in his voice brought her back to herself.

"You dreamed the sleeping princess sang for you,"
she said briskly. She offered him another spoon of bread.

"Yes. She would not be denied my love. And the
thorns shriveled around me. I strode through the gates of
the castle and woke her where she lay."

"How I wish . . ." Rose Mary began wistfully. *How I
wish I had killed every traveling storyteller at the borders of
our kingdom. How I wish I had torn their tongues from their
living heads and fed them to the swine.*

"Do you?" John said. "Really?" The edge was back in
his voice. He spat bread onto the ground at his feet. She
had asked him a dozen times not to do such things. It
attracted rats.

Rose Mary turned her head, pretending to put the long
spoon down, but really so that John would not see her
face. She could feel it reddening with irritation. She
turned back a moment later. "Would you like to hear the
next chapter of the book your father sent?"

"No," he said. "Leave me. I want to be alone a while.
I feel like that prize bull you coddled when I was a child."

Rose Mary smiled a little. "You are sometimes not so
biddable as that bull, John."

"Sometimes I wonder, Mother, whether you don't like
me trussed up here in this place. I'm like that bull to you."

She looked at her once handsome young son. *Oh, yes,
child, I like slogging through mud and fighting this damned
hedge and living like a peasant for you while your father pines
for me at home and I rub my damp thighs together at night
dreaming of his fine weight on my stomach—his hot tongue in
my mouth.* But what she said was, "I am your mother. I
will take care of you until your father or the council can
think of a way to free you."

"Ma'am," Mariah said softly. "May I speak to you?"

The Queen nodded and turned from the frowning figure of her son.

When they were out of earshot, Mariah whispered to the Queen, "Ma'am, do you think you could spare some time to look at young Tristan, the duke's son around the curve of the tower? Ma'am, he looks bad. I'm worried and so's his servants."

Rose Mary felt the customary ache behind her eyes. There were seven men still alive in the thorns, betrayed in their quest for the sleeper in the tower by this living trap. Tristan was the youngest and the most recent to be caught. His rusted sword still hung just past his reach, grown around by three of the slim, flexible vines Rose Mary had named Hunter Branches. Tristan had made it in much further than John. It was almost impossible to do anything for him but extend food and water to him on long poles. He was so black with dirt and infection that she couldn't imagine what he must once have looked like. Yet he had lived on longer than anyone could have imagined.

"I had best go now, Mariah. Could you please begin chapter nine of the book the King last sent? I think John is finding it quite diverting."

Rose Mary took Jacob and the bag of herbals and walked the beaten path through high grass past the small north tower to the place where Tristan's prison lay. The castle was set on a high hill, its walls at the foot. Tristan had been trying to get through to the small south gate. His part of the hedge lay at a low spot in the land and so was darker and damper than John's.

His servants waited at their camp for her. There was only a woman and a boy—Tristan's family was not rich.

"I thank Your Majesty for coming. Things is in a bad way with the boy, I believe."

"So I heard from Mariah. How bad, do you think?"

"Bad enough, ma'am. He's been talking nonsense this morning and would eat nothing."

Rose Mary nodded. A fever. Should she dose him, or

was it a greater kindness to do nothing? A fatal fever might be the boy's best friend.

She crept as close to him as her tough leather bodice would allow.

"Lord Tristan. Sir! It is Queen Rose Mary, mother of Prince John. John, who is also a prisoner of the thorns? Can you hear me?"

A giggle, thin and drawn out as a string of saliva.

"Lord Tristan! Will you take a tonic if I make one for you?"

"You are a tonic, Lady Queen."

She saw his dim form, deep in its nest of foliage, try to turn to face her. She thought she heard the drawn-out scratch of thorn against bare skin and she winced.

"Please don't move, my dear. You will only cause the brush to grow thicker. How do you do?"

There was a pause and a sigh. "I am so lonely," Tristan said.

"It is hard, sir. I know it is," she answered. "I would come more often, but it is so hard. Every hour means a new challenge. We fight the rain or a new thorn or Hunter Branches. And it is so hard to know what to do. If we do too much, the thing retaliates. The thorns almost bent John in two last year when we spread salt on the ground to kill it. And when I tried to weave a roof over John's head with thatch, it sent out a dozen suckers. And yet it allowed a shelter made of cloth . . ."

She heard the thin giggle again and blushed red. What was she doing, boring this sufferer with her own sufferings? "Prince Tristan?"

"Yes?" he said pleasantly.

"Please forgive me for burdening you with our griefs. I will brew the tonic."

"Do not ask for forgiveness, ma'am. You have given me meat for a week's daydreams. Imagine. A shelter to keep out the weather!" And he began to giggle again.

Rose Mary strode from the dark ugliness of Tristan's camp to the house she had had built near the castle walls.

She did not often have time to play her lute, and she

did not play well. But since no one else among the suffering princes or their caretakers played or sang much, she was greatly appreciated. She brought the instrument back to her camp near the thorns. Mariah was working at the endless pile of mending. Jacob and the other men were playing at cards and John, it appeared, was dozing.

Rose Mary sat on her camp stool and began to quietly play.

"Good morrow, dame. Can you tell me, is this the tower of the sleeping princess?"

The deep voice, heavily accented, badly startled Rose Mary, so that she nearly dropped her instrument. She stood and turned to face a dusty young man.

He was not large but well built, with broad shoulders and long, dark hair that framed large brown eyes. He had neither horse nor livery, but was dressed in strange, well-made clothes fashioned of some sort of thin, shining leather. He carried a sort of lance tipped with three parallel iron spikes and a net slung over one shoulder. He looked chagrined at her startled expression and made an odd movement with one arm, bowing from the waist.

"I did not mean to startle you, good woman."

He is very young, she thought.

"I am Rose Mary. I am Queen of a land many days to the east. May I inquire of you your name and rank?" It was more abrupt than she meant to sound, but she was still shaken and so took refuge in ceremony.

The boy bowed deeper and answered shyly, "I beg your pardon, Majesty. I am Terpen. Mine are the sea people to the north. We have no kings or titles, but my father has slain a whale single-handed and so is the ruler of our fleet. I have come to land seeking adventure and truth. I heard of the princess and have decided to rescue her."

Rose Mary smiled gently and shook her head. "No. No, Terpen, you must not attempt such a foolish thing. This evil hedge of thorns that guards the castle has killed twenty boys as brave and noble as yourself. And seven more have been trapped in its briars and suffer unspeakably in its grasp."

"I do not fear enchantment, Majesty. We people of the

water have enchantments all our own. I am trained. I will do it if any man can."

"Any man! Terpen, no man can do it. Do you not see my own son there in the clutches of the thing? These are mummers' tales you've heard. The nattering of Gypsies. The hedge is not to be beaten, not by land and certainly not by sea. I wager that if the princess in that castle ever was alive, she is dead now, the victim of hunger and thirst or consumed by these damned thorns."

Terpen made a gesture of impatience. "The sea is greater than the land, Majesty. Greater in size and, forgive me, greater in spirit. If this hedge is enchanted, then the enchantment can be broken. If it is merely a hedge, then I'll cut through. My people have traded ivory and oil for steel blades from far, foreign places. My trident and my sword are stronger than your weapons."

He is so young, Rose Mary thought. *He is, perhaps, the same age as John was when he tried the castle. He thinks nothing can touch him because he is strong and beautiful and he has never known defeat.*

"Young Terpen, meet my son. Please. Look at his wasted, scarred body. He will tell you what you face. The invincible sword he used now rusts on the ground where he dropped it when the thorns first covered him over. He will tell you the truth of the hedge."

Terpen smiled gently at her. She hated that look. It was polite and . . . dismissive. You are a woman, it said. But I have good manners, so I will indulge you.

She took Terpen's hand and led him to the mud-encrusted wooden boards in front of her son's prison in the thorns. The stranger looked carefully at the half-naked form of her John and bowed again.

"Prince, your mother tells me the briar hedge has captured you."

John stared at the boy and then at Rose Mary.

"Tell him, John," she said gently. "Tell him not to risk your fate. He is from a people who live on the sea and he thinks he has powers that we do not. He is a stranger here and will have no one to look after him when the thorns take him—if they do not kill him first."

John hung silent in the twisted branches for a moment, and then his eyes glinted and he smiled at Terpen, a broader smile than she had seen on his face since his father had given him his first horse. It was a look of triumph and challenge. "Don't listen, boy. She is my mother and a lady queen, but she is only a woman, and no longer young. What can old women know of true passion or courage? Where is a woman's lust for adventure? Your courage will win you through, I am certain of it. And your love will win your love. Attack the castle, sir, and win!"

"John!"

"Silence, Mother." His voice trembled, then held firm. "Go, Terpen, and God be with you."

As she watched, horrified, Terpen held open some part of his clothes and pulled out a vicious-looking curved sword, turned abruptly and walked down the line of the hedge.

He waved a farewell salute to John, and her son answered back, "Have at it, hero!"

'How could you do such a thing, John?" She turned on her son, horrified and furious. "Has your own ill fortune taught you nothing?"

"It has taught me much, Mother. I hang here each day and I think more about my future than about all the philosophers you read to me or the music you play. I think about it more, even, than I think about how much I suffer and how miserable I am. I am only five and twenty, but my life is over. I will die here in this hedge. Sooner or later I will be dead and my life will be—"

"Don't you dare!" Rose Mary nearly screamed. "Don't you dare say it, you coward! Don't you dare lose hope, when we who have struggled for five long years to save you have not lost it. You have no right!"

She put her hands on her face, stunned at what she had said to him. She went on more calmly. "We will free you, darling. It is only a matter of time before we will conjure up some solution. But we cannot have foolish foreign lads angering the power of this thing anytime they take a notion to play hero."

He laughed then, a sound as frightening as Lord Tristan's laugh had been before. "I have failed, Mother. It is true. It is not so hard a thing to accept. Can you not fail as well?"

She stared at him for some moments, frozen and unbelieving. "No," she said softly.

And she left him, ignoring whatever it was he said next.

She followed Terpen several hundred yards along the hedge to the place where the main gates stood. He finally stopped.

"Please, dear boy, please don't do this."

"Majesty," he said as gently as before, but firmly. "I know spirit power that the makers of this hedge never knew."

"But what if you are wrong? What if your magic and your blades are no better than the efforts of those poor souls now in the hedge? What then?"

Terpen would not look at her. He only shrugged and said, "Would you stay to witness what I do? I would consider it a favor."

Her throat constricted. She looked at the angular oval of his tanned face, the sweep of his shoulders and the narrowness of his waist. She could not imagine watching as the monster before them destroyed such beauty. But she was not a soft woman and no longer weak.

"Yes. To please you, I will stay."

"Thank you," he said. But he had turned away from her before the words had left his lips. He threw the net he had been wearing over his shoulder down onto the ground. He carefully placed his trident and his sword upon it, and crossing his legs at the ankles, sank onto the damp ground and began to sing.

Rose Mary felt a ripple of shock run through her and then, oddly, embarrassment so acute she wished she could turn away. The beautiful young warrior sat in the dirt like a child, tipped his head back and chanted. His voice whistled, and shivered up and down the scale like the sound of wind on rocks or water and the answering rush of waves. His eyes were closed, his brow wrinkled in concentration, his weapons lying useless before him.

She looked up at the hedge to see if there was any reaction. She could detect nothing.

When her ears were buzzing and she had truly begun to believe he would never stop, Terpen grew quiet. He picked up the curved sword in his right hand and the three-pronged lance in his left, stood and walked to the hedge.

He lifted the sword and the lance over his head and began again the loud, wavering chant. He struck the hedge with the lance.

Rose Mary knew the briars well. She had manipulated them, to her own ends, as carefully as she had nursed her son. She could feel the roots under her feet give a soft shudder.

Terpen continued to chant. He lifted the short, curved sword and brought it down on the snarl of branches. A deeper shudder went through the roots in the ground under her feet. Far off, down toward Tristan's camp, a scream rose up, long and fatal.

"Stop!" she cried. "It is punishing the others for what you do here. It may kill them! You must stop!"

"Too late," Terpen shouted. "What I have begun must be finished."

She grabbed at his arm, risking the hedge with him, but he was much stronger than she was and he shook her off and brought the short blade down on the briars again. A large section fell before him and Terpen stepped into the gap.

"It will grow back up around you before you can get any further. Stop! Now! Stop or I will break your damned skull!"

But now the boy's attention was entirely on the gray wall looming over them. His voice rose in a keening ululation. The hedge shivered more deeply at every change of pitch. He struck the hedge a third, fourth, fifth time with his gleaming curved sword, pushing the broken undergrowth away with his lance.

Rose Mary watched in horror and fascination. Terpen made his way through the deep thickness of the briars and to the small door in the great gates. Behind him the slashed sections of hedge were turning from gray to black and crumbling into brittle dust.

"MOTHER!" John's voice sent the blood screaming into her ears. She raced back to her son's place in the thorns to find Mariah, Jacob and the others deep in the thorns, hacking frantically at the growth, all semblance of caution abandoned.

And she saw why.

The hedge was sprouting frantically. Even as she watched, a thorn pierced one of John's blue eyes while a Hunter Branch encircled the fingers of his left hand, popping the joints out of their sockets as it squeezed.

She snatched at a free knife and dove in. The brush attacked them all, but she no longer cared. She hacked at the vine by his face and pulled the thorns away. The section around his chest tightened until she broke it away in bleeding fingers and stomped it underfoot.

The wild growth slowed and then ceased.

With almost the speed of the thing's earlier arousal, the briar hedge began to blacken and fall away in shreds from around them all.

For the first time in five years, both of John's feet touched the ground, and he fell forward into his mother's outstretched arms.

Her hand went to the spot on his back where an old, festering thorn wound lay. It was an angry, callused spot the size of her thumb. With the thorn gone, she could look down into the wound and see bone. God, how it must have hurt him, she thought.

They gently rolled Prince John over onto his back. He was dead.

They might all have sat in the black mud for a moment or two, or it might have been longer, when they heard sounds coming from inside the castle.

Rose Mary looked up and in the embrasure of the tallest tower stood Terpen, strong and straight. A captivating young girl in a slim white dress clung to his side. She might have looked like the painting Rose Mary remembered, or she might not. She smiled rapturously at the boy who had risked death or worse to save her. They both gazed up at the sky, enraptured by the light like two children emerging from a cave.

"He did it." Mariah sat next to her, bleeding and in tears. "I didn't think he could. I didn't think anybody could. He must have been right. The magic of the ocean must have been stronger than the hedge."

"I've never seen salt water," Jacob said. "It must be very strange."

Terpen and the young princess walked away from them and out of sight.

Slowly a sound like a distant bird flock began to rise from within the walls of the castle. The noise began to distinguish itself as cheering and the sounds of animals bellowing. The thought cut idly through Rose Mary's despair that any number of chickens spared the kitchen maid's ax for the past five years would lose their heads tonight.

Pipes skirled and the dim thunder of a deep voice called out something she could not hear from the tower where the two young people had stood.

Time passed and then a little more time passed. Rose Mary felt the firm hand of her maid on her shoulder. She bent away from her son's body to look behind her. Mariah sat with her skirts in the musty softness of the dead hedge. Stains smeared down the bloody creases in her face. One of the men was binding up Jacob's leg. The soft plop, plop of blood dripping onto the ground punctuated his efforts. Another of her men stood looking up at the castle wall, rubbing the back of his hand across one cheek, then his chest, then back to his cheek again.

Old habits fell again around Rose Mary, clicking into place like John's baby toys had fallen in armfuls into his toy chest. "We must bury my son," she said wearily, "but I will not bury him like this. Walter, Simon, if you can lift him between you, take him up to the house. Mariah, we must wash him carefully. You will find a set of his clothes in the good chest. I had saved them for . . ." Her voice caught, but she would not give in to it. She paused until she felt it steady in her throat. "For the time when he would be free of this place. Well, he is free now. I . . . I want to do this well."

Mariah helped the men carry John away.

Rose Mary went down onto her knees in front of Jacob and unbound the bandage. He had a deep cut in the calf of his leg and she could see a wood splinter still buried in it. She pulled hard; he cried out and then was silent. She salved the wound and it finally stopped bleeding. She bound it up tightly and bade the young man go home.

"Excuse me, Majesty," he said, "but let me collect some of our things first. Your good chair and your lute."

"Leave them," she said. "I am done with them now."

There was a brave cheer from inside the castle walls. A speech, Rose Mary supposed, to describe delight in a daughter returned from danger and welcome to a son who had risked his life to save her.

"How can they cheer," Jacob said, and, man though he was, he cried out loud, "when we have lost everything?"

Rose Mary felt very old at that moment. She leaned on Jacob's arm and began to walk to her house. "They cheer because it is we who lost and not them. As we would cheer if it were us there now."

Jacob nodded. "Terpen was a fine, brave knight, was he not, majesty, to try the enchanted thorns after all you'd told him?"

Rose Mary paused. *He was stupid,* she thought. *Stupid and careless and firm in the belief that he would live forever. And careless. Terribly, horribly careless of what harm he might do. Careless as all young people are.*

But what she said was, "He is brave, indeed, Jacob. Now, I am so very tired and there is so much yet to do. Come away. Come away and leave this castle to its happy inhabitants. We have no place here."

And slowly she walked toward her son and the last hard duty he would force on her with the heavy club of her own love. But she was no longer weak and this job would give her a chance for once to be gentle with her John. Once more.

Arabian Phoenix

INDIA EDGHILL

*India Edghill credits her interest in fantasy to
her father, who read her* The Wizard of Oz,
The Five Children and It, *and* Alf's Button.
*Later she discovered Andrew Lang's multicol-
ored fairy books and Edward Eager. She has
sold stories to* Catfantastic IV, Marion Zimmer Bradley's Fantasy Magazine, *and* The
Magazine of Fantasy and Science Fiction.
*Edghill admits that she and her cats own too
many books on far too many subjects.*

*Most of the stories in our fairy-tale anthol-
ogy series are based on Western fairy tales. Edghill, in her version of "Scheherazade," from* The
Arabian Nights *(of which she owns three different translations), gives the traditional tale a
thoroughly modern twist that is entertaining as
well as instructive.*

Arabian Phoenix

"**O**h, look—I can see the bride's limousine now. It's just turning the corner from the bazaar." Leaning out the narrow window at a precariously acute angle, Dunyazad stared entranced at the royal wedding procession below. Her long hair billowed over the windowsill like a banner of black silk.

Shahrazad looked up from *Golden Compromise: A Comparative Study of International Monetary Reform and Its Impact on the Third World* and frowned. "Be careful, Dunya. If any of the Protectors of Virtue see you—or more to the point, if they see your bare face—"

"I'm being careful," Dunyazad announced in complete defiance of observed fact. "And you're a fine one to talk, considering what you— Oh, now the car's in *our* street— ooh, and this time it's covered in *blankets* of roses and *masses* of pearls—"

"The white Cadillac again?" Shahrazad asked. She

turned a page, and tried to concentrate on the chart delineating ratios of import expenditure to export income for seventeen new African nations.

"Um-hum. Oh, Shari, *do* put down that stupid book and come watch with me!"

"I'm busy, and there's no room anyway." The window at which Dunyazad stood was old, and narrow, and usually covered by a rather valuable antique sandalwood lattice which Dunyazad had thrown cavalierly open to get a better view of the day's events.

"There's plenty of space." Making a great sacrifice, Dunyazad edged sideways and indicated the space freed by her move. "And what's the point of reading books like that? You know Father will never let you go to college. He'll never let us out of Badour. Not," Dunyazad announced with all the authority of her thirteen years, "in a million billion years. So you might as well give up."

"Never," said Shahrazad, who was sixteen and stubborn. "But I'll come and look, if you like." So saying, Shahrazad set aside *Golden Compromise*, unfolded her blue-jean-clad legs, and rose gracefully from the cushion-strewn sofa upon which she had been studying. After stretching, she ambled over to press next to her sister in the narrow window embrasure. Being only human, Shahrazad also wished to view the latest of King Haroun al-Raschid's extravagant marriage processions.

"I don't see why you aren't more excited," Dunyazad complained, putting her arm around her older sister's waist and hauling her into viewing position. "Just *look*— it's like something out of a movie. It's a pity the king isn't here, though. He's *so* handsome. Like—like Tom Cruise or somebody like that."

"I suppose he is," said Shahrazad, gazing down at the wedding procession speculatively. "But I also suppose he's gotten tired of playing the eager bridegroom. What's he up to now? Three dozen?"

"Forty-seven," Dunyazad informed her, and shuddered dramatically. "It's horrible, Shari. Like something out of the Middle Ages."

"Or the Arabian Nights." Shahrazad's response was

almost absentminded; as Dunyazad chattered on, Shahrazad studied the glorious festival passing below her with
the intent gaze of a keen young hawk.

The wedding procession rambling through the narrow
old streets was an overelaborate spectacle of gems and
silver, roses and gold. Prancing horses, their coats polished to an oiled gloss, bore proud-faced men in flowing
robes of sun-bright brocade before a blindingly white
Cadillac limousine draped in hot-pink roses. Pearl tassels
hung awkwardly from the car's fenders and antenna.
Walking behind the bride's fancifully decorated Cadillac
were men even more lavishly garbed than the dazzling
outriders. They carried silver trays heaped with coins. At
suitable intervals, pageboys dashed up and flung double
handfuls of the coins into the watching crowd. The crowd
was duly appreciative of this largesse.

The groom—who should have been the cynosure of
all Badouri eyes on his Day of Days—was conspicuous
by his absence.

But then, Shahrazad reflected, this was hardly their
respected ruler's first Day of Days. Or even his fourth.
Doubtless by now he'd grown rather bored with riding
forth upon a cloud-white stallion, both he and horse
clothed in cloth of gold and enough diamonds, pearls,
and rubies to choke a roc. And when the sun splashed
down upon him (and it always did; Badour rejoiced in
364 cloudless days each year) spectators had been nearly
blinded.

The gap in the procession left by the groom was now
filled by a vintage Rolls-Royce. Shahrazad felt that as a
representative of the ardent bridegroom, the vehicle left
something to be desired. Still, the entire exhibition of the
first of His Royal Highness's many wedding processions
was available on videocassette; if you wanted to see the
king riding a white horse, you only had to press "Play."

All the royal weddings looked exactly alike, at least
from the observer's viewpoint. Perhaps the king's brides
had a different view; something unique.

But, of course, no one heard of the brides again after
their wedding days. . . .

"I wonder what he does with them. What do *you* think, Shari? You're so clever; *do* tell me what you think."

Shahrazad blinked and realized that her little sister had, as usual, been chattering nonstop, and that she hadn't really heard a word. "Think about what, Dunya?"

"The king's brides, of course!" Dunyazad sighed with exasperation at her sister's denseness.

"What about them?"

Dunyazad stared, eyes wide. "Oh, Shari, don't you *ever* pay attention to anything important? Every month the king marries a girl, and every month the bride just"— here Dunyazad lowered her voice to a dramatic whisper— *"disappears,* never to be heard of again!"

Shahrazad knew; all Badour knew. A minuscule country, Badour clung to the edge of the Arabian peninsula, and like all the countries fortunate enough to be so located, Badour possessed untold wealth in oil, the Black Gold of the industrial present. Despite this flood of petroleum-based profits, Badour had remained proudly ambered in the past.

Until the ascension to the throne five years ago of His Royal Highness Haroun al-Raschid. The new king had been educated in the West; probably the reason the self-styled Protectors of Virtue called him by such old-fashioned titles as Spawn of Satan. King Haroun had earned *that* title by announcing during his maiden speech to the nation that henceforth *all* children must attend school until the age of twelve.

That political bombshell had been followed by half a year of increasingly progressive decrees from the king and increasingly menacing rhetoric from Badour's religious reactionaries. Accusations of heresy finally provoked the royal suggestion that the Protectors of Virtue should *read* the Koran instead of replacing the Prophet's holy words with their own. For a week afterward, there had been a sundown curfew throughout the city, and the king's own Guard patrolled the streets to ensure peace.

To everyone's surprise, a lull had followed the storm; odd as it seemed, King Haroun apparently had taken to heart strictures of the Protectors of Virtue, and abandoned his most liberal policies. In fact, he began committing a most proper act. A year after his accession to the throne of Badour, King Haroun commenced to marry.

And then continued to do so, with quite amazing frequency. . . .

It seemed to Shahrazad that she should be able to deduce the reason for this, but it was hard to think with Dunyazad hissing royal scandal into her ear. "Don't you know what they *say*, Shari?"

"Nothing sensible, I'm sure." Shahrazad craned to see the last of the gold-plated Rolls-Royce as it majestically rounded the corner into the next street.

"Pay attention! You remember he was married to that Western whore—"

"And she divorced him when he became king," Shahrazad said without much interest. "Of course I remember."

"*Well*, what *I* heard—Gulnar's maid heard it from someone who works at the palace—he swore that a woman would never again betray him. And so each month he marries a new bride and then . . ." Dunyazad paused for dramatic effect before uttering, in a low, throbbing whisper, ". . . when he's had his way with her, she's executed!"

"Really," said Shahrazad. "And what does he do with all the bodies?"

"Buries them in the desert sands," said Dunyazad promptly. "And *that's* why the royal brides are never seen or heard of again after their wedding days!"

"That's the silliest thing I've ever heard," Shahrazad announced after a moment's thought.

"It's *true!*"

"It's nonsense, and I don't believe it."

"It's true, I tell you. I heard it from Gulnar, who heard it from her maid, who—"

"Heard it from the goldfish in the fountain, I suppose. Gulnar's an idiot."

"You never believe anything." Dunyazad flounced, losing her viewing-place at the window. "It's all those books you read. You're—you're unwomanly."

Uninjured by this devastating attack, Shahrazad continued staring down into the crowded street below. Abandoning her attempts to insult her sister, Dunyazad squeezed in beside Shahrazad at the narrow window.

"Isn't it *fabulous?*" Dunyazad sighed, looking down on the fierce riders, the pages bearing golden trays, the masked dancers circling across the petal-strewn road. "Rose petals all over *everything,* and outriders in cloth of gold—oh, how I wish *my* wedding could be like that!"

"Including the execution after the wedding night?"

"I thought you didn't believe that!"

"I don't," said Shahrazad, "but you said you did."

"No, I didn't; I said that Gulnar said her maid said—" Dunyazad stopped and eyed her sister suspiciously. "Why don't you believe it? Everyone says it's true. Why, it was even reported in *The Badouri Crescent!*"

Too late, Dunyazad realized this was an unfortunate admission; Shahrazad shook her head, assuming an expression of pious sorrow. "So you read the newspaper? Who's being unwomanly now? How immodest, how shameless, how—"

"Oh, shut up, Shari! I just happened to glance at it, that's all."

"And thought this silly rumor very romantic, I suppose." Shahrazad went back to staring out the window, sunlight for once unshadowed on her face. She looked thoughtful, like a waiting cat. Forty-seven brides, married and vanished. . . .

"Well, sad, anyway. Shove over," Dunyazad demanded, "I can't see."

Shahrazad gave way without argument. Dunyazad continued staring and talking.

"How do you think he does it? One of my friends thinks he has them beheaded with the Royal Scimitar. She says it has a ruby the size of a woman's heart set into the hilt. Do you think he has them beheaded?"

Smiling absently, Shahrazad shook her head. Forty-seven brides. Girls she had played with as children, girls she had attended school with. Girls who had been her friends, girls as convinced as she was of the need for education, and change—

"Drowns them in the swimming pool?"

"And then swims in it afterward? Dunya, you *must* stop reading those silly American books!"

"Well, he's the king—perhaps he has two swimming pools!"

"One for swimming, one for sinking?"

"Oh, really, Shari, you never take anything seriously!"

"Oh, yes, I do," said Shahrazad, who had suddenly realized what the king's brides had in common.

"*What*, may I ask, sister dear?" Dunyazad inquired with awful sarcasm.

"I take serious matters seriously," Shahrazad said and pulled the lattice closed. "That's enough, I think. The Protectors will be prowling along any minute sniffing for wantonness and immodesty, and I don't want them throwing stones up at us. Oh, don't pout, sister—you've been the most enormous help."

"I have?" said Dunyazad doubtfully.

"You have. And I think," Shahrazad finished, "that it's time I talked to Father about this."

Bowing to her father's well-known fondness for the hallowed past, Shahrazad dressed with great care before approaching him. Although he ignored as beneath his lofty male dignity what his two daughters chose to do within the confines of the household's harem (and graciously provided them with American Express Gold Cards so that they might, in keeping with the family's rank and wealth, indulge their every girlish whim, provided they did it via the telephone), their father liked to think of himself as an advocate of the old-fashioned virtues.

It would have been truer to say, Shahrazad thought, that their father was a cautious conservative. And frustrating though his attitude was, it was hard for Shahrazad to condemn him for it. Challenging the combined might of centuries of tradition and modern violence as purveyed by the so-called Protectors of Virtue was a martyr's task. What truly angered her was that "virtue" was demanded chiefly of women. Women lived secluded and veiled, and supposedly remained innocent of any notion that hadn't been purified by the fires of hundreds of years of practice. But the telephone and the television—not to mention the international postal service and the Internet—liberated even life behind the all-encompassing veil.

However, in deference to her father's delicacy of mind, Shahrazad obligingly donned gandoura and gold-embroidered vest, slid turquoise-and-silver bracelets onto her wrists, and wove coins into the dozen intricate braids it had taken her and her Pakistani maid several hours to create. She even circled her eyes with kohl, emphasizing their long, doelike softness. She drew the line, however, at her eyebrows. Authentic and historic it might be, but Shahrazad refused to paint two thick black lines from one side of her forehead to the other. The natural half-moon arch of her brows would simply have to suffice.

A coating of Revlon's Fire and Ice to redden her lips, and Shahrazad decided her costume was finally complete.

"Wish me luck," she told Dunyazad, who had spent the morning watching Shahrazad's transformation with wide-eyed astonishment.

"Why?" Dunyazad demanded. "What *are* you going to do, Shari?"

Moving carefully in her layers of silk and gold-embroidered velvet, Shahrazad walked to her bedroom door. There she paused and smiled at Dunyazad.

"I'm going to ask Father to let me marry the king," Shahrazad said.

"Are you mad, girl?"

"No, Father. I don't think so." Shahrazad stood with her hands modestly tucked into her flowing sleeves and tried to look meek.

"Well, I say you're too stupid to find sand in the desert!" Her father began pacing back and forth in front of his mahogany desk. "Tell the king you want to marry him—I never heard such nonsense. Where do you get these ideas? You aren't watching American television, are you?"

Prudence and a respect for truth dictated that Shahrazad dodge such a ridiculous question. After all, it was Father himself who had ordered the satellite dish installed on the roof. "But, Father—"

"No, I said, and no I meant." Here he thumped his fist on the desk for emphasis. "Where do you think you're living, my girl? In The Thousand Nights and a Night?"

"Father, surely you don't think the king is actually killing his brides, do you?"

"I don't know and I don't care; a man's women are his to do with as he likes. What I do know is that my daughters are going to be good, pious, obedient wives, and that I'm not marrying either of them off to a man who deals with the devil!"

When her father assumed that patriarchal tone, Shahrazad knew reasoned argument was futile. She bowed her head, apparently docile.

Appeased, her father patted her head. "There, I knew you'd be a good girl. That's what comes of keeping women in their proper place: proper women."

"Yes, Father." Shahrazad knew her father's definition of a proper woman: an ignorant one who never questioned a man's decision.

"I understand—you're a kind, pious girl; you want to save the king from his own evil nature. But you're too young and innocent to know that can't be done. His corruption runs too deep."

"I could try, Father," she murmured.

Her father drew himself to his full height, puffing up like an outraged toad. "This subject is closed, daughter. I forbid you to speak another word about it. Now leave my office, Shahrazad; I haven't time for your nonsense today. I'm a very busy man, you know."

Back in her own room, Shahrazad thought for a few moments, then sat at her cream-and-gilt Louis XVI writing desk. She took out her pale pink writing paper and her crimson-lacquer Cross fountain pen, and began to write.

Your Highness: Although you of course do not know me, I of course, know you. As Your Highness's most humble and

obedient handmaiden, I wish to serve to the limits of my capac-
ity. In short, although I know the risks involved, I wish to offer
myself as a candidate for marriage to Your Highness. . . .

There were more ways to catch a cat than by setting
hounds upon it.

After Shahrazad managed to smuggle the fateful letter
into the post, six days passed without a word or sign.
Then, on the seventh day, Dunyazad came flying into the
library, calling Shahrazad's name.

"A car, Shari! Here, from the palace! And asking
about you!"

"A car is asking about me?" Shahrazad raised her
moon-arched eyebrows and closed the book she'd been
reading.

"Don't be a pain, Shari! It's a woman from the palace—I bet it's the Mistress of Girls! She's asking to see
you. And Father's turned as purple as a rotten fig!" In her
excitement, Dunyazad bounced about with the enthusiastic energy of Jane Fonda demonstrating aerobics.

"In that case," said Shahrazad, setting aside *Forbidden
Sands: the Effect of Alien Flora on a Closed-System Desert
Ecology,* "I'd better come down at once, don't you think?"

She rose, and Dunyazad caught her arm. "Oh, Shari,
you don't think that *he*—"

"I certainly hope so," Shahrazad said. Then she
smiled, and smoothed her little sister's hair out of her
eyes. "Don't worry, Dunya, this is my chance to win our
freedom. Somebody's got to do it, and I'm the elder."

"But, Shari—"

"Don't worry," Shahrazad repeated. "I have a plan."

Despite her father's apoplectic objections, an hour later
Shahrazad was signing her name to a betrothal contract
that bound her to marry His Royal Highness Haroun al-
Raschid of Badour, on the day of the next full moon. The
contract specified a marriage of precisely one week's dura-
tion. As soon as the contract was signed, Dunyazad flung
her arms around Shahrazad, crying on her shoulder so

hard Shahrazad's blue silk crepe-de-chine blouse was soaked.

"Oh, Shari, you'll be gone and I'll never see you again! I'll be alone in this house, and Father will never let *me* do anything interesting!"

"Nonsense," Shahrazad told her, just as she had many times before. "I told you, I'll take care of you. Just wait, Dunya. And trust me."

Dunyazad sniffed back more tears. "You really have a plan, Shari?"

"I really do." Shahrazad smiled, hoping to encourage Dunyazad to stop crying.

"Yes, but, Shari, you *always* have a plan. Do you really think this one will *work*? I don't *want* you to be beheaded!"

"His name's Haroun al-Raschid, not Shahryar! Oh, Dunya, do *try* to think logically for once! *Who* has the king married? Which girls? *Think*."

Baffled, Dunyazad merely stared at her in damp-eyed misery. "I don't know," she said at last.

Sighing, Shahrazad hugged Dunyazad again. "Well, never mind, darling. Just trust me, all right?"

"I will." Semi-consoled, Dunyazad sniffed back more tears. "And at least," she added, cheering up perceptibly, "you'll have a *splendid* wedding, Shari!"

"All the king's brides do," Shahrazad agreed. "Now come and help me choose something to wear to my betrothal feast. I have a new Calvin Klein dress—"

"Oh, yes," said Dunyazad, distracted from grief by the all-important question of what her sister should wear, "that will be perfect!"

"I hope so," Shahrazad said.

On the day of the next full moon, Shahrazad's marriage to HRH Haroun al-Raschid of Badour was celebrated with all the pseudo-medieval pomp and circumstance that provided free monthly entertainment to the critical populace. In other words, a melancholy imam asked Shahrazad if she were really willing, and upon her answering in the affirmative, Shahrazad's father reluctantly signed the marriage contract, his signature thin and timid below the king's authoritative scrawl. Smiling demurely behind the concealment of her wedding veil (a heavy sea-foam mass of silk illusion hastily imported from Paris, where it had been hand-embroidered with seed pearls and crystals by overworked nuns), Shahrazad allowed herself to be handed into the bride's rose-and-pearl-draped Cadillac. A slow parade through the streets to the royal palace, and then—

Then I will discover at last whether or not I am correct in my deductions, Shahrazad thought as the snow-white limousine began its slow progress away from her father's house. Now that there was no retreat, she felt the chill fingers of unease (she would not admit to fear) caress her skin. Powerful tool though logic was, disciplined as her clever mind was, Shahrazad found herself dwelling inexorably upon sword blades and swimming pools.

"Nonsense," she said aloud. The word seemed to disappear even as she spoke it, the sound smothered by the limo's upholstery—Italian cut velvet dyed a shocking pink. Who could possibly have chosen that lurid color? As that question was unanswerable, Shahrazad tried to soothe her jumpy nerves by telling her own private litany: the names and reputations of each of the forty-seven girls whom her new husband, His Royal Highness Haroun al-Raschid, had previously honored with his hand in marriage.

In the royal palace, Shahrazad was ushered to a suite of magnificent rooms in the palace harem. With the giggling assistance of a Filipino maid, Shahrazad removed her wedding veil and dress and then locked herself into the pink marble bathroom. There she spent several industrious hours soaking, polishing, oiling, anointing, and brushing, until she at last emerged glowing like a deep-sea pearl and redolent of Floris's Damask Rose.

She had made up her face with extreme care (she wished to appear neither too old nor too young) and French-braided her glossy hair. Then the next decision, the momentous one: what should she wear?

After trying on and discarding every item of apparel

that had been hung tidily in the cedar-lined walk-in closet, Shahrazad started another sorting of her clothes.

Abaya? Too reactionary.

Jeans? Too Western.

Turkish trousers? Too theatrical.

Despite owning a trousseau fit for a queen, Shahrazad realized with rising panic that she possessed nothing whatever that was suitable for this vital occasion. Clad only in cream silk tap pants edged with coffee-colored lace and a matching brassiere, she surveyed the multi-garment heap on the bed in dismay. What was she going to do?

"I'll *die*," she wailed to the piled clothing. "I have *nothing to wear*."

"Are you sure?" asked a curious male voice behind her. "There seems to be quite enough there to clothe the entire Topkapi harem in its heyday."

Uttering a shriek that always made her blush when she remembered it in later life, Shahrazad whirled around and found herself staring straight into her husband's eyes. Of course she'd seen his picture (both still and moving) many times, but somehow the king in photographs and the king in warm flesh were two entirely different kings.

The difference became particularly pellucid when all you were wearing was a rather revealing set of thirties-style undergarments. Shahrazad (who was, after all, only sixteen) made a faint squeaking noise; an eavesdropper would have been justified in suspecting the room harbored a distressed mouse.

"Excuse me," said Haroun al-Raschid, not even pretending not to stare, "are you quite all right?"

Unable, for once, to speak, Shahrazad managed to nod her head.

"Oh, good. Perhaps . . . would you be good enough to put something on?"

"What?" Shahrazad managed to say. After all, if His Highness her husband had a preference for a particular garment—

"Anything." Tearing his gaze away from the delectable sight of his latest wife in her underwear, the king grabbed up the first garment that his groping hand encountered and thrust it at Shahrazad. "This will do."

Clutching the dress to her, Shahrazad prudently retreated into the pink marble bathroom. There she hastily dragged the dress (a Laura Ashley floral chintz) over her head. After a quick check in the bathroom mirror to assure herself that her appearance was still adequate, Shahrazad took a deep breath and walked slowly and regally back into the bedroom.

King Haroun waited there, idly flipping the pages in the silver-bound Koran that had been placed upon the nightstand. At Shahrazad's entrance, he looked up. "Do you know the first commandment in the Holy Koran?"

" 'Read.' "

"Yes." He set the holy book carefully back in its place. "You are quite a reader, I understand."

Cautious, Shahrazad nodded.

"Cat got your tongue? You had enough to say in your most persuasive proposal letter."

Shahrazad blushed. "I—"

"Please, speak freely—or are you afraid I'll have you thrown to the lions?"

"We don't have any lions in Badour, Your Highness."

"No." The king smiled.

There was a pause; Shahrazad looked at the king, and he at her. After a few moments, she said, "You liked my letter? It wasn't too . . . forward?"

"You reminded me of Khadijah, the Prophet's first wife," said Haroun al-Raschid. "Firm-minded and strong. Yes, I liked your letter. It was short and to the point. I wish I could persuade my ministers to take lessons from you."

"Thank you," said Shahrazad, and watched him with grave attention.

"What most interests me," Haroun said, "is why you chose to write it. I'm sure you know that none of my brides remains my wife more than a week, and none has been heard of again after her wedding."

"Oh, yes," said Shahrazad. "It's the talk of Badour."

"I thought it would be," said Haroun with what

sounded almost like malicious satisfaction. "Well, then, wife number forty-eight—what do you think happens to my disappearing brides?"

Shahrazad took a deep breath, vowing to be a model of modesty, piety, and obedience forever if only she were right in her assumptions. "They go where I most devoutly wish to go, Highness."

"And where is that? Remember, rumor has it that I slay them all after a night because my first wife left me."

"Then rumor's an idiot," Shahrazad said.

"Frequently, and a rather conservative idiot at that. So you don't believe in the beheaded brides?"

"No." After a moment's pause, she added, "But my little sister believes you drown them in the swimming pool."

"Sewn in a silken sack, no doubt? And what do you believe—Shahrazad, isn't it?"

"Yes, Highness. I believe—" She regarded Haroun closely; he looked encouraging, and rather younger than she'd thought from his photographs. "I, too, wish to go to school. To college. To be educated."

"To be Western? Americanized?"

Shahrazad shook her head. "I am not Western; I am not American. I am Badouri. But Badour could be—oh, so much more than it is! If only—"

"Yes," said Haroun al-Raschid. "If only."

"Oil has made us rich," Shahrazad said, "but the oil won't last forever, and what will happen then? Badour *must* be prepared for the future—" Realizing she was lecturing the king, Shahrazad stopped abruptly and blushed.

"Instead of being admirably fitted for the past. I agree." Haroun smiled at her. "Tell me, Shahrazad, how did you discover what I was doing?"

Frowning, she considered carefully before answering. "All the marriages were contracted for only one week's time. You didn't even have to divorce the women you married. And—I knew some of the brides, or had heard of them. They were the girls who were discontented, or the ones who showed promise in scholarship. I used logical deduction to reason it out."

"Just the sort of woman I delight to marry."

"And I listened to all your speeches," she added.

"What, all of them? You are dedicated." Haroun smiled again, looking rather rueful. "And what did you think of them?"

"They were very well reasoned," Shahrazad told him with prim reserve. "You sounded—" She considered and rejected words, and finally selected "moderate."

"Thank you." Haroun's face remained perfectly bland. "I appreciate praise from informed critics. Anything else?"

Although she knew he was laughing at her, Shahrazad refused to take offense. Laughter could not harm her, and certainly a beleaguered king was entitled to such minor amusements as he could discover. "Yes. I— If I had not written to you, Your Highness, would you have selected me? As one of your wives, I mean."

"Perhaps," said Haroun. "I like to think I'm not a fool; I have my spies in the women's world, you know. Your intelligence is formidable, and your school marks were most impressive."

"Yes," said Shahrazad. "It's a pity girls are required by law to attend school only until they're twelve."

"It's better than no schooling at all."

"But not as good as a proper education."

The king sighed. "I know; I do what I can. But I don't want a revolution here, and I don't want my throne yanked out from under me. True progress has to come slowly, and the people must be willing for it to occur."

"Thank you," said Shahrazad.

He regarded her with curiosity. "For what?"

"For not treating me like a child—or like a woman."

The king smiled, and suddenly looked much younger. "I wouldn't dare; you're too intimidating."

"I am?" Shahrazad considered this, then smiled back. "I suppose I must consider that a compliment, Your Highness."

"So to answer your question—perhaps. Your father's an important man, and he's—shall we just say, very conservative?"

"He thinks a woman's place is in the fifteenth century," Shahrazad said.

This time Haroun laughed. "I didn't want to offend him if I didn't have to. But then I received your letter, and I knew I must intervene in your case."

"Thank you," said Shahrazad. She hesitated, then added, "I have a sister. . . ."

"Dunyazad," he said. "Thirteen, isn't she?" When Shahrazad stared, Haroun smiled. "I, too, do my homework," he pointed out.

Impressed, Shahrazad vowed that she, too, would always have all facts and figures ready to fling into verbal battle. "Yes. And she's really very bright—"

"I'm sure she is. But does she also want what you so desire? Or is it only your wish for her?"

"I don't know," Shahrazad said, "but I think Dunyazad should be allowed to find out for herself."

"That's true. But since she's my wife's sister, I can't demand her for my next bride, you know."

"No, but . . . surely there must be something you can do?"

"The queen's command?" Haroun considered the matter, absently sliding makeup tubes and perfume bottles over the dressing table as if they were chessmen. "Well, I'll think about it and see what I can devise for her. Ask me again in a few months, after you've settled in."

"Settled in where?"

"Ah," said Haroun al-Raschid to his latest bride, "that is what we must now discuss."

Shahrazad had her heart set on Vassar, or Radcliffe; Haroun al-Raschid favored Cambridge, or the Sorbonne.

"But first you must qualify academically; there are excellent boarding schools in Switzerland. You'll need to spend a year or two there first. Then we can decide on a college for you." He held up his hand, stopping her eager thanks. "But there are conditions."

"Conditions?"

"Yes. First, you must maintain decent marks. Second, you must remember that you represent Badour and at all

times act accordingly. And if you haven't the good sense
to know what that entails, I'll have you brought home
and married off to a Bedouin camel trader."

"I understand." Shahrazad regarded him with grave
intensity.

"Good. Third, you must return and give Badour at
least seven years of service once you've finished training
for your career."

"That's fair," said Shahrazad.

"Well," said the king, "I think so.

"And now," said her new husband, "let us consider
which boarding school you should attend. I have here
some brochures from those I regard as most suitable. . . ."

Three days later Shahrazad stood beside Haroun al-
Raschid at Badour International Airport, waiting for her
Swissair flight to board. She wore a trendy angora sweater
set and retro bell-bottomed trousers, an ensemble con-
cealed from prying Badouri eyes by the obligatory swath-
ings of black. "BMOs," the foreign soldiers had called
local women during the Gulf War crisis. Black Moving
Objects. But that would change. Someday.

The announcement of her flight echoed over the loud-
speakers; Haroun touched her arm.

"Are you ready?"

Shahrazad nodded. Haroun al-Raschid had been more
than generous; she had an English chaperone, a round-
trip first-class ticket to Geneva, and an ample bank account in her own name awaiting her there.

"Remember, if you change your mind, don't be afraid
to come back. You're young, and you've chosen a hard
road. If—"

"I won't change my mind." Shahrazad's voice was
muffled by the thick black cloth veiling her face. "But
thank you."

"Just remember what I said. And when you've finished your studies—"

"I will return to Badour, as I promised." Shahrazad
looked through the thick tinted glass out onto the runway

where the Swissair jet awaited her. Once on the plane, she could remove the veil, perhaps forever. . . .

"Perhaps," said Haroun, "you would consider returning to something more personal than a country. Sooner or later, you know, I will need a real queen."

Shahrazad looked through the veil into Haroun's steady eyes, and smiled behind her mask. "Perhaps I will. If," she added, for Shahrazad was nothing if not sensible, "we are both still of the same mind then. After all," she reminded him, "we may be married, but we hardly know each other."

"I know how that can be remedied," Haroun said, and gestured at the overanxious flight attendant who was calling for passenger Shahrazad Wazir to board. For His Highness, even punctual Swissair must wait.

"How?" Shahrazad asked.

Haroun smiled. "Write me a letter."

Toad-Rich

MICHAEL CADNUM

Michael Cadnum lives in northern California and is a poet and novelist. He has published fourteen novels, most recently In a Darkwood, *a novel about Robin Hood and the Sheriff of Nottingham, and* Heat. *His most recent collection of poetry is* The Cities We Will Never See, *and a picture book for children,* The Lost and Found House, *was recently published. "The Flounder's Kiss," from* Black Swan, White Raven, *was selected for* The Year's Best Fantasy and Horror: Eleventh Annual Collection.*

Cadnum is the master of the pithy, nasty, clever tale. The narrator of "Toad-Rich" is surprisingly sympathetic despite her lack of warmth in this volume's second version of Charles Perrault's "The Fairy Gifts."

Toad-Rich

I have a mouth. Some people have eyes, beauty, smarts—
I've got a mouth. Lydia, my pretty sister, has baby blues
and walks around looking at the sky, the birds, wide-eyed
and breathless. Dumb as my left tit but lovely, and when
a knight-at-arms eased himself off his war-horse and
stepped into the shade, you could see him crane his neck
to follow Lydia as she made her way out to the ducks.

Which is about all she was good for, domestic fowl,
fed on old bread mixed with maize, the same stuff we set
out for the geese. If a gosling choked on a crust, it's one
less for the weasels, is the way I looked at it. Lydia grew
all tearful watching a duckling pump its neck, trying to
not choke on a cob-butt, while I watched and laughed.
That was about the only funny thing all day around here,
barnyard fowl in fits.

Despite what you might think, we got along pretty
well. I handled the thinking for Mama and Lyd, and I

bred those hounds you've heard of, eyes like weep holes but capable of following a vixen from here to Sodom. The approach I took was: drown the runts, keep the stud hounds full of fresh meat, and don't be too fussy what kind, duck, goose, mutt. I kept the bitches in heat feeding them witherwort and musk-of-rut I boiled down to a paste. They whelped until they staggered. Then I axed them, chopped them up, and kept the kennel fat. Courtiers cantered up from all directions, fingering their florins. I weighed my apron down with gold some summer days, no silver here, only the finest coin. I kept the prices up by thinning out the yappers.

One day a dog bit my shank, a little nip, and it went puffy. I had to stay indoors, watching the progress of the duck parade Lyd led from pond to pen. The sight warmed my heart, my guileless sibling, marching with her birds. I cooked a poultice with mama's help, and thonged it onto my lame limb.

I called for Lydia. "Take the goat-hide buckets and fetch some water from the well, and don't stand around blinking at the serving lads on the path. Go there, come back, and get back to your sewing." I had to blush, talking to Lydia this way, but it was an iron habit.

Lyd curtsied, kind to me, no matter what, and Mama stared at both of us like a woman cursed with knowledge of the past and present. She didn't hate life, but gave that impression, stony-faced and hard—brave men looked away when she entered a room. But Mama and I share a humor, granite on the outside, almost human in the heart.

Truth to tell, I do indulge a weakness, and sometimes stroke a pup or let a brood bitch take a morsel from my hand. When no one's looking. And I confess to a fondness for Mama and my Lyd. I can't resist this tender feeling, almost foreign to my soul.

That terrible morning Lyd ran back panting, out of breath, bodice laces bursting. She couldn't speak at first.

The pinkness was subsiding from my bite and I was feeling half happy with the world.

"Becky!" cried Lyd at last. "Mama!" Each familiar syllable sounding like a burp, glittering cough-up flying through the air to our feet, two jewels. Topaz and a ruby, well set and fine.

Lyd puked out her tale, an emerald for each noun, a diamond for each verb, and when she coughed, pure gold. Painful and frightening both, and yet by the end of her narration a little mountain of treasure glittered on the straw.

"Dear Lydia," I said, caressing her. "Such a trial." All I could think was: who did this to poor Lyd? Only half believing her tale. No old woman waits at wells in this county, not if she knows what's smart. You find your way to the wellhead fast and nimbly. The last old woman who loitered was the one who had an infant just fallen in, bawling for her baby. The woman was twenty years past childbearing, a freakish thing. We burned her.

We don't tarry at anything in this part of God's earth, and we don't say good day, or fare-thee-well. We use our mouths for telling people what we think of them, and as a result a nice silence is all we hear from Sunday till Christmas. Someone wears a new stocking, or sings a new song, we step right up and tell him the one he wore last year was better, and too bad his voice is as ugly as his face.

So it wasn't a desire to be a bijoux spewer that flounced me out into the lane, all skirt and bad leg. I was looking out for the virtue of the countryside, and ready to find this stranger who had nothing better to do than blast an innocent and witless girl with an affliction. I was hunting for the wayfarer who had harmed my Lyd.

There was no one at the well. One or two goodwives peeped out of the hedging, saw it was me and peeped back in again. I dropped the buckets one by one—for in her frightened haste Lyd had neglected her duty—when this witch dragged herself, all wens and gums, right up to where I sweated, hauling a billy-goat skin full of well water from the very bottom of the hole.

"Give me but a drink, good lass," said this insult to appearance, this counter to the faith that God is imaged in the human form.

I had heard Lyd's coin-throttled recitation of this greeting, but couldn't help but maintain the standards of our town. "Call that a face, dear friend? Call that a way of making way upon the summer landscape, grinning like a wound, squinting like a pig's sphincter? Let me favor you with an honest piece of advice—"

I coughed.

Just a frog in my throat, I reckoned, hawking, spitting out a toad glistening with my saliva and quite satisfied to belly-down, solemn as Solomon, right there in the mud, blink, blink.

"The water you need's for bathing," I belched, uttering a lizard, two snakes, and a moth.

The old woman grinned.

"I'll skin you to the bone," I said, seizing her bony frame, cloak and gristle. Spiders scurried down my chin. "I'll have you flogged!" I cried, crickets scuttling to the dust. "You'll be pilloried in the market until All Saints'," I cried, each word the eruption of a worm.

But then I remembered my manners, the tradition of honesty and good faith that makes our town renowned, frankness and outspokenness our pride. No longer would I dally with this hag. I strangled her with the well rope then and there, cursing bugs into her face.

There were weeks of fury, ruined sleep, bitterness. Mama swept larva, daddy longlegs, thrips, and patiently shoveled garnets, opals, cameos, rings. I endured an era of unhappiness. I felt sorry for myself, and wept myself dry of tears.

One morning a prince rode into the barnyard, tickled by rumor into soft words, kissing poor Lydia's hand. And taking it in marriage. "And the two of you as welcome guests." The prince smiled, all teeth cheek and chin.

The wedding was celebrated three long nights, all Lydia-produced gold and tiaras, even on the serving wenches. Mama went perfumed and dimpled, a new woman. I attended veiled, silent as a nun.

All so just, the goodwives whispered. The one with

the mouth cursed, the demure and kindly blessed and honored.

But then the whispers changed.

Merchants rumored the infamy from lake to sea, the beautiful, weak-minded Lydia, kept by a king's son in a tower. Stewards pinched her into utterance when inspiration failed. She gasped out even more brilliant gems now, pearls, and amber, and all but worthless.

Worse than worthless. You've heard how these days diamonds are used as gizzard stones for geese, how gold is melted into leading for the spires. You've heard how silver is nailed into boot heels. Rubies are ground for sandpaper. Opals are employed as sling stones. Some byways drift with topaz, other are cobbled with sapphire. All because poor Lydia whispers her prayers each night, more gems by the bushel basket, a countinghouse rendered worthless by sheer glut. Her groom the prince despairs, the shadow of a man.

While I no longer weep. I have sold off the last of my pups, and tend a lowlier, more exotic breed. The midge and the silverfish I pinch and rinse from my fingers. The common tadpole I feed to the viper, the salamanders to the asp. I cull my tribe of scuttlebugs and wasps, drowning, burning, thrashing lifeless all but the beautiful, all but the rare.

It takes time, but I have enough of that.

I do a fruitful, thriving business in pilgrims, in errant squires, in knights bound for the Holy Sepulcher. My banners flutter in the breeze: This way to the adder, Cleopatra's bane. This way to the serpent, scourge of Eden. This way to the silk moth, prize of the East—watch him feed, watch him weave, watch him sleep.

Friars queue, ambassadors jostle. Tinkers bribe their way to the head of the line. Mama guides them from pen to cage, showing off poison spiders for the spiteful, butterflies for the betrothed, scarabs and centipedes for the curious, all marvelous, all rare.

Mama and I are going to buy Lydia back with a dragonfly, and a wasp's nest. The prince will sell her for any price—snails, snakeskin, moth-glitter, poison-arrow toad.

Or if he'd prefer, then with a bee swarm, wax, and apple-blossom honey. The sphinx moth, the chameleon, the bat-wing. Each more precious than a gem.

We bolt our windows nightly against potential dragon-fly thieves, armed with clubs of gold. Highwaymen brood with emerald dirks, and children skim silver plates across the pond. No living thing is too small or common—lizard's kid or circus flea—and no vermin is without wonder, even so lowly a creature as I myself, rich in love and toads.

Skin So Green and Fine

WENDY WHEELER

Wendy Wheeler has written short fiction for anthologies and magazines including Snow White, Blood Red; The Crafters *volumes 1 and 2;* Analog; Aboriginal SF; Gorezone; *and* Pandora. *She teaches fiction writing for the University of Texas. She has turned two of her stories into screenplays and has started to design games.*

The idea for "Skin So Green" came from Wheeler's reading of two books. In The Uses of Enchantment, *Bruno Bettelheim asserted that the ending of "Beauty and the Beast" shows the healthy resolution of the Oedipal conflict—which mostly means that Beauty is not supposed to find the Beast lovable (and, hence, sexually attractive) until she's transferred her warm feelings for her father to another man. At the same time, Wheeler was reading Anton Gersi's book of cultural investigation,* Faces in the Smoke. *She especially liked the concept of possession by spirits as a component of religious ecstasy, which she extrapolated into another, more erotic, ecstatic experience.*

Skin So Green and Fine

The day of her wedding to the Snake Man, Bonita made *pastelitos* to be sold on the streets of Santa Domingo just as if it were any other day. But because she was leaving her beloved Papi and the family bakery on Calle El Conde, she made these turnovers very special, with the chicken spicy the way her father liked it, extra raisins, nuts, and peas.

Bonita still had the grit on her fingers from scrubbing the last iron pot when her father got back from sending the boy off with the *pastelito* cart. Papi's curly black hair shone with pomade and many combings. Bonita thought her father in his rented tuxedo was more handsome than ever.

"A joyous day, daughter." Papi's smile was bright, but he wiped the sweat from his lip with a handkerchief that Bonita had laundered, pressed and scented with citrus cologne the night before.

Who would do for her Papi after she left? wondered
Bonita, suddenly a little dizzy now that her adventure
had begun. "A lucky marriage indeed," she said dutifully.
Now was not the time to be selfish. Her bridegroom's
wealth had saved them—the bakery's debts melted like
spun sugar, even the business with the Cuban laid to rest.
Her Papi was too trusting to deal with men of that nature.

"And who has your heart?" her father said, an old
game with them. "Where is your heart, little one?"

Bonita peered into one of his tuxedo pockets. "Is this
my heart, Papi?"

He gave a gasp of surprise. "Oh, there is the heart of
my favorite daughter!" He hugged Bonita to him. Her
cheek rubbed against stiff gabardine. "Had not the rich
man asked me for you, I would not have believed you
old enough," he said. "Your sisters could not wait to paint
their faces and go to the clubs."

As if on cue, Bonita's two older sisters came through
the bakery door.

"What are you doing in this kitchen?" scolded Raquella. "Take off that apron, *chica*, and show us the gown
your rich bridegroom sent you!" Raquella and Ysabel had
themselves only recently married, their father's new prosperity allowing them to find husbands in the *mercado*.
Now they were grand señoras, with tall, lacquered hair
and shining red nails.

Bonita took one last look at the tiny kitchen. "Remember when Papi bought this place? The funny name painted
across the front window? Happily-God-Loves-Me-Bakery-
Messenger-of-Happiness."

"A crazy thing, using the name of Our Father like
that," said Ysabel. "Just like a Haitian."

There was silence. Raquella narrowed her eyes at Ysabel, who ducked her head and wiped at the countertop.

Bonita's bridegroom was a Haitian, albeit one with a
sugarcane plantation somewhere in the Cibao Valley. Although the two races, brown and black, shared the island
of Hispaniola, they rarely mixed. This marriage was something of a scandal.

Bonita merely smiled. "But soon you'll have a Haitian for your brother-in-law."

"Yes," Raquella said. "And soon little babies running around! Of whatever color!"

Bonita felt her smile stiffen. "Babies?"

She had resolved to be happy in this marriage. Indeed, the part of her that spent hours gazing out the window of the bakery, wishing for the life of an adventurous woman, that part was happy.

But she had seen her future husband only once, had never touched him. How was she to make babies with this man when she was only a baby herself? For, despite being known as the most beautiful girl on El Conde Street, Bonita had done no more than hold hands with a boy. She had a face like a saint, her sisters told her. Everybody wanted to admire it, but no boys would ever want to kiss it.

As she followed them upstairs, Bonita studied the backsides of her sisters, resplendent in their snug brides-maid dresses. They waggled before her like two heavy blooms on a fuchsia bush, one red satin and one pink. Raquella and Ysabel were married women now. Did they talk differently? With more . . . experience?

"Raquella, Ysabel," Bonita began. "About the wedding night . . ."

"Ah, the young virgin!" squealed Ysabel. "Wondering about the mysteries of the bedroom, Bonita?"

"Well, I had hoped . . ." said Bonita. "Mama, God bless her soul, is not here to tell me." All three sisters crossed themselves. "The good Father Cristos counsels me to honor my husband's needs. But when I try to imagine it . . ." She made a face.

At the top of the stairs, Ysabel turned to grab Bonita, her neck flushed red. "Your heart is beating, beating faster just thinking about it? *This* is the best part. Afterward you will realize how lucky you are to be innocent!"

Raquella tugged Bonita gently away. "You are right to shudder, little sister," she said. "The bedroom is where the woman's burden weighs the heaviest. When you see for yourself the animal nature of men . . . well, it is a secret all wives share." She looked pointedly in Bonita's bedroom, with its small bed, plain walls, and altar to Saint Theresa. "How like a little nun you have been living."

Ysabel snorted. "That will change!"

"Mother of God, it is one of those places," said Bonita's father when his old sedan creaked to a stop. The cars holding Bonita's sisters and three brothers pulled up alongside them. "This changes everything! No, not for my daughter!"

They had parked before her bridegroom's church, a large building tucked away amidst yucca plants in the Barrio Menor, the Haitian quarter. Colorful images writhed and twined across the stucco walls: candles, crosses, saints, and snakes—snakes wrapped around tree branches, snakes entwined and facing each other, snakes swallowing fruit—all had been painted with more enthusiasm than skill. To the right of the front doors, a cross festooned with plastic flowers stood in what appeared to be a child-sized grave.

"Papi, don't be so quick!" Bonita said, heart sinking despite her resolve. "Surely this can't be a temple of the Devil's religion!" All her life, Bonita had heard stories of the Haitian religion—frightening, terrible stories. She pulled again at the gaudy red dress her future husband had sent her. It squeezed her breasts and hips and made her constantly aware of the curves of her body. The white ruffles of the plunging neckline frothed around her face like meringue on a cherry tart.

"Why didn't I ask?" her Papi rubbed at his face, looking years older. "I want a happy marriage for you, not this heathen voodoo. We can break our promise to the rich man, give him back his money. And your sisters' dowries, well, I can fix that, given time."

Through the open car windows, the muffled rhythm of drums flowed across the warm air. God knew what wickedness those people did inside, in the dark.

Bonita closed her eyes and heard Father Cristos's voice telling her again that her pure heart was proof against whatever might come. She'd wondered what he meant; now it made more sense to her.

Then Bonita imagined her father, her family, with all their debts back and new debts added. What did she actually know of voodoo, anyway? Only stories told to frighten children.

"We mustn't be silly, Papi," she said. "This will be a matter for me and my husband. Let us gather my brothers and sisters and go inside."

Two ancient black women in immaculate white cotton dresses led the Arregon family through rooms lit with dozens of candles, heavy with the scent of jasmine and goat and burned feathers. With every step, the music of the drums grew louder. They arrived at a large room swirling with dancing people, more people standing along the walls clapping, all black, many with eyes closed as if in ecstatic prayer. Six drummers bent over brown leather drums. Bonita felt her father's hand tighten on her own. A rope dangled from a hole in the thatch roof to the dusty cement floor.

The floor vibrated with the pounding of the drums, rhythms Bonita could feel deep in her belly. The bodies that whirled around her radiated heat; their blank faces seemed to have no human soul inside them.

A heavyset man appeared before them and waved at the far wall. "Father André has been calling the saints; everything is almost ready." Bonita could see a large shelf crowded with flowers, fruits, bead necklaces, and bottles of rum. Two red wooden chairs sat in front of it. "Please sit before the altar. Your bridegroom, the good monsieur, is preparing himself in the *djévo* and will attend us."

He seemed to notice the apprehension of the Arregon family. "This is your first time at a *houmfor*? We have a very fine temple, and Father André is a very good *houngan*." He smiled broadly. "He practices only the highest vodoun, only the right-hand magic."

I am the leader in this event, Bonita realized, and led the way to the red chairs and sat in one. Her Papi came to stand behind her, his hand on her shoulder. Father

André a thin, older man in an embroidered cassock, looked over and nodded at them.

Bonita glanced down and saw, touching the toe of her new red shoe, a design in scuffed white-and-black powder. She pulled her foot back and peered closer. Flour and ashes. And beyond, more curls and loops leading right to the altar, where lay the bodies of six headless chickens. Spatters of blood across the floor showed dark as chocolate.

Bonita gulped and looked away, then silently chastised herself. Was she so dainty? How many chickens had she bought at market and plucked herself? Ah, but never in a church, a part of her said.

Then the rhythms of the drums changed. A new group appeared from a side room, carrying several spangled flags. A low moan went up and a path cleared for them through the writhing, shaking dancers.

Another person joined the flag-bearers: a tall man in a brown felt fedora, a long, stylishly cut coat hanging from his broad shoulders, his eyes hidden behind black sunglasses. He followed the marchers with a sinuous grace only slightly marred by the way he dragged his left foot.

The Snake Man. Monsieur Aspic.

Bonita watched her bridegroom approach. He seemed all power and confidence—surely good qualities in a husband. But despite the sweat dripping between her breasts, Bonita shivered.

Monsieur Aspic paused before the other red chair, then turned and sat. Watching him with sidelong glances, Bonita noticed his small ears and almost-bald scalp. The Snake Man's skin was a color between olive and black-brown. And yes, there was a mottled pattern on his cheeks and neck. So the stories were true.

Bonita turned her eyes back to the front.

Monsieur Aspic reached across with a gloved hand to touch her arm. "You honor me with this marriage, *chérie*," he said, leaning close to speak his Haitian-accented Spanish into her ear. "The old ways say to ask the papa. But now, *moi*, I need to ask you. Do you want this thing yourself?" When Bonita hesitated, he added, "Ah, your face is as beautiful and pure as a saint's. *Alors?*"

Blushing from the spicy scent of him, the feel of his breath upon her cheek, Bonita could only say, "Yes."

Father André appeared before them, a white ceramic cup in his hands. Another black man, this one in the dark suit of a civil employee, stood beside him. Father André chanted something in singsong French, then sprinkled scented water on them. Bonita gasped at the cool drops. Father André gave the white cup to an assistant and picked up a lacquered gourd cup. He then took a chicken carcass by its legs and held it upside down over this gourd until blood trickled from the neck hole.

As Father André put the chicken back down, took the gourd cup, and held it high, Bonita began to feel true panic. If he splashed that blood on her, she didn't think she could bear it!

Again the rhythm of the drums changed, faster and more frantic. The priest held the cup out to Monsieur Aspic, who leaned forward and drank a few drops. Another moan went up from the crowd. Horrified, Bonita found herself wondering what the blood tasted like, if it was thick on the tongue. Then the priest held the cup out to Bonita, his old eyes sharp on her face. *She* was to take their sacrament?

A flood of saliva filled Bonita's mouth, and her throat closed. Her soul fluttered in her chest, but Bonita knew her duty. Honor my husband, she told herself. My heart is pure. She leaned forward until the mouth of the cup loomed before her, deep and brown, the blood black inside it with a sour smell of copper. Another smell too— the breath of her husband?"

I will be lost, she thought. She jerked her head away.

The old priest just nodded and held the cup up again. Several other worshippers gathered now to sip the blood, many gasping and arching as if in ecstasy. Bonita's eyes stung with tears; then she felt Monsieur Aspic's gloved hand pat her leg comfortingly.

Father André gestured to the government official, who stepped forward. This man spoke to Monsieur Aspic. "I will handle the legalities of this marriage in the eyes of the state and this community. You signify your vows, both legal and spiritual, by the placing of the ring on her finger." Monsieur Aspic took from his breast pocket a gold ring. The official frowned. "Please, sir, remove your gloves for so important a ceremony!"

Monsieur Aspic hesitated, then with a stony expression removed his glove. Over the noise of the drums, Bonita could hear the gasps of her family behind her. She watched, her mind whirling, as Monsieur Aspic reached across her. His hand was large, the fingers long. But the skin . . .

The skin of her bridegroom was covered with dusky green scales.

Monsieur Aspic drove them home himself, the Cadillac sedan heading northwest from the city toward the rich fields of the Cibao Valley. "Why are you wearing that schoolgirl jumper, pose?" he had said to Bonita when she changed for the long trip. "And you a married woman now."

He seemed to be teasing, but he didn't smile much. What am I supposed to wear, she thought, tight red dresses and loose red shoes? "These? These are the clothes of a baker's daughter," she said. He seemed to accept that.

How her father had held her and wept when they left. Bonita watched out the back window as Santa Domingo became nothing more than a distant sprawl of buildings. That is my childhood behind me, she thought. She turned back in her seat and looked at the impassive profile of her husband, still in his hat, glasses, gloves. She tried to think up conversation, but after the early morning at the bakery, the wedding, the food and wine afterward, she couldn't stay awake despite the bumpy road.

Her husband woke her three hours later with a brush of his gloved hand on her cheek.

"It becomes easier each time I drive this journey," he said as she blinked sticky eyes.

"Oh," said Bonita, happy to learn about him. "Because you so rarely go into town?"

Monsieur Aspic stiffened. *"Pas de tout.* I often go into town. Just usually, *moi,* with a chauffeur."

Bonita wondered how she'd offended him. "Then I am impressed with your driving skill," she said. "I never took the lessons to get my license."

He seemed to relax. "Now you can see Bosquet Aspic ahead, which means the 'Aspic Grove.' *Entendu."* Before them stood a water tower painted blue, many white buildings with orange clay roofs, fences around lush gardens.

"Will someone be there to meet us?" asked Bonita, straining forward.

Monsieur Aspic froze again. *"Non.* My parents, they die many years ago. I have no other family."

Puzzled, Bonita asked, "And no servants either?"

"None." Monsieur Aspic trod harder on the gas pedal, and the sedan jumped quietly forward. "Not anymore." They drove between two gateposts, and the road became smooth and quiet beneath their wheels.

When they pulled up before the huge house, Bonita's heart fell. All over the walls were painted the symbols she'd seen on the temple in the Barrio Menor. And more images: she saw a smiling Saint Patricio, a snake in his hands, and one of Saint Theresa. By far the biggest image was a red-and-orange snake about five meters long with rays of yellow painted around it.

"Such a big snake!" Bonita said.

"That is Lord Djamballah-Wedo, whom we honor in my household," said Monsieur Aspic in a light tone. "His other name is Saint Patricio. He is the lord of fecundity." When Bonita looked quizzical, he added, "The lord of much prosperity and many babies."

"Oh," said Bonita.

Inside, her new home had great expanses of red tile floors and whitewashed stucco walls. Bonita smelled spicy rose perfume and the freshness of well-scrubbed wood. A large tiled fountain stood in the center of the entryway, itself the size of a chapel. Hallways went off to the left and right. Down one of those hallways was her marriage bed.

Quickly, Bonita turned back toward the front door. Two altars were built into the front walls, with jewelry and food laid upon them, fresh flowers, some candies. "Surely someone else tended the house while you were gone?" she asked.

Her husband shook his head. "I honor *Les Invisibles*, so they take care of me. It is the saints I have to thank for my life and sanity." He took off his hat, showing a finely shaped skull. After a moment's hesitation, he took off his gloves also, then his dark glasses, and laid them on a table.

When he turned back to Bonita, she realized she had never seen his eyes before. They were widely set with irises so pale brown as to be gold. Scant lashes, very thin brows, but an intelligent gaze. The snakeskin pattern ended at his jawline.

"I am very tired from the sunlight and the driving, *moi*," Monsieur Aspic told her. "Your rooms are down that hall; mine are down this one. Food and drink are ready for us, and our bathwater is waiting." He stepped close and took her two hands in his. His fingers were hot around hers. "You can stay the night in whichever bed you choose, *ma femme*. I hope it will be mine."

She looked up into those gold eyes, then down at the thin, scaled hands. I should be a wife, she thought, but she imagined those hands touching her. Snake's skin touching her private flesh. She pulled away. "Please, not yet."

"I married you for your generous heart," said the Snake Man, moving away. "And for your saintly beauty. Don't worry, *petite fille*, I won't force you. You must want to be a wife to me. *À bientôt*, then."

Beneath his lids, Bonita thought she saw a glint of pain in the gold eyes.

Though alone, throughout that night Bonita slept fitfully in her huge, luxurious bed. She would awaken, heart beating, sure that someone had caressed her in the dark, but each time it was only the satin sheets and duvet sliding across her skin.

The next morning, she checked the large bedroom closet and found none of her usual cotton jumpers and dresses. Instead, all these clothes were brilliantly colored, silky—and slight. Bonita finally put on a very short green skirt, a tight yellow sweater, and shoes with heels high enough to make her totter.

As she combed and braided her long hair, a strange thing happened. The braids seemed much easier to plait, almost as if other hands helped her. She found it easier to arrange her hair on the crown of her head in a new, elegant style. She looked at herself in the mirror; not the same Bonita at all. Her transformation had already begun.

When she opened her bedroom door, the supper tray with the remains of last night's chicken-and-pea soup was gone. But no note or message from her husband. Had he cleared up? Put her luggage away? Bonita couldn't easily imagine him doing such work.

As she made her way toward what she hoped was the center of the house, she saw a door open onto a back balcony. A table was set with breakfast. With some relief, Bonita went forward to greet Monsieur Aspic. "My husband?" she called, but got no answer. Only one chair here, too. If they indeed had no servants, it was lovely of Monsieur Aspic to cook this meal for her. She soon finished the white cheese omelet and slices of grilled bread.

From her high vantage point, Bonita could see only grazing animals in the nearby pens and the waving cane plants in the distance. No people for miles. So different from the busy shop on Calle El Conde. Then she shook herself. There was a whole plantation to explore! And her husband to find . . .

Bonita wandered throughout the house all that day, never seeing her husband, not even a note to tell her where he was. She thought she found his room—the vodoun drawing on the door looked familiar—but it was locked, and no one answered when she tapped. She tried walking down halls calling the name she'd learned from her marriage license: "Michél? Michél? Are you here?"

She finally gave up the hunt, a little sick at heart. As the youngest of six children, Bonita had never spent a day alone before. If her husband was gone for good, how would she find her way back home? And she had yet to see a telephone. Why, oh, why did such a rich man have no servants?

So Bonita let the large, immaculate house distract her. She could use it to learn about her husband and her circumstance. She avoided the altar with the rum and candies on it because the red, orange, and yellow flowers told her it was for Djamballah-Wedo, the snake god. Once or twice she imagined she heard voices inside a room, only to open the door and find the room empty. Sometimes footsteps seemed to be pacing, just behind her. It felt very lively for an empty house.

And it seemed there was a room here for everything. From the well-stocked pantry and Deepfreeze in the kitchen, Bonita conjectured that she could cook every dish she knew and still have inventory left. She used some rice, beans, and pork to make a *bandera* for lunch. She hoped the smell of cooking food would draw Monsieur Aspic to her, but it was not to be.

Then more investigating. Whenever she came upon them, she studied carefully the many photos of black strangers in prosperous clothes, doing things rich people did. The women in particular seemed sultry, looking at the camera with knowing eyes beneath expensive hats. Was this her future, then?

Finally, as the outdoor light grew dim, Bonita found her way back to the dining room, where a candelabra lit a long walnut table. Savory smells came from a chafing dish, and chopped fresh vegetables filled a large bowl. She walked to the food and stirred the fragrant stew wonderingly. How had Monsieur Aspic managed to cook such a meal without her seeing?

A voice from behind her said, "You've found our dinner, *ma femme*. Shall we sit and eat?"

Monsieur Aspic lounged in a chair, wearing pleated trousers and a pale linen shirt. No sunglasses covered his yellow eyes.

"Where have you been?" Bonita cried before she thought. "You just abandon me all day?" She stopped, aghast. This was not what Father Christos had meant by being a dutiful wife.

Monsieur Aspic merely smiled and shrugged. "I had to sleep extra long, *moi*, to restore my charge. You know this word? It means a special energy. And then I must spend many hours before my altar to feed the saints. They were restless after my time away." He rose and bent down as if to kiss her. Bonita shied away. "I knew that you would be well taken care of," he said. "And you were fine, were you not?"

"Y-yes." Was she being unreasonable? She didn't know how the wife of a rich man filled her days. "But why have you no servants? That's so odd."

Monsieur Aspic turned abruptly to the casserole dish. "They were sent away. You and I can make do by ourselves, with the help of the saints. Ask me no more about it."

"Ask you no more—?" Bonita flopped down on a silk-upholstered dining chair.

"You have too many questions for a new bride, Bonita." He dished up a plate and put it before her. "We must take patience to learn each other. And how did you spend *your* day?"

After a sigh, Bonita picked up her fork. "I—I looked around the house, then found the library and read some, mostly from a collection of essays on science and man." She did not tell him about the book she'd found on vodoun.

"The Montaigne book!" said Monsieur Aspic. He sat to Bonita's left, close enough that she could touch him. "My tutor, Monsieur Henri, had me write my own essays on some of those same subjects."

"Tell me more about your childhood, my husband," said Bonita, half pleased with the married sound of that sentence. And though he wouldn't answer her questions, surely she could glean something from his history.

Monsieur Aspic responded to her efforts, as though her questions were insightful and her comments witty. He became altogether relaxed and engaging, yet smiling seldom. After a while, Bonita almost forgot about his yellow eyes and green scales.

But her husband's eyes traveled often to her smile, to

her hands, her shoulders, her chest, her bare legs where the disgraceful skirt didn't cover her properly. A fluttering began in her stomach. "You are very beautiful tonight, *ma femme*," Monsieur Aspic finally said. "It is nice to see you in women's clothing."

"Thank you." Bonita blushed. "These are the clothes you put in my closet for me."

"I did not put them there, but they are for you." Monsieur Aspic put his large hand on her bare knee. His palm was hot. "Bonita, *petite*, you should know. I need you to be a wife to me."

But the wall was up again, at least for Bonita. "If you didn't put the clothes there, then who—?"

"The saints," said her husband. He leaned back in his chair. "*C'est bien*, you need more patience." His voice seemed too casual. "Until tomorrow. Enjoy your dreams." He threw his napkin to the table and left Bonita to find her way to her room alone.

The next morning, Bonita found a tight, aqua-colored dress whose ruffled neckline kept sliding down her shoulders. On the dresser lay silver jewelry inset with turquoise and carnelians. She pulled her hair back and clasped it high, so that waves fell down her back. She chose the lowest heels in her closet because today her quest was outside.

She suspected Monsieur Aspic had a workroom or office in one of the many smaller buildings clustered behind the house. She remembered a set of doors in the west hallway that opened onto a courtyard. After another solitary breakfast and fruitless calling of her husband's name, Bonita hunted for and found the west wing.

She also found an alcove with a beautiful, intricately carved altar as long as her arm. Tiny yellow and pink roses sent up a fresh scent from where they surrounded a graceful statue of Saint Theresa, only half a meter tall. The white marble of her praying hands looked soft as flesh. The marble hair on the statue was pulled back from the face with waves down the shoulders. Bonita's jewelry matched the turquoise beads around the statue's neck.

How charming, thought Bonita, then crossed herself.
Saint Theresa was her patron. "Bless me in this marriage,"
she whispered. "And help me solve its many mysteries."

The courtyard seemed overgrown, with wrought-iron
benches and tables. Once through a narrow but tall gate,
Bonita turned to look around her. So many buildings, so
many twisty paths to take. Where was her husband?

Soon she heard muffled music from behind a fence
wall. A short walk brought her to a whitewashed hut with
a thatch roof. The walls swarmed with the familiar signs
of crosses and snakes, and the blue-painted door stood
ajar. From the doorway of the *houmfor* came drumbeats,
many rhythms and tones that wove together in a rich
texture.

People! Thought Bonita, for surely she heard the work
of three dummers at least. Her heart pounding as loudly
as the drums, she crept up to the dark doorway. The
blackness inside seemed to absorb the light of the candles
flickering on the familiar crowded altar. This time she also
saw a box of fine Cuban cigars.

But no drummers. The music came from a portable
tape player, and the *houmfor* was empty. Then Bonita saw
movement on the floor and jumped back, startled. It startled her even more when she recognized him.

It was the Snake Man. His eyes showed only white as
he lay belly-down on the dirt-floor, flicking his tongue in
and out and hissing. He didn't seem to hear Bonita's startled cry. She ran away, shaking, back to the house, ulti-
mately, back to the sensible words in the library.

The book on vodoun, when she finally dared to open
it, was a scientific, almost dry, discussion of the Haitian
religion. There was indeed a difference, according to the
author, between right-hand magic and left-hand magic.
Left-hand magic was the stuff of nightmares, those frightening childhood stories she'd heard of curses and zom-
bies. Wasn't the temple in Santa Domingo of the good
kind?

To calm herself, Bonita prepared a dinner of spiced
chicken in rum that night. At the dinner table, Monsieur
Aspic again looked immaculate, even if he did drag his

foot a little more. Bonita kept glancing at his face, relieved to see the intelligence that flickered there.

"Wonderful food, *ma femme*," he said. Then, "Bonita," he began in a coaxing voice. "You must learn a little of my religion, of my *société*. Are you still afraid of voudoun?"

"Father Cristos says vodoun is wrong," Bonita said shortly. "B-but I will honor your beliefs, for you are my husband."

"Father Christos gives me the sacrament also, and takes my tithes," said Monsieur Aspic. "Has he judged me evil? No, *ma femme*. I honor the saints and ask their help and their good magic in my life. By feeding and calling upon *Les Invisibles*, by letting myself be possessed by the saints, I keep Divine Protection. And another thing." His face looked almost dreamy. "The breath of the saints, when it fills you, it, it—"

"But," Bonita pushed away her plate of chicken. "It's bloody—and blasphemous. And it looks dangerous!"

Monsieur Aspic set his jaw. "It is dangerous. That's why the members of a *société* must be devout, and why the *houngan* leader must be very wise and strong in his spirit."

"Is your *houngan* strong? Is your *société* devout?"

"My *houngan* was my father, and he is dead. My *société* is . . . gone away." Monsieur Aspic bent his head and slumped a little over his meal.

"My husband, I'm sorry." How would she get him to trust her if she challenged him so? "I think maybe I am sharp tonight because I am a little homesick. I—I've never even gone a day before without seeing my Papi. How you must miss your own father."

Monsieur Aspic pushed his chair back. "Maybe my religion can comfort you." He left. Bonita heard a door open and close in a nearby room; then he was back with a small silver pitcher. "This is a *govi*. Because it has held the sacred saints, it has certain power." He filled the *govi* with water and held it out to her.

"Look into it, *ma femme*, and wish to see the face of the person you love most." His golden eyes looked deep into hers.

The silver pitcher felt cool and slick and heavy in her hands. Bonita looked inside it, at the ripples on the surface. Then the water seemed to grow smooth and hard, as if it were a mirror. Bonita saw her father, her beloved Papi, sitting at his place at the yellow kitchen table. He held a cigarette between his thumb and forefinger.

Bonita gasped. "I see him! Papi, oh, Papi!"

The image of her father took a puff of the cigarette, squinted, and gestured toward someone.

"It is your papa's face you see, is it?" asked Monsieur Aspic, back in his chair.

"This is wonderful, my husband. How do you do this?" she said. "No, never mind. I don't want to know." She stood, the *govi* in her arms. "I'm too excited to eat, so please excuse me." Impulsively she leaned toward Monsieur Aspic to hug his neck.

He sat impassively as she put one arm across his broad shoulders. "*Le bon Dieu* give me strength as I wait for a wife to come to me," he said as she left the room.

The next morning, determined to search the other buildings for more clues, Bonita met her husband again. She'd heard a furious bleating and the sound of splashing water. The noise drew her to a cobbled courtyard where Monsieur Aspic, dressed in a damp linen shirt and trousers, wearing a fedora and sunglasses, washed a goat.

The beige nanny gave a twist that almost pulled the rope from Monsieur Aspic's hands. The water hose flopped, soaking his shoulder.

Bonita called out, "Here, my husband, let me help you with her." She took the rope in one hand and with the other began scratching behind the goat's ears.

Monsieur Aspic looked surprised to see Bonita, then picked up a bar of soap and began washing the nanny in earnest. His snakeskin arms showed a sickly olive in the sun. "A good thing you happened by, *ma femme*."

Bonita realized her skirt had ridden up, showing her thigh. "Oh!" she said to distract him. "Now I remember to ask you. What is that beautiful little statue by the courtyard door?"

Monsieur Aspic looked up at her through his dark glasses. "Erzulie. You know her as Saint Theresa. She is the owner of the sweet waters and the teacher of pleasure and happiness."

"Oh. Such a devout saint." Bonita noticed the goat had yellow eyes like her husband's. "What's your pet goat's name?"

"This is not a pet; it has no name."

Bonita ceased the ear scratching. "Then why is it getting bathed?"

"To honor the saints." Monsieur Aspic shook the water from his hands, then walked to the faucet and turned off the hose. "*Merci* for your help. My marshal, he prepared these sacrifices for me. These contrary animals make such a fuss. I hope the saints are pleased with her." Taking the rope from Bonita's hand, he led the goat away. "You may come, too, if you like."

Bonita just looked at him and shook her head. She walked quickly away, but not before she imagined a bleating scream from the direction of the *houmfor*.

That day, Bonita found barns filled with feed and implements. Then she found an odd circle of small, abandoned houses, all with weeds covering their whitewashed foundations and vines overgrowing the orange tile roofs. These mystified her. She knocked on doors and looked in windows to see furniture, books. But no one was home. Why would they just abandon such pleasant, sturdy houses?

Another surprise awaited within the garage. The black sedan they had driven from Santo Domingo was there, along with five other, slightly dusty automobiles. The small red convertible with a black roof seemed to call out to her.

Bonita slid into the driver's seat, a place she'd never before sat at. The red leather upholstery felt warm as human skin. She turned the steering wheel and practiced waving at passersby. "Hello!" she called out. "See my car?"

The garage door in front of her suddenly rumbled up.

Monsieur Aspic stood grinning just outside, a set of keys jingling in his hand. He tossed them onto the front seat.

"Drive the car, *petite*," he said.

"I can't drive." Bonita rubbed the wheel and sighed.

"My woman must take care of herself. You'll learn to drive today. *Et voilà*." Monsieur Aspic jumped smoothly over the side of the car, guiding his feet onto the floorboard on the front passenger side. For the first time, Bonita noticed one shoe had a thicker sole.

"I—I don't know," said Bonita. He smelled of soap and cologne.

"Don't fear it. It gets easier once you've started." Monsieur Aspic slid close and reached across her chest, causing Bonita to press back against the seat. "*Tranquilment*, Bonita," he said. "I am just buckling your belt." His muscular thigh pressed against hers. "It will be a wild ride."

At his coaxing, Bonita started the motor, put her feet on two of the three floor pedals, shifted into gear, and they were off, out of the garage and down the driveway. The car jerked and sputtered, but her husband remained calm. A few times he put his green hand over hers to guide the gearshift. Soon they were in fourth gear, speeding down the country road.

"This is fun!" she crowed to the cane fields.

At the dinner that night of fried plantains and pork, Monsieur Aspic promised her the red car for her own once she'd mastered driving. She wanted to ask him about the cluster of abandoned houses, but feared to ruin the happy mood.

After another long look at the neckline of her blouse, her husband finally asked, "Thinking of lessons, *ma femme*, will you come to my room tonight? I want to teach you something else." He smiled a tense smile.

Bonita recalled his strong grip on the wheel, his sturdy thigh next to hers. It gets easier once you've started, she told herself. She opened her mouth to say yes; then his eyes caught the light, reminding her of the golden eyes of the goat. How like the Devil's eyes they looked.

"Can we wait just a little longer, husband?"

"*D'accord*. You must be ready in your heart." His tone

was patient, but Bonita saw him look down at his scaly hands as if he hated them.

Monsieur Aspic helped with her lunch preparations the next day, quickly tearing apart a head of cabbage with his clever fingers, attending her instructions closely on how to trim the beef and tenderize it with the edge of a plate.

"*Très bon!*" she called, which made him laugh aloud.

When he began to dice the onions thin at her direction, he stopped, wiping his eyes with his sleeves. "Oh, *ma femme!* What have you done to magic these tears from me?"

"It's just the onions." She laughed. "Everybody knows about onions."

"What about them?" Monsieur Aspic had the stony look again on his face.

"That they, that they—" Now Bonita paused, flour on her hands from breading the meat. "Oh, come. You cooked them in many of the breakfasts you left for me."

Monsieur Aspic sighed. "Once, this room was full of noisy women making delicious things. *Moi,* they chased me off, though sometimes with a treat in my hand." His face looked so lonely as he turned to her. "I tell you, I have not been in this kitchen since we returned. When will you believe what I tell you about the saints, about my religion?"

Bonita ducked her head, unsure. "I—I doubt most boys in the *mercado* know much about kitchens either, what with their mothers and sisters and sweethearts to cook for them. It is a special husband who will learn such skills."

Monsieur Aspic blinked, then grinned. "And a special sweetheart who can teach so well."

Bonita's heart warmed, but she knew she could ask him no more questions that day.

In her solitary bath, Bonita would rub soaps and lotions on her body and wonder what it felt like for other hands to touch her all over. Here, maybe. And here. She'd taken to going to bed in her panties, the better for the satin sheets to stroke her. She saw daily in the mirror what fine clothes and leisure hours did to make her look rested and wealthy. And older—almost a woman.

But when it came time each night to say, "Yes, I will be a wife to you," Bonita couldn't do it. Monsieur Aspic had not answered her question about the abandoned houses. He evaded other questions about the fresh flowers in the vases each day, the floors that seemed to sweep themselves, the dust that never gathered.

If he would just show her a little trust, a little faith, maybe she could find the strength to take that long walk to his bedroom. But he didn't. So she put him off for weeks, then a month. With each refusal he grew a little more tense, a little more icily polite.

Then one morning, Bonita was astonished when, breakfasting on her balcony, she saw her husband hacking plants out in the cane fields. She put on the sturdiest of her clothes and went to meet him. He was angry at her offer to help, but finally accepted. "It shames me to do this, for my father raised no field worker," he said. "But this is not a matter the saints can help us with. If we don't bring it in, the cane will rot in the fields. *Entendu,* I thought my life would be different by now."

They traveled the cane fields with massive machetes, hacking off the brown stalks of sugarcane near the ground so new shoots would grow. Monsieur Aspic did this, sweeping from side to side with the knife, his dusty green skin streaked with sweat. Bonita trimmed each stalk of its fronds and stacked them in a flatbed truck. At night they had barely enough energy to bathe and eat.

After three days of this, Bonita surveyed the acres of uncut cane. "How can the two of us finish this in time, husband? Why can't we call in some workers?"

"We cannot," Monsieur Aspic said. "If you had my pride, if you knew the situation, you would know that is impossible."

"Well." This time Bonita didn't accept his evasion. "Pride can kill you if you let it. And if I don't know the situation, it's because you never told me." She turned her back on him and hacked clean another cane stalk. Each leaf she visualized as his forked snake tongue that never told her the truth. That night her exhaustion was even greater.

The next morning, Bonita went to her *govi* and filled it with water. At the image inside, she gasped and almost dropped the pitcher.

Her Papi lay thin and still in a strange bed in a very white room. Lines of pain marked his forehead.

Bonita burst into tears and went to find Monsieur Aspic.

"I cannot see what you see," he told her when she held the *govi* up. "You must tell me why you are crying, *ma femme*. What has happened?"

"My—my Papi," she sobbed. "He is ill, and all I can think of is how much I miss him. How much I miss the bakery. How much—" She put a hand to her face, words gone.

Monsieur Aspic, in work clothes, was headed to the cane fields. "Do you wish to visit them, then?"

She looked at him through wet lashes. "Will you take me?"

Monsieur Aspic shook his head, his jaw set. "I cannot. But if you wish to go so badly, you can drive yourself."

"In the red car? Drive myself?" Bonita's heart jumped into her throat at the thought. But . . . it was for her Papi. "I suppose I could, with a map and many stops to rest."

The next day, Bonita set two leather suitcases and a well-marked map on the front seat of the red car. She smoothed the jacket of her stylish dress. "See you in a week, husband," she said to Monsieur Aspic. They had agreed a week was long enough. When he bent his head to hers, she wrapped her arms around his chest and gave him a hug instead.

"You must come back," he said over the top of her head. "You promised to come back and be my wife."

Three hours was not so long a trip after all. Bonita found a spot to park right in front of the Happiness Bakery, and was gratified to see Esteban loading a cart with *pastelitos.* He raised his eyebrows at the car, then recognized Bonita.

"Bonita? Little *chica*, is that you? My God, girl." He flung open the door of the bakery and shouted, "It's Bonita! The Snake Man has let her come back—and in such a car!"

Between kisses, Bonita inquired, "Where's Papi? Is he sick?"

"He's upstairs, supposed to be resting from the grippe," said Raquella. "Scared us when the doctors put him in the hospital to get fluids into his veins. But he thinks he must run the business or it will fall into ruin."

Ysabel interrupted. "Did you hear about our catering contracts, *chica*? Now we do all the food for weddings, for christenings—"

"Later for that! Papi will be so happy to see her," said Esteban.

When Señor Arregon saw Bonita, tears sprang to his eyes. "Oh, my darling girl!" He hugged her hard. "Are you here for a visit? Is the marriage a happy one?"

"Yes, Papi. But now I am here to make you well and happy. Monsieur Aspic sends his good wishes too."

"Monsieur Aspic?" Raquella laughed. "Don't you call your husband by his Christian name?"

"Christian?" snorted Ysabel. "Not after what we saw in that wedding."

"Your servants must groom you well," said Raquella. "You're looking so sleek and fit."

"Oh, we have no servants," said Bonita shortly, aware for the first time that her sisters envied her.

It turned out her sisters' husbands were too lazy or too arrogant to do any work themselves. The new catering business was for extra income. Bonita was glad to help them make a success of it. She rose early in the morning to cook, stayed up late discussing food presentation. Her father accepted her back as if she'd never left. A flash of memory stopped her one day: was it Tuesday she was supposed to return? Oh, surely not seven days yet. Her sisters needed her so badly.

But she grew to resent their improper questions. "Does

he kiss you with a forked tongue, Bonita?" Ysabel asked one evening as the three of them trimmed sugar roses in the upstairs apartment.

She'd ignored all the other taunts, but today she felt tired. "Monsieur Aspic does not. He respects my wishes."

"Ah, Raquella, this *chica* is still a virgin!" cried Ysabel.

"Oh, you poor girl," cried Raquella. "Six weeks, and he's not forced you or seduced you?"

Ysabel put a hand to her mouth. "Bonita, this one must not like girls. I know! Papi can have the marriage annulled, and we will make this rich man pay us to keep his shameful secret."

"No, we won't," said Bonita. "My husband is kind and wise, and knows magical things."

The sisters exchanged glances. "What kind of magic?" Raquella asked.

Bonita retrieved the *govi* she had packed in her suitcase. Raquella reached out and stroked the metal pitcher. "This is solid silver, I'll bet."

"Whenever I filled this with water, I could see Papi whenever I wanted. Look." Bonita got water from the kitchen tap. As she handed it to Raquella, she looked inside, expecting to see her Papi reading in his bedroom. Instead, the water stiffened, and she saw Monsieur Aspic. "Oh, I see Michél," she cried. There was something terribly wrong, though.

"Let me," said Ysabel. She snatched the *govi*. "I don't see anything in here except my own reflection!"

"Give it back, sister," Bonita said, her voice fierce. "Now."

Ogling her baby sister, Ysabel returned the pitcher. Bonita hugged the *govi* and looked inside.

Monsieur Aspic was dead!

He must be dead; she had never seen him look so thin and still. He lay alone in a large bed, sheets up to his bare chest.

Leaving her sisters to the confectionary, Bonita ran back to her room and began frantically folding and packing her clothes. Her father came upstairs, still in his baker's apron. "Are you leaving tomorrow, Bonita? It seems too early."

"I'm leaving today, Papi." She kept packing. "My husband needs me."

"You know that I will miss you too, don't you?" Her father hugged her shoulders. "And who has your heart? Where is your heart, little one?"

Bonita stopped dead still. "Why, I believe my heart is in a sugarcane plantation in the Cibao Valley," she said. "And pray God it's not too late."

Driving alone for hours in the dark could have frightened Bonita. But she didn't let it. She was more afraid of what she'd find when she returned home. And finally, an hour or two past midnight, she was there. When she opened the heavy door, the house smelled musty and stale. Dirt had blown under the front door, and colored centipedes floated in the entryway fountain.

"Monsieur Aspic?" she called. "My husband? I'm back."

No answer.

Bonita went down the hall to Monsieur Aspic's room and knocked at his door. Did she hear a moan? "Michél? Are you there?" She threw open the doors to a large bedroom with many shuttered windows. Crosses and vodoun paintings filled the walls. Several large designs in flour and ash covered the floor. In a wrought-iron bed against the far wall lay her husband.

She ran to him, aghast.

He was bone-thin and unshaven, his body a field of gray-green scales amidst tangled sheets. "Oh, Michél." She dropped to her knees by the bed. "Your skin is so dry."

"Bonita," Monsieur Aspic said weakly. His eyes opened. "You're back. I thought you had finally had enough of me."

"I'm sorry I'm late," Bonita said, her voice trembling. "I broke my promise to you . . ."

"How could you keep such a promise?" He spoke low. "I wished for too much. Too much . . ."

"Not at all. You are my husband." Bonita stood up and looked around for a water jug. "Any food? What has become of the house and all the helpful spirits?"

"I grew too sad to call on the saints, and they will come only when I honor them." Monsieur Aspic reached out his hand. "Can you bring me water? I drank the last this morning." Bonita found the empty jug and filled it from the bathroom faucet. Her husband gulped down two glassfuls.

"Rest now, husband," she said, "and I will make you soup."

With braised onions and vegetables simmering in the kitchen, Bonita felt the immense emptiness of the house weigh down on her. "Come back, you saints," she called out. "He needs you here."

Her voice just echoed on the air.

She had never believed him before when he talked of magic, of the invisible saints. But now she compared this empty house with the one she had seen ten days ago. Someone, something, was missing now. If she believed that, then what of the rest? The sacrifices. The possession. The . . . ecstasy?

A good wife honored the beliefs of her new household.

Bonita took a haunch of rabbit with her and went out into the dark night to find the *houmfor*. She passed Saint Theresa on the way and shivered at the dry, dead roses.

The paintings on the *houmfor* walls seemed to dance in the candlelight. The open doorway yawned like a dark mouth. Bonita stood on the threshold and felt her skin crawl. "I can't speak French to make you hear me," she said aloud to the darkness within. "But I am here to honor you with this good rabbit—ah, *lapin*—which you can feed on, as is your way." She stepped inside and could smell old candle wax, rum, burned feathers, the scent of washed goat. She lit the candles that still had wicks. "I make this sacrifice in place of my beloved husband." She found a spot on the crowded altar to put the meat. "My husband is ill and needs your help. Please come back. And in return, I will learn to perform the rituals that are permitted an initiate."

The soup was ready when she returned to the kitchen. She filled a bowl, found some fruit and bread, and carried a tray to Monsieur Aspic's room. He sat up so she could feed him. "It is healing food," he said, his voice already stronger. Tears stood in his eyes. "If you wait a moment, I will cover myself to shield your sensibilities."

"Hush and eat," she said. "You're not shocking me." He seemed so frail and young without any clothes. Bonita was able to sit right next to him without trembling.

He ate the rest of the soup himself, and a handful of grapes.

"I can imagine how sticky and uncomfortable you are," said Bonita. She found a basin and some towels and soap. "Pull this down." She tugged at the sheet drawn up to his chest. Beneath, he wore silk briefs. The snakeskin pattern covered all his torso. "Much better," said Bonita. "Who better to tend you than your own wife?"

Monsieur Aspic just set his teeth and avoided her eyes.

She began to sponge him, first on his face and neck, then down to his chest. She held his arms up, the better to wash the curly hair in his armpits. The curve of his biceps struck her as so beautiful she stopped the bathing just to observe him. How long and lean! How fine-boned his face, how full his lips! She began to wash his chest, paying close attention to the flat dark nipples in their nests of hair.

But Monsieur Aspic lay beneath her hands tense and shivering.

"What is it, my husband?" she asked. "Am I hurting you?"

"Only with your kindness," he muttered. Then louder, "You think I don't know what you're thinking? What everybody thinks?"

"And what is that?" Bonita said gently.

"That ugliness is the sign of a diseased soul. You, with your saint's face and generous heart, are proof that beauty inside and beauty outside go together. That is why I hide my skin and my deformity from other people's eyes."

"Deformity?" Bonita then noticed how one bare foot was turned in a little with curled toes. She took the foot in one hand. "This is nothing. And you should meet all the pretty women and handsome men I know who are not worth a *phffft. You* have a good soul, Michél. A little too proud, but honorable and generous and willing to sacrifice."

"Hmmm," said Monsieur Aspic, but now finally he began to relax.

"And your skin, my husband, is so fascinating close up." It had a pattern like tiny overlapping feathers, each flake of skin marked with a fine dark edge. It gave the effects of scales. "It is different, but beautiful," Bonita said. Skin so green and fine. She began to kiss it as she washed up the leg now, past the muscular calf with its fine, thick hair, to the knee, the thigh. The skin was warm and soft beneath her lips. Her husband caught his breath and sighed.

Her eyes traveled to that other place at the juncture of his legs, which swelled so round and full beneath the silk. Was this it, then? Was this the secret that married women shared?

At the edge of the mystery, Bonita stopped, trembling, until her husband reached down with surprisingly strong hands, and drew her across his chest. Her face was level with his. His hands were warm against her back.

"Will you stay with me tonight, *ma femme?*" he asked. "Will you be a wife to me?"

As he spoke, his breath filled her mouth, a flavor new yet familiar too. She felt passion ripple through her, possess her thoughts, her heart. She put her lips on his.

The next morning, Bonita awakened to voices and music. She drew the sheet up against the cool morning air on her naked skin. The soreness in her groin made her smile with memories of the night before. Then she heard laughing outside, the slamming of car doors.

The Saints had never sounded like this.

Now wide awake, Bonita sat up and looked around. Her husband was gone, but a note on the bedside table said simply, "To work! Love, M."

A chorus of voices sounded just outside the window.

Bonita recovered her dress from the floor and opened the shutters. She blinked at the sun, and then again at the sight.

A full dozen cars and trucks were parked around the house. Groups of plainly and cleanly dressed people, most black or mulatto, unloaded boxes, groceries, and suitcases. Six small children ran down the driveway. When her shutters opened, the children called out something in French and waved.

Still wondering, Bonita waved back and closed the shutters.

The bedroom door opened and her husband came in, smiling like a bright angel. *"Ma femme,"* he said, enveloping her in an embrace. "You have slept long, and my *société* is already here! Imagine it! Léon, my marshal, says an orange snake spoke from their fire and told them to return. It must have been He. I am so honored."

"Your *société*?" said Bonita. "The other members of your temple?"

"More than that," said her husband, rubbing her arms. "My father's people, and now mine, for I am their *houngan*. I think they grew impatient over my pride." At her quizzical look, he added, "Yes, I was raised and trained as a priest in the right-hand magic. Only I didn't think I was worthy. I became so obsessed with my own ugliness, I didn't have the faith that I could lead these people. They finally left me one day."

"And they abandoned those homes I saw, while you had to do by yourself the work of many?" Now it made sense.

"Pride can kill you if you let it, someone said to me. But I thought if I waited for your heart to tell you to be a wife to me, that would prove my worth." He kissed her again, and she turned in his arms to face him, breast against breast, so that their hearts thudded against each other's chests.

When they left the bedroom an hour later, Bonita made Monsieur Aspic stop at the altar of Saint Theresa. "There were moments in last night's ecstasy when I think

I felt her spirit overshadow me. What did you say her other name was?"

Her husband whispered it in her ear, his hand warm on the skin above her heart. "She is Erzulie, the energy of love and the teacher of fulfillment."

Bonita dropped jasmine blooms around the statue, its small marble face so expressive of its full heart. "Send me another lesson tonight, sweet Erzulie," she whispered.

The Willful Child, the Black Dog, and the Beanstalk

MELANIE TEM

Melanie Tem lives with her husband, writer and editor Steve Rasnic Tem, in Denver. They have four children and two granddaughters. Tem's most recent novels are Witch-Light *with Nancy Holder,* Tides, *and* There Be Dragons. *Her short fiction has recently appeared in the anthologies* Peter Beagle's Immortal Unicorn, Dark Terrors, Hot Blood 9 *and* 10, Snapshots, Gargoyles, *and* Imagination Fully Dilated *(with Steve Rasnic Tem) in the magazine* Cemetery Dance.

Tem's story grew out of the interplay between her two professions—social work and fiction writing. She feels that both ways of looking at human experience—social work more analytical and positing a linear cause and effect, fiction more metaphorical and suggestive and evocative—have truth to tell, and it's reductionist to ignore any of it.

Fairy tales, being even more metaphorical and multilayered than some other kinds of fiction, can take our understanding that much farther. Tem weaves the Brothers Grimm's "The Stubborn Child" and several other fairy tales skillfully, enabling her troubled characters to tell their own stories.

The Willful Child, the Black Dog, and the Beanstalk

This was the fourteenth year I'd taught, so at least the fourteenth time I'd sat through the diagnosis discussion about which first-year social work students always cared passionately. Early in the semester I'd made my pronouncement on the subject: "In our zeal to 'understand,' let's not confuse the metaphor with the referent. Diagnosis, mythology, even language suggest a certain truth, but they're constructs. Stories. They don't have an inherent reality, only what we impute to them." As usual, no one had asked what I meant, which was fine with me because I'd have been hard pressed to explain any more. I was, more or less, thinking about my daughter.

I became conscious of a woman I'd noticed before, rather peripherally, because she had the look and manner of the perpetual outsider. Although she was paying close attention, she wasn't participating in this discussion, and I didn't think I'd ever seen her talking to any of her classmates.

I looked for some characteristic that would help me recall her name or something else about her. She was tall, broad-shouldered, broad-hipped, with a broad, pretty face. Her drab blond hair was further dulled by gray— premature, since otherwise she looked no more than thirty-five; nervously she kept trying to tuck it behind her ears, which made me notice sculpted sideburns, the only attempt at styling. She wore jeans neither fashionably baggy nor form-fitting and a man's lumberjack shirt with sleeves rolled up over strong forearms made to appear delicate by the pale underside of the flannel.

Kathleen, I thought, or Kathryn. I glanced down at the roster. By this point in the semester most students had staked out their territory in the classroom and sat in roughly the same place every time, but she, I was fairly sure, had moved all over the room, sometimes even changing places at the break, as though she couldn't find a chair that suited her. Now she sat on the floor, although several desks were unoccupied.

Katharine, it was. Katharine Watrous. Once I'd have noted in the margin whether she used a diminutive. Despite the allure of ready-made aliases, I'd generally been grateful my name wasn't Margaret or Katharine or Elizabeth. You couldn't do much with the name Ruth; "Ruthie" never lasted long, thank God. "Jill" was a name like that, too. Probably she'd long since changed it.

I sighed, regretted it. One of these budding therapists was sure to note such nonverbal communication, even when it wasn't intended to communicate anything.

The bell rang, mercifully interrupting a spirited argument over whether a particular client was a borderline or inadequate personality. Gathering my notes together and testily trying to come up with a more-or-less believable excuse for being very tardy to the noon faculty meeting, I looked up into Katharine Watrous's gray gaze. "Dr. Torgesson," she said. I was drawn by her voice, smaller than I'd have expected from a person her size. "I'm Katha Watrous."

Katha. I wouldn't have thought of that. I smiled and held out my hand and said, as I've always said to students when they haven't already assumed it, "Call me Ruth." Her handshake, though, was solid and somehow soothing, and I realized I'd held on longer than etiquette strictly required.

She inclined her head as if I'd shamed her. "I'd like to make an appointment to talk with you. Privately."

Thinking happily of the faculty meeting due to start in ten minutes, I said, "I could meet with you right now if you'd like."

As we made our way to my office, my impulse was to demand of her then and there what she wanted, to get it over with, even if it meant having to go to the faculty meeting. Most things students wanted of me had used up my interest a long time ago. Career or curriculum advice. Intercession with another instructor about grades or assignments. Ethical guidance. Counseling about rigid parents or recalcitrant lovers. Over the years there'd been, too, sexual and academic propositions ranging from the patently ridiculous to those worth fleeting consideration.

The third-floor hallway looked exactly like the hallways on the second and fourth floors; I had yet to find any distinguishing characteristics other than room numbers and names on small, removable plaques. The old building, abandoned several years ago and razed, had had clattering pipes, radiators that had emitted veils of dust, and a general blurry-brown ambience with yellow underlighting. You knew without conscious thought where you were and why.

I'd brought over all my things. Professional certificates and publications. The odd, bright, self-stimulating drawings by the autistic kids I'd worked with so long that the drawings and the noises and the staring into space had started to make sense to me. A pen set given to me early in my career by a student I barely remembered, for a reason I'd completely forgotten. Pictures of Jill, each associated in my memory with some small or monumental difficulty. Surely there'd been more to my life with my child than problems, but by this time she'd been gone four years and seven months (and sixteen days, but I disliked knowing that) and I couldn't have sworn to it.

The baby pictures, adorable as they were, brought back memories of how demanding she'd been, impossible to please, how I'd been chronically sleep-deprived for so long that it had come to seem a natural condition. The charming shot of her on her tricycle when she was about three reminded me unpleasantly of the battles we'd waged over where she was allowed to ride; I'd finally confiscated it, which had served only to change her method of escape from the yard, the block, my thoroughly inadequate maternal supervision. By the time of her fourth-grade school picture, she'd been refusing to do her homework, and I had never found an effective consequence, logical or otherwise. In the portrait of her at fourteen, strikingly plain though she had been an attractive enough girl, defiance was clearly detectable.

There was, however, nothing in any of the pictures, including the snapshot from the summer she'd turned seventeen, to indicate that she was sick. But she had been. We never had a firm diagnosis, but the doctors had suspected some sort of progressive autoimmune disease, her body treating as enemies things that were not. In that last snapshot Jill, not wanting to be seen with me, was moving out of the frame, and my hand was extended after her, for all time.

Shaking myself out of the dolorous reverie inspired by the gallery of Jill, I turned to find Katha Watrous sitting in my chair. There was an immediate, visceral feeling of violation. Katha all but scrambled up, a motion made awkward by her size. I didn't tell her it was all right, stay where she was. I pushed past her, aware of her warmth and bulk relative to mine, and sat down in my chair, which, I swore, had taken her imprint.

There were two other chairs in the office, but now Katha remained standing. "Did you hear about the woman who was murdered last week by the girl she was about to adopt?"

Startled, I nodded. In professional journals and the popular press, I made a point to read accounts of children who killed their parents. In some perverse way, it made me less likely to lie awake worrying about my own child. For all her willfulness, she hadn't killed me.

"I placed that girl. She called me at home to tell me what she'd done."

I said hopefully, "And you called the police."

"Regina already had. They were there when I got there. Regina was curled up on the bedroom floor screaming that her mother was still alive, her mother wouldn't die. Her mother, Carol, was on the bed. Regina had stabbed her in the belly. I read in the paper later that it was thirty-seven times, from sternum to pelvis." Katha took a breath. "That was my case."

"Oh, dear," was all I could think of to say, other than something flip about developing assessment skills the hard way or about this being a learning experience.

"I have to find out why she did it," Katha said.

I considered her statement. "I should think there are obvious, almost generic reasons," I said. "Adoption issues. Adolescent issues." "Issue" was high on my list of odious terms from the language of social work, which was not precisely English, but I couldn't think of another way to say it, which was more than a little distressing.

Katha shook her head. "All those things are true. There's some truth. But they don't explain anything."

This woman, I thought, had potential. "No warning signs?"

"I don't know. Carol once told me that Regina tried to push her into the hot oven." I raised my eyebrows. "Regina insisted she was just trying to hug her."

There was something almost laughable in the mental image of that scene. I restrained myself.

"She rigged a bucket of water over the kitchen doorway so it would fall on Carol. She made little bonfires in her shoes."

With an effort I said, more or less soberly, "And you think all those things are connected. To each other and to the murder."

"I want to find out. And I want you to help me. Will you?"

I visualized the faculty meeting and all the others just

like it. I considered Jill, for whom grief and anger and worry had become commonplace background noise to my everyday existence, enervating now rather than energizing.

I looked at sweet, ponderous, displaced Katha Watrous shifting her weight, and thought I could do worse than pursue her obsessions instead of my own. "Why not?" I said. "Have a seat."

I stayed late at the office that night, reading through the materials Katha had left. It was not unusual for me to work late; more than a few times I'd even spent the night in the old wingback in the corner. Though I didn't feel at home in my office, I felt less at home at home.

Katha had said that the file contained all the information on Regina. That wasn't true, of course, despite its bulk; Katha obviously hadn't thought about how information gets gathered and stored about all of us, formally and informally, deliberately and with no one's conscious intent.

What was there would have said as much about the observers as about the subject if the observers had been more clearly identified. As it was, presented in official form as reports to the court or to the Department of Social Services, the information relied on the dangerous presumption of its truth.

Regina Lauren Dempsey had been born a little over fourteen years ago in a local general hospital. Mother's name and age and race duly noted; father unknown. No problems at birth. Foster placements and returns home, neglect and abuse complaints against the mother, and failed treatment plans began when she was about a year old. This went on for six years, a sheaf half an inch thick, of poorly photocopied case notes.

Then, when Regina was seven, her mother had vanished. There was no death certificate in the file. I counted thirteen foster homes for Regina in the next seven years. They were collected into stark columns on one sheet: the dates she'd lived there, the names and addresses of the families, and, under the heading "Reason for Move," thirteen identical entries: "Child's disruptive behavior."

Eventually she'd been placed in one of those residential treatment facilities from which most adolescents never emerged. There were reports from psychologists and social workers, some slightly more interesting than others because they seemed to be talking about an actual person, but none very illuminating. Then, slightly less than a year ago, Regina had been placed for the purpose of adoption in the home of Carol Burroughs. I read Carol's adoptive-home study, signed by Katharine Watrous and countersigned by her supervisor, and found it creditable if not inspired. Carol sounded like a sensible, easygoing, thoughtful woman with considerable capacity to give and receive love. I'd probably have liked her. I'd surely have approved her to adopt.

Katha's post-placement reports, one a month for eleven months, were notable because they didn't mention the adjustment problems typical of older adopted kids and their families. No conflicts over homework or curfew or household chores. No sexual acting out. No runaways. No violence or even unusual anger. With the eleventh report, in which there was mention of the upcoming finalization, the record stopped. There was, of course, nothing about Carol's death; Katha wouldn't have had time to write a closing summary even if she'd known what to write. The event's absence gave the file an ironic tone, as if all the information in it were nothing but foreshadowing. As if the meaning of a tale were all in the way it would end.

"I've talked to one of her foster families," Katha told me the next evening in my living room. She had taken the chair I thought of as mine, an odd fancy for a person who lived alone in a house full of places to sit. The threadbare Queen Anne wasn't even the most comfortable chair in the room, and it hunkered inconspicuously in a corner. I didn't much like her appropriation of it, and the urge to move her was distracting.

It wasn't common for students to come to my house; I'd passed through the comradely stage long ago. But something about Katha—the waiflike quality heightened by her size; the lostness and unease accentuated by her competence—had me offering homemade vegetable soup. Who knew what in her or in me led her to accept.

She'd brought a six-pack of Beck's Dark, but was, unforgivably, letting hers go warm and flat at her elbow. Dark beer, bitey and very cold, was one of life's few certain pleasures. I sipped mine steadily and savored the happy image of more glass mugs frosting in the freezer.

Katha was consulting her notes. "They mentioned her obsession with cartoons. She used to get up in the middle of the night and go sit in the TV room all huddled up in a blanket until cartoons came on. On weekends Mrs. Floss would shoo all the kids outside, and pretty soon she'd find Regina with the volume down low and her nose practically touching the screen. A few times she even played hooky from school and somehow managed to sneak in to the TV."

"Power struggle," I said dismissively.

"They also kept saying how much she liked to read. That made quite an impression on them, not entirely positive. There aren't many books in their house."

"What did she read?" I had no particular reason for wanting to know this, but I'd lived to regret recalcitrance more often than inquisitiveness.

"Fairy tales and mythology," Katha answered at once. "The meaner the better, Mrs. Floss said."

It was easy to understand why a little girl powerless and repeatedly hurt in a world populated by unreliable adults would be drawn to tales of princes coming to the rescue, goddesses ruling at swordpoint, children pushing wicked witches into ovens.

The pit of my stomach buzzed. There was a clue here, but I couldn't quite see what it was. "Didn't you tell me Regina tried to push Carol into the oven?"

Katha caught my tone and fixed her gaze on me. "Both my supervisor and I thought Regina's version made more sense, that she was just running up to give Carol a hug from behind. In fact, one of the dynamics we looked at in this case was Carol's paranoia. But she did get a nasty burn on her leg."

"Hansel and Gretel pushed the witch into the oven," I reminded her. "That's how they got rid of her."

Katha regarded me for a long moment. "Why would she think Carol was a witch?"

"Maybe she just wanted to get rid of her. Maybe she didn't want to be adopted." I knew I was reaching, but I couldn't shake the conviction that there was some connection here.

Katha was unconvinced. "They'd known each other for a while. Carol was a volunteer at the treatment facility. Regina always seemed a lot more invested in making the placement work than most kids are. And anyway, kids over twelve have to consent to their own adoptions in this state."

"So is that why the foster family had her moved? Because she read too much and watched too much TV?" Having encountered excuses more ludicrous than that for adoptive parents giving up on kids, I was almost afraid to hear the answer.

"They felt really bad about giving her up," Katha said a little defensively. "Mrs. Floss said she became especially attached." I snorted. "Then Regina tried to kill her."

Excitement cut with dread made me want to postpone the telling of this tale. Holding up a hand, I stood. "Let me check the soup. I'll be right back."

The soup was simmering nicely. I tasted it, added unnecessary pinches of oregano and sage to justify myself, then gave in and got a second Beck's, taking care to restock the freezer with a fresh mug. Courage fortified by the first icy, sharp sip, I went back to the living room. Katha's eyes had been fixed on the doorway, and I thought I saw inordinate relief, as if she hadn't been sure I would come back. "So," I said, settling myself, "I'm listening."

"The Flosses' house is one of those tall Victorians, three full stories with high peaks. Mrs. Floss was up on an extension ladder painting the gingerbread at the roofline, and when she started down, Regina got more and more upset, screaming and crying. Mrs. Floss climbed down faster to get to her and find out what was wrong.

Then Regina got a little brush saw and was sawing away at the rungs and she almost knocked the ladder over with Mrs. Floss on it, coming down."

"Odd," I mused, holding the mug in both hands and mourning its rapid progress toward room temperature, "that she didn't just push it. I wonder what the point of the saw was."

A thought struck us both. Katha's gray eyes widened, and she pushed both hands through her hair, exposing those endearing sideburns against full cheeks. "The giant," I said, amazed. "Jack and the Beanstalk."

We were silent, both of us waiting to see what else we would come to understand. At first we stared more or less at each other, but our gazes wandered. It wasn't long before I was thinking about my daughter, which was where my thoughts always settled when no place else would have them. I wondered if Katha had a spot like that for her thoughts.

Finally I gave up and served dinner. Katha offered to help but I declined; I loathe having people in my kitchen. I had ladled soup into nice white bowls when I heard something at the back door. *Jill*, I thought before I could censor myself, *Jill alive. Jill coming home*, and, with trepidation and yearning equally ridiculous, went to investigate.

A gaunt black dog stood on my patio. I took a step back, then rapped imperiously on the door pane. The dog was looking in my direction with eyes made yellow, probably by the house lights they reflected, and it didn't move.

I hadn't had pets in years, no small maternal sacrifice. When Jill's symptoms had first started, one doctor had thought she might be allergic to animals, so we'd gotten rid of our cat and dog. I'd tried not to show how heartbroken I was. Jill had shown hardly any reaction, including amelioration of her sickness. It had taken me some time to adjust to living without a pet, and now my first impulse at the sight of this black dog at my door was to invite it in. But it was too late, I told myself. I was too set in my ways. And I couldn't have a dog when Jill came home.

I called through the glass, "Go away! Get out of here!" I opened the door and repeated my order. The dog didn't move, except to swing its long head more precisely toward me. *Just like a kid,* I thought in great annoyance. *Doing whatever it damn well pleases.*

I stepped outside into the spring evening redolent with my neighbors' lilacs, a lovely fragrance that used to make Jill sneeze. I advanced toward the black dog, meaning to threaten. It didn't move. I was certain that it hadn't moved. But it was gone. I stalked back into the house.

Both soup bowls on the table were empty, spoons still in them. Frowning, I peered into the pot on the stove. Only a faint skim of broth remained. "Katha?" A note was propped on the end table in the cone of light from under the orange sod. Katha's script was childish. "Sorry. I had to go. Thanks for dinner."

They let me in to see Regina because I said I was her therapist, and as if to prove it, flashed my card, which stated only that I had a doctorate in social work and accepted clients for short- and long-term psychotherapy, revealing nothing about my relationship or lack thereof to Regina Dempsey. But the middle-aged, gum-popping guard behind the desk doubtless cared rather little about relationships. After a perfunctory inspection of my bogus credentials, his expression, minimal at its peak, went utterly blank, and he made no move to unlock the door to the visitors' area.

I did my best to return his gaze in kind, but he was much better at it. I seethed at being subjected again to petty authority. Just that morning I'd lost an argument to the pinched-faced manager of the local dry cleaner, where I'd traded for years: I couldn't find the claim check and she couldn't find my burgundy dress; she'd accused me of accusing her of stealing it, which hadn't occurred to me until then, and she refused to do any more of my clothes. Daily life was full of little object lessons about who held real power.

Finally the guard roused himself from his hostile torpor long enough to reach behind him and push the button that buzzed open the door. Into a mike on the desk he informed somebody that Dempsey had a visitor. Not thanking him made me feel better.

At eye level around three walls drooped a single frayed strand of red crepe paper, left over from Valentine's Day or early for the Fourth of July. Accentuating the barrenness of the place might well have been its function. This was a jail, after all; the inmates weren't supposed to be happy. It seemed to me, though, that some of them were.

At the table on my right, a bent old man and a boy who looked no more than twelve played cards. They didn't say a word to each other. The cards snapped and fluttered. I was briefly fascinated, first in an unsuccessful attempt to decipher what game they were playing, then in sheer aesthetic appreciation of the rhythms and patterns they kept going.

"Who the fuck are you?"

Regina Dempsey wore chartreuse plastic sandals, a black lace midriff top that hardly covered her breasts, skintight silver shorts. Her hair—blond, intense black, hot pink, purple—kinked into her face. I was surprised they let her dress like that in here, and that she wasn't in handcuffs. The first time Jill had been picked up for shoplifting, eleven years old, they'd cuffed her. That day, in the echoing brown hall of the courthouse, with an armed deputy cruelly holding her arm, she'd blushed and refused to look at me, and I'd been shocked to tears. In time, as our story took form, we'd both become accustomed to props like manacles and guns.

I told Regina my name and that I was a friend of Katha's. She shrugged. I said I was there to talk about "what happened." She sneered at the euphemism, as well she should. "Since when are you my fucking therapist? I don't need no shrink."

"I notice you didn't tell them I wasn't."

She put one foot up on the rung of the chair, cocking her hip. The chair was too unsteady and the rung too high for her to maintain that stance for long; impatiently she took her foot down again. "Shit, anything's better than sitting in that fucking room. Cell. My roommate's fucking crazy." She rolled her eyes, which were dark blue inside rings and arcs of lavender and black. I wondered, somewhat resentfully, why they allowed makeup in here.

"Why don't you sit down," I suggested through gritted teeth, sounding in my own ears like any other irritable adult, "so we can talk." I'd always been an easy mark for adolescent insolence; my private practice, such as it was, specialized in children and adults.

"Why should I?"

"Don't, then."

"You got a cigarette?"

"No," I said, and added smugly, "I've never smoked." Jill had started smoking at twelve— maybe earlier, for all I knew. The sicker she'd got, the more she'd smoked.

"Well, ain't that special." Abruptly Regina sat down, close enough now that I could smell the slightly sweet, slightly rank odors of her young body. The boy and the old man finished a game; I couldn't tell who had won. The boy shuffled the cards with an expertise I found distressing, whizzing noise and motion between his small hands.

From the several opening questions I'd considered, I chose: "What do you think is going to happen to you, Regina?"

"I don't know, Ruth," she answered at once, mocking my tone, curling her pale lip. "What do you think is going to happen to me?"

"I don't know, Regina." I stopped myself before I repeated the entire syntax and tone, pressed my lips together, and waited.

After a while, she turned directly to me and said, with an air of speaking the simple truth, "I'll burn in hell."

I looked at her sharply and detected no sarcasm now, no hint of an ambush or trick. Still, I proceeded with caution. "What do you mean?"

"I'll burn in hell," she repeated. She seemed almost pleased by what she was saying. Her lips, buffed as though with black shoe polish, were slightly parted. "Murder is a mortal sin. The devil is waiting for me right now. He's got a pitchfork." I didn't think her ghoulish smile was for my benefit.

I was stymied. In good conscience, I couldn't disabuse her of her guilt; this child was a confessed murderer. And it was almost always pointless and often harmful to debate somebody's personal symbolism. What I wanted to know—admittedly, for no reason much better than prurience—was why she'd killed Carol, and I didn't quite know how to get us there from where we were in this dialogue.

Mulling various conversational gambits, I was thoroughly blindsided when Regina said, "That's where your kid is, too, you know. In hell. On the devil's pitchfork." She laughed.

Outrage swept me to my feet. "What did you say?"

She was grinning. "You don't know where your daughter is, huh? She's dead, Ruth. She's in hell."

I yearned to slap her. I closed my fists to keep from strangling her. Breathing heavily, I rasped, "What do you know about Jill? Do you know my daughter?"

She chuckled. "She was bad. So now she's burning in hell."

"What happened to her? Do you know what happened to her?"

She leaned back in her chair and stretched her legs out in front of her. "Wouldn't you like to know?"

I reached for her shoulder, missed. *"Tell me."*

"Somebody put her in a barrel that had nails sticking out inside it and rolled her down a hill."

Struggling for control, I tried to say calmly, "Regina, please. If you really know something about Jill, please tell me. Don't play games about this."

"Oh, that's right. My house landed on her and all that was left was her shoes!" She chortled. I slammed my fists down on the rickety table and stamped my foot on the peeling linoleum. Her eyes widened disingenuously. "Wow. So now you'll fall through a big crack in the ground and I won't ever have to look at your ugly face again. Right?"

"Regina—"

She stood up. Her chair tipped over backward, and some people, including the guard nearest us, looked in the direction of the clatter. The boy and the old man had apparently finished a game; the boy was dealing again, cards snapping smartly into two piles with a kitty in the middle. Regina said evenly, "I know all kinds of ways for getting rid of bad guys. But my mother's too powerful. I have to keep trying to kill her, but my mother'll never die."

The next day I was to go with Katha to interview another of Regina's foster families. Their farm was miles east of town and our appointment, for reasons that escaped me, was first thing in the morning, so we'd have to be on the road at the crack of dawn.

I couldn't sleep. I couldn't even go to bed. I paced around the house, the yard, the block, puzzling over whether Regina's comments about Jill could have been anything other than throwaway digs at me, cruel scatter-shot bait; whether she could possibly have known my daughter and have information about her; whether I would ever know.

The night was misty. I guessed I was seeing things that weren't there and missing things that were. A knob on the side of a street maple so persistently suggested someone hiding, much like one of the forms monsters had taken in my childhood, that I circled the tree twice, stumbling off the curb. A black dog, shaggier and lower to the ground than the one that had come to my door, probably had been trotting along beside me for a while, because when he turned off into an alley I was aware of his absence. I heard a child's call in the distance, as if it had been repeating itself for some time, but the instant my attention caught and focused on it, it ceased.

I had never dreamed about Jill; maybe she'd been too much in my conscious mind. But frequently there'd been what I'd come to think of, somewhat wryly, as hypna-gogues, whose reality was of a different nature than that of either dreams or waking experiences. That night I was visited by one of those.

Somewhere in the middle distance, I saw Jill being stuffed into her grave. Although she was patently dead, she refused to do what she was told. Her arm kept shooting up out of the hole, middle finger extended. They'd throw more dirt on the arm and it would pretend to be subdued, but then it would spring up again, a gesture of defiance both tragic and infuriating, horrifying and falsely hopeful.

The vision stayed with me, as they do, but it faded from physical sight, and I went home.

The living room couch had been disturbed, pillows askew, upholstery fabric rumpled. I searched, afraid of what I would and would not find. My bed had been lain on, too, the spread still pulled up but holding the outline of a body. Katha was in Jill's bed. I was incredulous. She raised herself on her elbows, gray-blond hair in her face, sideburns shaggy and childlike down her cheeks. "I hope you don't mind," she murmured sleepily. "We have to start so early in the morning, I just thought it'd be easier. I tried to call, but there wasn't any answer. Your door was unlocked. I hope you don't mind—" She sank back among Jill's pillows and I had neither the heart nor the energy to roust her.

Scant hours later, on the way to the Bernardinos' farm in her chugging old pickup so high off the ground I could hardly climb into it without a boost, I demanded, "Did you tell Regina about my daughter?"

Katha glanced at me, then away again. "I thought having a child with troubles might make you credible."

"What did you tell her?"

"Just that your daughter ran away and you hadn't heard from her, and that she'd been in trouble before that."

I pressed grimly. "And how did you know that? We've never talked about her."

Katha hesitated. "Everybody knows, Ruth. It's part of what everybody knows about you."

Molly Bernardino was a dark-haired, energetic woman in her late thirties, several inches taller than I but not unusually tall. Her husband, David, was much taller, considerably heavier, and probably a few years younger, with a full blond beard. They both met us at the door, and their knee-high black dog, too. David, I noticed, was all but scowling, while his wife fluttered and chattered; I had no way of knowing yet whether this was their usual manner or whether our visit was making her nervous and him angry.

We sat on comfortable, dusty, overstuffed chairs in a cluttered little living room. Books were stacked on end tables, piled on the floor. One wall was completely covered by an intricate bookcase, obviously handmade, with nary a right angle and numerous visible gaps where boards didn't quite meet. Under David Bernardino's baleful gaze, I moved several books in order to sit down.

Molly brought strong coffee in colorful mismatched mugs and apple muffins on a cracked blue Rivieraware plate. I was glad then for the rapidity of her movements and the steady talk she kept up from the kitchen, because David made no attempt whatsoever at small talk. Increasingly awkward, we all sat eating and drinking and petting the dog.

Tired of waiting for Katha to take charge, I was about to start the interview when Molly said, "You're here to talk about Regina," and her voice broke.

Yes," said Katha, consulting her notes, although I'd have bet she didn't need to. "She was with you the longest she's been any one place."

"Shouldn't have been that long," David said.

When he didn't continue, I cued him. "Why is that?"

He shook his head. "Suppose you first tell us what's going on." Katha told them, bluntly and without much elaboration.

Molly's hands had flown to her mouth and her eyes were large. "Oh, my God. Oh, my God. That's why we gave her up,"

"We gave her up," David said sternly, getting to his feet, "because we wanted a child." He was addressing Katha and me, although he seemed to be looking at Molly. "Especially my wife. My wife wanted a daughter. That girl was nowhere near a daughter."

Then he strode out of the room, the black dog at his heels. Out of the house; we heard the back door slam. I considered this peculiar, not to mention rude. Katha made a note on her yellow pad, which sometimes is all you can do. Gazing after her husband, Molly said, and I suspected she'd said it numerous times, to outsiders and to David and to herself: "We weren't the right parents for her. We just didn't know how to help her."

Having heard nearly those exact words from countless other adoptive parents as they reneged on promises to children, I became impatient. I saw no point, though, in saying to any of them that the purpose of parenting was somehow both more and less than "helping" your child. What did I, the mother of Jill, know about parenting, anyway?

Katha had nodded and now didn't seem to know what to do next. Molly was lost in a sorrowful reverie. I stifled an exasperated sigh and asked, "What did she do that was so difficult?"

From Katha's glance in my direction, I guessed I hadn't been entirely successful at keeping my tone neutral. Molly looked at me, too, then seemed to make a decision and settled into her chair to tell the story which must by now have had the feel of a legend. "When Regina came to us," she began, "she was a very bright, very loving, very scared little girl. We thought, and the social workers thought, we could build on the first two. But her fear was so deep and pervasive that it consumed more and more of her reality."

Katha brightened. "Do you mean she was schizophrenic?"

"That's what one psychiatrist thought. Another one said she was a borderline personality with psychotic tendencies. There was even one who thought she was a split personality, but Regina never blacked out or anything, and later we found out that that guy was doing his thesis on split personality, so practically every kid he saw got that diagnosis." She laughed bleakly.

"What did she do?" I pressed.

Molly wasn't ready yet to quit the theoretical framework. "She had to construct detailed fantasies in order for her fear to make sense and to keep it under some semblance of control. Otherwise it would have overwhelmed her. She was just a little kid." There were tears in her eyes.

She's worked on this, I thought rather uncharitably, until she's come up with words that give her a semblance of control. "What," I repeated, "did she *do?*"

Molly must have sensed my growing skepticism, for she leaned toward me and began to tick off examples on her fingers. "She was afraid to cross the footbridge over the irrigation ditch. This was early on, so she was still telling us why she did things, and she said her birth mother was a troll hiding under the bridge to eat her. Then for a long time we couldn't have mirrors in the house. She'd smash them and leave the pieces all over the place, sometimes in little barricades along with all the combs and brushes she could find, sometimes just scattered. She had to have stitches in her hands three or four times. She'd go through my purse and break the mirror out of my compact because it was dangerous for me to carry her birth mother around like that."

"I take it she didn't worry about seven years' bad luck," I said, all but laughing. Katha scowled.

"I think," Molly replied solemnly, "she figured she had that coming no matter what she did."

"So she was trying to protect you," Katha said.

Molly nodded. "She loved us. Called David Daddy right from the start." Tears fell. "She never quite knew what to call me."

"I don't think she ever knew her father," Katha said. "It would have been mothers she had an issue with." She was probably right, but I gritted my teeth.

"Once she set fires inside my shoes."

Katha's head shot up. I let her ask, "Why?"

Molly sighed in both regret and, I thought, satisfaction. "It took us a while to figure that one out, because by then she wasn't talking to us much. We finally decided it must have to do with those original Grimm fairy tales, before they were toned down. The evil mother figure was often forced to dance in red-hot slippers until she died." I heard Katha let out her breath.

David never did reappear, and Molly, having told her story, had not much more to tell us except what I already knew, that Regina had gone from their house into a short-term treatment center. They'd lost touch with her, she said. They'd been afraid something like this would happen. As we were taking our leave, the dog came back unaccompanied and pushed his nose into my palm.

On the way home, Katha, breathing a longish silence, asked me, "Did you get the feeling they weren't telling us everything?"

"Nobody ever tells anybody everything." It was one of those unhelpful declarations purporting to mean more than they really do. Katha made no reply to that, for which I couldn't blame her. After a while I deigned to add wryly, "I'd bet on the husband," and Katha nodded.

But it was Molly Bernardino who showed up at my office a few days later. I was immersed in a journal article positing that some infants, because of physical abnormalities in their nervous systems, are born cranky and hard to please. The nature-nurture debate, spurious as it had always seemed to me, showed no sign of running its course any time soon.

I was reading the article with more attention than I thought it deserved when I heard a quick loud knock on my open door. Thinking it was a student come to offer some plea or bargain for a better grade on last week's exam, or my department chair with another committee assignment for me to refuse, I snapped, "Come in," without looking up and finished the "conclusions" section, which concluded, remarkably, that we are products of a complex interaction between nature and nurture.

Disgusted, and gratified to be so, I tossed the journal into the chaos on my overburdened desk. I couldn't quite place the woman standing before me with a book in her hands.

When she spoke, though, I knew who she was; her context for me was in her voice, telling a story, making sense of things. "Dr. Torgesson?" It was a question, but since she obviously knew who I was, I didn't know what I was being asked.

"Last time I looked," I said stupidly.

Katha loomed behind her then. "I said we could meet in your office," she explained a little breathlessly. "I hope you don't mind. I don't have any place—Mrs. Bernardino says there's something else we should know about Regina." They both came on in and Katha pulled the door shut, a mostly symbolic gesture, since sounds traveled with astonishing clarity through various ducts above the ceiling tiles.

Molly had already started. "Regina almost broke up my marriage. David really resented her. He's the one who insisted we had to give her up. I wanted to keep on being her family even if she couldn't live with us. I wanted to adopt her." She was crying again. "I loved her. I still love her. He never did."

On the one hand, I couldn't imagine why any sane person would love a child like Regina. On the other hand, more dangerously, I couldn't imagine why anyone would not. Left, then, with nothing to say on the matter, I waited.

Finally Molly went on grimly. "I didn't tell him everything. I didn't tell him about this book."

Vaguely she held it out, in neither Katha's direction nor mine. A beat or two passed, and then I was the one who reached to take it.

The young-adult hardcover mythology primer had a fringed bookmark at about the midpoint. "I found this under her bed after she left," Molly said.

When no instructions were forthcoming, I sighed resignedly, opened the book, and read aloud the passage girlishly underlined, highlighted, and bracketed in lavender ink:

" 'The people believed that the king was right next to the gods. So it was his fault when the crops failed or they lost a battle or something else went wrong. He ought to be punished. But they couldn't afford to really lose the king, and besides, he wouldn't allow it.

" 'So somebody would be chosen to be sacrificed instead. It was a great honor. For a little while the stand-in was treated like a king, wore fancy clothes and jewels, and told everybody what to do. Then they burned him at the stake or buried him alive.' "

In the margin, Regina, I presumed, had printed, "So did it work?"

"I was her stand-in," Molly explained eagerly. "She couldn't afford to really get rid of her mother, or her mother wouldn't allow it, so she was going to get rid of me instead."

"She'd have killed you," Katha breathed.

Molly drew herself up. I swore she was proud. "Because she loved me," she declared. "Because I was starting to be her mother." The neatness and plausibility of it made me shiver.

By the end of the summer, Regina Dempsey had been sentenced to a juvenile detention facility until she turned eighteen. Katha tried twice to visit, but Regina wouldn't see her; I didn't try. She had become less than completely real to me, as if I'd imperfectly made her up. But here I am, telling her story.

Katha, though, worried the mystery a while longer. Why, specifically, had Regina *stabbed* Carol Burroughs, and why in a line like an incision from her throat to her pubis? Eventually she settled on Little Red Riding Hood for her paradigm, the version in which the wolf is slit open and filled with stones, so when he bends to get a drink from the river he topples in and drowns. This had always seemed like overkill to me, so to speak; as if having your belly cut open and filled with rocks wouldn't be enough.

After that, Katha dropped out of school. I haven't seen her again. For a while I thought about her, spun out her story if she found a place for herself and if she didn't. Neither ending ever quite seemed to fit.

I haven't seen Jill again, either. Hers is every tale—and there are many—of a child lost in the woods, lost to the grave, lost to her own willful spirit. Doubtless that's not what she'd have recounted about herself, but it works for me, and it's become so much a part of my own story that I hardly have to think about her anymore.

But I did get a dog. A huge black dog, waist-high on me, from the Dumb Friends' League; the woman guessed that his size alone had kept him unclaimed, and he was on the euthanasia list by the time I came looking for him. Intensely black, he has yellow eyes that sometimes, in the right stray light, glow like balls of fire. He never willingly leaves my side, and I'm less and less willing to leave him; when classes resume next term, I think I'll take him to school with me. I won't say why. People can come up with their own interpretations.

Or maybe I'll say: He's my guardian. He's my familiar. He's the spectral representation of everything I've lost. He's my guide.

Late last night he and I went for a walk, as we often do when neither of us can sleep. I keep a leash in my pocket for the sake of appearance, but it's silly to think of this dog on a leash.

At some point in our wanderings he left my side, and just as I began to worry he danced up to me and laid something at my feet. An arm. A young girl's arm and hand, middle finger extended, a ring I recognized.

I cried out, stepped back, dropped to my knees. It was a branch with twigs and leaves, and the dog was dancing eagerly for me to toss it. I grasped the defiant branch by its thicker end and threw it as hard as I could along the sidewalk in a direction I did not intend to go. The black dog bounded after it and brought it back.

Three times the big dog materialized out of the mist ambered by streetlights and deposited the arm-shaped branch in my path. At last, desperate, I scrabbled in somebody's flower bed next to the sidewalk and managed to bury the thing. The dog didn't try to stop me, nor did he offer help.

Afraid it wasn't deep enough, I pounded on the soil with a brick from the hapless gardener's border, tamping, beating, keeping Jill's image firm in my mind, saying her name. At last it stayed where I put it, out of my sight.

This is a story only the black dog and I know.

Locks

NEIL GAIMAN

*Neil Gaiman is a transplanted Briton who now
lives in the American Midwest. He is the author
of the award-winning* Sandman *series of
graphic novels, co-author (with Terry Pratchett)
of the novel* Good Omens, *and most recently
author of the novel and BBC TV series* Nev-
erwhere. *He also collaborated with artist Dave
McKean on the brilliant book* Mr. Punch, *and
the children's book,* The Day I Swapped My
Dad for Two Goldfish. *In addition, Gaiman
is a talented poet and short-story writer whose
work has been published in* Snow White,
Blood Red; Touch Wood: Narrow Houses
2; Ruby Slippers, Golden Tears; Midnight
Graffiti; *and several editions of* The Year's
Best Fantasy and Horror. *The recent collection* Smoke and Mirrors *reprints most of his
shorter work.*

*"Locks" was inspired by the experience of
telling his young daughter "Goldilocks"—over
and over and over. Within three months of its
writing, "Goldilocks" became a slightly odder
story, because by then, his daughter was convinced that a witch ought to live in the three
bears' house too, and nothing Gaiman said
could disabuse her of this, despite the fact that
the witch never turned up in the story. And,
Gaiman says, "if you'd asked for the poem now,*

you might have got something very different—after all, she's now a fan of 'Cinderella,' and 'Rumpelstiltskin,' and 'The Sleeping Beauty,' and 'Dick Whittington' . . ." (And this was back during the winter of 1997.)

Locks

We owe it to each other to tell stories,
as people simply, not as father and daughter.
I tell it to you for the hundredth time:

"There was a little girl, called Goldilocks,
for her hair was long and golden,
and she was walking in the Wood and she saw—"

"—cows." You say it with certainty,
remembering the strayed heifers we saw in the woods
behind the house, last month.

"Well, yes, perhaps she saw cows,
but also she saw a house."

"—a great big house," you tell me.

"No, a little house, all painted, neat and tidy."

"A great big house."
You have the conviction of all two-year-olds.
I wish I had such certitude.

"Ah. Yes. A great big house.
And she went in . . ."

I remember, as I tell it, that the locks
of Southey's heroine had silvered with age.
The Old Woman and the Three Bears . . .
Perhaps they had been golden once, when she was
     a child.

And now, we are already up to the porridge,
"And it was too—"
"—hot!"
"And it was too—"
"—cold!"
And then it was, we chorus, *"just right."*

The porridge is eaten, the baby's chair is shattered,
Goldilocks goes upstairs, examines beds, and sleeps,
unwisely.

But then the bears return.
Remembering Southey still, I do the voices:
Father Bear's gruff boom scares you, and you delight
     in it.

When I was a small child and heard the tale,
if I was anyone I was Baby Bear,
my porridge eaten, and my chair destroyed,
my bed inhabited by some strange girl.

You giggle when I do the baby's wail,
"Someone's been eating my porridge, and they've eaten
     it—"

"All up," you say. A response it is,
Or an amen.

The bears go upstairs hesitantly,
their house now feels desecrated. They realize
what locks are for. They reach the bedroom.

"Someone's been sleeping in my bed."
And here I hesitate, echoes of old jokes,
soft-core cartoons, crude headlines, in my head.

One day your mouth will curl at that line.
A loss of interest, later, innocence.
Innocence; as if it were a commodity.
"And if I could," my father wrote to me,
huge as a bear himself, when I was younger,
"I would dower you with experience, without
    experience."
And I, in my turn, would pass that on to you.
But we make our own mistakes. We sleep
unwisely.
It is our right. It is our madness and our glory.
The repetition echoes down the years.
When your children grow; when your dark locks
    begin to silver,
when you are an old woman, alone with your three
    bears,
what will you see? What stories will you tell?

*"And then Goldilocks jumped out of the window
and she ran—*
Together, now: *"All the way home."*

And then you say, *"Again. Again. Again."*

We owe it to each other to tell stories.

These days my sympathy's with Father Bear.
Before I leave my house I lock the door,
and check each bed and chair on my return.

Again.

Again.

Again.

Marsh-Magic

ROBIN MCKINLEY

Robin McKinley lives in Hampshire, England, with her husband, writer Peter Dickinson, three whippets, and over four hundred rose bushes. Two of her previous novels, Beauty: A Retelling of the Story of Beauty and the Beast *and* Deerskin, *have been inspired by fairy tales, as is her most recent novel,* Rose Daughter. *Perhaps her best-known books are* The Blue Sword *and* The Hero and the Crown, *laid in the magical kingdom of Damar. Damar is also the setting for several of the stories in her most recent collection,* The Knot in the Grain and Other Stories. *McKinley also edited the World Fantasy Award-winning anthology* Imaginary Lands.*

McKinley and Dickinson are planning a joint anthology of "wet stories"—stories about water magic. McKinley wanted to be in one of our fairy-tale anthologies and realized one of the things she and her husband missed in roughing out their anthology was a "marsh story." McKinley is also ". . . very hot on Girls Who Do Things and . . . 'Rumpelstiltskin' is very high on my list of Get Rid of That Hopeless Git of a Girl. But I wouldn't go so far as to say that 'Marsh-Magic' is based on 'Rumpelstiltskin.' It's more like one of the bigger turnips that went in the pot."

Marsh-Magic

There was a family of kings who had been the rulers of their country for many generations, son following father and his son after him and then his son's son; and they were thereby a wonder in the countries of their neighbors, whose ruling families rose and fell and conquered and were conquered in the ordinary way.

The very first king of that unbroken line, Rustafulus I, had had a mage, and this mage had said to his master, "Lord, you will rule long and the country will prosper under your rule, and the people will smile as they say your name. But you need to get a son who will rule as long and as wisely, for this is your immortality, that Rustafulus II shall be the name that the sons of your people speak smiling, and Rustafulus III after him shall be in the mouths of your people's sons' sons."

The king said, "I have thought of all this myself already; but how is it to be achieved? For often, it seems to me, the stronger the father the weaker the son."

Said the mage: "I was myself an orphan, raised by lions in the desert, as you know."

"So often you have told the story in my hearing," replied the king.

"Thus," the mage continued, unperturbed by the king's interruption, "I see all people differently than you who have lived among them from your first moments breathing in this world, wet from your mother's womb. And what I have seen which pertains to your future sons is this: there are women who live in the wild marsh country within the borders of your kingdom who are as strong and brave as any man, and cleverer than any other woman. You could buy the haughtiest princess on the continent, for you are a great man, and all who watched would know what this meant; which is what an ordinary man would do. But I say to you: you shall marry a marshwoman."

Said the king: "I am no farmer, to take a wife with marsh-mud on her face to bed, because she has good bone, as one might buy a mare." For his pride was strong in him, and uncanny things were said of the folk of the marshes; and he looked at his mage with suspicion, for a mage was an uncanny creature himself, and the king had spoken to no lion who claimed him as a foster son.

The mage, knowing what was in his master's mind, said smoothly: "You are yourself and unique, my king, and a marshwoman is a princess when her face and hands are washed and she is dressed in the gowns of a princess. I say to you, the weakness of the women of the marshes is less than the weakness of other women. A marshwoman will not sap your son's strength in the womb as another might. For the way of the mother on an unborn babe is mysterious, and even I cannot control it, I who may order all else—the rising of winds and the falling of seas; even can I call fire out of the heart of a mountain—all answer to my command, my lord, but you, and a mother's gifts to the child she carries."

Said the king: "I have heard a tale that the marshfolk never stand in battle, for they are cowards to the heart of them, and cannot. The women may be as strong as cart-horses and I will have none of them to breed my son."

Said the mage: "It is true, the story you have heard, that the men cannot stand in battle. But that is because all the virtue of the race is in its women. There is a magic in the wild marshes that lie on the border of your land, a woman's magic, which runs under the dry lands, invisible, like a seam of old stone beneath a field, that you know not till you go to plow the field, and break your coulter. I say to you, marry a marshwoman, as you would marry the daughter of the king you conquer, that his people will follow you without question. Marry a marshwoman, and see she does your will; and the land will know your sovereignty as the cart-horse knows the collar and bit."

Said the king grandly: "I have a mind to drain the marshes, and plant them, for after so many years the land there must be even richer than the rest of my land; and the crops that grew there, or what is wrought of them, would fetch a high price anywhere in the world."

There was a pause while the mage considered, for he was not so skilled in handling kings as he would become. At last he said: "This land has lain vacant of a king's hand for how long?"

"Twenty generations of man," said the king carelessly, "but that is all myth and nursery tale."

"I do not listen to myths and nursery-tales," said the mage. "Lions have no use for them, for the cubs are quiet on command of their elders. But I know the history of this land because I am a mage, and I say to you that these dry lands are yours, and the crops that will grow there, and what is wrought of them, will fetch good prices in many cities of the world—but that you will lose all you have gained if you waste your strength upon so hopeless a project as draining the marshes."

The king looked at his mage, and said, "What is it you do not tell me? First you say that I am to marry a marshwoman because she will bear me a strong son, and

then you say I hold my kingdom only so long as I do not
trouble the stinking bogland that divides it. I administer
my kingdom by no man's permission, neither dirty
marsh-hopper nor . . . mage."

The mage, who had not yet learned never to be angry
at the pettiness of kings, said, "You are strong beyond
most mortals; if I stood against you with nothing but a
sword, you would strike me down; nor could I lead an
army, for I do not speak the language of the common
soldier. But I am a mage, and I have been of use to you
with my mage's wisdom, which has so little to do with
the language of the common soldier.

"I know certain things about the balance between your
dry lands and its marshes, for the chief thing a mage is
always concerned with is balance. It is through the strivings of the mages of this world that the world continues
to possess such good things as sunlight and water and
beasts and the turning of the seasons that gives us crops;
and through the strivings of mages it has thus far happened that the world has survived even the vanity and
arrogance of kings."

Muttered the king: "My people will not like it; they
will know she is only a marshwoman despite her fine
gown; and a king's rule finally depends on his people's
goodwill, however strong he be."

The mage laughed. "Your people will revere you for
your boldness. Do you not know that the goddess of
spring, to whom they pray the most fervently, to whom
they dedicate the grandest of the seasonal festivals, who
they believe makes the seeds germinate and the rain fall,
is the spirit of the marshlands? No dry-lander dares marry
a marshwoman."

The king looked at his mage and thought, I do not
know anything of this man but what he chooses to tell
me, because he is a mage. But his advice has been good
and his help unwearying in these long, hard years just
past that have earned me this kingdom. If he wished the
kingship for himself, would he not merely take it? For the
king was unaware of certain bindings that lay upon a
mage by virtue of his mageship. Aloud he said: "Very

well. I believe you, for you have called the stormwind, and pulled the top off a mountain, and I have seen you do it. Find me a marshwoman to marry, and make for me a son as strong as I am, who will hold the country I have won for him. But never again do I wish to hear of the vanity and arrogance of kings."

"The making of the son I leave to you," said the mage more smoothly than ever, as if no harsh words had been spoken on either side, "but I will stand by you and him till he comes of age. I will go now, and begin the search, and by this time next year you will have a wife to bear you a strong son."

A year from the day of this conversation, the king's new wife had been carrying the king's son for six months.

The mage, too, had married at about this time, although no one knew it for some years. The news, when it came quietly twisting through the people's talk as gossip, was a surprise and a relief. The king's people might have admired their king for taking a marshwoman to wife; their feelings about his chief counselor were more mixed.

There were no stories of mages living among ordinary folk as Rustafulus's mage did; there were tales, of course, of the mages who lived alone for centuries in the mountains, and of the wandering mages who stayed occasionally in a village for purposes they did not reveal, carelessly healing sheep and pigs in exchange for nights in someone's hayloft and a few good meals. (No one ever offered to feed a mage anything but the best he had.) But everyone knew that a mage's formidable powers did not end with the healing of domestic animals, and it was not only Rustafulus I who had seen his mage tear the top off a mountain and call up a stormwind. Were the stories of the centuries-old mages accurate? That was the question that came up the most often. Perhaps they were a series of mages dedicated to one enchanted spot, like solitary priests serving a lonely temple generation after generation. Surely a mage's powers are too dangerous to be held by anyone with more than one human lifetime's experience of the world? What could not such a person do? Would not ordinary mortals seem no more than dogs?

But no one knew these answers, and no one dared ask the mage. So the news of the mage's marriage was welcome; so welcome, perhaps, that no one wished to question it, just as no one questioned the mage's cool comment that he had kept it a secret for so long only because his wife was a quiet creature and wanted no fuss made. That no one even met her seemed quite like the sort of thing a mage would do; just as it seemed fully in character that he should not have mentioned that his wife bore a son close to the time the king's wife had borne the king's son, till both were half grown. Even then the mage's son was but rarely seen at court, till he had won his mage-mark and was ready to stand at Rustafulus II's elbow, as his father had stood at Rustafulus I's.

Rustafulus II was strong and brave and wise, as kings are wise, as his father had been; and Rustafulus II's mage appeared as deep in magecraft as his father had been. So like his father he was indeed that Rustafulus I had once joked that there had been no mother at all; that his mage had boiled up a brew which shaped itself solid into two legs and two arms and one head and one body, and that the mage had then drawn his own lineaments upon the form and breathed his own breath into it till it had become yet another of himself. The mage had smiled with a faint air of dutiful politeness, but had remarked, in a voice that was rather too smooth, that a mage was still a man. The king had come to dislike his mage's voice when it was too smooth, and perhaps for this reason chose not to comment upon the astonishing similarity between father and son again.

The king's death was an occasion of much pomp and gloomy ritual, but the first mage's death went unrecorded. He had appeared at his master's great funeral but had said no word to anyone; it was his son, soon after, who informed the court that his father had retired, and would not be seen among them again.

But the mage's son served the king's son as his father had served Rustafulus I (though there were fewer wars to be fought), including, when Rustafulus II was two-and-thirty years of age, shortly after his father's death and the first mage's retirement, bringing to him a marshwoman, whom he married and got with child. Thus was born Rustafulus III, and in due course IV, who also was as strong and brave as his father and grandfather and great-grandfather—or nearly; for perhaps he was a little marked by the sadness of his childhood, which was that his mother, when he was but one year of age, grew ill of a wasting sickness, and withdrew to apartments at the center of the palace, and was not seen again by any but her few maidservants, chosen for their discretion, for the remainder of her short life.

Rustafulus IV was named The Merciful, and the country prospered under him no less than it had under any Rustafulus before; but while Rustafulus V was born in due course to a bride Rustafulus IV's mage had brought to him, Rustafulus V was a different sort of man than his grandsires, no less strong and brave—as was proven when a new ruling family in a neighboring country thought to annex some of Rustafulus's territory—but possessing a wisdom of a different sort, a sort that made his people a little afraid of him, unlike that of the first four kings of his line.

Well, said his people of him, a line that goes on too long without change weakens at last; unless, perhaps, you are a mage. Rustafulus's people had adjusted to the fact that for every new king there was a new mage, because there now lay a tale in the folklore that the mage served the unequivocal purpose of finding the correct new marshwoman for that king to marry; though no one could remember where the story had first come from. Nor did their belief in their queens' binding their country together, wet and dry, so that it was one country in a way no dryland king had ever before held it, stop them from noticing that each mage looked exactly like the last: tall, pale, dark-haired and dark-eyed, ageless and expressionless. Everyone knew that Rustafulus II had been shorter than his father, and Rustafulus III taller than either; that Rustafulus IV had been his grandfather's height but more slightly

built than any of his sires, and his hair had been paler,
and had curled, while the others' hair hung straight. The
knowledge that the kings' mages married and got sons
and died was reassuring, as far as it went, if a little scant-
ily proven; for the wives of the kings were seen, dim in
the refulgent glory of their husbands, whereas no mage's
wife, so far as anyone knew, had ever been seen at all.

There was one universal characteristic about the de-
scendants of Rustafulus I, which was that they all died
much younger than their patriarch. Rustafulus I had been
well into middle age when he had finished winning his
country; he had sired Rustafulus II when he was fifty-
three, and had died at eighty-six. But Rustafulus II and
all those kings after him died at around sixty, and in the
year after each old king's death the new king married a
marshwoman, found for him by his new mage.

So it went on, generation after generation, each king
seeming the reincarnation of some one of his grandsires:
either Rustafulus I, Rustafulus IV, or Rustafulus V—although the type of Rustafulus V became more common,
and that of Rustafulus I less so. And with Rustafulus XIX
there was a new rumor among the people: that the line
of these kings appeared at last to be weakening.

Nonetheless Rustafulus XIX, who was one of those
who resembled Rustafulus IV, though he was not particularly merciful, ruled a quiet land, and got a son by the
bride his mage brought him, like all his sires before him.
But after an uneventful life, Rustafulus XIX did something
very extraordinary: he lived past the age of sixty-three.

In his sixty-fifth year it was plain that more sheaves
had been laid upon the spring goddess's altar than was
usual, and anyone who was looking might have noticed
that the people averted their eyes when the king's processions passed—though they cheered just as loudly. There
was another new tale told, even more disturbing than the
increasingly inauspicious fact of the king's age, which was
that Rustafulus XIX's mage, during those unprecedented
years the king lived past sixty-three, began to look haggard and old.

He was accustomed to stand at the king's right elbow

on the days the king heard civil cases, and to ride beside, or in the carriage with, the king on his processions; and so although he had little if anything to do directly with his king's people, they not infrequently saw him. The sword-straight bearing and silent but startling presence, promising great secrets and unimaginable strengths, of each of the nineteen mages were part of the tale of the Rustafulus kings. Yet, in those last years of Rustafulus XIX's life, this mage was seen to stoop, to lean on the king's chair, even to mutter to himself; and occasionally he turned his head round suddenly, as if he heard something no one else had heard.

But Rustafulus XIX did finally die, at the age of seventy-one, and the mourning at his funeral was very pronounced, as if his people felt they needed to make up for something. The mage was there—or was it his son?—looking as cool and potent and self-possessed as all the stories told of his forebears.

While the symptoms of decline were perhaps more conspicuous in Rustafulus XX, it is possible that the difference was only that Rustafulus XIX's temper had not been tried by too many years as crown prince. When his mage came, a few weeks after his father's funeral, to speak to Rustafulus XX of his future bride, the new king was not in a good mood. He had not been overfond of his father and resented the extra years of waiting for his marriage on no better grounds than that it was the tradition he not marry till he was king. "She must be beautiful," said Rustafulus XX to his mage.

"She will be beautiful," said his mage, neither his voice nor his face offering any clue to his thoughts. "If I have your will, my lord, I will go in search of her at once."

"Yes, yes," said Rustafulus XX, "and in a year and a day you will have brought me a wife, except that it never takes you—has taken any of you," he added, and giggled, "that long." He turned away abruptly, found himself facing a small table with a carafe of wine and a goblet on it, picked up the goblet, and stood staring at it vaguely. The light twinkled off the dark surface of the wine; the king smiled. He looked up, saw his mage still motionless, and said, "Well, go on, then," sharply, as if he were ordering a page to bring him more wine. He turned his back this time, raised the goblet, and drank.

The mage stared at the back of his master for a long moment and then turned and left him, without turning and bowing at the door, as all the king's servants were required to do, although if anyone had been there to see the omission, there was no one in all the kingdom who would have said a word to the mage about it.

The country of the Rustafulus kings was low and green. It had no mountains, though it had many knobby hills and much fine forest; and it had good rivers and good seaports, and its merchant trade was brisk. Mountains might have been useful to protect it from its enemies, but it had not had enemies for a long time; and while a Rustafulus sat on the throne, its neighbors had thus far continued to prefer peace. Its one obvious geographic drawback was its marshland.

It had many marshes. Not far from the capital city was a vast fenland, stretching many leagues. It might have provided some deterrent to hypothetical enemies if it had lain on a border, but it lay instead inconveniently between the country's biggest seaport and the farmland that produced much of its best exportable goods. It was dank and dreary enough, with thin, poor, acid soil, useless to the farmland which pressed up against its one side, or as any extension of the docks and shipyards of the port, which crowded in as much as they could on the other side; and when the wind was in the wrong quarter, furthermore, it stank. Portions of it had been dragged a number of times over the generations, and while this had yielded peat for local fires, nothing seemed possible to be done about its drainage, or lack of it, and it persistently refilled itself within a few years and became just as damp, ugly, and treacherous as it had been before. But it was not truly wild, and there were paths through it, and a cautious traveler was safe enough, and certain traders earned their

living by carrying other folks' goods between the farmland and the sea.

To the east, however, there were marshes that were
dangerous for any to cross, where unwary travelers might
go so far astray that they died before they found their
way out again; or where one might fall into a sucking
mire, and drown or suffocate. If there had been anything
beyond those marshes but rocks and, beyond the rocks,
desert, where lions roamed, there might have been more
travelers and more accidents; as it was, it was rare that
anyone wished to go that way.

There were tales, of course, about the denizens of this
marsh. The goddess of the spring festival lived there,
somewhere, but no one really believed she breathed and
took up space and walked on the ground like an ordinary
mortal. And there were the usual sorts of stories about
ghosts and fairies and slimy monsters with mossy teeth,
and the figures of voluptuous women who sang to lost
traveling men, and drew them to the bogs where they
drowned. But people lived there too, almost-ordinary hu-
mankind, who had learned the safe ways, and how to tell
when they became unsafe, and how to find new safe ones
instead; who lived meagerly off the young shoots of the
dubl tree, which no one but a marsh-dweller (it was said)
could be bothered to gather, and off the fruits of the
chork-berry bush, which no one telling the tales had ever
seen. One of the few things that was well known about
the marshfolk was that they ate no meat; one of the others
was that they knew where the goddess lived. It was a
term of half derision, but the other half awe, to call someone a marsh-dweller; it meant the person was dreamy in
a way that the namer did not understand and was inclined to be alarmed by. And while the dry-landers re-
vered their kings for marrying marshwomen, they were
pleased that the queens were so little seen abroad, except
at the spring festivals, when sometimes the queens laid
flowers and a sheaf of last year's corn on the goddess's
altar.

It was to the eastern marshes that the mage of Rustafulus XX went after his brief conversation with the king

about his future queen. He walked a trail that no one but
a mage, or a marsh-dweller, could have seen or followed,
and on the second day after he had crossed the marshland
border, he came upon a young woman washing her hair
in a pool. The pool was clear, though the water of the
marshes was generally not clear, and the mage said to
her, "Rustafulus XX needs a queen."

The woman looked up at him, pulling her fingers
through her hair, and as the waterdrops fell from her
hands they sparkled in a manner not at all like water. "I
will tell my people what you say," she said, and bent
again, and dipped her hair into the water. She was very
lithe, for she sat on the bank with her legs crossed, and
leaned forward, and rubbed her scalp with her fingers,
and all the mage could see of her was the nape of her
neck above the water, and her back, lying smoothly over
her crossed legs.

The mage did not allow his temper to rise, for he was
a mage, and she was a mere marsh-dweller, but he said
very coldly: "You know the terms of our bond."

The woman could hear underwater, for all the marsh-
dwellers could, and she sat up straight again, and threw
her hair back, arching her spine so that it did not fall
against her clothing but down toward the ground; and it
was so long that it trailed upon the ground behind her
hips. She picked up a length of cloth that lay beside her,
gray as the water and green as the bank, and wrapped it
once around her head, and then curled the tail of her hair
into its folds, and twisted it round again, till she wore a
turban almost as high as she was, sitting cross-legged on
the bank. Then she looked at the mage again and spoke
as coolly as he had done: "Yes. I know the terms of our
bond."

She rose to her feet as easily as she had bent low over
her crossed legs. With her turban, she was taller than he
was. She would have turned and walked away from him,
but he reached out and seized her wrist.

"You shall not play with me," he said.

She said nothing at all, but waited, and finally he
loosed her. "Tomorrow morning," she said, "we will be

ready for you. If you wish, you may sleep under my parents' roof tonight, and eat our food."

"The roof of a marsh-dweller?" said the mage. "I prefer my cloak."

She did not think he would waste his mage-sight on her—or perhaps she did not care if he did. As soon as she knew the trees hid her from any ordinary following gaze, she broke into a run. The cloth around her hair came loose and fell behind her, and she did not notice, and her wet hair soaked her shoulders and back and chilled her skin, and she did not notice. She came to the small clearing where her parents' house was, and threw herself down upon the soft green moss at their doorstep, and wept.

Her mother found her, and knelt beside her, and put a hand on her damp shoulder. She sat up, and turned around. "I did not believe it," she said. "I did not believe. But he has come, and we must meet tomorrow, and one of us go with him! Ah! She will die in that hard, dry city; she will die, whoever she is. Oh, Mother, it is a cruel fate that we still bear, after twenty generations!"

Her mother stroked her daughter's wet hair back from her tear-stained face, and said, "It is. It is the best our mothers and fathers of twenty generations ago could find to do; none of us had been forced to bargain with a mage before, and we were . . . we were . . ." Her mother stopped, and looked away from her, over her shoulder.

The daughter said, "What is it?"

Her mother sighed. "Ah, dearest heart, it is nothing. The story has been told for twenty generations and some of the details have doubtless gone a little wrong in all those years. I have often thought if it had been I who was chosen, on the last meeting day, I would not have had the strength. . . . Come. We must tell the others."

The marshfolk knew the time of summons was near, for even they had heard of the death of the king, though none had left their beloved wetlands to attend his funeral. When the news of the mage's arrival went round, the young unmarried women whose moon-cycles had begun at least four years ago gathered together, separately from the rest, and looked into each other's eyes, thinking to see some token, some brand, that would tell who must go with the mage; looked eagerly and cravenly into each other's eyes, each wanting the mage's companion not to be herself, each wanting the next queen not to be any of her friends, her cousins; and they were all cousins, in fact as well as in affections, for the numbers of the marshfolk were few.

That night, the story was told once again of how, twenty generations ago, a mage had come from nowhere, over mountains, over deserts, over clouds in the skies, had come to one small corner of a large continent, and said to one battling lord rather than another, "I can make you king, I am a mage, and these are my powers, if you will allow me to align my strength with yours."

But before the mage had gone to the battling lordling who became Rustafulus I, he had had another interview of another sort.

Now, the marsh-dwellers have their own magic. The stories of the dry-landers are true so far. It is also true that they are bound to peace on account of that magic; that their magic runs in their blood so strongly that should any one of them do murder, the murderer would fall dead even as did the victim; and it made no difference if this happened on the battlefield or in a private duel; face-to-face, or from ambush. Or so went the story, for no marsh-dweller had tested it for more generations than twenty.

Now, mages, too, are bound to peace; but the magic a mage learns to handle is a trickier thing, and it does not run in the blood in the same way; the talent for it does, but not the thing itself, and a clever enough mage may hold it in his hand, as he might hold the end of a chain looped around the neck of a dragon or a tiger, and use it as he will, so long as he is clever enough to keep the chain tight, and not let the beast turn upon him. Rustafulus's mage was one of this sort, and the chains he held were around the neck of a dragon called Power and a tiger called Glory. He could not make Rustafulus his puppet, for true mortal strength may not be sapped by magic, it can only be killed outright. But the mage guessed he might stand less than half a step behind a strong mortal king, at the king's shoulder, whispering in his ear and gesturing with his hand; and the mage thought that, with time, more yet might be done. He knew the rules of the magic he wielded, but he had even greater confidence in his own strength to win his heart's desire.

The mage, because this is the sort of thing mages know, knew of the country that became Rustafulus's kingdom. He knew of the marshes, and of the particular magic that runs in the marshfolk's blood, and of how that magic ties the wet lands to the dry; and it was for these reasons that he came to this land rather than to some other, to stand behind the shoulder of a king of this country, rather than of some other; and he was pleased that circumstances gave him so ready a binding to this king. And perhaps it amazed him—so went the marshfolk's tales—that no mage like him had ever tried what he would win. But perhaps there had never been a mage like him—one strong enough to see a chance and squeeze it in his hand till its shape was what he desired.

But—so too went the tales of the marshfolk—that mage, first come to the lands he would shortly help win for the battling lordling who would become Rustafulus I, walked far into the marshes, paying little heed to what he did, for he was preoccupied with thoughts of his own future. When he came to himself from his deep thoughts, he realized he was lost; for the air of the marsh confused him, and his sense of direction went round and round, and he felt himself in the grip of a magic he did not know, and he was afraid. But fear, to him, was an anathema almost as potent as poison, and as he walked he cried aloud, not in fear but in fury. And so it was that when he met with the marshfolk, he wanted only to curse them, and narrowly missed forgetting why he had come among them at all.

And so it was that when he struck his bargain with them, it was as bitter a bargain as he could make it, and this was very bitter indeed, for he was a powerful mage.

He came out of the marshes again, and perhaps he

seemed much the same as before, for there was no one to say otherwise. Rustafulus went on winning all his battles, because he now had the strength of a mage following his own strength and that of his army; and when Rustafulus was crowned, there was no question but that he had created with blood and sweat the right to call himself king.

Then his mage said to him, "You shall marry a woman of the marshes, for the blood of this country runs in their veins, and as you tie your blood to theirs, so shall your sons and your sons' sons rule forever."

And Rustafulus said, "I will do it."

Her name was Mthonel, and she bore her husband a son a year and a day after their wedding, and though she lived many years, she was rarely seen after that; not even, so went the rumors, by the king. But she emerged once a year to lay a sheaf of last year's corn at the feet of the altar of the goddess during the spring festival, and the king's people looked at her greedily, and wished her to smile at them, and then were glad when she disappeared for another year.

Nor did she bear any other children but the first.

But Rustafulus II held the kingdom after his father, and when he married a woman of the marshes she too bore him a son a year and a day after their wedding, and she too bore no further children to the king, but Rustafulus II also grew to be a strong king, whose understanding of how to hold his country seemed instinctive, as if the blood of the land itself ran in his veins.

The marshfolk knew older stories than those of the conquering Rustafulus I. Forty generations before Rustafulus XX, there had been another king, and he had tried to fight the marsh-dwellers. He knew the story that they could not kill any human being, and he supposed they could kill no animal either, for they were said to live on green honey and btharrum, which was an herb so bitter that even those dry-folk with catarrh, for which btharrum was a known remedy, could rarely bring themselves to use it. This king thought he would exterminate the marsh-folk, and drain their wetland, and have a fine kingdom.

But somehow his armies never found the marsh-dwellers to do battle with them; nor would the trees burn, even when dry tinder was brought many miles by those same armies (increasingly afflicted by a form of wasting fever with catarrh). Nor would any drained marshland stay drained. The smaller boglands near the capital city and the port silently grew boggy again, however many channels were laid and banks built, as soon as the work stopped; but the wild eastern marshes never grew one whit less wet in the first place, however deep the diggers plunged their spades.

But the marsh-dwellers knew they were in danger, and spoke among themselves, for their seers told them there would come a day that another, and more crafty, king would seize their land for his kingdom; and that when that day came, mislaying the safe paths and sending catarrhs would not do to prevent his victory. That was forty generations ago; that was where their tales began.

When Rustafulus I's mage came to them, other questions had arisen among them, for in the last twenty generations they had watched many would-be kings attempt to set their hold over the dry lands that were woven among the marshlands, and fail. And they had come to believe that while they themselves set hand to no weapon, that although their own hands were clean of a violence they knew would kill them, that was not the whole truth. The marshfolk knew the dry-folk carried no binding magic in their blood. They had despised the dry-folk for this lack; but they came to wonder if perhaps they bore some responsibility to their dry-land kin, who sank wells deep into their dry lands for the water they too needed to live; water that ran into their lands from the marshes. The marshfolk feared that the deaths of the many dry-folk in the battles of would-be kings were on their consciences.

Their seers had no help for them. Over the generations the marshfolk's vitality declined, and they believed that a curse had fallen on them as a result of all the dry-land lives lost. As the marshland shared its underground watercourses with the dry lands it lay among, so the blood of those fallen in battle soaked into the ground and was carried back to the marshland by those same watercourses, and the tang of blood shed to no purpose sapped the marshlanders' strength and will.

Once there had been many communities of marshfolk, scattered over all the marshlands; at last there was but one left, buried at the heart of the wild eastern marsh, wearied by a long, nameless grief. When Rustafulus I's mage came to them, they were ready for him, or so they thought; but they were dismayed by the violence in him, and perhaps did not make so good a bargain as they might have done. But this much they won: that their wetland should be left to them in peace; and that wet and dry should be united under one king. And by the strength of this king and that of his heirs, there should be no more fighting, no more killing, no more blood soaking into the earth and the earth's waters.

All the young women who gathered at dawn the next morning knew the stories, and knew that so long as the kings of the dry-folk held the land through their marsh-dweller mothers, the marshes were safe. That their ancestors twenty generations ago had made the right decision was proved by the fact that the babies born to the marsh-folk since then had almost without exception been healthy and thriving, and had grown up to be wise and purposeful adults; surely this was enough. For twenty generations no marsh-dweller had wished to think long about the exchange of one guilt for another, the many deaths of strangers exchanged for the sacrifice once a generation of one of their own; nor did they wish to consider that while there were no fewer marsh-dwellers than there had been those twenty generations ago, there were no more either.

The young women looked round themselves at the trees and pools they loved, and each tried to resign herself to leaving, and failed; and each knew she would not wish the leaving on anyone, on any marsh-dweller.

The young women made a circle round a certain pool, and around them their kinfolk gathered. Each would kneel, one by one, and touch the water; for all but one of them, the pool would lie as it always lay, cool and green and apparently depthless, motionless but for the tiny ripples made by the fingers of a slender hand; like any other cool green pool. But for the one, this pool would seem to clear, and at its bottom there would be a picture, in eye-dazzling white and vivid blue, of a pale city set under a hot sky; this was the city of the Rustafulus kings. And she who called it up would be the next queen.

This pool was at no great distance from the marsh-folk's chief village, and lay near one of the paths that, in most years, was often used. But the marshfolk knew something of what was occurring beyond their marshes— not only on account of the bargain they had with the Rustafulus kings—and as the time came for the next queen to be selected, that path and that pool were increasingly shunned. So it had been this time; not a one of the marshfolk now gathered around it had been this way in over a year.

This was the pool beside which Rustafulus I's mage had first met with the marsh-dwellers, but it was the marshfolk themselves who put the spell on it, that they might not have the smell of the mage forever hanging over their beloved fenland—although this was not how they put it to him. It was as gentle a spell as they could make it, yet in the twenty generations since, it had become unlucky to drink or bathe in that pool. Some people said it gave bad dreams; some people said that it made the skin dry and sore.

There was no ritual for which of the young women should kneel and touch the water first, although once the first woman had done so, the woman on her right, and then the one next on her right, and on around, did so after—till the image of the city wavered out of the darkness and doomed someone. The tradition had it that there was a pause of some little time after the circle of young women had formed, before any one of them knelt to touch the surface of the water. But this time there was almost no pause. The last women had barely set their feet upon the brink when one of their number sank down so quickly that she might almost have been fainting—except that she stretched her hand out calmly enough, and touched the water.

The image of the city burst upon them like a blow,

and not only the young women but those behind them
took an involuntary step backward. When they had
blinked themselves into seeing again, they saw that the
future queen had indeed fainted, and several people
rushed forward to drag her out of the water, for not even
a marshwoman can breathe underwater.

The mage was waiting for them by the pool where he
had met the young woman washing her hair the day before. It was as if he had not stirred a foot since that time.
They knew little of the daily habits of mages; perhaps he
had not. All the marshfolk came, to see Rustafulus XX's
mage, to see their daughter and sister and cousin for the
last time. She was dressed in the blue that was their
wedding-color; presumably Rustafulus XX's mage had
been told by his father about the precise shade of blue
that the woman he would take away with him to be his
king's queen would be wearing or perhaps it was only
that he was a mage, for his eyes found her at once, though
there was nothing else to mark her out.

"*You,*" he said.

It was the woman who had been washing her hair
the day before. She raised her eyes to look at him. "*I,*"
she said.

She did not know what it had been like for all the women
who had followed all the mages before, for no stories ever
came back to the marshes about them; only that the heirs
were born, and grew up, and became kings, and the ageless mage or his son came for the next woman. All she
knew of them was that they were alone and lonely, and
that eleven of them had died soon after their sons were
born.

What she did know was that she set eyes on Rustafulus XX and hated him; just as she knew that he saw in
her nothing that he desired, and hated her for that. She
said no word, for she knew why she was where she was;
and she stood at his side during the wedding, while the
priests said words over them and gave them the same
cup to drink from. Even she bore with the wedding

night—which the king took no more pleasure in than did she.

A year and a day passed and she was as slender as she had been on her wedding day, and no heir had been born. Dutifully the king attended her, in the evenings, and when she said to him, "Tonight is a good night, my lord," he lay with her, but nothing came of it. She watched the moon wax and wane in puzzlement, for she knew her body's rhythms. In the marshlands, on the day a girl sees her woman's blood for the first time, a feast is held, and all her girl cousins, and sisters if she has any, come, and their mothers and aunts and all the elder women tell them everything they need to know, which by the time they have attended all each other's feasts they know so well it has become as much a part of living in their bodies as their speech and vision are, and they will be ready to tell the woman's-knowledge in turn to their daughters and nieces and younger friends. Fiheri knew when she should conceive; but she did not.

Fiheri knew that in her marsh-blood ran the magic that held the kingdom together; knew that although it was Rustafulus XX who sat on a chair the dry-landers called a throne, this was not the only thing that mattered. She also knew her spirit shrank away from the king's touch while her body suffered it. There were no special woman's-knowledge tales for future queens, only the stories of the welcome a baby receives from the womb; only stories of tenderness and accord between the man and the woman who hope to create a child between them.

Some of her waiting-women were mothers and were gentle and kind to the queen they served; but she knew their proffered friendship was based on the fact that she asked nothing of them. There was no one in the king's court whom she might speak to; anyone who might be worthy of trust would not trust her. It was only the marshfolk who knew the truth of the queens' bargain.

Two years and two days since her wedding passed; and in the third year the king stopped attending her. Neither did he request her appearance at court anymore. Such occasions had been rare enough from the beginning, but she would still have been glad of them; even in this king's court there was some bustle of human conversation and activity, some faint, familiar echo of what she had known in her marshland home. Her own rooms in the palace were large and empty, and her waiting-women kept their eyes cast down even when they smiled at her, and spoke in whispers even when their words were compassionate. But no summons came and she dared not go unsummoned; even living as she did, she knew something of what stories were being told of her, and she shrank from the consequences.

The mage, whom she had not seen in three years, came to her rooms and requested an audience; and she met him calmly.

"If you do this for spite," said the mage, and it was obvious he thought she did, "you are but killing your own people."

She saw his eyes dilate as he said the word *killing*, and he watched her closely. She saw that the ban on the marsh-dwellers to shed no blood fascinated him even as he despised them for it—even as, so the marshfolk's story went, he had chosen this land instead of some other to rule, in his way, because of it. His eyes shifted to the tray her women-in-waiting had not yet taken away from her solitary supper table; there were only bread crumbs upon it, and the cores of fruit.

"I do not," she said, and maintained her calm.

The mage paced once across the room and once back. "The king would set you aside and choose another wife," he said; and Fiheri saw with a shock that he too was afraid; and she realized that he must understand the truth of the bargain with her people very nearly as they did. Or perhaps he only feared any appearance of his own failure; for it had been he who brought back this queen. Fiheri had not understood the references she had heard of Rustafulus XIX's long age; nor had she paid any attention to the fragments of tales she overheard about the mages' impassivity, so she thought nothing of his restless pacing, nor the ease with which she read his face.

She looked out of her window, a window that faced

her marshes, though they were too far away to see, and said nothing, for she had nothing to say.

"I will lie with you myself," said the mage.

Calmly she said from the window: "You will not."

"You would not know," said the mage, "for I can seem to be the king as readily as I can appear as myself."

"I would know," she said, and turned her eyes, green-brown as the pools of her homeland, toward him; and it was the mage's eyes that slid away. Again he paced the length of her long room and back again.

The mage stood close to her as he said, "I have ordered the king to sleep alone for the next month. When that month is up, he will come to you again. Count your days carefully, for in a year's time I wish to hear the cries of a healthy babe."

She counted the days no less carefully than she ever had, but the night before the night on which she would say to the king that it was a good night, she slipped away from the king's city. It was a long walk she would have before daylight, and her waiting-women were accustomed to bringing her breakfast soon after dawn. The marsh that lay near the king's city was not her marsh, but perhaps it would do.

The night was more than half over when she found a pool she could use. She sank swiftly down beside it, and touched her fingers to the water. Its night-black opacity thinned, as if a light shone from its bed; and in the light was the face of a child. The child blinked, and looked up at her with her own eyes, and was then lost in a dazzling burst of gleams and flashes, as if someone had stood up abruptly behind her on the bank holding a torch, though her kneeling figure cast no shadow. Then the light died, and the pool became black water again.

She flew back to the king's house, and arrived with the first rays of daylight slipping over her bedchamber's windowsills. She had no time, but thrust her muddy feet under the bedclothes, and tried to look as if she had been sleeping. Her favorite waiting-woman brought her breakfast, and smiled at her. "My lady has fought dragons in her dreams, I think," she said, and patted the hands that were clenched on the pillow, and touched the tangle of wind-rumpled hair.

In nine months' time, Fiheri was brought to bed and delivered of a daughter.

In her dreams she had imagined that when the babe was born she would declare her part of the bargain finished and return to the marshes, as she had never understood why none of her predecessors had done so. But when she first felt the baby stir, beneath her ribs, under her heart, her resolution wavered; and when the baby lay in her arms she understood why all the other queens had stayed; and so she stayed also. Her own days were gladly given over to her child's needs, and the baby-nurses were sent away. The only change in her staff was an increase in laundresses.

When the baby was six months old, the mage came to her again.

"It is old enough to be weaned," he said.

"That is for me to say," replied Fiheri. "Little you know of mothering."

In six months more, the mage came to her again and said, "It is time it was weaned."

"It is no it," said Fiheri, smoothing the baby's soft hair; "she is a she, and her name is Liath."

"I do not care what you call it," said the mage, "for it will grow up to be Rustafulus XXI; the country has already been told that the king has a fine son, now a year old."

Fiheri stared at him, not taking it in. "You cannot," she said at last, slowly, for speaking anything in answer to such a statement was hard.

"I can and will," said the mage. "Starting now." And he reached out to seize the child from Fiheri's arms.

"No!" she said, and jerked away. Liath grasped her mother's dress with her small hands and began to cry.

The mage smiled. Fiheri had never seen him smile. "Three more days you may keep it," he said. "*Her*. But the king already knows that you are a little—mad: and has agreed that you should retire, now that your child is weaned and ready to go to its first proper tutor, to the rooms at the heart of the palace, where many other queens have lived. There is a pond there, and gray, smooth stones with moss upon them, and a tree whose leaves weep into the water. Rustafulus IV was a kind man, after his fashion, and felt generous to the woman who had given him such a strong son."

"But—you cannot," said Fiheri, breathing quickly. "You cannot give a one-year-old child to a tutor. There will be a nurse—the nurse will know—"

"The nurses and tutors will believe their charge is a boy," said the mage, smiling, "for my seemings are not limited to the face and form I myself wear."

"And when my daughter is old enough to marry?"

"Rustafulus XXI shall marry a marshwoman, as did his father," said the mage, still smiling.

And Fiheri suddenly realized why she had hated Rustafulus XX on sight; his smile was identical to the smile she now was seeing on the mage's face; his habitual expression of faintly bored distaste was much like his mage's expression, only on the king's face it was also petulant. The implications pressed against her; she thought again of the long tale of queens who had borne precisely one son each to their kings, and how the mother-knowledge given marshwomen on their first blood-day does not guarantee the sex of a child; she remembered that the characters of the Rustafulus kings were said to fall with curious regularity into one of only three patterns. For a moment her heart stopped beating and her mind staggered, and she wrestled with madness. But her child was crying, and she bade her heart beat again, and shook her intellect free of madness, for her daughter needed her to know what to do.

"I will not let you do this," she said.

"Three days," said the mage, and left her.

Fiheri did not have to check the doors and windows to know that guards were posted there. There had been, she supposed, guards posted since Liath was born; but since she had chosen to take care of the baby herself, she had had little time or attention for anything that went on beyond the walls of her rooms and the small garden where she took Liath when the sun was shining.

Three days. What could she do in three days? She felt sick, and it was hard to get her breath; she understood now why eleven of the mothers of the kings of this country had died upon their sons' first birthdays, or had withdrawn into the rooms at the center of the palace and never been seen again.

She rocked her daughter till she stopped crying, and then set her down to play upon the floor. But the little girl knew there was something wrong, and clung to her mother till Fiheri picked her up again, and stood for a moment deep in thought. Then she wrapped the two of them snugly in a great scarf, and went out into the corridor, and turned in a direction she did not normally turn, and waited until someone stepped out to bar her way.

"Pardon, lady," said a young man in an honor guard's uniform.

She looked up at him, and saw a kind young man's face, and saw he believed the mage's story and was sorry for her.

"I would like to see the rooms prepared for me," she said. "Those at the center of the palace. The mage has told me . . ."

Her voice drifted away, but the young man waited politely till he was sure she was not going to finish her sentence before he said, "Yes, lady. I will take you there, if you wish it."

"Yes," said Fiheri. "I do wish it."

Liath stirred in her arms, and the young man looked wistful. "May I see—your child?" he said.

Fiheri dropped the edge of the scarf and Liath smiled at the young man, and offered to pull his hair when he bent toward her. Can you not see she is a girl? Fiheri thought, but did not say it aloud. The young man smiled. "My wife is expecting our first," he said. And then he brought himself back to attention and said, "Thank you, lady. Your pardon, lady. If I may lead the way, lady."

He left her at the door into the Queen's Apartments, by which she understood that there was no other way out.

She breathed deeply and smelled long lives and sorrow; she walked a little bent forward as if she could thus somehow protect the child in her arms. Liath was half asleep, one hand clenched around two of her mother's fingers.

The rooms were large and handsome, and the pond at their center, open to the sky three stories up, was cool and deep and reminded her painfully of her home. She turned her back on it and walked hastily away; but the rooms all opened off it, and kept leading her back to it. She looked at it from the shade of a lintel, as if she were hiding from a predatory animal, watching it cautiously for signs of its intentions, trying to gauge if it were hungry or no. She remembered the beautiful, leaf-shaded pool that had shown her the king's city; and she remembered the smaller, muddier, bleaker pool that had filled up with stars and shown her her daughter's face.

She walked quickly forward and stooped abruptly by the edge of this pool at the center of the Queen's Apartments deep within the walls of the palace of the Rustafulus kings. She put her hand out and touched her fingers to the water.

His name. If you can find out his name.

She paused, bent awkwardly by the pool, curled over the small body of her sleeping child.

His name. Find his name. Even a mage has a name. Especially a mage.

But how can I?

There was no answer; it was a message only, left by eleven women before her, as if written in their blood, like a series of prisoners scratching their names and dates on the walls of their prison.

She knelt, slowly, settled down cross-legged, laying Liath in her lap. She bent over her till she could dip both her hands in the water, and she lifted enough water in them that she could sip a few drops, wet her face with it. She put her damp hands against her daughter's face; Liath made a little, sleepy murmur, and put her fist in her mouth.

Fiheri, still cross-legged, bowed over her, and fell into a waking dream.

At first all she saw was water; but slowly its level sank, or land rose up beneath it, and low islands appeared. And the water drained away yet more, and the islands became land, and the water became pools, and trees grew on the land, and for a long time that was all, except that this wet, pool-glinting land threw back the light that fell upon it like no other land did, every fog full of rainbows no matter how the sun lay, every leaf silver with starlight on nights too dark for stars. And then came people.

They were small at first, and moved in small, darting steps like mice that fear the hawk; they wore no clothes, and they did not speak. But they grew taller, and learned of fire, and of clothing, and of language. And then they learned of magic.

It was the magic of the land they learned, and they learned it by living there, by breathing its air and drinking its water; and much of what they learned they did not know they had learned: like that its price was that they could eat no meat, could carry no weapon against any person, animal, bird, or fish. They had been doing these things for many generations before their seers told them that these things they did were connected with other things: like that they could throw a handful of water-drops in the air, and speak a word, and each droplet became a lily or a wren; that they could hurl rainbows from treetop to treetop even at midnight. That they could make lovers happy together, and sick children well, and they could find lost treasures, however large or small.

But with that knowledge came pride: that they were not as other people. The marshfolk traveled out of their marshes, and met the dry-landers, and discovered that the dry-landers, who ate meat and murdered each other, could do no magic; and the marshfolk learned to despise them. They withdrew to their marshes again, saying to themselves that the dry-landers' ways were nothing to do with them, and their fate none of the marshfolk's.

It was many more generations before they discovered the price of this division. By that time there was far less marsh than there had been. Rainbows were visible only when the light was right, and leaves were silver in star-light only on clear nights. The marshfolk sometimes found lost treasures, big and small, but sometimes they did not; and not all their sick children recovered.

When a king, forty generations before Rustafulus XX, had invaded the marshlands, the marshfolk applied their obstinacy, which was very nearly all they had left, and it saved them. But they knew their weakness; and they loved their land.

And then Fiheri, dreaming, saw the mage come among them, and saw her people agree to a bargain based on the tales of but twenty generations. She wanted to cry out to them, No, wait! You do not know what will come of this! This is not the way to do what must be done! But she was caught where she was, far away from her people, too far away for them to hear her voice. She was not sure if she had spoken aloud or not; it was the mage's voice she heard in her ears, hard and domineering, just as his twenty-generations' son spoke; his son. . . . His son.

Did magehood run in a family so straight, so flawlessly?

As firstborn sons ran so flawlessly in the line of the Rustafulus kings?

Still half dreaming, still with the seeing of the mage and her people in her mind, Fiheri dipped her hands again in the water, and this time she let the drops run off her fingers and into her ears. The mage's voice was hushed, and the water against her skin felt like balm, or like her own mother's hands. She relaxed gratefully—but she had no time to relax—she startled in her place, bruis-ing her hipbones on the paving stones that lined the wa-ter's edge, involuntarily reaching out as if she could snatch at the fading vision with her hands. Her eyes flew open and for a moment the mage seemed to stand, poised, like a shape in some evil smoke, coiled over the pool at the heart of the Queen's Apartments.

"Ah!" she said, and this time she knew she spoke aloud. Liath murmured, moved in her sleep, resettled as her mother quieted. One of Fiheri's hands touched her daughter; the other reached out toward the stark, ominous shape of the mage.

Though her eyes remained open, the Queen's Apartments faded from her sight, yet still she could see the mage standing before her. But Fiheri's magic was marsh-magic, and tied to its land, and as she tried to look farther, the magic weakened. The water on her outstretched hand twinkled and dizzied her. As a new landscape took shape around the mage, he too grew dim and vague, and she could recognize him now only from having recognized him before; and she was afraid, for she knew this was not good enough, and she also knew that this was the best she could do. She dropped her distracting hand to her knee. She felt the tiny, soft rise and fall of her daughter's chest with her other hand. *Help me,* she said; but she heard no reply.

Blurry figures moved out of the misty background and stood near the figure that had been the mage; she thought they were talking, and she strained to hear.

". . . often I have wished to show you the shadow of your strength, but you will not see; and because you are too strong for me, you think you are strong enough. But I, who know more about shadows than you do—perhaps because of my lesser acquaintance with strength—could tell you, if you would listen to this either, that you are not strong enough to defeat yourself."

I shall know no defeat, for I have learned how to seek victory; unlike you, cow-minder, baby-tender, tree-listener, frog-friend.

his name

". . . cannot deny you the mage-mark, for you have earned it three times over, as you know," came another voice, stronger and clearer than the first. "But I can do this much. I can tie your name to the reality of what you do; and should that reality serve to do any person ill, let that person cry your name aloud."

I will say I was raised by lions, for lions give not their children names; the mage I will be, which will be enough for them, and my roar will be that of forty lions in their ears.

HIS NAME

And the blurred picture, and the voices, faded to nothing.

"No!" cried Fiheri. "I must know his name! I *must!*"

Distantly, whisperingly, she heard the first voice; no, it was a third voice, so faint it was almost as if Fiheri imagined the words: ". . . you underestimate the toughness of ordinary mortals, and the inertia of natural force, which it is beyond even a mage to bend for more than a few centuries, and even that no more than a finger's dam against a snowmelt torrent in the mountains. How can you not know that a mage's striving for balance is but making a virtue of necessity? Beware your own desires; I say this to you as your teacher. I do not say it as your master, for master of you I have not been for many long years. Beware your own desires. . . ."

"Cincarnac," said Liath clearly.

Fiheri opened her eyes, and for a moment she saw what her daughter would be in twenty years; and she saw her wearing a garment that shaped itself to her body, so that her flat belly and crotch and the curve of her breasts left no doubt of what she was. And then the vision faded with the rest, and her daughter was a bright-eyed one-year-old, just woken from her nap. "Ah—aah!" said her daughter.

Cincarnac.

Slowly she gathered herself together, and stood, and went back to the door into the Queen's Apartments, and there she found the young man still waiting for her. He looked at her anxiously, and she guessed that she appeared tired and dazed. "Take me to the mage and the king," she said.

"I—" said the young man.

She made an effort. "They are in the great hall, are they not?" she said, and the young man remembered that she was a marshwoman, and that the marsh-dwellers had a magic that lay upon them like other people might wear a cloak. He had seen her often before, in the garden set aside for her, and had liked her for the happiness in her face as she watched her baby, but he had never seen her like this. There was a glamour upon her, and he feared to touch her, though his orders were that she could not go farther than certain rooms. She was certainly not allowed in the king's hall.

"I will go there," she said, looking into his eyes, "and you will follow me." He broke her gaze only to bow his head in acquiescence.

There was no assembly that day, but the king was there, with certain beautiful young women, and half a dozen courtiers or ministers, and one young man kneeling upon one knee and holding a tray with a jug upon it, and a number of tall, thin cups. They glanced up, astonished, at the marshwoman, in her plain gown, and with a scarf wrapped around her in such a way that they knew she carried her child; and slowly they remembered that this marshwoman was the queen, whom no one had seen for a year, since her child had been born.

Fiheri looked at the king, and at the mage who stood at his shoulder, and grew angry.

"Do you know, *husband*," she began, "that your mage is to take my child from me, the day after tomorrow, and order me to retire to the rooms at the center of the palace for the rest of my life? The rooms called the Queen's Apartments, where no one goes, for they smell of bad omens and sorrow?"

She saw at once in his face that he did know; but she wondered what he thought he knew of why.

"Your mage is planning on turning our daughter into a son," she said. "Did you know that?"

The ministers looked embarrassed; she remembered the mage had told her that she was already known to be a little mad. "Yes, I see you did know that. But I am not mad, for we have no son but a fine daughter; and while our mage can make her seem as he wills, there is one thing such a seeming cannot do. Have you never wondered how it is that all of the kings before you had but one child each of their queens? And that every one of those children was a son? Have you not ever looked into a mirror and wondered that your mage's smile smiled out at you, and not your father's?"

The court was hushed in horror; the queen was truly

mad. Soon the guards would take her away, gently, for she was still queen; and they would all forget this had ever happened, and she would be safe, immured in the Queen's Apartments.

"I declare the reality of what you have done," said Fiheri, "and I call upon you to account for it. I call *you*, Cincarnac!"

At the sound of his name, the mage threw up his arm as if to shield his face. No one moved; even the young man balanced upon one knee appeared frozen to his place. And then, with a low cry, the mage rushed out of the hall.

"Take her back to her rooms, and see that she stays there!" said Rustafulus XX, and went in the direction that his mage had fled. But no one had ever seen the mage flee anything before; and no one wished to lay hands upon the one who had caused it. No one tried to stop her as she turned away from the little group which had stood round the king and his mage; the young honor guard who had accompanied her came to attention, as if he would be the queen's guard in truth, and not her jailer; but she did not look at him. The other guards stood away from the door as she walked toward it.

She went down the grand, wide stairs to the courtyard where she had come four years before to be married to the king; and, carrying the king's child, she walked away from the palace, and the city around it, and the farms that lay around the city. Over a week it took her, for she had the child to think of; but people were kind to the young woman in her plain dress with her young child, and they never went hungry, and Fiheri's own people were waiting for them at the edge of their marshland, which none but the next queen ever went beyond, nor had for eighty generations.

Soon after the first birthday of Rustafulus XXI, Rustafulus XX lost a series of battles led against him by the generals of his armies, the first of which broke out shortly after the disappearance of his queen and his mage. It was a long time before his people were sure that the tales of the disappearances were anything but rumor; and no one connected a certain plainly dressed young woman and her daughter with the queen—who was known to have had a son. What became of the son no dry-lander ever heard. The battles led to war, and what had been the country of twenty kings in an unbroken line from father to son was cut up into many tiny princedoms that warred with each other for many years. But no one ever saw the mage again, and the story of his disappearance became connected somehow with the magic of the marshfolk, with the result that no dry-lander dared set foot in the wild marshes next to the desert for many generations, for the magic there was even stronger than a mage's. And in the marshlands the daughter of a king taught her mother's people that there were other truths and other bargains than those made by blood and sacrifice; but that is another story.

Toad

PATRICIA A. MCKILLIP

Patricia A . McKillip has written a number of fantasy novels, among them The Riddle-Master of Hed *and* The Book of Atrix Wolfe. *She has also dabbled in science fiction with* Fool's Run, *and the mainstream with* Stepping from the Shadows. *Her most recent novels are* Winter Rose *and* Song for the Basilisk. *Her short fiction has been primarily fantasy. McKillip currently lives in New York, in the Catskills.*

"Toad" was written as a response to some unanswered questions she has always had about "The Frog King," among them why any self-respecting frog would want to marry such a spoiled brat.

It is the perfect complement to the Tanith Lee story that opened this anthology.

Toad

The first thing that leaps to the eye is that my beloved had no manners. She behaved like a spoiled brat, once she had what she wanted. If it had not been for her father, where would I have been? Still hanging around the well, instead of dressed in silks and wearing a crown, and being bowed and scraped to, not to mention diving in and out of the dark, moist cave of our marriage sheets, cresting waves of satin like seals, barking and tossing figs to one another, then diving back down, bearing soft, plump fruit in our mouths. "Old waddler," she called me at first, with a degree of accuracy missing from subsequent complaints. She never could tell a frog from a toad.

Why, you might wonder, would any self-respecting toad, having been slammed against a wall by a furious brat of a princess, want, upon regaining his own shape, to marry her? Not only was she devious, promising me things and then ignoring her promises when threatened by the cold proximity of toad, she was bad-tempered to boot. The story that has come down doesn't make a lot of sense here: why are lies and temper rewarded with the handsome prince? She didn't want to let me into the castle, she didn't want to feed me, she didn't want to touch me, above all she didn't want me in her bed. When I pleaded with her to show mercy, to become again that sweet, weeping, charming child beside the well who promised me everything I asked for, she picked me up as if I were the golden ball that I had rescued for her, and bounced me off the stones. If she had missed the wall and I had gone flying out a window, what might have happened? Would I have waddled away, muttering and limping, under the moonlight, to slide back into the well until fate tossed another golden ball my way?

Maybe.

She'll never know.

Her father comes out well in the stories. A man of honor, harassed by his exasperating daughter, who tries to wheedle and whine her way out of her promises. A king, who would consent to eat with a toad at his table, for no other reason than to make his daughter keep her word. "Papa, please, no," she begged, her gray eyes awash with tears, the way I had first seen her, her curly hair, golden as her ball, tumbling out of its pins to her shoulders. "Papa, please don't make me let it in. Don't make me share my food with it. Don't make me touch it. I'll die if I have to touch a frog."

"It's a toad," he said at one point, watching me drink wine out of her goblet. She had his gray eyes; he saw a bit more clearly than she, but not enough: only enough to use me as a lesson in his daughter's life.

"Frog, toad, what's the difference? Papa, please don't make me!"

"Toads," he said accurately, "are generally uglier than frogs. Most have nubby, bumpy skin—"

"I'll get warts, Papa!"

"That's a fairy tale. Look at its squat body, its short legs, made for insignificant hops, or even for walking, like a dog. Observe its drab coloring." He added, warming to his subject while I finished his daughter's dessert, "They have quite interesting breeding habits. Some lay eggs on land instead of water. Others give birth to tiny toads, already fully formed. Among midwife toads, the male carries the eggs with him until they hatch, moistening them in—"

"That's disgusting!"

"I would like to be taken to bed now," I said, wiping my mouth with her embroidered linen.

"Papa!"

"You promised," I reminded her reproachfully. "I can't get up the stairs; you'll have to carry me. As your father pointed out, my limbs are short."

"Papa, please!"

"You promised," he said coldly: an honorable man. A lesson was to be learned simply at the expense of a stain of well-water on her sheets, a certain clamminess in the atmosphere. What harm could possibly come to her?

I have always thought that her instincts were quite sound. For one thing: consider her age. Young, beautiful, barely marriageable, she might have kissed—though, contrary to common belief, not me—but she had most certainly never taken anyone to bed with her besides her nurse and her dolls. Who would want an ugly, dank and warty toad in her bed instead of what she must have had vague yearnings for? And after all that talk of breeding habits! Something bloated and insistent, moving formlessly under her sheets while she tried to sleep, something cold, damp, humorless—who could blame her for losing her temper?

Then why did she make those promises?

Because something in her heart, in her marrow, recognized me.

Let's begin with the child sitting beside the well, beneath the linden tree. She thinks she is alone, though her world, she knows, proceeds in familiar and satisfactory fashion within the elegant castle beyond the trees. The linden is in bloom; its creamy flowers drift down into her hair, drop and float upon the dark water. Breeze strokes her hair, her cheeks. She tosses her favorite plaything, her

golden ball, absently toward the sky, enjoying the sup-
pleness and grace of her body, the thin silk blowing
against her skin. She wears her favorite dress, green as
the heart-shaped linden leaves; it makes her feel like a
leaf, blown lightly in the wind. She throws her ball, takes
a breath of air made complex and intoxicating by scents
from the tree, the gardens, the moist earth at the lip of
the well. She catches her ball, throws it again, thinks of
nothing. She misses the ball.

It falls with a splash into the middle of the well, and,
weighted with its tracery of gold, sinks out of sight. She
has no idea how deep the water is, what snakes and silver
eels might live in it, what long grasses might reach up to
twine around her if she dares leap into it. She does what
has always worked in her short life: she weeps.

I appear.

Her grief is genuine and quite moving: she might have
dropped a child into the well instead of a ball. She
scarcely sees me. I make little impression on her sorrow
except as a means to end it. In her experience, help answers when she calls; her desperation transforms the
world so that even toads can talk.

All her attention is on the water when she hears my
voice. She speaks impatiently, wiping her eyes with her
silks, to see better into the rippling shadows. "Oh, it's a
frog. Old waddler, I dropped my ball in the water—I must
have it back! I'll die without it! I'll give you anything if
you get it for me—these pearls, my crown—anything! So
will my papa."

She scarcely listens to herself, or to me. I am nothing
but a frog, I while away the time eating flies, swimming
in the slime, sitting in the reeds and croaking. Her pearls
might resemble the translucent eggs of frogs, but I would
have no real interest in them. Yes, of course I can be
her playmate, her companion; she has had fantasy friends
before. Yes, I can eat out of her plate; they all do. Yes, I
can drink from her cup. Yes, I can sleep in her bed—yes,
yes, anything! Just stop croaking and fetch my ball for me.

I drop it at her feet. I am no longer visible; I have
become a fantasy, a dream. A talking frog? Don't be silly.

Frogs don't talk. Even when I cry out to her as she runs away, laughing and tossing her ball, that's what she knows: frogs don't talk. Wait for me! I cry. You promised! But she no longer hears me. All her fantasy friends vanish when she no longer needs them.

So it must have been with a first, faint sense of terror that she heard my watery squelching across the marble floor as she sat eating with her father. They were not alone, but who among her father's elegantly bored courtiers would have questioned the existence of a talking frog? The court went on with their meal, secretly delighting in the argument at the royal table. I ate silently and listened to their discreet murmurings. Most took the princess's view, and wished me removed with the salmon bones, the fruit peelings, and tossed unceremoniously out the kitchen door. Others thought her father right: I would be a harmless lesson for a spoiled daughter. Most saw a frog. A toad with its poisonous skin touching the princess's goblet, leaving traces of its spittle on her plate? Unthinkable! Therefore: I was a frog. Others were not so sure. The king recognized me, of course, but, setting aside the fact that I could talk, seemed to believe that for all other purposes, I would behave in predictable toad-fashion toward humans, desiring mainly to be ignored and not to be squashed.

But the princess knew: to journey up the stairs with me dangling between her reluctant fingers would be to turn her back to that fair afternoon, the sweet linden blossoms, the golden-haired child tossing her ball, spinning and glinting, toward the sun, then watching it fall down light cascading over leaves into shadow, until it fell, unerringly, back into her hands. When the ball plummeted into the depths of the well, she wept for her lost self. Faced with the future in the form of a toad, she bargained badly: she exchanged her childhood for me.

Who am I?

Some of the courtiers knew me. Their wealth and finery did not shelter them from air or mud, or from the tales that are breathed into the heart, that cling to boot-soles and breed life. They whisper among themselves. Listen.

"Toads mean pain, death. Think of the ugly toadfish that ejects its spines into the hands of the unwary fisher. Think of the poisonous toadstool."

"If you kill a toad with your hands, the skin of your face and hands will become hardened, lumpy, pimpled. Toads suck the breath of the sleeper, bring death."

"But consider the midwife toad, both male and female involved with life."

"If you spit and hit a toad, you will die."

"A toad placed on a cut will heal it."

"If you anger a toad it will inflate itself with a terrible poison and burst, taking you with it as it dies."

"Toads portend life. Consider the Egyptians, who believe that the toad represents the womb, and its cries are the cries of unborn children."

"She is life."

"It is death."

"She belongs to the moon, she croaks to the crescent moon. Consider the Northerners, who believe she rescues life itself, when it ripens into the shape of a red apple, and falls down into the well."

"She is life."

"It is death."

"She is both."

To the princess, carrying me with loathing up the stairs, a wisp of linen separating the shapeless, lumpy sack of my body from her fingers. I am the source of an enormous and irrational irritation. I rescued her golden ball; why could she not be gracious? I would be gone by morning. But she knew, she knew, deep in her; she heard the croaking of tiny, invisible frogs; she recognized the midwife toad.

If she had been gracious, I would indeed have been gone by morning. But her instincts held fast: I was danger, I was the unknown. I was what she wanted and did not want. She could not rid herself of me fast enough, or violently enough. But because she knew me, and part of her cried Not yet! Not yet!, she flung me as far from her as she could without losing sight of me.

Changing shape is easy; I do it all the time.

The moment she saw me on the floor, with my strong young limbs and dazed expression, rubbing my head and wondering groggily if I were still frog-naked, she tossed her heart into my well and dove after it herself. She covered me with a blanket, though not without a startled and curious glance at essentials. She accepted her future with remarkable composure. She stroked my curly hair, whose color, along with the color of my eyes, I had taken from her favorite doll, and listened to my sad tale.

A prince, I told her. A witch I had accidentally offended; they offend so easily, it seems. She had turned me into a toad and said . . .

"You rescued me," I said gratefully, overlooking her rudeness, as did she. "Those who love me will be overjoyed to see me again. How beautiful you are," I added. "Is it just because yours is the first kind face I have seen in so long?"

"Yes," she said breathlessly. "No." Somehow our hands became entwined before she remembered propriety. "I must take you to meet my father."

"Perhaps I should dress first."

"Perhaps you should."

And so I increase and multiply, trying to keep up with all the voices in the rivers and ponds, bogs and swamps, that cry out to be born. Some tales are simpler than others. This, like pond-water, seems at first glance as clear as day. Then, when you scoop water in your hand and look at it, you begin to see all the little mysteries swarming in it, which, if you had drunk the water without looking first, you never would have seen. But now that you have seen, you stand there under the hot sun, thirsty, but not sure what you will be drinking, and wishing, perhaps, that you had not looked so closely, that you had just swallowed me down and gone your way, refreshed.

Some tales are simpler than others. But go ahead and drink: the ending is always the same.

Recommended Reading

Fiction and Poetry

The Robber Bride and Bluebeard's Egg, by Margaret Atwood
   This Canadian writer often uses fairy-tale themes in her excellent contemporary mainstream fiction.

Snow White, by Donald Barthelme
   This is an early postmodern short novel that would be politically incorrect by today's standards.

Katie Crackernuts, by Katherine Briggs
   A charming short novel retelling the Katie Crackernuts tale, by one of the world's foremost folklore authorities.

Beginning with O, by Olga Broumas
   Broumas's poetry makes use of many fairy-tale motifs in this collection.

The Sun, the Moon and the Stars, by Steven Brust
A contemporary novel mixing ruminations on art and creation with a lively Hungarian fairy tale.

Possession, by A. S. Byatt
A Booker Prize–winning novel that makes wonderful use of the Fairy Melusine legend.

Nine Fairy Tales and One More Thrown in for Good Measure, by Karel Capek
Charming stories inspired by the Czech folk tradition.

Sleeping in Flame, by Jonathan Carroll
Excellent, quirky dark fantasy using the Rumplestiltskin tale.

The Bloody Chamber and *Burning Your Boats* by Angela Carter
Angela Carter is grand dame of modern adult fairy tales. Her extraordinary, dark, sensual fairy-tale retellings are collected in *The Bloody Chamber,* and can also be found in *Burning Your Boats:* a posthumous collection of Carter's complete short fiction.

The Sleeping Beauty, by Hayden Carruth
A poetry sequence using the Sleeping Beauty legend.

Briar Rose and *Pinocchio in Venice* by Robert Coover
Coover often works with fairy-tale themes in his fiction; these two books are particularly recommended. The first is a highly literary exploration of the Briar Rose theme, dense and lush as a briar rose hedge; the second is a more satiric work.

Beyond the Looking Glass, edited by Jonathan Cott
A collection of Victorian fairy-tale prose and poetry.

The Nightingale, by Kara Dalkey
An evocative Oriental historical novel based on the Hans Christian Andersen story.

The Printed Alphabet, by Diana Darling
This novel is a rich fantasia inspired by Balinese myth and folklore.

The Girl Who Trod on a Loaf, by Kathryn Davis
Uses the fairy tale of the title as the basis for a story of two women, and the opera, at the beginning of the twentieth century. A lovely little book.

Blue Bamboo, by Osamu Dazai
This volume of fantasy stories by a Japanese writer of the early twentieth century contains lovely fairy-tale work.

Provençal Tales, by Michael de Larrabeiti
An absolutely gorgeous collection containing tales drawn from the Provençal region of France.

Jack the Giant-Killer and *Drink Down the Moon,* by Charles de Lint
Wonderful urban fantasy novels bringing "Jack" and magic to the streets of modern Canada.

Tam Lin, by Pamela Dean
A lyrical novel setting the old Scottish fairy story (and folk ballad) Tam Lin among theater majors on a Midwestern college campus.

Vinegar Jar, by Berle Doherty
An eerie, disturbing contemporary novel weaving traditional fairy tales into the story of a disintegrating marriage.

Like Water for Chocolate, by Laura Esquivel
Esquivel's book (and the wonderful film of the same title) wraps Mexican folklore and tales into a turn-of-the-century story about love and food on the Mexico/Texas border. Complete with recipes.

The King's Indian, by John Gardner
A collection of peculiar and entertaining stories using fairy-tale motifs.

Crucifax Autumn, by Ray Garton
One of the first splatterpunk horror novels; Garton makes use of the Pied Piper theme in very nasty ways. Violent and visceral.

Blood Pressure, by Sandra M. Gilbert
A number of the poems in this powerful collection make use of fairy-tale motifs.

Strange Devices of the Sun and Moon, by Lisa Goldstein
A lyrical little novel mixing English fairy tales with English history in Christopher Marlowe's London.

The Seventh Swan, by Nicholas Stuart Gray
An engaging Scottish novel that starts off where the "Seven Swans" fairy tale ends.

Fire and Hemlock, by Diana Wynne Jones
A beautifully written, haunting novel that brings the Thomas the Rhymer and Tam Lin tales into modern day England.

Seven Fairy Tales and a Fable, by Gwyneth Jones
Eight enchanting, thought-provoking, adult fairy tales by this British writer.

Green Grass Running Water, by Thomas King
This delightful Magical Realist novel uses Native American myths and folk tales to hilarious effect.

Thomas the Rhymer, by Ellen Kushner
A sensuous and musical rendition of this old Scottish story and folk ballad.

The Wandering Unicorn, by Manuel Mujica Lainez
A fairy-tale novel based on the "Fairy Melusine" legend by an award-winning Argentinean writer. Translated from the Spanish.

Red as Blood, Or Tales from the Sisters Grimmer, by Tanith Lee
A striking and versatile collection of adult fairy-tale retellings.

Terrors of Earth, by Tom Le Farge
This poetic little collection of stories weaves sensual, surreal imagery out of old French "fabliaux."

The Tricksters, by Margaret Mahy
This beautifully told, contemporary New Zealand story draws upon pancultural Trickster legends.

Angel Maker, by Sarah Maitland
A collection gathering the short fiction by this excellent English author, including stories making rich use of themes from fairy tales and myth.

Winter Rose and *Something Rich and Strange* by Patricia A. McKillip
The first is a gorgeous, poetic, magical fantasy set at the edge of an English forest, using themes from Tam Lin and other English tales. The second, also beautifully penned, is a sparkling short novel (with art by Brian Froud) using fairy tales of the sea as the basis for a contemporary story set in the Pacific Northwest.

Beauty, by Robin McKinley
Masterfully written, gentle and magical, this novel retells the story of "Beauty and the Beast."

Deerskin, by Robin McKinley
A retelling of Charles Perrault's "Donkeyskin," a dark fairy tale with incest themes.

The Door in the Hedge, by Robin McKinley
"The Twelve Dancing Princesses" and "The Frog Prince" retold in McKinley's gorgeous, clear prose, along with two original tales.

Disenchantments, edited by Wolfgang Mieder
An excellent compilation of adult fairy-tale poetry.

The Book of Laughter and Forgetting, by Milan Kundera
This literate and cosmopolitan work makes use of Moravian folk music, rituals, and stories.

Sleeping Beauty, by Susanna Moore
An eloquent, entertaining contemporary novel that uses the "Sleeping Beauty" legend mixed with native Hawaiian folklore.

The Private Life and *Waving from the Shore,* by Lisel Mueller
Terrific poetry collections with many fairy-tale themes.

Zel by Donna Jo Napoli
Published as young-adult fiction, this is a dark and engrossing retelling of Rapunzel.

Godmother Night, by Rachel Pollack
A unique contemporary fantasy, based on the Godfather Death fairy tale, about two gay women, their child, and the angel of death—surrounded by her coterie of leatherclad bikers.

Haroun and the Sea of Stories, by Salman Rushdie
A delightful Eastern fantasia by this Booker Prize–winning author.

Kindergarten, by Peter Rushford
A contemporary British story beautifully wrapped around the "Hansel and Gretel" tale, highly recommended.

Transformations, by Anne Sexton
Sexton's brilliant collection of modern fairy-tale poetry.

The Porcelain Dove, by Delia Sherman
This gorgeous fantasy set during the French Revolution makes excellent use of French fairy tales.

The Flight of Michael McBride, by Midori Snyder
A lovely, deftly written fantasy set in the old American West, this magical novel mixes the folklore traditions of immigrant and indigenous American cultures.

Fair Peril, by Nancy Springer
A droll, wise, adult fairy tale set in the land of Fair Peril—between two stores at the local mall.

Trail of Stones, by Gwenn Strauss
Evocative fairy-tale poems, beautifully illustrated by Anthony Browne.

Swan's Wing, by Ursula Synge
A lovely, magical fantasy novel using the "Seven Swans" fairy tale.

Beauty, by Sheri S. Tepper
Dark fantasy incorporating several fairy tales from an original and iconoclastic writer.

Indigo, by Marina Warner
Fairy tales are woven into the fabric of this lush contemporary novel (by one of England's foremost fairy-tale scholars) about family life in the Caribbean.

Wonder Tales, edited by Marina Warner
Gilbert Adair, John Ashberry, Ranjit Bolt, A. S. Byatt, and Terence Cave retell six French fairy tales in this beautiful little edition, with an excellent introduction by Warner.

Kingdoms of Elfin, by Sylvia Townsend Warner
These stories drawn from British folklore are arch, elegant, and enchanting. Many were first published in *The New Yorker.*

The Coachman Rat, by David Henry Wilson
Excellent dark fantasy retelling the story of "Cinderella" from the coachman's point of view.

Beauty, by Susan Wilson
A romantic contemporary retelling of "Beauty and the Beast," set in an isolated house in New England.

The Armless Maiden, edited by Terri Windling
Original fairy tales exploring the darker themes of childhood by Patricia McKillip, Tanith Lee, Charles de Lint, Jane Yolen, and many others.

Snow White and Rose Red, by Patricia C. Wrede
A charming Elizabethan historical novel retelling this romantic Grimm's fairy tale.

Briar Rose, by Jane Yolen
An unforgettable short novel setting the Briar Rose/ Sleeping Beauty story against the background of World War II.

Don't Bet on the Prince, edited by Jack Zipes
A collection of contemporary feminist fairy tales compiled by a leading fairy-tale scholar, containing prose and

poetry by Angela Carter, Joanna Russ, Jane Yolen, Tanith Lee, Margaret Atwood, Olga Broumas, and others.

The Outspoken Princess and the Gentle Knight: A Treasury of Modern Fairy Tales, edited by Jack Zipes
Presents fifteen modern fairy tales from England and the United States including works by Ernest Hemingway, A. S. Byatt, John Gardner, Jane Yolen, and Tanith Lee.

Modern Day Fairy-tale Creators

The Faber Book of Modern Fairy Tales, by Sara and Stephen Corrin
Gudgekin the Thistle Girl and Other Tales, by John Gardner
Mainly by Moonlight, by Nicholas Stuart Gray
Collected Stories, by Richard Kennedy
Dark Hills, Hollow Clocks, by Garry Kilworth
Heart of Wood, by William Kotzwinkle
Five Men and a Swan, by Naomi Mitchison
The White Deer and The Thirteen Clocks, by James Thurber
Fairy Tales, by Alison Uttley
Tales of Wonder, by Jane Yolen

Nonfiction

The Power of Myth, by Joseph Campbell
The Erotic World of Fairy, by Maureen Duffy
Dreams and Wishes, collected essays by Susan Cooper
Cinderella: A Casebook, edited by Alan Dundes
Tales from Eternity: The World of Fairy Tales and the Spiritual Search, by Rosemary Haughton
Beauty and the Beast: Visions and Revisions of an Old Tale, by Betsy Hearne
The Arabian Nights: A Companion, by Robert Irwin
Woman, Earth and Spirit, by Helen M. Luke
Once Upon a Time, collected essays by Alison Lurie
The Classic Fairy Tales, by Iona and Peter Opie
What the Bee Knows, collected essays by P. L. Travers

Problems of the Feminine in Fairy Tales, by Marie-Louise von Franz

    Collected lectures originally presented at the C. G. Jung Institute

From the Beast to the Blonde: On Fairy Tales and their Tellers, by Marina Warner (highly recommended)

Six Myths of Our Time, by Marina Warner

Touch Magic, collected essays by Jane Yolen

Fantasists on Fantasy, edited by Robert H. Boyer and Kenneth J. Zahorski

    Includes Tolkien's "On Fairy Stories," G. K. Chesterton's "Fairy Tales," and other essays

Fairy Tales as Myths, by Jack Zipes

Fairy-tale Source Collections

Old Wives' Fairy Tale Book, edited by Angela Carter

The Tales of Charles Perrault, translated by Angela Carter

Italian Folktales, translated by Italo Calvino

Daughters of the Moon, edited by Shahrukh Husain

The Complete Hans Christian Andersen, edited by Lily Owens

The Maid of the North: Feminist Folk Tales from Around the World, edited by Ethel Johnston Phelps

Gypsy Folktales, edited by Diane Tong

Favorite Folk Tales from Around the World, edited by Jane Yolen

The Complete Brothers Grimm, edited by Jack Zipes

Spells of Enchantment: The Wondrous Fairy Tales of Western Culture, edited by Jack Zipes (highly recommended)

(For volumes of fairy tales from individual countries— Russian fairy tales, French, African, Japanese, etc.—see the excellent Pantheon Books Fairy Tale and Folklore Library.)

Terri Windling has worked with adult fairy tales for many years: as an editor of over twenty anthologies, as a novelist and nonfiction writer, and as a visual artist. She is a consulting editor for Tor Books, and has won five

World Fantasy Awards. She lives in Devon, England, and Tucson, Arizona.

Ellen Datlow was the fiction editor of *OMNI* Magazine and Omni Internet for over fifteen years. In that position she published many of the best writers in and out of the science fiction and fantasy genres. She is currently the editor of the webzine *Event Horizon*. She is also the editor of various anthologies, including, with her co-editor Terri Windling, the award-winning *The Year's Best Fantasy and Horror* series; two anthologies on vampirism, *Alien Sex* and *Off Limits; Twists of the Tale: Tales of Cat Horror;* the World Fantasy Award–winning *Little Deaths;* and *Lethal Kisses.*